Life First

R J Crayton

This book is dedicated to Fred, Eric and Ella, who provided love, support and, often, distraction.

CONTENTS

ACKNOWLEDGMENTS

Writing a book takes time, effort and revision. I'd like to thank all those who contributed. A special thanks to Joan Conway for her thoughtful comments and advice. Also thanks to Frank Childress for being an early reader. Another word of thanks to Jim Brown for all his helpful advice on the publishing process. Finally, a second thank you to my wonderful husband Fred, who suffered through several drafts and offered helpful advice on each.

1. DECEPTION

As I walk down the hallway with my father, I stare at the Persian rug beneath my feet, wanting more than anything to be like it. Yes, a strange desire. But, well placed, as the rug is a fake. It is good at pretending to be something it is not. Tonight, my fate depends on me pretending.

The rug is better than me. Most people would think it is a handmade Persian rug. It is pristinely woven with a medallion at center, surrounded by intricate flowers, and red and blue swirls spaced perfectly apart in a repeating pattern — a little too perfect. That is the telltale sign the rug is a fake. Machines are flawless. Real loom maidens who labor for hours by hand make mistakes. There's a certain irony to it: the rug shows it's imperfect by being too perfect.

I keep my head down, face hidden, in case I have a telltale sign. I stare at the rug, feel it squish softly beneath my feet and do not speak to my father. That seems easier than facing him.

No one needs to walk a 23-year-old to her bedroom, so I know he wants to talk. But I'm afraid if he gets a good look at me, he'll realize what I'm planning. Even if I were as good as the rug, he's the equivalent of a Persian rug expert. He's hard to fool. So I stare at the swirls and watch one sock-clad foot step in front of the other.

The little white tassels appear. Rug is done. It ends at my room. I lift my gaze to the polished mahogany door. Centered a little lower than eye level is a nameplate made of baked dough decorated in pink and yellow flowers. KELSEY, it reads. It has held up well, considering I made it in fourth grade.

I focus on that nameplate, but from the corner of my eye I see my father turn toward me. Though I feel his stare, I don't return his gaze. Not yet. I can't.

"Kelsey," he says, just above a whisper, but authoritatively. I turn and tilt my head up to meet his eyes. My father is a half-foot taller than me at 6 feet even. His face always appears accessible — a hazard of his job, I suppose. He is trying to look accessible now, in hopes that I will confide in him. He is using his most effective trait — his penetrating, soulful blue-gray eyes — to his advantage. Those eyes can either make you open up and pour out your most cherished thoughts or cower with fear.

Tonight, he eyes me sympathetically. "Honey, I know you're worried about tomorrow," he says in the "I really care" tone perfected in his early career. I nod. It's true. I am worried, but not for the reasons he thinks. "You'll be fine," he assures me. "This is a very safe procedure."

I try not to move the muscles in my face — no twitching or grimaces — nothing to hint I'm being dishonest. I just nod again. Yes, the procedure is very safe. Incredibly safe, unless you're in the five percent who suffer major complications.

His lips are pressed together tightly and his eyes stoic. Does he know I'm hiding the truth? I want a moment more to analyze him, to try to decipher all the body language he's worked so hard to keep controlled so he presents only the information he wants out. But at that moment, he pulls me into a hug. I don't expect it. My father is many things: strong, brave, courageous, stubborn, idealistic. Touchy-feely, not so much. Despite the shock of the embrace, I manage to lift my arms and wrap them around him. I try not to wrinkle his suit jacket too much. A wrinkled suit jacket won't look good if a reporter snaps his picture.

"You're doing the right thing," he whispers in my ear.

"I know," I whisper back. This is true. I know I am doing the right thing. Only, what I'm going to do isn't what he wants me to do.

He releases me, takes a step back and smiles — a genuine one. As a politician, my father smiles a lot. Most smiles are for show, because no one wants to see a grim man kissing babies or shaking hands. The public smile means nothing. Pulling his lips into that friendly curl is as easy as breathing to my father. Seeing the public smile is about as endearing as seeing him scratch his forehead. The genuine smile, the one my mother showed me the hallmarks of, is the one I love. If he blesses you with it, it means you truly have his heart.

I pray my actions tonight won't break that heart. Part of me wants to tell him I'm sorry, so sorry, for what I'm about to do. To make amends before I leave. The other part of me, the part that knows I can't let him find out, not prematurely, not when he can still stop me, just wants him to leave. I smile back, but this time it's my public smile.

I wonder if he can tell. If so, he doesn't let on. He looks down at the thin black watch wrapped around his wrist. "It's eight o'clock. That means nothing else to eat tonight, though you can have a few sips of water if you're thirsty."

I nod, relaxing the muscles in my face to look calm. I lean back against the hallway wall, trying to look like someone ready to do what Dad wants.

Dad wears a neutral expression, but frustration is etched in his blue-gray eyes. "I can see you're still worried, sweetheart," he says. "Do you want me to stay here tonight?"

Panic. I feel like my heart stops, and wonder if my face is giving me away. Quickly, I look down at the rug's swirls, hoping to hide any fear visible in my expression. This is bad. He has to leave. Has to go to his meeting, then stay at the condo he owns in the city. I force a smile, meet his eyes again, do my best to look reassuring and shake my head. "No, you should go, Daddy," I say encouragingly, moving off the wall and lightly patting his jacket sleeve. "You're already dressed and ready to go, and I'd like some peace tonight. I want to think, get a good night's sleep. I'd feel bad if I kept you from work for no reason."

I'm rambling. I need to wrap it up. But how? I glance at the rug for inspiration. It makes faking look so easy. My eyes find my father again. "Plus, Haleema's here," I finish, letting him draw his own conclusions.

Haleema is technically my father's assistant, but nowadays she mainly looks after the house, because we are rarely here. Since my mother died, Haleema has been a godsend for me. She's provided maternal advice and a nurturing presence. I appreciate her more than I can say, because my father is gone so often. My father, I believe, recognizes his reliance on Haleema. I think he's always felt that if there were something he didn't see because he wasn't a mother, she would catch it and help me.

I watch my father closely, trying to look OK, trying not to show panic. I lift my hand to pull a strand of hair and twirl it around my finger, but stop myself just in time. Instead, I smoothly redirect and scratch my ear, then return the hand to my side. Playing with my hair will ensure he stays.

My father is unnaturally still as he watches me. He's looking for a sign of what to do. Debating whether to take me at my word. Debating if I want some woman-to-woman bonding time with Haleema, to really be alone, or if he should delve deeper. Debating whether he needs to be fatherly in some way he isn't right now. I've seen this internal debate play out across his furrowed brow too often lately. He takes in a breath, and I can tell he has decided to try again to be fatherly.

"I can stay if you want," he says, measuring my reaction. "It's not really work, Kelsey. It's just a strategy meeting and cocktails with a couple of donors."

"Big donors," I retort, raising an eyebrow. "Go ahead, I'll be fine. No need to worry about me, OK?" I proffer another smile, trying to make it look genuine.

He doesn't move. Instead, he fixes his eyes on me, as if by looking hard enough he might see some secret hidden in my expression, some clue as to what he should do. I wonder if all fathers feel this level of uncertainty when dealing with their children, or only widowers.

After a moment more of thought, he nods, then kisses my forehead. "You know, you will be fine. The doctors are very good. Not to mention," he adds with a chuckle, "You're the daughter of the lead gubernatorial candidate. Your dad also happens to be a sitting state senator. They'll take extra good care of you."

I smile again, step toward my room, grab the knob, turn it and push the door open. Dad still watches, refusing to leave me just yet. I turn back to him, breathe out and say affectionately and truthfully, "I love you, Dad." I know these are the last words I'll say to him in person.

He replies in kind, clearly assuming this is just like any other night. Then he turns around and walks back down the hallway. I step inside, close the door. Safe. For now.

2. WAITING

I lean against my door, thankful my father is gone. The first hurdle is complete. The next will be getting out of here unseen.

If all goes well, I'll be leaving in two hours. If things go perfectly, I'll be safe, truly safe and out of harm's way, by this time tomorrow. If things don't go well ... I don't want to think about that.

I relinquish my spot at the door and take another step in. Even though I've been here for more than a week, I am suddenly struck by how much this room no longer represents me. The best way to describe my room is girly. The bed has been here since I was 12: an oak, four-poster with a pink canopy and matching ruffled covers. Photos of friends dot the wall. Teddy bears, dolls and other stuffed animals adorn the dresser and desk. The pale pink walls still bear the flowers I painted on them when I was pubescent. Definitely girly.

This is a room for the naïve, the innocent, those who don't know what I do.

Even though I can't leave yet — I need an important signal first — I don't want to be idle. I decide to get ready.

I go to my dresser, cattycorner to the door, and take out a black turtleneck. I considered wearing it to dinner, but thought it would make me look grim and unhappy. I pull the yellow shirt I'm wearing over my head and toss it in the dirty clothes bin. Then, I slide the turtleneck on and walk a few steps to the full-length mirror affixed to the wall.

My wavy brown hair is hanging naturally, fanning out across my shoulders. That won't do. I pull it back it into a bun. Now, the blonde wig will be easier to put on. In the mirror, giving myself the

5

once over, I can't help concentrating on my eyes. They're brown. Nothing out of the ordinary, flashy or particularly memorable, but the brown suits me, I think. I have a pair of blue contact lenses in my bag — another part of my disguise. I tried them on the other day, and my eyes looked mutant. I hope this was just because I'm not used to the look, and to passersby, I'll appear normal. With luck, I won't need the wig or blue mutant eyes.

I turn my body for a profile view. The black pants and top make the perfect stealth outfit. I run my fingers across my midsection, then lift my shirt so I can see the area where they plan to make the incision tomorrow. I shake my head. I won't let them. They aren't going to cut me open and take what's mine.

I lower my shirt, turn away from the mirror, away from this line of thought, then look at my watch: 8:12. Nothing to do until 10:15 but wait, watch the hands tick by, then get up and flee the only life I've ever really known.

I head over to my bed. It's a stupid move, really, but I'm floundering a little and don't know what to do. So I sit on the bed, positioned against the wall. The bed is comfy and inviting, not something I want to leave. Clearly this is not a good place to sit. However, I find myself drawn to it. A corkboard pinned with pictures hangs on the wall above the bed. I home in on a photo of my father and me at a rally a couple of years ago. The big "Life First" banner hangs prominently above us. It's such hypocrisy, I think, absentmindedly brushing my fingers across my midsection. If this is Life First, I want no part of it.

Beneath that picture is one of me and Susan when we were 13 and both at Camp Picklewick — a ridiculously silly name for a camp, if you ask me. Anyway, the photo was taken before the incident at the lake. Susan's arms are wrapped around me, and she's showing off her wide-mouthed, goofy grin. Her eyes are fearless. I wish I could be bold like her. It feels like she's been my best friend forever, but the summer that picture was taken is the one that forever bonded us together.

I blow out a long breath, close my eyes and lean back on the stack of pillows at the head of my bed. Stupider still, I'm sure. I shouldn't get comfortable when I have to leave soon.

I sit up, trying to yank myself out of this plush, comforting bed. I need to be ready to leave. I go over my plan in my head: escape the house with our dog, go through the woods, meet up with Luke and

Dr. Grant at the church.

Really simple. I hope.

I wish Luke were here already. I'd feel better. Luke has always had that effect on me. Even the first time I met him — in a pub near campus my sophomore year of college — he made me feel glad I'd met him. And that's saying something, as he was drunk and unpleasant that night. I next saw him a year later — walking across the quad talking conspiratorially with Dr. Grant. I was immediately glad to see him. So glad, I stopped in my tracks and watched them. He noticed and came over. Despite my embarrassment at being caught staring, I was happy that the tall guy with the mop of brown hair was striding toward me.

"I remember you," he said.

"Really?" I hadn't been able to hide my surprise. From the moment I saw him, I knew it was him. But the idea of him remembering me, a year later, when we hadn't spoken or seen each other again, made me feel happier than it should have

"Moe's Pub. A year ago," he offered, in case I hadn't remembered. "I was a total jerk, and you walked out."

He had it perfectly clear. "I'm surprised you remember me."

"Of course I do," he said, winking. "You're the one that got away."

I could feel myself blushing, but had no way to stop it. He was definitely charming, when he wasn't ogling. "So, are you still a total jerk?"

"Not a total jerk," he said, emphasizing the word total. "Though, I still have my moments."

He'd said it to be funny. It wasn't true. Luke is refreshingly "moment" free. That's why I wish he were here. He helps me stay calm. Luke is the one person in this world whom I'd be completely lost without. And tonight Luke is going to help me escape. I pray we succeed. For, if we don't, tomorrow my government will strap me to a gurney, slice me open, take my kidney and give it to someone else.

3. LMS

If I could bounce off the walls, I would. The wait is getting to me. It's hard knowing what you want is within reach, but untouchable at the moment. I urge my students to be patient daily, yet here I am unable to take my own advice. I temporarily calm myself by reading a novel about space adventures. It is trite and silly, but I enjoy it because it's a gift from Luke. And anything from Luke makes me happy.

I sit "crisscross applesauce," as we kindergarten teachers love to say, with my back against the wall. The room feels too warm, so I roll up my sleeves and fan myself with the book. I glide the book through the air slowly, but consistently, bringing a weak, but steady, breeze. Then it occurs to me that maybe it isn't hot. Maybe it's just nerves. Maybe fleeing has put me on edge.

I look at my arm, midway between wrist and elbow, at the slightly raised square of flesh that used to give me such comfort. Just under the skin is my life monitoring system (LMS): a tiny computer chip that tracks the body's major systems to make sure they're functioning correctly. Each LMS is linked wirelessly to a government database. If my blood pressure were to dip dramatically due to a stab wound, the LMS would signal the government for help. Because all LMS chips emit a low-level tracking beacon, the government can easily find anyone and send aid.

I've always felt comforted knowing my LMS would bring help. It was like the ultimate safety blanket. But tonight, I feel the opposite. The LMS means I can be tracked, and that is the last thing I want. If the rumors are true, authorities are monitoring my LMS data. If I leave, the LMS will lead them to me within minutes.

Under normal circumstances, that is. But, a few well-placed dollars allowed Luke and I to change the circumstances. A source inside the LMS monitoring group promised to alter my identity data temporarily. For a period overnight, the source will switch Haleema's LMS data with mine. When I leave, it will look like Haleema is leaving. No reason for anyone to get alarmed. I feel guilty about involving Haleema. There weren't a lot of choices about whom to switch ID with, and I've convinced myself that she'll be OK with it. Hopefully, this is not wishful thinking.

Once I leave here, I'll travel about a mile to the safe house, where Dr. Grant will remove my LMS and place it in Buddy, our five-year-old Black Russian Terrier. Normally, removing an LMS causes the device's alarm to go off. However, Dr. Grant knows a way to stop the alarm from sounding long enough to reinsert the LMS into Buddy. A regulator chip will make sure Buddy's data looks enough like a person's that techs shouldn't notice any difference. Unfortunately, the chip can only regulate data, not forge it, so the LMS must be implanted into another mammal in order for the regulator to work. Mainly it will control for minor differences in heart rate and temperature between dogs and humans. It would be better if we could simply take my chip out, slap the regulator on it and leave it in my room. But, this is the best we can do. The tech will switch Haleema's and my data back in the morning. When I don't show for surgery, authorities will track my LMS and find only Buddy. I'll be long gone.

That's the plan at least. All I need now is Susan's call — at 10:15 — to say my LMS data has been switched with Haleema's.

The mobile phone in my pocket is set to vibrate, so Haleema won't hear. I don't want to involve Susan in my escape. She's already had more trouble than anyone deserves in life. Yet, she wants to be a part of this. She wants to help set me free.

Given all she's been through, I feel I owe it to her. Owe her the opportunity to help me. We're uneven in our relationship. Not in any tangible way, but in a more ethereal way. Susan thinks about it like Yin and Yang or tit-for-tat or basic Karma. She believes things need to be balanced, equal. In reality, things are, but she doesn't see it that way. She is hung up on Camp Picklewick. That was the summer I saved Susan's life.

Even back then, Susan was an overachiever. She wanted to be the best at everything. And that summer, being the best meant winning the camp triathlon. She had everything down, except for swimming, so she dragged me out to the lake to watch her practice. She told me the only way to improve was to "push yourself to the brink, then go one step more." She couldn't go one step more that day, though. From the shore, 50 yards away, I saw her go under.

Survival statistics had taught me well. If I called for help and waited, she would die. If I saved her myself, she had a chance at life. So, I jumped in and swam to her, reminding myself that the average swimmer had an 87 percent chance of pulling this off. Thank God Susan's hair is as bright and fiery red as her personality. It was the only thing that helped me find her. She'd been sinking and resurfacing, so I could keep track of her, and execute my sorry attempt at a rescue. As I got close enough to almost grab her, she sank and didn't bob back to the top. I managed to duck my head under and see that dazzling red plume of hair in the murky water. Reaching her, grabbing hold and pulling her head above water was the most satisfying moment of my life. I had saved my best friend from certain death.

That rescue threw us out-of-whack. Susan feels she owes me for that day, owes me something more than she owes the rest of society. Frankly, any average swimmer would have done for her what I did. Only, it was me who saved her, so she wants to repay me. She thinks helping me now will somehow even the slate.

Truth is, the slate's always been even. I was a shy child, and having a friend like Susan, an outgoing, dynamic, full-force personality, helped me immeasurably in making new friends and fitting in. But, she's never seen it that way. So, tonight, she's my signal that it's time to go, that I don't have to worry about my LMS betraying me. After tonight, we'll be even in her mind.

4. GO

The buzzing on my thigh startles me. Realizing it's my phone, I pull it from my pocket and glance at the screen. Susan's number. I press "answer" and put the phone to my ear. "Hello," I say softly.

"Hey former roomy," Susan says.

"Don't start," I retort, full of mock indignation. "I'm coming back to our apartment — after I recover."

She chuckles. "I know. I miss you," she says. "I just wanted to make sure you were alright. I didn't wake you, did I?"

"No, no. I wasn't quite ready for sleep yet. I'm glad you called."

This has all been rehearsed, in the event my line is being recorded. There are rumors that once you've been marked, nothing is private. That everything is monitored to make sure no one does precisely what I am attempting to do. It's not clear if this rumor is true, so we don't want to chance it.

Susan and I came up with plausible patter. It's all true. I'm glad she called; I would go back to our apartment, if I were really going through with the surgery. I miss her. I miss our apartment. I wish I could be there. Sadly, the escape plan requires me to leave from here.

"Are you worried?" Susan asks me, following the script to a tee.

"A little," I lie. I'm incredibly worried. "It's normal to be a little nervous before surgery, right?"

"Yeah, it is, but don't worry. Everything will be fine. You're all set to go."

That's it. That's the signal. Simple and clear: You're all set to go. My entire body relaxes. At least a hundred muscles I hadn't realized were tight unfurl all at once. I know Susan will hear the relief in my

11

voice. "Yeah, you're right Susan. I shouldn't worry."

Her tone changes subtly, and I know she has picked up on the fact that I am no longer a heap of tangled nerves. She continues her part. "It's late, Kelsey. You ought to get some sleep."

"Yeah, I think I will," I say, just as we rehearsed. "Good night."

She responds in kind, and with that, I press "end call," tuck the phone under my pillow and climb out of bed. This is it. Do or die. Now or never.

My stomach churns as I grab my shoulder bag. It has cash, the wig, contact lenses, and a fake ID. I'm not sure how helpful the fake ID will be. If someone's asking for my ID, I'm already in trouble.

Securing the satchel over my shoulder, I stop at my dresser and pull out two envelopes: a letter for my father and another for Haleema. It's the best I can do at good-bye, since I can't say it personally. I set the letters on the dresser, quickly feeling my father's to make sure the chip with the video recording is sealed inside.

* * *

Skulking out of the house with Buddy is simpler than I expected. I don't run into Haleema or anyone else. I simply creep down the stairs, secure my wig, grab Buddy, slide open the door and cross the yard. I look back at the stately brick house and mouth a final good-bye. This place will always hold a special place in my heart because I lived here with my mother. But, I can't stay any longer.

After a few quick paces, I am in the forest and out of sight.

All night, I've been avoiding thinking about my fate, but here in the darkness, I can't help feeling slightly bitter knowing that society hasn't always been like this. That there was a time when things were different. A time before the pandemics that wiped out 80 percent of the world's population. A time before society decided we owed our fellow man all that we could safely give, if it meant survival. A time before there were statistical charts that told you when you should sacrifice to save others and when it was too risky to save a life. A time before you had to give blood biennially during the month of your birth to maintain an efficient, healthy blood supply. A time before everyone got DNA-typed, with the info stuck in a database to use if someone get really sick and need a donation.

It's been 100 years since the pandemics hit, and 50 years since the era of Life First swept in. It was a little more than three weeks ago I learned I was likely the best match for a man in Virginia with failing kidneys. Two weeks ago, the results of extra testing came back and confirmed I was indeed the best match. I was officially marked for donation. And once you're marked, there is no turning back.

So, I won't. I can't. Instead, I look ahead, into the pit of darkness before me and take heart knowing that not everyone fell in love with Life First. Jerry Maylee didn't. He took his band of people opposed to Life First laws and set up shop in what used to be called Florida. The joke at the time was that the strip of land would erode away in a few hundred years, and the world would finally be rid of those who refused to preserve life.

When he was no longer part of the nation, Mr. Maylee and his band of followers decided to name their new country Peoria after Maylee's hometown. The original Peoria, the one Mr. Maylee was from, was in Illinois. There was an ancient entertainment slogan that evolved among performers who tested their shows in small towns before taking them to big cities: "If it won't play in Peoria, it won't play anywhere." Well, for Mr. Maylee, "Life First" didn't play in Peoria, and it never would.

So that's where I am headed tonight: Peoria. I will take the midnight train to Georgia. It's some odd historical thing that runs twice a month. Luckily, tonight is one of the runs. Once I get to Georgia, I'll get a one-way rental car, saying that I am going to visit family, and drive to the border town of Valdosta. Then I will sneak across the border, using a hidden crossing. And at last I'll be safe.

5. TROUBLE

Crossing the forest is a process that requires the bulk of my concentration. Not because it is particularly arduous, but because it is so pitch black. There is cloud cover so the moon — and it's beautiful, guiding light — is hidden. I can't use a flashlight for fear someone will see me. Maybe that's an irrational fear. Who in their right mind is in the woods in the middle of the night?

So, I march ahead with Buddy padding along almost noiselessly at my side. He's a good dog that way. I wish he didn't have to be part of this. I'm dragging everyone — Haleema, Buddy, Susan — into my escape. I must not get distracted by those thoughts. I must focus on moving forward.

I count off seconds in my head, trying to approximate the ticking of a clock. My test walk through the forest the other day took 18 minutes, 1080 seconds. When I get to that magic number, I should be at the clearing and almost at the church.

That's the place Dr. Grant picked to meet. He's used it before, he said, though I don't know the reason. I haven't asked, nor will I. Dr. Grant's services require secrecy, and I have no interest in violating that mandate. Fittingly, the church was a stop on the Underground Railroad hundreds of years ago and its secret cellar still exists.

I stop just short of the edge of the woods that separate my family's home from St. Ignatius. I need to go it alone for the moment, so I tie Buddy to a tree, a few yards into the woods, tell him to stay and that I'll be back soon. He seems hesitant, but remains still as I walk to the tree line adjacent to the church's lawn.

Like the woods, the church rests at an elevation higher than the street. The grounds are dimly lit, as are all things. Light pollution is bad for the earth, and therefore people, so all lights remain dim, unless a person is nearby. The grounds won't illuminate until I get close enough to be picked up by the motion sensors.

I scan the area. Down the hill, parked on the street is a tan sedan that will serve as my escape car. Once Dr. Grant has removed my LMS, I will drive that unmemorable vehicle to the train station.

I take a deep breath, close my eyes, whisper a quick prayer, and step out of the woods. When I am halfway across the field separating the woods from the church, headlights appear on the road. I contemplate dashing to the building, but see red strobes illuminate the night like a disco ball. A police car. Shit.

Do they know already? Did my father come back to check on me and find me missing? Are they here to take me back to him? Or worse, to take me to a holding facility? No, it's early. Even if I am caught, I won't be sent to a holding facility. I haven't, technically, done anything wrong yet. It won't be a crime until I don't show up in the morning.

I consider running back to the woods, but an officer would catch me. Not to mention, what if I am wrong? What if they haven't realized I am running? What if they aren't trying to bring me back home? What if this is coincidence? Then, I'll definitely look suspicious.

The police car parks on the road in front of the church. A stone path cuts downhill through the field connecting the road to the church's front door. The officer gets out and begins climbing the path toward me.

I quickly lift one hand to my head, and feel to make sure the wig remains in place. Although it seems fine, there is no way to know for sure without a mirror. I turn my head, then reach into my shoulder bag and put on a pair of glasses Dr. Grant gave me. The lenses have no magnification; but he felt they would make my real features less memorable. As I turn back, the officer is cresting the top step and heading my direction. I wait for him to come closer, then smile. "Good evening, officer," I say.

He looks me over as if I don't belong, releases a long sigh, then forces a smile. "Evening, Ma'am," he says, removing his cap. He inclines his head in the direction of the car parked on the street a few feet in front of his cruiser. "Is that your car?"

I nod, trying to perfect a confused expression. I pretend to be the normal one. He is the weirdo for asking about a strange woman and a strange car at a church late at night.

He looks back toward the car, then at me, fidgeting with the cap in his hands. "Are you alright?"

Now, I genuinely am confused. I nod again.

He puts his cap back on. "Can you speak your answers, so I can make sure you're OK?"

"Sure," I say, nodding my head yet again for reinforcement. It feels like it's becoming a nervous tic. I'll have to stop nodding. "I'm fine. Why do you ask?"

He shifts his weight from his left foot to his right and shakes his head sheepishly. "Governor Wannabe is a do-gooder," he says.

I raise an eyebrow. "Which candidate?"

"Reed. He has a house not far from here. He called to report a vehicle parked in front of the church. Said it had been here when he arrived three hours ago, and was still here when he left. He thought the church was closed, and wanted an officer to come check out the area, make sure no one had been hurt."

I feign another puzzled look as I privately wish my father would mind his own business. "LMS would've reported someone hurt, right?"

He chuckles. "Yeah, but you know how these bigwigs get. They want someone to check it out. How'd it look if he saw this, didn't report it and we found someone dead due to a damaged sensor."

I touch my forearm. "Damaged? These things are great. Never had a moment of trouble with mine."

He briefly eyes the little square protrusion between his wrist and elbow, then me. "Yeah, me neither."

We share a moment of silence, as neither of us has much else to say. As I hear the crickets singing their night song, I pray Buddy will stay quiet. He isn't much of a barker, but he also isn't used to being left alone in the woods.

I need to move this along. I tilt my head toward the church. "Well," I say, as I begin walking. "If that's it, I'm going to get back to church."

He follows me a second, then reaches out and grabs hold of my shoulder. "Wait," he barks. I turn to face him, and he lets go of me. Clearly puzzled, he looks at the church and says, "It's closed."

I start to shake my head, but stop, as I'm concerned about the wig. "No, it's open," I explain. "For prayer and candle lighting."

He looks toward the church, where light is emanating from one of the chapel's stained-glass windows, then back to me. He pauses, asks. "So, you've been here, for several hours?"

I wish this guy would leave. I want to bolt, but being too urgent will do me no good. I smile, as if he's just said the silliest thing in the world. "No, of course not." I lower my voice, cast my eyes down and pause through my words as if I'm choked up. "This was my mother's favorite church. She died when I was six, in a crash at 11 o'clock. I wanted to light a candle at her exact time of death. I stopped in earlier to check with the chaplain that this was still a 24-hour church. I just came back a little while ago."

Now he looks ashamed for asking. I feel guilty. So guilty. He's going to realize tomorrow he's been fooled, and he might even get punished for not realizing I'm a fraud. He offers up a respectful nod. "I'm sorry to hear that, Ma'am" he declares. "I won't intrude on you anymore then."

He turns and walks down the grass, to his car. "Be safe, Ma'am," he says right before hopping in and driving off.

I wait until he's out of sight, then scurry to the church. The main door is open. A sign at the entry reads, "All welcome in the House of the Lord at all times." It is, in fact, a 24-hour church. I look around. No one is inside. I need to get to the meeting place.

I walk down the aisle, take a right at the altar, and enter a door labeled, "Staff only."

Down a flight of stairs, into a dark basement, through another doorway, and finally to a floor-to-ceiling shelf filled with metal pots and pans. I pull the entire shelf forward, just as Dr. Grant told me. The shelf, on a hinge, easily pivots out of my way. Behind it, is a door with no knob on my side. Only a keyhole. I knock five times, wait 10 seconds, knock three times, wait 10 seconds and knock five times again.

A moment later, Dr. Grant opens the door.

6. LUKE'S LAW

I smile. Dr. Grant does not. His face is overwhelmingly serious. I notice his left cheek is darkish purple, as if he's suffered some injury. My insides turn uneasily as the first inkling of something wrong hits me. I've only been in the tiny secret room a moment, and things are going downhill.

The room is only about 12 feet by 12 feet, and reminds me of the tiny dorm rooms on campus dubbed "psycho singles" due to their claustrophobic nature. The wall's contours are curved, uneven, like a cavern. A few feet away, I see a figure sitting on the floor, back to the wall, head tucked down, knees pressed to chest. Even though his face isn't showing, I'd know that sandy brown mop of hair anywhere.

"Luke," I say softly, taking a couple of steps toward him. I am afraid that saying it louder or getting any closer means he'll hear me speak, look up, and confirm the sinking feeling I have. But, in truth, his very posture has already done that. Why would my Luke not get up and greet me? Why wouldn't he sweep me into his arms and murmur in my ear words of encouragement about tonight, if everything were alright?

Luke doesn't answer. I'm sure he heard me, and not answering further hammers in what I already know: something is terribly wrong.

I turn back to Dr. Grant. "What's going on? And what happened to your face?"

Dr. Grant looks away from me, closing the door to the secret room. When he turns back, he sighs and puts his hand to his chin, considering my question. I search his face for any clues about what has gone wrong.

From behind me, Luke speaks. "I hit him."

Frozen momentarily by what he said, I take my time to slowly turn and face him. "What?" He can't have said what I thought he did. I wonder if saying the words aloud will help them make sense. "You hit him?"

He doesn't speak but nods and inclines his head toward the doctor. My lips part slightly, then I stop myself from giving into the jaw-dropping shock I feel. Instead, I take a deep breath and hope a moment of silence will help me compose myself. I don't want to be angry at Luke. Not now. Not when time is of the essence. Not when I am barely holding it together as is. But I do want answers.

Feeling silly in this ridiculous blonde wig and wanting Luke to see the real me, I pull it off my head, and shove it in my shoulder bag. I do the same with the stocking cap and rubber band that had been holding my hair in a bun. Yanking the shoulder strap over my head, I drop my satchel to the floor and take the few remaining steps to get to Luke, who is blanketed in shadow in the crevice he's chosen. I kneel and look at his face. His blue eyes are moist at the edges and he appears to be suppressing a deep urge to scream — or perhaps an urge to hit Dr. Grant again.

I whisper, "Why did you hit him?"

He looks past me, at Dr. Grant. "Tell her," he spits, with more venom than I've ever heard him direct at another human being.

"I made a mistake," Dr. Grant admits, moving closer to us. I stand, doing a 180 to face Dr. Grant and strategically placing myself between the men, afraid Luke might have another outburst.

I dig my toes deep into my shoes, trying to plant myself, steel myself for whatever Dr. Grant must tell me about his mistake. Part of me doesn't want to hear it, but I know I must find out because it clearly is going to affect my escape. And it clearly isn't good.

"Is it something we can fix?" I ask, hopefully.

He shakes his head, still looking severe. After a moment, he puts a hand on my shoulder, then sets his amber-eyed gaze on me. "Do you remember when I asked you if you had your original LMS?"

I nod, though I am confused. This is irrelevant. "Yes, I remember. I still have the original."

He looks at the dirt floor briefly, then back at me and shakes his head.

"You should have checked sooner," Luke mutters from behind me.

The doctor ignores me, instead eyeing Luke. "I know," he says remorsefully.

"What are you talking about?" I ask, still confused. "I have my original LMS. It's never been replaced. I would know if it had been replaced."

Both men are silent a moment. Then, Dr. Grant turns his attention to me again. "Did you break your arm when you were six?"

My knees suddenly feel weak, and gravity's force seems to have gained extra pull. I nod, as I can't muster any sound from my throat. Knowing I can't stand anymore, that my legs won't support me, that they will succumb to this overwhelming urge to sink into a hole, I lower myself down, landing not far from Luke. The ground is cold and hard, just like the new reality settling around me. I feel Luke's hand on my back, rubbing lightly.

"Well, according to the medical records," Dr. Grant says, "it was a fairly bad break, with the bone splintering."

"I had to have surgery," I say flatly. I don't remember everything about the incident. The haziness of my memory is probably due to the trauma of being thrown from a horse. At the time, we were all thankful I was still alive, safe. A broken bone was getting off easy, the doctors had said. My parents had arranged what should have been a safe ride. Although the instructor had held the reigns the entire time, a fox darted out of the forest and spooked the Saddlebred. It was so sudden, the instructor lost his grip, the horse bolted, and I slammed into the ground, landing on my arm.

Dr. Grant speaks softly. "The records show they decided to replace the LMS while they already had the arm opened up for the bone repair. It was the latest model at the time. It's the one they still use today." I know the ramifications of what he is saying, but he spells it out anyway. "I can't take it out, Kelsey."

I feel my heartbeat pick up, my breathing increase. This is insane. Ridiculous. He has to take it out. If he doesn't take it out, they will find me. The air suddenly seems thinner in this tiny room. I look to Dr. Grant, praying there's something more he can do.

"What about changing the information. Just switch the information again," I say in a voice that sounds too high and pitchy, even to my own ears.

He shakes his head. "My guy can't do that, Kelsey. He has a family, too. He was at his risk limit in switching the data overnight. In a little more than nine hours, you're going to be Kelsey Reed again."

"Nine hours," I repeat. It's not enough time. They will find me. And then they'll strap me to a gurney and take my kidney.

"It'll be OK, Kelsey," Luke whispers in my ear as he wraps his arms around me. "We'll think of something."

If anyone else had said that, I would have thought it was a lie, a lie meant to soothe. And I suppose it's possible it is just that. Only, Luke doesn't say things lightly. He pulls no punches, and speaks only of the possible. If he says we can think of something, then maybe we can.

Dr. Grant looks at us and begins walking toward the door. Clearly feeling like the third wheel he is, he excuses himself to check messages.

We're alone, and I am trying to let the warmth of Luke's embrace drown out the nightmare of what I've just been told.

"Kelsey," he says. He is so close, I feel his warm breath tickle my ear. My whole body lights up when he speaks my name. He says it as if he's a thirst-quenched man in the desert and I am his oasis. I want to sit here with him, like this, forever. Only, I know I can't. I sigh, as I pivot around on my bottom to face him. Our knees touch now, as we sit cross-legged on the ground.

"Now do you believe in Murphy's Law?" I ask. This is a running joke between us. He thinks Murphy's Law — "whatever can go wrong, will go wrong, and at the worst possible time" — is a ridiculous adage. Hokum, he calls it. Instead, he thinks we should abide by Luke's Law: whenever something goes wrong, fix it.

Tonight, instead of chiming in about Luke's Law, he says, "Maybe I should become a believer."

He looks unsure, unsteady. I have never seen that in him before. He strokes my cheek, then looks down at the ground or my hand or at anything but my eyes. Finally, he looks back up. The uncertainty in his eyes scares me. It's the antithesis of Luke. Luke is self-assured, confident, someone who protects and keeps others safe. The Luke in front of me now seems to need protection.

I try to be brave for him. "Don't give up on Luke's Law," I say, mustering my best look of encouragement. "We can think of something."

He looks down again and doesn't speak for a few seconds. The silence unnerves me. It's so unlike him to be silent when he clearly has something on his mind. His unease is spreading to me. If his jitters infect me, I'll be up and pacing this tiny room in a minute. I need him to speak.

As if in answer to my silent request, he meets my eyes and begins. "What if the simplest fix is the one staring us in the face?"

I lean back, confused. "What would that be?"

He doesn't say it for the longest time, then whispers, "Maybe you could just go through with it?"

The words hang there in the air, as I try to comprehend. Go through with it? Give up my kidney for a stranger when it could leave me disabled, or even dead? He wants me to do something he knows I don't want. I am rebuking society and everything in FoSS by trying to run. I have to live with that, and I've reconciled that. Now he wants me to question it again.

The horror I am feeling — that he now wants me to do this, when he has been so against it from the beginning — must show on my face, because he immediately follows up. "Kelsey, there's very little risk," he says like a speed-talking salesman. "You'll be very safe. I know the doctors will be very careful, especially because you're Senator Reed's daughter. And losing a kidney is not the end of the world. People do it all the time."

I stand up, turn my back to him, and walk across the room. I want to get away from him. The idea that he wants me to do this is beyond my comprehension. He introduced me to the underground pro-choice movement on campus. He has all sorts of banned historical books and pamphlets discussing individual rights and freedoms. He hates the Life First mantra. How could he, of all people, say this?

"Why would you want me to do this?" I ask, the bitterness seeping out, despite my best efforts to control it. "Aren't you for personal choice as much as I am?"

He stands, crosses the room and positions himself right behind me. I can't turn to face him, though. He's stopped short of touching me, but I can feel the warmth radiating from his body. His voice is low, yet clear.

"I am for personal choice," he declares. "My choice is to be with you. Always. And I don't care if you have one kidney or two."

He slips his arms around my waist and kisses my neck. "I can't lose you to a holding facility over something as small as a kidney. Please, for me, consider just doing it."

Part of me wants to say, longs to say, "Of course." That's the effect Luke has on me. I want to give him every part of me. And if the kidney were for Luke, I would give it up in a heartbeat. I'd give him both without a second thought. But, for a stranger? When losing a kidney means I could ultimately lose my health, my ability to enjoy my time with Luke or, worse, my own life?

I slowly circle around to face him. Still nestled in his protective arms, I peek up at him and find his pale blue eyes, desperation deep within them, staring at me. He's afraid, I realize.

"Please," he says.

I can't look at him anymore. If I do, I will tell him yes. So, I close my eyes and bury my face in his chest. He smells slightly sweaty and salty. It's a very manly scent, and I inhale deeply to get more of it, more to remember him by, in case the fears he's dreaming up materialize.

"Kelsey, I know I'm asking a lot of you, but you're the best thing I've ever had in my life," he whispers. "I don't want to lose you because of a stupid principle."

I pause. Then I speak words that are, on every level, wrong, but still leave my lips: "Would you love me if I were like Susan?"

"Yes," he says, so quickly, so definitively, so firmly, that I know he means it unequivocally. And for that alone, I love him dearly. The problem is, I won't love me if I'm like Susan. Not because there is something innately wrong with Susan's condition. But, because I could never forgive myself for going in, knowing the risks, and letting it happen. I would always blame myself, wish I'd not gone through it, wish I'd run, if I did turn out like Susan. For Susan, there had been no warning. Her odds were as good as mine, better in fact, but everything had gone wrong and now, after she was marked and had surgery, she is paralyzed. The thought of ending up like Susan — forever damaged by surgical error — terrifies me.

Luke pulls me tighter. "I know what happened to Susan scared you, but it won't happen to you, too. The odds are ridiculously low. You'll be fine, and we can be together if you just do this."

On the most rational level, his words make sense. So much sense. Yet, emotionally, they're all wrong. I don't know I won't be like Susan. And even if everything turns out fine, I won't be me anymore. Won't be Kelsey. I'll be Kelsey without a kidney. Not just Kelsey without a kidney, but Kelsey who didn't fight for her kidney. Kelsey who willingly gave up without a fight, even though she knew it was wrong. How do I make him understand? I close my eyes, and enjoy his comforting arms.

As contented as I am in his arms, I know what I have to ask. "Do you love me?"

"Of course."

"Why do you love me?" I finally bring myself to look him directly in the eyes.

He smiles that darling, cocky, light-up-the-room smile only he has, and says, "We don't have enough time for me to tell you all the reasons I love you."

Classic Luke. It takes a few seconds to get over the swoon and respond. "Tell me three."

"You're beautiful."

I roll my eyes. Of course he goes for one that isn't actually true, and is easy to think up. "And?" I prod.

"You're smart and sexy and honest. And you follow your heart, and try to do what's right."

I nod, thankful he'd gone in the direction I wanted. "And would it be right for me to give up my kidney, Luke, even though I don't want to? To give it to this stranger, when my choice is no?"

His smile fades, he lets go of me and walks across the room, back to his corner. It's my turn to follow. To stand behind him, wrap my arms around him, and warm him in my loving arms. He is silent as we stand huddled in this secret cellar. And when he decides to turn and face me, he asks in a desperate whisper: "Is it so wrong to not do the right thing?"

He looks so wounded that I want to say yes to his request, to say I will give up my kidney if it will wash away the hurt and anguish he's feeling. But I know I can't. Instead, I say: "Ask me again, Luke. If you think it's the right thing to do, ask me again to go through with it so we can be together."

He closes his eyes and pulls me tighter, holding me so snugly that I feel completely loved. But I know he is torn, that he is struggling with what to say. Eventually, he slackens his grip, leans to my ear, and whispers. "Kelsey, will you promise to always be the Kelsey I love, and always fight for what you believe is right?"

"Yes," I whisper back. I'm not sure how I would have answered the alternative question, so I'm glad he didn't ask it. Glad he loves and accepts me for me.

He tilts his head downward and our lips meet. His mouth is warm, soft, and a bit minty from the breath fresheners he chews. The heat from the kiss radiates outward, pulsing from my lips to chin to cheeks, down my neck and spreading like a warm sunrise through my entire body. It's enough to make me forget the damp, chilliness of this subterranean room.

As if on cue, Dr. Grant knocks. "Come in," I call as I detangle myself from Luke. When Dr. Grant has closed the hidden room's door, Luke and I are simply standing next to each other holding hands.

As we stand there, it hits me that the real work begins now. We have to figure out what to do next.

7. A NEW PLAN

I look at Dr. Grant, then my watch. "When does the tech switch us back?"

"Eight a.m."

The time hasn't changed. There is no way I can get out of FoSS.

I shudder involuntarily. Luke squeezes my hand. As bad as things are, Luke's presence keeps me from panicking. In fact, I can think clearly when he is in arm's reach.

Right now, I need answers. Luke and I are holding hands, leaning against the wall at the far end of the room. Dr. Grant stands a few feet in front of us. I take a step closer to him, though my hand still lingers inside Luke's.

"So, give me the short version of why you can't take it out," I say.

He nods briefly, glances nervously at Luke, then back at me. "The older LMS sends an alarm if a person experiences a drop in temperature below 95 degrees. That is nearly four degrees beneath normal body temperature, indicating it's not just a slightly below normal temperature, which some people do have. Something lower than 95 means something is wrong with the user, or that the chip has been forcefully removed."

I nod understanding, so he continues. "Well, this worked fine until people figured out a way to keep the chip warm while it was being removed."

I nod, pull my hand free of Luke's and begin lightly tapping on my thigh. "So, they changed the chip?"

"Not immediately. There wasn't some rash of people removing their chips. But, aware of the problem, they quietly worked on a fix. There was no rush until the Dr. Elkin case."

A shiver runs down my spine at hearing that name. I was too young to understand at the time Elkin committed his crimes, but the name is infamous enough everyone my age has heard it. He was crazy, tortured people.

"You would have been too young to remember the particulars," Dr. Grant says. "But, in a nutshell, Dr. Elkin was a mentally ill veterinarian who stopped taking his psychiatric medication. Authorities were using the LMS to monitor his medication. But, he didn't like the meds. He felt they made him sluggish, so eventually he implanted his LMS chip in a chimpanzee. Elkin gave the ape his medication, so it would show up in the monitoring report. After being off his meds for several weeks, he went on a killing spree. You would have been about three at the time this happened."

I nod. Dr. Grant continues. "Within a year, they'd drastically reduced the rights of the mentally ill and come up with a replacement chip. The newest LMS regularly shoots nanoparticles into the body. They're microscopic electronics that travel through the bloodstream and return to the sensor every three hours. If a nanoparticle doesn't return to the system at the proper interval, an alarm goes off. The nanoparticle then begins emitting a low-level pulse that can be detected by government sensors. So, if I remove the LMS, even controlling for temperature and put it into another mammal, the government will know something is wrong when the nanoparticles don't return. Your LMS will send the distress signal. Once they realize you're gone, they'll send out a team with equipment that detects the nanoparticles. That team will find you."

I begin pacing and wringing my hands. This is bad. I don't have a nine hour escape window. I have a three hour window. Three hours and then they'll start looking for me — and find me. I stop in front of the low curved wall and turn back to Dr. Grant. "So what do I do?"

Dr. Grant looks at me, then at Luke, then back to me. He speaks hesitantly, to Luke. "Maybe she can turn herself in, and refuse to go through with it. She's Senator Reed's daughter. She might get more leeway than others."

Luke's face flushes with anger, and he shoots back, "This is not about furthering your pet causes, Dr. Grant."

Dr. Grant takes a few steps back, stopping when he bumps against the door. He looks from Luke to me. "Kelsey, I'm not interested in this for politics and pet causes. You, of all people, know that. I just thought it was something to consider. It was just an option."

Looking at Dr. Grant, I wonder if it's a viable option. We are all silent for a moment. As Luke realizes I am seriously considering this, he reaches out, grabs my arm and pulls me closer to him, or perhaps away from Dr. Grant.

Ignoring Luke's resistance to the idea, I ask Dr. Grant, "You think they will consider what I say?"

He nods, and appears poised to say more, when Luke blurts out: "All they'd consider is which holding facility to lock you away in."

Dr. Grant treads carefully. "If she showed up, she wouldn't be charged with fleeing. And then, maybe they could figure out a way she wouldn't have to do it." He looks at me tentatively. "Your father is an influential man, and I've heard a rumor that the Virginia governor got his cousin off a match list somehow."

I hold my breath a moment, not sure if this is a real option. My father wants me to do this. If I thought he'd use his sway to get me out of surgery, I would have picked that route first. I shake my head. "My father's not going to be able to help," I tell him. "Do you think, if I turn myself in without him, it will still work?"

Dr. Grant purses his lips, and folds his arms across his chest. "Maybe they still might help you. The movement for choice has picked up steam. We could be at a tipping point. Maybe yours would be the case to tip the scales in favor of allowing people to refuse."

It seems too easy. Are we at a tipping point? Part of me wants to believe that's possible, that people are beginning to see things my way. Even if people are changing, there are still laws. Saying no and sticking around would put me afoul of those laws. "You think I'd have to go to a short-term holding facility while they decided?" I ask Dr. Grant.

"No," Luke growls. Dr. Grant and I both turn to face him. "She's not going into ANY holding facility!"

Luke is adamantly opposed to anything that would put me in or even near a holding facility. I know why, but I'm not sure I agree with him. His father worked in a holding facility his entire career. Luke hates them, believes they are the vilest places on Earth. He views them as if they are prisons. But, they're not. They got rid of prisons after the pandemics. There were so few criminals, so few people that would do anything to upset the tender balance that tilted things towards life, that they weren't really needed.

But, over the years, there have been enough bad apples, enough problem souls who committed crimes and owed society a debt. So, we have holding facilities. The smaller crimes require short-term holding facilities. There, people can get some rehabilitation therapy and serve their debt to society through donation of living goods — like blood or tissue or stem cells. The long-term holding facilities are places for the most depraved in society. They hold those sentenced to death. Not some purposeless killing, but death by giving life — a heart, lungs, liver, both kidneys, whatever a person who truly believes in Life First needs.

Holding facilities aren't great places, but Luke's experience is solely with long-term facilities. Surely, a short-term facility has to be better. I wonder if Dr. Grant is onto something. A short-term holding facility won't be the end of the world, especially if it buys me more time.

"Maybe he's right, Luke," I say, a tinge of hope in my voice. "Maybe, if I go willingly, there might be an opportunity for me to escape."

"No one's ever escaped from a holding facility," Luke spits. Then he pauses, reconsiders. "At least, not the way you mean."

I close my eyes. Suicides. Those have been the only escapees. And that was only in the beginning. Most of the inmates in long-term holding facilities go insane and are kept heavily sedated or straight jacketed. They can't stand the waiting, the knowing that at any moment, without notice, they'll be told they're dying today. That their heart is needed for a transplant to someone who puts life first. That their time here is done. That Life First, the mantra drummed into their heads since childhood, means nothing. The hypocrisy alone would drive one mad, let alone the prospect of being the parts drawer society reaches into to cure its neediest patients.

OK, maybe Luke has a point. I don't want to go to a holding facility, even a short-term one. But, we're running out of options. "Then what?" I plead.

Luke begins to pace. "Let me think a minute."

A minute. The minutes are running out for me. I need a solution, and nothing is coming to mind. I turn away from Luke, addressing Dr. Grant. "If we take it out, is there a way to extract the nanoparticles, to call them home, back to the LMS?"

Dr. Grant shakes his head. "Kelsey, I've gone over the data, time and time again, trying to figure out a way to do it. I've reviewed all the literature on the modern LMS, and I can't see a way to get rid of it. Not immediately, at least. The nanoparticle has a short shelf life. It recharges at the LMS, so it can only go about 24 hours before dying. But, generally, the nanoparticles will lead authorities to you before they expire."

My brain churns, trying to outsmart the sensor created to avoid people outsmarting it.

"What if you take it out and Kelsey leaves while the LMS signals are still switched?" Luke asks.

Dr. Grant thinks for a second. "You mean, while she's still showing up as Haleema?"

Luke nods.

Dr. Grant puts his hand under his chin, thinks a moment more, then gives a hopeful shrug. "It might work," he says. "At least in terms of more time. It would probably give her five hours, tops, then the search would be on."

I look from Luke to Dr. Grant, then take a second to make sure I'm following properly. They want to cut it out and let the nanoparticle alarm sound. Only the authorities won't be worried about me. They'll think it's Haleema, who'll be asleep in the house. "So, what's the first thing FoSS will do when the nanoparticles don't come back?" I ask Dr. Grant.

"Well, if we follow the original plan, and transplant it to Buddy, they'll want to check the accuracy of the information. A nanoparticle not returning could be a blip, not a sign of removal. Since it's not a life-threatening emergency, and all the other readings should be fine, they'll call Haleema."

"She'll answer the phone and tell them she's fine," I chime in.

"Right," Dr. Grant says, offering his first smile tonight. "Then, they'll tell her there might be a problem with her chip. They'll wait a couple more hours for the next nanoparticle to return, but because it's in Buddy, it won't."

I frown. This is where they'll have the best chance of finding me, I realize. "So, then they call out the cavalry?"

"Not yet. They'll probably ask Haleema to come in and have her chip looked at. If Haleema isn't concerned, they might tell her she can wait 'til morning. If she is, and she goes to the hospital right away, they'll realize they've got the wrong LMS chip data when she arrives there, and the location beacon shows her — or more precisely Buddy — still at the house. At that point, someone will probably figure out what's happened, and they'll come looking for you. That will be 3 to 5 hours, most, depending on when your nanoparticles last charged at the sensor. And remember, the nanoparticles will still be in your system, emitting a signal, and trying to return to the LMS, even though it's been removed."

Luke moves to my side, a hopeful glint in his eye. He asks Dr. Grant, "How far does the nanoparticle signal emit?"

"They can usually pick it up from as far as 30 feet."

"So," Luke continues. "If we're gone by the time they get here, they won't find her through the nanoparticles signal?"

"Not directly," Dr. Grant says, soberly. "Once they realize she's fled, Kelsey's picture will be all over the news. If anyone sees her, they're going to report her. The fact that she's too far from the spot where her sensor last tracked doesn't mean the authorities won't find her. If someone spots her, they'll go to that location, fan out, and search for the nanoparticle signal."

Luke pulls me closer. "I'll keep her safe, and out of sight."

I gape at him. "You can't go with me," I sputter.

He laughs, defiantly. "Yes, I can."

"You don't have a ticket."

Dr. Grant shakes his head. "You can't take the train, if we do it this way, Kelsey. They'll know in as few as three hours about the switch and start broadcasting your photo. If the conductor spots you, you're sunk. The safest bet is to drive, and stay out of sight. Stay away from people. Stay in your car."

I am silent, trying to think through what he said. Stay in the car, out of sight, and drive. I can do that, but I'll have to stop for gas. There are very few full service places anymore. Most are self-serve. Even with the electric/gas hybrid car, I'll need to stop at some point. I'll have to get out and pump gas. That means people will see me.

Luke is stroking my neck now. I always have difficulty thinking when he does that. He's doing it on purpose. Trying to stop me from forming any reasonable arguments against his plan. It's working.

"It'll be better this way," he murmurs soothingly. "You'll enjoy the company."

"Yes, but if I'm caught, you'll be caught too."

He kisses my neck. "You won't be caught."

8. SURVIVOR MENTALITY

Luke doesn't want to chance anything else going wrong tonight. So, he's gone to get Buddy from the woods. I wouldn't have let anyone else do it. In fact, no one else could do it. Despite the cuteness of the name, Buddy is no pushover. He is a 120-pound guard dog who is vicious towards anyone he doesn't like, and that's most people. Only my father, me or Haleema have much luck getting Buddy to do anything he is told. Mostly, Buddy growls at strangers who come too close, bares his teeth and approaches with biting in mind.

Strangely, or perhaps that's part of Luke's charm, Buddy took an instant liking to Luke. I swear, he practically purred upon meeting him. Haleema insists it's because Buddy knows I love Luke and therefore treats him well. But, I think it has more to do with Luke than anything Buddy senses about my affection for him. Luke had Buddy charmed from the first smile.

I know Buddy will come back with Luke, no problem. I left Buddy in the woods mainly to make sure things were ready, because I know he hates enclosed spaces. I'm glad I did. Buddy would not have done well with the cop, nor would he have been able to sit still while we hashed out a new plan.

Dr. Grant is busy turning a small corner of our secret cellar into a sterile environment. The whole room smells like antiseptic. He has set out sterile cloths, gauze pads and stainless steel instruments. While our seating is limited to a couple of overturned crates, the equipment area looks like something you'd see in a hospital. That's good. I want the process to be clean. Last thing I need is to get to Peoria and die of an infection that started at the site of my removed

LMS.

Since Luke won't be back for a couple of minutes, I decide to probe a little more into the LMS debacle, without worrying that Luke will further batter the man about to perform minor surgery on me.

"Dr. Grant," I say. He glances up at me as he places a scalpel on a metal tray. "Why did you decide to look up my records?"

He shakes his head. "I didn't just decide to do it," he says, softly, yet very warm, very friendly. That's the way he usually is with me, when Luke isn't standing by ready to pound him. "I was always going to do it," Dr. Grant continues. "I just was doing other things first. It wasn't high on my priority list. There were three models of LMS given around the time of your birth. All the same manufacturer, but slightly different in series. Think first generation versus second or third. Well, generations A and B are very similar. I can use the same tool to remove them. The generation C LMS requires a different tool. I was looking up your record tonight just to make sure I had the right tool. That's when I found out you have a new one."

I sigh. An early look at the records would have shown the problem. We could have come up with a better plan earlier, if we'd known. I must stop thinking about this. There is no room for regrets. Right now, we have to deal with the present.

"Luke should be back soon," Dr. Grant says. "If you don't mind, I'll go ahead and apply the topical anesthetic. It should make it more comfortable when I take your LMS out."

I walk over and sit on a crate next to Dr. Grant. He takes out a gauze pad, then opens a brown glass bottle. A fresh antiseptic smell wafts out, making the room feel even more stifling. Dr. Grant, clad in latex gloves, pours a glob of clear ointment onto the gauze pad, then wipes it on my arm, just atop the spot where my LMS is implanted. The ointment feels cool and tingles. Dr. Grant, his slick brown hair dotted with gray, smiles gently at me. He's been so helpful throughout this whole thing. I know he takes risks for his patients. But, I'm not one of his patients, and still he's helping me.

"Thank you so much for doing this for me," I say.

He waves me off with a smile. "Kelsey, this is the least I can do for you. I'm just sorry I can't do more, and that I messed up with the LMS."

I shake my head. "It's going to be fine," I tell him, meaning it. He's done more than enough to help me.

Dr. Grant gives me a reassuring look, then tosses the used gauze into a red bag with a biohazard symbol on it. How doctorly. He seems well-suited to this profession. "Do you still like being a doctor?" I ask.

For a moment, he is silent; then a smile creeps across his face. "I do, Kelsey," he says. "I like helping people." His gloved hand touches where he rubbed ointment. "How does it feel?"

"Tingly."

His eyes meet mine. "Good. That means it's getting numb. In a minute, the skin should feel heavy there." He focuses in on my arm, then back up at me. His head droops a little. "Sometimes I feel like doctors today are asked to make too many compromises in pursuit of Life First," he says, leaning back, shaking his head. "I feel awful that it was a doctor that started us on this path. Too many doctors today are like Ilsa's doctor."

Yes, I am sorry, too. Ilsa Wagoner's case is the reason we live under Life First. She was a woman who lived 50 years ago. She left her small hometown to visit a friend, and while she was gone, an epidemic struck, wiping out most of her town, including all her siblings and husband. Using the knowledge gained in the pandemics, the authorities contained the outbreak, saving lives. Ilsa was able to return home, but there was no one left. Then, she learned what should have been good news — that she was pregnant. Historians tell us Ilsa wasn't happy. She fell into a state of extreme grief and wanted an abortion. Only, her doctor refused to give it to her. He instead had her committed to an institution.

"Yes, if he'd only just told her no and left it at that," I say as Dr. Grant looks over the tools on his tray. Ilsa's doctor sought to have her barred from having the procedure, arguing it was barbaric. Ilsa's attorney took a different stance, contending Ilsa had no interest in "killing" the child per se, but that she wanted the child removed from her body, where it would either survive or flounder on its own. The attorney said forcing Ilsa to continue with the pregnancy would be like forcing Ilsa to give blood to a stranger so he could survive, or forcing her to donate a kidney or some other body part solely for the benefit of another human being. The judges agreed with the attorney's analysis and kept Ilsa locked away. We do owe our fellow man our bodies to survive. So now, as long as the chance of significant or fatal harm is less than 20 percent, people are expected to help. I am expected to help.

"What are you thinking?" Dr. Grant asks me, and I realize I've zoned out.

"Just about Ilsa, about how one case can have such a huge impact."

"Yeah," Dr. Grant sighs. "It changed everything. Especially how doctors practice. Did you know doctors used to take a different oath?"

I sit up straighter. While this makes sense, it never occurred to me before now that doctors made a different pledge when they were sworn into the profession. "Something other than the Oath to Preserve Life?"

"Yeah, they used to take something called the Hippocratic Oath. One of its key tenets was: 'First, do no harm.' I wish we still took an oath like that. I feel like I'm hurting my patients by not helping them the way they need to be helped, by always balancing their needs against someone else's."

Yeah, that would be tough. His colleagues, apparently, don't share the same concerns. "Why aren't more doctors upset by it?"

"Some are," he says plainly. "Others are just of a different breed. They're immersed in Life First. Sometimes I think people have forgotten just how much society changed after the pandemics. So many people died, and many of them carried practical knowledge that wasn't necessarily in the books. It took two decades just to get back on track with returning the normal chain of supply of goods, and get people out of their houses and trusting again. And while the medical community has probably made the most strides since the pandemics, the people who emerged from it weren't the doctors and nurses that went into it. A lot of the people who ended up in medicine during the pandemics weren't trained physicians. They were warm bodies willing to come in contact with a deadly virus. After the pandemics, these new doctors were people who had survived, who had immunity. They were taught on the fly how to care for sick people. They had to make due with their own notions, and those notions have shaped medicine today.

"That survivor mentality among doctors has managed to prevail. People don't believe saving lives is doing harm. But, sometimes it is."

I want to say something, to respond in some way that makes sense, that lets him know I understand. But all I can muster is a nod of my head. There is a knock at the door. We each turn and look at the door, holding our breaths ever so slightly. Once it is clear it is Luke doing the secret knock, we each breathe out. Dr Grant jettisons his gloves and lets Luke in. I look down at my arm, which has stopped tingling and feels heavy.

Panting as he pads into the room, Buddy comes straight to me. I pat his head, rub from the top of his ears down his back, then give him a kiss on the nose.

"You're a good boy, Buddy," I coo.

He barks, then sits at my side.

"You ready?" Luke asks me, taking hold of Buddy's collar. I nod.

Dr. Grant touches my arm to make sure it is numb. Satisfied, he turns his attention to Buddy, using scissors to cut hair on Buddy's back, then wiping it with numbing ointment. Buddy whimpers apprehensively, but stays fairly still. I'm not sure this will continue once the numbing kicks in.

Luke lets go of Buddy's collar, and the dog pads over to the door.

Dr. Grant removes the latex gloves he's been wearing and puts on another pair. He reaches over to his tray to find the instrument he wants. When he lifts the scalpel, I turn my head. The sight of blood — particularly my own — makes me squeamish. Despite the numbness, I feel the pressure of the blade when he makes the incision; feel a small, unpleasant jostling; hear a click; then feel the sensation of tugging.

With curiosity winning out over squeamishness, I turn my head to watch. Dr. Grant has a small machine in his hand that reminds me of an electric razor. Instead of a razor at the tip of the device, there are two pincers holding my LMS. Using his free hand, Dr. Grant gives me a two-inch square of thick gauze.

"Hold this over your incision, please," Dr. Grant tells me. Then he turns to Luke in the corner. "Bring Buddy back."

Luke grabs Buddy's collar and leads him back. The dog walks hesitantly, and I fear he'll bolt. Then, Dr. Grant does something unexpected — at least to me: reaches into a black bag near his feet, and pulls out a plastic zip-top bag stuffed with chunks of raw meat. He opens the bag and dumps the meat onto a metal tray on the floor.

Buddy's gate increases, and in a flash, he's at our feet gobbling up the meat. Just like that, as quick as I've ever seen hands move, Dr. Grant makes an incision with his right hand, and then shoves the

LMS in with his left. If Buddy notices, he doesn't show it. Though I doubt he's noticed, the way he's still gobbling down the meat.

After removing yet another pair of gloves, the doctor grabs a tube and squeezes a clear goo on top of the area he's inserted the LMS into Buddy.

He notices me staring. "Liquid bandage," Dr. Grant says. "Should seal over the wound so it doesn't get infected, and the LMS doesn't pop out."

I watch Buddy, who is now licking the tray. "That was awfully quick. Doesn't the LMS have to be attached better?"

He shrugs. "Ideally," Dr. Grant says, as he pours the same liquid bandage on my own wound. Only, with me, he takes more care. "But, it will still take readings even if it's only loosely inserted. It will usually bond itself, and even if it's not deep in, the regulator I attached will keep the readings steady." He pats Buddy's head gently. "Plus, we know they're going to figure this out in a few hours. There's no sense in upsetting your dog with me trying to do a perfect fit if it's only going to be in him till morning."

Makes sense. I look over at Luke, who's standing patiently in the corner. Dr. Grant puts on a new pair of gloves and finishes bandaging my incision. Once he is done, he removes the gloves and places the used, disposable medical items into the waste bag. "So what now?" I ask.

Luke pipes in. "I'll run Buddy over to your place, then come back for you."

"You think it will work?" I ask.

Luke shines his full-of-bravado thousand-megawatt smile. "Of course."

I hope he's right.

9. DR. GRANT

Luke is taking Buddy back to the house and getting Susan's car. Even though she couldn't use her car after surgery, Susan hadn't wanted to give up the little red convertible, so she stores it in our garage. Luke thinks it's best to trade cars. Both the officer and my father saw the tan sedan. I don't want to further involve Susan, but I'm at a loss for other options. On the plus side, she can say honestly she didn't know I would take it. Red is a bit bold, but not so out of the ordinary as to be conspicuous.

Dr. Grant and I clean the room. It just takes a couple of minutes to remove all traces we've been here. We leave the secret room together, and he locks the door with his key. When we reach the exit of the little church, I say, "Thank you," and hug him tightly, not quite ready to let go. He kisses my forehead, and whispers "Be safe. Good luck." And he's off.

It feels odd, watching him slink into the darkness, not sure when or if I'll see him again. I've only known him three years, but in that time, everything has changed.

I first met Dr. Grant during my third year at the state university. I'd planned to spend the weekend at the beach with my boyfriend. However, a couple of days before the trip, Tyler broke up with me, claiming he'd fallen madly in love with someone else. I was sure Susan would drop everything to console me. I'd envisioned a girls' weekend shopping and bashing Tyler relentlessly. Only I was wrong. Susan had agreed to welcome doctors attending a campus conference. The gathering would culminate with the opening ceremony for a new research lab on campus.

I hadn't been paying much attention to the whole hullabaloo, as

I'd been too absorbed with my relationship. Everything else had just been background noise.

Once Tyler was gone, it seemed clear this new lab was a really big deal. Media from around the country were descending on campus. Susan, a go-getter to the core, wanted to be a part of it. Instead of wallowing, she suggested we use the conference to forget Tyler, and I became part of the welcoming committee.

Our job was to greet the new lab director, Dr. Stephen Grant, and give him a short tour of campus, ending at U Hotel.

We were waiting outside the administration building when a taxi pulled up. Watching as he got out and tipped the driver, I realized Dr. Grant looked oddly familiar. He was a large man with wavy black hair and a matching beard. Clearly of hearty stock, he was well-proportioned enough that he looked like a lumberjack stuffed in a business suit. His face was eye-catching; not classically handsome, but intriguing. Something about his broad face and square chin, and the serene gleam in his eyes made you stop and take notice.

Susan strode over to him, smiled and introduced herself, while I stood several feet back, watching. He smiled professionally and extended his hand to shake hers. Susan motioned to me, then he turned, caught me in his sights and didn't let go. His gaze was laser like and unsettling. It was filled with wonder, curiosity, and something else, something unnerving. I didn't understand why he looked at me that way, nor could I look away.

Susan, for once, seemed oblivious. She didn't notice his unbreakable gaze. Instead, she chuckled at something he said, then guided Dr. Grant to the spot where I was standing. "Dr. Grant, this is Kelsey Reed," Susan said, inclining her head in my direction.

Despite my discomfort from his gaze, I extended my hand affably and said, "Nice to meet you."

He shook my hand; it was firm and kind, if handshakes can be kind. Dr. Grant stared at me a moment more with that same intense look, then turned to Susan. "Do you think you'd be able to find me a bottle of water? I'm parched."

Susan smiled and said, "Sure." As she grabbed my hand to take me with her, the doctor cleared his throat and Susan stopped in her tracks. "I was hoping Kelsey could tell me a bit about the school. We'll wait here."

Susan nodded, but was clearly irritated at being dismissed. I turned to face Susan, so the doctor couldn't see, and rolled my eyes. I hoped she realized I had no interest in schmoozing with the doctor. She didn't seem comforted. My choice or not, I had managed to upstage her. And that rarely happened.

As Susan walked into the administration building, I turned back to Dr. Grant and masked my discomfort with a friendly façade. "What do you want to know about the campus?"

He didn't answer. Instead, he maintained a wonder-laden stare. "You look just like her, you know?"

I narrowed my eyes, trying to understand. "Like Susan?" I asked, though I knew he couldn't mean her. Susan was three inches taller than me, svelte, with fiery red hair and attitude to match. Nothing like me.

"No, no," Dr. Grant said, almost laughing. "You look just like Maya."

I felt like I'd been slapped. I wasn't sure why, but the words hit me hard. What he was saying was true. Anyone who'd known my mother and now knew me said I looked just like her when she was this age. But, the doctor using her name as if he knew her, hurt.

"You've seen pictures of her?" was the only response I could manage.

He shook his head. "No," he said, his shoulders drooping, as he let out a sigh. "I was her obstetrician."

A lie. I had only been seven when she died, but I remembered her heading off to obstetrics appointments. She would say, "I'm off to Dr. Rice's office." And I always thought it was silly that her doctor was named after food.

Something about my expression must have told him I didn't believe him. For, he added quickly, "I practiced with Dr. Rice. I saw her the last three appointments."

I'm not sure when my jaw dropped. I just remember feeling a strong April breeze blow in and thinking I should close my mouth.

"There's something I need to talk to you about," he said. I nodded reflexively, too stunned to do anything else. "Would you meet me at my hotel tonight, say around 9 o'clock?"

A thousand thoughts crossed my mind, of things I should say, of things I should ask, but no words sprung from my mouth. Just another nod. From behind, I heard the clanging of high heels on pavement. I turned and saw Susan, in her light blue blouse and beige skirt, striding toward us, a bottle of water in hand.

She closed the distance quickly, handing Dr. Grant the bottle as soon as she reached us.

"Thank you," he said to her. "I'm afraid I'm not really interested in a campus tour. If you don't mind, I'll walk to the hotel myself."

Susan kept her public smile plastered across her face, but gave me a look that said I had some massive explaining to do once he left.

The doctor reached into his pocket, pulled out a card and handed it to me. "This is my number. Please call if you can't make it, so we can reschedule. It's very important."

I nodded, and he walked off.

When he appeared to be out of earshot, Susan gave me a hard look. "What was that about?"

My voice was monotone. I was too raw, still trying to process the emotions I was feeling. "He wants me to meet him at his hotel to-night."

Now, Susan's expression turned from anger to alarm. "You can't go, Kelsey," she practically shouted, then lowered her voice, realizing she would attract attention. "Good doctors don't ask students to meet them in their rooms after hours. He must be some kind of a pervert. Why else would he want you alone in his hotel room?"

The answer to that was easy. I knew it the moment he admitted seeing my mother for her last three appointments. "Because he wants to apologize. He wants to say he's sorry for killing my mother."

10. DRIVING

It is still dark and I've been asleep for what seems like an hour. Luke is doing marvelously at keeping awake and chauffeuring me to Georgia. It's a long drive, but there's nothing we can do about that.

Part of me is glad he's here. It makes me happy knowing he will be with me on what could be a scary journey. The other part of me hates it and wishes he were safe somewhere else; wishes I were going it alone, and he would join me later. I don't know what I'll do if we're captured. If Luke has to go to a holding facility because he helped me, I will never forgive myself.

I am in my seat belt, curled into a ball to sleep better. I stretch out, figuring I should keep Luke company. I mean, this is technically my escape. Yet, he is the one taking the active role. I wanted to drive, but Luke said it would be safer for him to be at the wheel if we got pulled over by the police. He insisted he could talk to the officer while I pretended to sleep. He didn't seem to think the officer would notice I was a fugitive. Why Luke thinks the police are so ridiculously inept that they wouldn't ask me to show my face, I don't know. Actually, I don't think he believes that. I think he just wanted to be useful and grasped for any excuse to drive. I let it stand, without pointing out the silliness of his assumption. Plus, when he proposed driving, I actually was tired. I hadn't been sleeping well in the days leading up to this.

I look over at Luke. He is concentrating on the road. Very few cars are out. My watch says 4:30 a.m. I've slept too long. Still dark, yet morning.

Luke notices me awake. "You should sleep, if you're tired.".

I yawn, stretch out. "Nope, I'm fine. I'd like to keep you company."

"No, I'm good," he protests. "Really, sleep."

I decide not to argue, at least not with words. My staying awake will get my point across.

I shift in my seat slightly. My arm still throbs where the LMS was removed, but I don't dare look at it. I don't want Luke to worry I'm in pain. Instead, I stare out the window, watching the steady white line separating the road from the shoulder. A green road sign says, "Welcome to South Carolina"

My heart does a stutter step as I glance at the dashboard gauges, and realize we have been in mortal peril whilst I slept. "How fast have you been driving?"

"Fast enough to get us through a couple of states," he says. "Go back to sleep."

"I can't now. I'm afraid if we hit something at this speed we'll instantly disintegrate."

He rolls his eyes. "Very funny."

The speedometer reads 94. "We don't want to get pulled over," I say, the uneasiness I feel creeping into my voice. Luke sighs, and then I feel the car slow and watch as we decelerate to 65 m.p.h.

"Very few police on these roads at night," he says. "My friend Jack, his father's an officer. He told me most of the officers sleep on the overnight shift unless they have a call. Very few are out looking around for speeders."

I raise an eyebrow. "Jack is full of it."

"Yeah, he is," he agrees, "but not about that."

We drive for awhile more in silence, passing exit ramps promising food, gas and other amenities.

"Are you ready?" Luke asks.

No, but I don't really have a choice. "As ready as I'll ever be. I'm going to miss my dad, Haleema, Susan, you. But, you're gonna come in just two months, so it won't be too long."

He nods, keeps his eyes on the road. Neither of us really wants to talk about the new life I am heading to. So, we watch the road for a bit more. I see him steal a glance at me. "Do you remember what I asked you, after you told me you'd been marked?"

How could any woman forget the man she loves dropping to one knee and proposing? A guy who said you were his whole world, and he didn't want to go another moment without everyone knowing, without making you his wife. "I don't think I'll ever forget that night."

"Do you have an answer for me?"

I grimace. It had been hard enough not to say yes at the time. This feels like double jeopardy. "I think I gave you an answer," I say as gently as possible.

"You said to ask you later."

"I said to ask me when things were more settled," I correct. I had tried to explain this to him, then. It wasn't the right time for him to ask me. It was all about needing to be with me because there was a crisis ahead. That's never a good reason to get married. I want him to want to get married because he wants to spend a lifetime with me, not because he's afraid he's going to lose me during surgery. "I just think now's not the best time to make decisions like this."

He raises his voice. "And when is a good time, Kelsey?"

I purposely keep my tone low so he doesn't feel like I'm shouting at him. "When this part is over, when there's calm and we can make rational decisions."

He sighs, looks at me briefly, then returns his eyes to the road, shaking his head. "I don't know why you believe I can't think rationally now, that I'll somehow change my mind if there's not a crisis."

I bite my lip, and try to think of a response. He's right. I am worried he'll change his mind. Luke is wonderful in many ways, but sometimes he's ruled by the emotion of the moment. I wonder if he'll still feel the same when the moment of my jeopardy is over. I don't want to say yes if he's going to regret it later. "I don't think you'll change your mind," I say, though not as convincingly as I'd like it to sound.

"Kelsey, this refusal to say yes when I know you want to, is … very… frustrating. I'm not deluded with worry. I'm not going to change my mind once you're safely ensconced in Peoria and never show up. I really wish you would just say yes, and then we'd both feel better."

Maybe he's right. Maybe my reluctance is just my own anxiety, my own issues. I mean, he hasn't changed his mind in the three weeks since he found out. Why would he change his mind, now? Why can't I just tell him yes? I turn to him. "I love you, Luke, with all my heart. Can that just be enough for today, please?"

He glances at me, then the road. The answer in his eyes is clear. It's not enough. But, he looks back again, and smiles — same eyes, eyes that clearly say it's not enough — and says, "That's fine, Kelse. That's enough for now."

I smile back, turn to my window and close my eyes. I'm not sleepy, but I don't want to talk any more. Something about getting engaged while on the run from the law feels wrong to me. Like it's about doing everything for the wrong reasons, and I can't bring myself to say yes, even though I know it hurts him. Too much principle. I wonder if maybe I should just abandon my principles altogether, give up my kidney, like Luke suggested, and tell him yes.

"Kelsey," he says softly.

"Yes."

"I'm not gonna ask again, but I do have a question."

I feel weary of the question, but he deserves to be heard. "Yes," I respond, trying not to sound as ambivalent as I feel.

"Are you reluctant to say yes because your father doesn't like me?"

I wonder if I look as deer-caught-in-the-headlights as I feel. I have no idea where that came from. "No, this has nothing to do with my father."

He shrugs, and stays focused on the road. I start to say something more, to defend my position, but think better of it. I wonder if maybe there is a kernel of truth in what he's suggested. Not that my father's opinion matters above all, but he doesn't like Luke.

That isn't entirely Luke's fault. Luke works for Dr. Grant, and my father harbors an unparalleled hatred for Dr. Grant. So he naturally distrusts anyone working for the man.

Also, Luke is very unlike my father in some key ways. Luke likes to fly under the radar. He is low profile and tries to keep his life private, which is the antithesis of my father, who attempts to be an open book to his public.

Luke has attended a few pro-choice rallies. Being at the occasional rally probably matters less to my father than the fact that Luke was in the background of a photo that appeared in the newspaper. Pro-choice is not something my father wishes to be associated with.

I remember when I first told dad I was dating Luke Geary. He gave me the fatherly look that said, "I don't know about that, about my baby dating some strange guy." I waited for him to have Luke checked out — investigated by someone on his staff. Waited for him to speak to me about my beau.

He started with the hard stuff. "He works with that Dr. Grant," my father said. The implication was clear, though he decided to spell it out in case I'd missed it. "You know, Grant has more stillborns than the average doctor. Some people say he's not helping those babies on purpose."

I'd been ready for that question, of course. "Dr. Grant only works with high-risk pregnancies, Dad. He's going to have more deaths than other doctors," I said, trying to add a positive spin. "He mainly does research, now. He's got the support of the governor for his research, so he can't be all that bad. And, most importantly, Luke works for Dr. Grant. He's not Dr. Grant."

My father seemed unmoved. "Just because Dr. Grant knows the governor doesn't mean he's good. A lot of radicals hang out with that Grant fellow. Has this boy tried to convince you to attend a pro-choice rally?"

I laughed. "Dad, we hardly ever talk about the pro-choice movement or Dr. Grant."

"No Dr. Grant, no pro-choice? What is it that you talk about?"

Part of me wanted to say, "No talking, all sex." But, that little joke would have gone over like a lead balloon. Not to mention, it would have put the s-word out there with my father, and that's something that was outside both of our comfort zones. "Lots of things, Dad. We have classes together, and we see movies. He's very sweet. You'll like him."

Dad didn't. I'm not sure what it was. But, the two didn't get along. I got the sense my dad felt like Luke was an invader trying to stage a coup.

In the end, my father and I came to an understanding. We didn't talk about Luke, and Luke and I didn't flaunt our relationship publicly. My father believes controversy swirls around Dr. Grant, so he didn't want some issue with Luke or the doctor to pop up during his campaign because people knew we were dating. It seemed easy to just do as he wished.

For Luke's part, he prefers anonymity, at least in his personal relationships. He's quite content that most people see us as nothing more than two acquaintances. Our hot passion for each other is reserved for each other, and no one else. Er, at least it was until I'd been ordered to give a kidney and decided to flee the country. Suddenly Luke wanted to declare his love for me to the world and get married. That's another reason I can't say yes. It's too sudden a change from where we've been.

I sneak a peek at Luke as he drives, then turn back to the window. I need more time, yet I know ultimately I'll say yes. So does Luke. At least I'm pretty sure he knows what my answer will be. I just want things to be more settled.

"Luke," I say tentatively.

"Mmmhmm."

"Since you're driving me all the way to Georgia anyway, maybe you could just come to Peoria with me now. Then, maybe we could get settled in together."

The quiet seems to shout at me as he stares diligently ahead, occasionally checking the rearview mirror. "Is it the two months, Kelsey? Is that affecting your answering me?"

Touché. Good question. I'm not sure. The two month delay in Luke coming to Peoria was not the original plan. The first couple of times we discussed me fleeing, it had been the two of us going. Then, suddenly, with little explanation, it changed to him coming in two months. He suddenly thought it would be safer if he came later. Part of me feels like he's punishing me for not telling him yes. Like he's making me wait because I'm making him wait for his answer. But, that's not Luke's style. He wouldn't treat me like that. He knows I'd prefer he come now. So, gut-check time. Is the two month delay part of the reason I refuse to answer his proposal?

I look over at him and he looks briefly at me. In that minor glance when he takes his eyes off the road, I see how desperate he is for me to say it is indeed the two months, that I will tell him yes if he will come with me today. I swivel my head to look out the window and watch the fields flitter past as I search my soul for the answer.

It isn't the two months. I know that in my heart. It isn't his delayed arrival that makes me want to wait to answer him.

"No, it's not the two months," I tell him, trying to explain things in a way that won't hurt his feelings. Actually, to explain things in a way that won't further hurt his feelings. I turn back to face him, even though he watches the road. "I think we could feel settled sooner if we went together. The delay is really about letting things calm down, Luke."

Luke swallows, then says nothing. He drives with the singular focus I would expect of a brain surgeon. Finally, in a calm, measured voice, he says, "Kelsey, I still think it's safer for me to wait, OK? I can make sure things are settled here. You'll be fine for two months. You can stay at the Grant House, and then look for a more permanent place."

I take a deep breath. "You're right," I lie. Then, I turn back to face the window. "I'm gonna rest a little, if you're OK driving?"

"I'm great," he lies, too, adding false enthusiasm. "Get some rest."

11. A PROMISE KEPT

Three Years Ago

As I stood outside Dr. Grant's room at U Hotel, I wondered if I'd made a mistake agreeing to meet him.

Dr. Grant had the answers I wanted. He knew how my mother had died. I admit, I should have known more. It wasn't because I hadn't wanted answers; it was because my father hadn't given me any. I'd gotten the most basic explanation at the time: my mother's doctor had failed to diagnose a heart condition and she died. She was four months pregnant at the time.

Beyond that, my father said nothing about it. He wanted to move on. Our society had seen enough death to know that moving on is best, that you can't linger with those who have passed. So we don't. My father never explained exactly what happened. I had always wondered whether she had suffered. Had she thought of me in the end? Had she known it was coming, that death was near, or was it sudden and completely unexpected, laughing with her doctor one moment and dead the next?

These were things I could never ask my father. First, he hadn't been with her when she died, and second, even if he knew, he wouldn't tell me. He'd tell me to move on and live life. Life First and all, you know. The dead are gone.

Dr. Grant was different. He might tell me. That's why I'd agreed to meet him. I thought he felt guilty, and I could use that to my advantage. Use that to find out more about my mother's last day. Perhaps it was wrong of me to try to use him for this information. But, I thought, as her killer, he owed me whatever information he had.

So I went to Dr. Grant's hotel expecting he would usher me in and stammer through an apology. Expecting I would ask him my questions, and he would give me answers to ease his conscience. It hadn't occurred to me how those answers would impact me. Part of me wishes I had thought about that. But if I had, I never would have gone.

I stood in the hotel hallway an extra minute, debating whether I could do it. Finally, I knocked on the door of room 224. He opened it fairly quickly, looking pleased to see me, if not a little surprised. Perhaps he thought I wouldn't show. I had certainly thought about it, but my thirst for knowledge beat out my trepidation.

Dr. Grant's suite was furnished in the typical indistinct, yet comfortable-looking, hotel decor. There was a sofa, two chairs across from it, separated by a table, a desk in the corner and a television. A closed door probably led to the bedroom. Dr. Grant offered me a seat, and I chose one of the chairs.

"I'm glad you came, Kelsey," Dr. Grant said, still standing, as if waiting for some movement or action or speech I would give. Whatever he was expecting, I couldn't provide. I simply nodded in acknowledgment and waited for him to say more.

"I guess you're wondering why I asked you here," he said, as he perched on the sofa.

"You want to talk about my mother's death," I said flatly.

He shook his head and offered a nervous laugh. "I guess that was pretty obvious, huh?" Sighing, he looked down at the floor, then back up at me. "I just didn't think I'd ever get this chance, Kelsey. I wanted to talk to you soon after, but your father was adamant that he wanted to be left alone, that he didn't want anything to do with me."

That could not have been a surprise to him. You kill a man's wife, and then expect him to sit for tea with you? I wondered if I had made a mistake. Wondered if Dr. Grant was just one of those self-absorbed people who only sought to help himself. Someone who wanted to ease his conscious by seeing me, not caring if dredging up old wounds was good or bad for me. Yes, that perfectly summed up Dr. Grant, I decided. A selfish person. I suppose I knew that coming in. I had come for selfish reasons, too.

He flashed a friendly, nervous smile, then leaned forward. "What do you know about your mother's death?"

I was caught off guard by the question. I crinkled my brow as I tried to decipher why he'd ask. Maybe he knew my father hadn't told me all the particulars and wanted to know where he should start. Palms pressed tightly together in my lap, I met his eyes, then answered. "Just that she had an undiagnosed heart condition that caused her to die."

Disappointment flooded his face. Not quite a frown appeared, but the lines of his mouth turned downward and the expectant look he had in his eyes just moments before disappeared. It was as if I'd given the wrong answer completely.

"That was the public story, Kelsey. The true story of what happened to your mother is something very few people know: me, Dr. Rice, your father."

What he was saying was ridiculous. A public story? My father wouldn't tell me a public story. Why would he make up a public story? And if he made up this story for the public, why would the doctors go along with it? This wasn't making any sense, and part of me wanted to get up and go, get away from this man who had so wronged me already by taking away my mother. Wanted to leave before he could wrong me again by spinning some lie. But, the other part of me, the part that started leaning in closer to him, to appraise him, to hear him better, wanted to know what the Hell he was talking about.

"I can see you doubt what I'm saying, Kelsey," he said, opening his eyes a little wider, trying to appear honest, trying to gain my confidence. "I'll explain everything."

His eyes were calling to me, trying desperately to make some type of connection, but all I could return was a cold stare. He sighed, then began. "I was new to the practice the year your mother was pregnant with your brother," he said. A brother. I hadn't known the baby was a boy. I would have had a little brother if they hadn't died. It was strange news to hear. A wave of sadness and regret washed over me at learning the gender of the brother I would never know. Dr. Grant hadn't noticed my little emotional upheaval and was continuing on about how he was seeing a number of Dr. Rice's patients, including my mother.

"Your mother's symptoms, the fatigue, the ill-at-ease feeling, the constant malaise were typical in some respects, yet atypical in others," he said, pausing, as if remembering. "We did all the normal tests, changed her vitamins, boosted her iron, but nothing seemed to help.

So, I did a few extra tests and read some old journals, and finally, I figured it out. Your mother had a condition we hadn't seen in more than a century. They thought it had been eradicated — that people who had survived the pandemics had genetic immunity. So, no one even looked for it anymore. But, I was sure your mother had pre-eclampsia."

Whatever he said, I had never heard of it. It was an odd word. "What is it?"

"Exactly what it sounds like: the state you're in before eclampsia sets in. Eclampsia is a pregnancy-related disorder that causes convulsions and seizures that can result in severe brain damage, coma or death. Pre-eclampsia just lets us know we need to treat the mother before she goes into full-blown eclampsia. There's only one cure for pre-eclampsia: deliver the baby."

My mother was barely four months pregnant when she died. "No baby could survive that early."

"I know," Dr. Grant said, matter-of-factly. "I told Dr. Rice my conclusion, and he thought I was an overzealous, ambitious young doctor who wanted to make a name for myself by rediscovering a dead disease. He said I'd have to make strange and far-out diagnoses on my own time, once I took over the practice. I told him I wanted to go to the health board, so they could make a decision, so we could deliver the baby and save your mother."

Dr. Grant scowled indignantly and shook his head at the memory before continuing. "But, Dr. Rice refused. He said it was a ridiculous diagnosis and consulting the board would make him and me look ridiculous. Besides, he said, if it was pre-eclampsia, there was an 85 percent chance she would survive another week without intervention. We admitted her so we could keep an eye on her, and six hours later, she had the fatal seizure."

A fatal seizure. Not heart failure. I didn't understand. "Why? Why would they lie about it?"

Unfazed, Dr. Grant immediately answered. "Well, for several reasons, Kelsey. In the end, Dr. Rice realized he'd made a grave mistake and didn't want to end his career on that note. Also, your father wanted to believe it, wanted to believe he'd done all he could, I think."

"My father? What does he have to do with this?" I spat. "He didn't misdiagnose her!"

His amber eyes went wide — startled, unsure. My accusatory tone caught him off guard. He spoke quietly, as if by tamping down his voice he could tamp down my anger. "I called him," Dr. Grant said slowly. "He was out of town, in Chicago on business. I wanted him to back me on this, to help Maya. She wanted to go before the board, to get permission to birth the baby, even though doing so meant your brother would die. Your father was very influential. I figured if I could get him on my side, Dr. Rice would go to the board, and we could induce labor, save your mother."

I bit my lower lip, forced back the bile rising in my throat, and whispered: "He wouldn't do it?"

"He said he trusted Dr. Rice, but that he would fly back and judge for himself. He didn't make it back in time. She was gone before his plane landed."

I stood up. I'd had enough. Coming had been a mistake. This man was a liar. He had to be. He just had to be. I had to get out. What he said couldn't be true. It couldn't. I needed to breathe. I needed to get out. I stood and bolted toward the door.

"Wait!" he called out, following me.

"No," I yelled, refusing to look back. "You're a liar, Dr. Grant."

I was pulling the door open when he spoke. "I have something to give you, from your mother."

I stopped, stared at the door a moment. Finally, I turned back toward him, the doorknob still in my hand. "What did you say?"

He was standing a few feet from me now, his eyes locked on me like a tractor beam, as if he could will me to stay put simply by keeping me rapt in his gaze. "I have something your mother wanted to give you."

I pushed the door shut, but did not move from my spot. "I don't understand," I said, shaking my head. "How could you have something from my mother?"

He went to the laptop computer sitting on the desk in the corner, carried it over to the table and set it down. "The mobile phone I had with me that day recorded videos. Toward the end, your mother was feeling awful. She said she didn't think she'd make it. She wanted to record a message for you."

I still couldn't move. My limbs felt too heavy, but my brain still tried to process his words. "For me?"

He nodded.

That sounded wrong. "Not a message for my father?"

"Given his failure to push things forward, I think she was not really that happy with him at that moment. She wanted to record a message to you."

"What did she say?"

"I'm gonna let you watch it," he said, turning the laptop screen so I could see it fully. I walked toward the table, so I was standing next to him. He ran his cursor over a small icon, clicked it, and then a window appeared. On the screen was my mother, hair wet with sweat, wearing a hospital gown, frozen in time.

12. FAILURE

Present

We need more gas. It is 6 a.m., and they must be looking for me by now. Luke wants to go in and pay while I stay in the car. In theory, I agree. In reality, I have to pee.

The blonde wig seems good enough, and if I avoid eye contact, no one will notice me. Luke doesn't like the idea, and even suggests we pull over by the side of the road and I go in the woods. I counter that a car pulled over to the side of the road looks strange and might draw the attention of the police or a good Samaritan. It's best just to go now, before my face is everywhere. I can be in and out in a minute. I'll look at no one.

Luke grimaces, but finally assents. I slip on the wig while he drives. When he pulls into the station, I check in the mirror to make sure I look un-Kelsey enough. It'll do. While Luke pumps gas, I get out of the car and go inside. It's a typical gas station convenience store. Aisles of granola, vacuum sealed yogurt, trail mix, medicines for headaches and tummy aches, and car supplies. I walk past them, toward the back of the store, where a sign with a black silhouette of a woman in a dress marks the ladies room. I pull the door handle. It doesn't budge. Locked. Someone's inside. I lean on the opposite wall and wait.

I keep my head down, looking at the putrid brown tiles on the floor. In addition to the color being hideous, they're filthy. I hear the toilet flush, a sign the woman is almost done. This should make me feel better. It doesn't. I can't put my finger on why. I keep my eyes pointed toward the floor and hear the sink as the woman washes her hands. Next, the hum of the automatic dryer.

As she opens the door, I realize what I'm feeling: the sensation of being watched. I look at the bathroom door, then back into the main portion of the store. The man behind the counter, at the cash register, is staring at me. He looks intently at my face and I feel the color draining from my face as I panic beneath the wig.

The woman who's been inside the bathroom walks past. I hurry inside, pee, wash my hands, hold them under the automatic dryer for a few seconds, rub the wet hands on my pants, then leave. I don't look up, but I feel the man's gaze on my back as I cross the store and exit.

When I get to the car, Luke is just finishing pumping the gas. He takes one look at me and asks, "What's wrong?"

I have a split second to make a decision. So I do.

I walk closer to him, but not too close. "My stomach hurts," I say softly, touching my stomach with the palm of my hand, and scrunching up my face as if I'm in pain. "I don't want to go back in and take the chance of being spotted. Would you mind getting me some antacid?"

A look of relief washes across his face, and he smiles at me, that perfect Luke smile. "Of course," he says. "Get in the car, honey. You look really sick."

Well, I haven't lied, exactly. I do feel sick to my stomach. But not because of anything an antacid can cure. I am going to be caught, and they are going to take Luke, too, if he is with me. I can't stop my capture. I've blown that altogether. But I can stop Luke's.

I climb into the passenger side of Susan's car, mentally preparing to go as soon as Luke is out of sight. I glance at the starter and see the key fob is gone. Shit. I need it to start the car. I open the door and step out again. "Wait," I call, trying not to draw attention to myself. Luke is halfway across the parking lot.

He walks back toward me, concerned.

"I want to listen to the radio," I say.

He looks confused, then it dawns on him what I need. He reaches into his pocket, then tosses me the fob. I catch it with two hands cupped together and smile back at him. "Thanks," I say, as I duck back into the passenger seat.

I watch as Luke crosses the parking lot and enters the convenience store. As soon as the door shuts, I crawl over the gear shifter, slide into the driver's seat, and start the engine. I give one last look at the store, then drive away. Not too fast, nice and easy, so no one thinks it suspicious. However, fast enough that if Luke notices me leaving, he won't come out and try to stop me.

I know he'll be upset when he realizes I've left him and why. But, having a discussion with him at the gas station, convincing him that I have to go it alone, to be caught alone, is not something I'm capable of. He would want to stay with me, to come, to make sure everything goes OK.

He can't make this OK. I chose this risk when I decided to flee. It's not something I want for Luke. I want him free. I can't bear him facing the same fate as me: the wrong end of a holding facility.

I follow the interstate south, and wait. It is nerve-racking, and I sort of wish I actually had some type of stomach-calming serum. My nerves always rip apart my insides, making me feel queasy. It's one reason I hate being anxious.

I just have to ignore it and keep driving. There is nothing I can do. They're either going to find me or not. I have a map to Georgia, but not the specific place I'm going. That's all in my head. I memorized it, so that if I were caught, I wouldn't expose my route.

I've been driving almost an hour, and my stomach is beginning to calm. Just as I'm wondering if ditching Luke was a mistake, I hear the chopping of helicopter blades above me. They're looking for the car the man at the gas station must have clearly described.

I keep driving, at the speed limit, 65 m.p.h. The helicopter follows overhead, and finally, I hear a voice crackle from the helicopter's speaker system. "Driver in the red coupe, license plate 8BX TRC, please pull over."

I follow the instructions and pull to the side of the road. Several cars pass and nothing happens. Like a vulture before the feast, the helicopter flies in lazy circles above me for five minutes. It is a slow and unpleasant wait. In the rearview mirror, I see police cars, lights flashing, roll up. Two cruisers park behind me, and then another voice rings out over a speaker. This voice hails from one of the cruisers, rather than the air.

"Please exit the vehicle with your hands raised," the speaker voice says.

I do as I'm told. I stand there, on the side of a South Carolina highway, hands raised, looking and feeling like a criminal.

"Are you Kelsey Reed?" the voice over the speaker booms.

I nod.

An officer, clad in a black uniform, approaches me, and gently, professionally, says. "Ms. Reed, you're under arrest for fleeing a donation. Please come with me."

I follow the man back to the cruiser. He holds open the door, and I lower myself into the backseat. It is just as I expected. But this is the easy part. The hard part is the holding facility. That has yet to come.

13. LAST WORDS

Three Years Ago

Go ahead, Maya," I could hear Dr. Grant saying from off camera. "It's recording."

My mother was propped up in a hospital bed, wearing a white gown. Sweat beaded on her forehead, plastering stray auburn hairs to her face. Dark circles were under her eyes. Her breathing was shallow, as if she could barely draw in air, and her eyes were slits, lids struggling to stay open.

She closed her eyes momentarily, then strained to open them, winced and forced a smile.

"Kelsey, this is Mom. I want to talk to you, but I can't right now. Your father will be here soon. And that's good. He'll be able to help. But, in case he doesn't get here in time, I want you to know that I love you."

Her words were spaced out unevenly as she tried to breathe, which seemed increasingly harder for her.

"I also want you to know that you can believe in Life First, Kelsey. But, I want you to remember to always put your own life first. Putting someone else's life before your own, or the family you love isn't fair to you or your family," she gasped, then leaned back on her pillow, closing her eyes.

Dr. Grant, off camera, asked if she was alright. "Yeah," she said. "Just give me a minute." She took a few seconds, inhaling her shallow mishmash of breaths, then weakly lifted her hand and wiped sweat from her brow.

"This baby, I don't think can survive, Kelsey. And that's an unfortunate part of life. Not everyone can live. I wish everyone could, but they can't. Right now, this baby is killing me, and I don't want that, especially if it can't live. And even if there was a small chance he could live, I don't give as much weight to the could-be, as to the do-have. What I do have is you. I have you and your father, and I love you very much. I want to be with you, and see you grow up and get married and have your own children. I want to be there for your first date, see you graduate from college and get your first job. All those wonderful things; I want them all. Right now, I've been told no, because they think my chances are 85 percent. I don't feel 85 percent, Kelsey. And even if my chances were 90 percent, I can tell it's just heading downhill. I want my life weighed first, and that's not happening."

Tears streamed down her cheeks. "I know you won't see this now. Hopefully, your father will wait until you're older to show it to you. But, Kelsey, please remember, that you should put your life and your family first. I love you, and I tried to do that. When you get older, Kelsey, leave this place. No one should have their choices about life taken away. I love you."

Then, she looked beyond the recorder and said, "That's it, Dr. Grant. Has Lewis' plane taken off?" And that was it. It was over. The video was finished.

I waited for Dr. Grant to speak. To say something. Maybe sorry. Sorry for changing my view of my mother. Sorry for letting me know how hard her last moments were. Sorry for shattering the fantasy I had that it had been quick and painless, unexpected, even unpreventable. I looked down at the computer keys. I did not wish to see her like that anymore. Finally, Dr. Grant spoke. "I tried to give it to your father at the time, but he wouldn't take my calls or e-mails or letters. I was afraid if I sent just the chip, he would destroy it or throw it away unopened."

I had to leave. I stood. Dr. Grant watched me curiously, then hit a button on the computer. A small chip ejected. He put it into a plastic sleeve and handed it to me. "This is yours," he said.

Instinctively I curled my fingers around it, turned away from Dr. Grant and walked out of his hotel room. Despite what he'd given me, or maybe because of it, at that moment in time, I hoped I never saw Dr. Stephen Grant again.

14. HELD

Being the senator's daughter means one thing today: I get sent back to Maryland. Most people would be sent to a local holding facility with one or two cells. My father must want me home. I have not spoken to him, but it seems obvious he has pulled strings to get me moved, today, via helicopter, to Maryland's Holding Facility 2.

There isn't that much crime, so Holding Facility 2 serves Maryland, Virginia, the District of Columbia and Pennsylvania. Most of the facility holds long-term inmates, but the section I am taken to, the Evaluation Ward, is short-term.

When I arrive, my stomach begins to toss and turn again. I am queasy and fear I might vomit. Despite what I told Luke, despite my decision to run, both from the authorities, and later from Luke, I am not ready for this.

No one is mean or overly forceful. The guards simply state demands and expect compliance. No yelling, screaming, or obvious shows of force. No need with someone cooperating as I am, I suppose.

First, I am taken to a large empty room with a single chair perched in the center. A man enters carrying men's hair shears. "Sit," he says in a low, raspy voice, pointing to the chair. I follow instructions, even though I dread what is coming.

I sit, then the barber speaks in an oddly giddy tone. "I'm going to use the clippers to cut your hair," he says. "So, hold very still. It'll feel like a light tickle across your head." I hear the buzzing of the electric clippers as he turns them on. It is exactly as he said, a slight prickle over my scalp. I watch as long brown strands of my wavy hair fall in clumps around my feet. Part of me wants to cry, but there are worse things you can lose than hair, especially here.

While I knew they did this to long-term inmates, I now realize they do it to people who have yet to be convicted, people who might get sent home. Holding facilities shave heads to prevent suicides. In the early days, when facilities were just transitioning from prisons to the new system, holders didn't allow inmates to have anything they could use to hurt themselves, such as eating utensils or shoe strings. But, they didn't realize just how determined the condemned were. Inmates would pull strands of hair out, and weave them together into a noose. Now all inmates lose their hair, first thing. Though I do hope I won't be here long enough that I have time to weave my hair into a noose, let alone have the desire to do so.

Once I am sufficiently bald, a guard gives me a clear plastic cup and sends me to a restroom, instructing me to pee in the cup and leave it on the toilet lid. I do as I am told and wonder if all prisoners have to give a urine sample, or if I must do this because they are concerned about my kidney. Concerned I have somehow damaged it in my escape attempt and now it won't be usable for the transplant. There isn't much time to mull this over. The guard knocks on the door just as I finish filling my cup. Thankfully, my cup does not runneth over. I exit, leaving my sample behind for the holding facility pee fairies who apparently will whisk it away.

My clothes are next. I follow the guard to a plain space reminiscent of a gym locker room. It is completely empty except for two benches protruding from the floor and lockers without doors on the wall closest to the door. I walk to the bench and await instructions.

"Undress," the guard says, as he sets a plastic box on the floor and shoves it in my direction. "Put your clothes in here." I take the box from the floor and wait for him to leave. He just stands there. Apparently, privacy is not allowed, so I turn my back to him and undress as he watches. It feels as if his eyes never leave my body. Once I am naked, I turn back to the guard and give him the plastic box. In return he hands me a stack of neatly folded garments: standard issue prison clothing. A long-sleeved shirt and pants, as well as a pair of shoes with no laces, and thin soles.

The clothes are a tight-fitting material that stretches. It reminds me of spandex, only I know it isn't. Luke told me about this fabric once, but to see it in person is a little startling. I set the rest of the garments on the bench, and lift the shirt to the light to look at it better. I grab the sleeve and start to pull it slightly, watching as it stretches thinner.

"Stop," the guard says sternly. "It's HLFM."

I'd managed to forget he was there for a second. I turn to see what else he wants to say, but remember I'm naked as a jaybird. More importantly, I notice the guard enjoys seeing me like this, so I turn away again and begin dressing. As I pull on the shirt, the guard speaks. "HLFM stands for high-latency flexible material. It's made just for inmates. It's stretchy enough to fit most people, but it disintegrates if you put too much pressure on it. Pull too hard and you'll end up with a pile of dust. So, don't think about trying to hurt yourself or anyone else with your clothes."

I certainly wouldn't want to hurt myself. But the guard, that's another story.

Once fully dressed, I turn back to him. He smiles and adds, "Actually, I wouldn't mind if you kept pulling at your clothes. I think what the Lord blessed you with is much nicer than the HLFM anyway."

I look down at the floor and try to ignore the comment. What have I gotten myself into? The guard clears his throat. I look up and he has stopped smiling. He seems to be looking a little more professional now, as he opens the door to the room we are about to exit. I wonder if we are being watched in the hallways and that is the reason for his demeanor change. He issues the terse command, "Follow me."

I do. The guard wears a gray uniform, patent leather shoes and a billy club holstered on his side. I'm not sure where he is taking me, but I hope it is my cell. I don't want to be in his presence any more.

The halls are white and brightened with fluorescent light. After walking down the narrow corridors, making a turn here and there, we arrive at a white steel door. There is no window to peek in and see what the other side holds.

The guard swipes a plastic card in a reader next to the door. I hear a click as it electronically unlocks, and then the guard pulls the door's handle and swings it open. He points, and I enter what appears to be a white rubber room.

It is a cell, in every respect of the word. It is small and simple. Nothing in the room is movable. Nothing can be removed or broken off and used by an inmate to hurt himself or others. There are only two pieces of furniture, if you can call them furniture, even: a large rectangular block that will serve as my bed, and a ledge about knee height that protrudes about a foot-and-half from the wall. The bed block emerges directly from the floor, seamlessly, made of the same rubber as the floor, the walls and the ceiling. Same for the ledge, which I assume I can use as a table if I choose to sit on the floor to eat my meals. My room doesn't have a screen, so I apparently have no video or computer privileges, and no prospects of getting any.

I sit down on my rubber block. It isn't perfect, but it is soft enough. The guard closes the door behind him, leaving me alone with my thoughts. They immediately turn to Luke, my father, Susan and Haleema — in that order.

I hope Luke escaped and no one mentioned seeing us together or, if they did, that no one thought Luke a significant player in my escape. As miserable as I feel in this situation, the last thing I want is for Luke to be stuck in a holding facility, too. And my poor father. He now knows I have betrayed his trust and lied to his face. That all along, I had no intention of following through with donating my kidney to this stranger, but only pretended I would. He knows I left him without saying good-bye. He would never do that to me. I feel overwhelming guilt over how I have hurt him, how I have let him down.

And Susan. I've stolen her car and used it in an escape across the country. I hope no one thinks she is involved. I feel horrible, though I know Susan probably doesn't care. She has never given a damn about what other people think.

However, I am not so sure about Haleema. I wonder if she hates me. I used her, or at least her data, to escape. I hope they don't think she is complicit in this.

I will tell them she didn't know. She wasn't a part of it. Though hopefully they'll figure that out. I search my memory, thinking of the handful of cases I've read about where someone was caught attempting to flee a donation. No accomplices were ever prosecuted. Perhaps that is the trick to keeping society happy with the prospect of donation. No one is ever punished for aiding. It is always solely about the person who tried to escape. There isn't a witch-hunt, where people fear, "Might they think I was involved? Might I be punished?" There is little chance of collateral damage, so perhaps that's why people find it so easy to convict the wrongdoer and forget about him. When there's no chance you'll be touched by the problem, perhaps it's easy to forget it's a problem.

I will be punished for this, not Luke, Susan, Haleema or my father, even if FoSS suspects they helped. It will all be on me. If they want, they will be free to forget me and move on with their lives, never worrying their government will hurt them for my indiscretions.

I think about what Dr. Grant said and wonder if it is possible to get out of the donation. If giving my reasons against it might sway the people here.

I sigh, thinking Luke is probably right. I've never heard of a case where someone caught fleeing hasn't been forced to donate. And cases of people fleeing successfully — well, there are rumors of them — are nonexistent, according to the government. Though, Dr. Grant says he knows of two. The government has more reason to lie than Dr. Grant, so I believe some people have been successful. I wish I'd been one of them.

I shake my head. I can't think like this. No what ifs. I have to deal with the current situation. I have been caught. I try to remember the outcome of the other cases where people were caught. They all had to go through with the donation. A few years ago, one was sentenced to a year in a holding facility accompanied by psychiatric treatment, and another living donation (not an essential organ, but something). But, six months ago, a captured fleer was sentenced to death through donation. With the pro-choice movement ramping up on campuses, the government is taking a much harsher view on fleeing.

I stand. I don't want to think about that anymore. I don't want to sit on the rubber block anymore. I want to stretch, feel my legs, and think about something other than my fate or how I've hurt the people I care most about. The good news is that they are all out there, outside these cramped walls. If they are like most people whose friends and family end up here, they will write me off. They will make peace with my fate and say their good-byes, and that will be the end of it.

Except for Luke. He won't say good-bye to me. He will fight, fight to see me. My father, I'm not sure about. He brought me back to Maryland; that's one thing I am certain of. But, I have betrayed him by the very nature of what I've done. Does he understand my reasons and want to help, or is what I've done unforgivable? That thought sends a shiver through me. I am torn. The little girl in me hopes he doesn't feel that way. Yet, grown-up Kelsey knows writing me off is the best thing for him. It will keep him in the race for governor. Writing me off will let people know that I am an aberration, not the daughter he raised, but some stranger who has taken over her body. It will be right for him to keep his distance. And perhaps it will be justice for me. Justice for my betrayal. He's only ever had two passions in life: his family and his political career. When Mom died, politics and I were all he had left. But with me doing this, he should focus on the one passion still viable. And if he just writes me off, he can still have that.

I am walking away from my block, toward the opposite wall, pacing, when it turns pitch black. The lights are out. The darkness catches me so by surprise, I just stop moving, mid stride.

I put my foot down, so both feet are firmly planted on the floor as I try to discern what has happened. Is there a power outage? It seems unlikely. In homes, the power goes out occasionally. But government buildings have emergency generators. One might see the lights flicker if there is a power outage, as the emergency power source kicks in, but there would never be anything like this: something several seconds that is beginning to drag into minutes.

I don't move. It is so dark I can't see ahead or behind me. I can't see anything. Just darkness. I wait, hoping the lights will come back on.

The more I stand there, the more it truly begins to sink in that I am in the dark. I decide to turn around and try to make my way back to the rubber block. It should be easy, but I somehow get angled wrong and hit a wall. Not the one my block is on. I grope in the dark for a minute or two more before finding my way back to my rubber block. I sit first, making sure I am securely on it, then slowly stretch out to a lying position, and scoot close to the wall, so I am less likely to fall off.

I begin to wonder if sleeping on the floor would be a better idea. I toss and turn at night when I'm troubled. I don't want to roll to a thud on the floor. So, I test the floor, and it seems that even though it is made of substantively the same material, the bed block is indeed softer and more comfortable than the floor. It is a nuanced, but noticeable, difference. I stick with the bed.

I lie there in the silence, my eyes closed, having long since given up on them adjusting to this level of darkness, and try to think reassuring thoughts. A lights out time at a place like this is probably mandatory. This is not some power outage that will leave me without food or proper ventilation in this building for an indefinite period. I listen to the gentle whir coming from above. It is definitely a vent. Conditioned air is blowing in. I am getting air, and the lights will come on in the morning. I am not forgotten in this place.

The thoughts aren't really that reassuring. They just fill my head, and I realize that for me to sleep, I need my head empty. I concentrate on emptying my mind of clutter and thinking only of sleep. Eventually, my body takes over. I am tired from the restless night before and fall asleep. Even with my body doing what is needed, I can't really find peace. I awaken several times during the night, lifting my head for a few moments to listen for the whir of the vents. Soon after I fall asleep deeply enough to forget where I am, I awaken confused and addled. The complete darkness at first makes me wonder if I am dead. Wonder if I have gone through with the surgery but simply never awakened from the anesthesia. That's an incredibly rare occurrence. Less than one percent, but I've read about it happening, and in the fog of dreamland, this fact rushes to the forefront of my mind. Then I hear the screaming. You don't hear screams when you're dead. Do you? Finally, I divine it is me who is screaming, and stop.

I stay awake for what feels like an hour, but maybe it is less than that, 30 minutes. I can't see the room's digital clock in the dark. It's a gray monochrome display without backlighting. I remember seeing it at some point before the lights went out. The last I saw, the clock read 21:48. I have no idea what time is now. My internal clock thinks I've been up at least an hour after the screaming. I finally fall back asleep after that, but the sleep isn't good, just fits and bursts of rest.

When I wake up again, the lights are on and the digital clock says 6:22. Morning at last. I sigh in relief. The soft white light is soothing, and I manage to sleep a solid two hours, until I am awakened by a nurse named Keith. He barks out, "They need you to do some tests." A lanky, indifferent blond, Keith walks me through the bowels of the facility — dimly lit cement corridors — until we arrive in a medical area. There, doctors give me an ultrasound. It is irritating that I am so distrusted they believe I would harm my own kidney to prevent giving it away. They didn't need to check its healthiness via ultrasound. The whole point of avoiding the surgery is to preserve my own health, starting with that of my kidney.

While I am in the testing area, they also take my blood. Several vials. I suppose they will test me in every way to make sure I've done nothing odd to my body that could damage my kidney, making it unavailable for transplant. This mistrust bothers me immensely. I am not insane. I am simply a person who wants to live without fear of forced medical procedures.

Nurse Keith returns me to my room. There, I sit and wait, wondering what will happen next.

15. TIME FOR A CHAT

I sit in my room for two more hours, nothing but my thoughts to keep me company. I wonder again if Dr. Grant is right. If we are at a tipping point, if just telling them why I did it will help. Clearly, if they're testing to see if I've done damage to my own kidney, they haven't a clue why I fled.

The door to my cell opens, breaking me from my thoughts. I'm not sure who I expected to see, but it is doctors who appear. They waltz in with neutral faces and no talk, not even the customary hello.

One doctor is a man, the other a woman — both wear white coats. The man is large, towering over the woman. His muscles are visible even beneath the loose-fitting coat.

The woman, blonde hair swept into a bun, takes the lead. She gives me a quick once-over — sizing me up, I suppose. Her internal assessment made, she smiles. While the rest of their entrance seems deliberate, perhaps even planned to give nothing away, this smile feels unrehearsed, yet not entirely sincere. Perhaps something about the way I sit here, still and unmoving, makes her think I need someone to smile at me. While I wish it weren't true, she's right. I do need a smile.

"Kelsey," she says softly, as the man steps a little closer, still keeping his distance from me. I'm not sure if she is his superior, and he wants to show respect, or if he is concerned his size might frighten me. "I'm Dr. Klein," she says, then points to the man. "And this is Dr. Slate."

I stay seated on my bed block, look up at the woman, but don't speak.

She nods at the man. He leaves the room, then returns momentarily with two metal chairs. He sets them across from my bed. Dr. Slate leaves again, and returns with a camera, setting it up quickly on a tripod that unfolds with a jerk of one hand. The lady doctor sits. He follows her, sits politely, then looks toward her expectantly. The lady doctor, Klein, tells me they will be recording my interview. Dr. Klein is definitely in charge, I decide.

"Kelsey," she says again, in a low, smooth voice she clearly believes is soothing. "We want to talk to you about why you ran away. Would that be alright?"

I nod again.

She waits for me to speak. I'm not sure what to say. I'm tired from a restless night, irritated at being suspected of hurting my own kidney, and not certain what I should tell them. I look at my hands, hoping a brilliant explanation pops into my head. Only I don't do well on lack of sleep, and my thoughts feel slow to come.

The lady doctor is staring at me. "Kelsey," she purrs my name again, and I am beginning to hate the way it sounds rolling off her patronizing tongue. "Why did you run away?"

I maintain my hand-gazing to give myself a moment more to think. Then Dr. Grant's words pop into my mind. We are at a tipping point, he said. Is he right? If I just explain, will it make a difference?

Part of me wants to say the truth. The burden of hiding my belief has been heavy, but the price of being wrong is huge. The lady doctor is waiting.

"Kelsey," she says my name yet again in a low voice. "We're just looking for some answers."

Her expectant face means I must answer something. "I didn't want to give up my kidney," I blurt out, and it feels good. It feels good to say it.

Her expression remains momentarily neutral, then changes to curiosity. "Did you want the man who needed your kidney to die?"

I shake my head. "NO!" I screech. "No. Of course not."

Despite my shriekish reply, Dr. Klein speaks calmly. "What did you think would happen if you did not provide him your kidney?"

Her tone is patronizing, and I wonder if it is intentional, or if she intends the tone to sound merely nonthreatening. I'm not doing this right, I realize. I need to explain better. "I thought they'd find someone else," I respond, hopefully coolly, even though I am nervous about how things are going and upset that she accused me of wanting someone to die.

"Did you understand that you were the best match?"

I'm still not conveying this properly. I take a deep breath and try to match my tone to hers. "Yes, I understood that." I pause, searching for the right words. "It's just that I know other people participate in the system. I know my risk of death from the surgery is only 3 percent, but then there's also the risk of infection, or medical error. Something going wrong in general is 14 percent for a healthy person my age."

She nods her head gently to show she is following.

"It's just that, I, um, I got scared. After everything that happened to Susan, I just couldn't do it. Granted, hers wasn't a kidney transplant, and she had only a 12 percent chance of something going wrong, but something did go wrong. Terribly wrong. I just decided I didn't want to put myself at risk to help someone I don't even know."

Dr. Klein leans back in her chair, folds her arms, then, with genuine curiosity, asks, "Who is Susan?"

Well, that is a doozy of a question. I could spend hours answering it. Instead, I go simple. "She is my friend."

Lady doc looks surprised by my answer. She is now intrigued. I explain about Susan being marked last year for what should have been a simple bone marrow transplant, her operation, the infection, the paralysis, the low quality of life she has now. Dr. Klein listens without saying much, an occasional nod coupled with a "yes" or "go on." The man, Dr. Slate, watches me too, but shows almost no change in expression. I find myself wondering again why he is here. Is he a student tagging along to watch? Has he been told to remain neutral throughout, a passive observer? If so, he is very good at it.

Lady Klein notices me staring at her underling and clears her throat before speaking. She has my attention. "So, you're afraid Susan's misfortune will befall you if you have surgery."

I shake my head. "Not exactly." Putting my fears into words is hard because they're not concrete, but I know that if I'm unsuccessful at it, I will remain in this awful place. "It's not likely what happened to Susan will happen to me. The odds are totally in my favor. I mean survival statistics classes have hammered that in, over and over. The odds were in Susan's favor, too. They just didn't go her way. It's fine if the odds go against you, if you choose to take that risk. It's just that I don't want to take that risk."

The doctor crinkles her brow. "But the odds are in your favor. The surgery is a minimal risk."

"Of course it's minimal. And if Susan were the patient, I would risk it without a second thought. If it were my father. Or Haleema. Or, or," I want to say Luke, but know I can't bring him into this mess. "Or anyone else I loved, I'd do it in a heartbeat. But, for this stranger, for this person I don't know, I don't want to take the risk."

"Even though he'd take the risk for you?" she shoots back, dropping her doctor's veneer of impartiality.

"Yes, even if he'd take that risk for me," I say, trying to sound calm. Speaking the truth feels good and now that I've started, I feel the urge to spill every feeling I have on this subject, even though I know I need to avoid inflaming this doctor. "He would take that risk for me because society demands it. Because if he didn't, he'd end up in a place like this. If he would do it for me, on his own, out of the generosity of his heart, I would love that, but I would never force him to put anything about the life he's come to know in jeopardy to save me. If I have a problem, it's my problem to solve. If he wants to help, of course, I'd take it. But, I don't believe I'm owed it. Therefore, I don't believe I owe it to him."

She adjusts herself in her chair, crosses her legs. It seems to be a stalling tactic, something my father might do if he were feeling the need to regain his composure during a debate or contentious meeting. She leans forward, apparently back on track with her evaluation. "Do you believe you owe your fellow human being nothing?"

The question is the type that could be laced with venom, and I wonder if secretly she wants it to be, but it comes across monotone and dispassionate.

I put on my best look of incredulity. "Of course not. I owe my fellow man much. I just don't believe I owe him my body."

She lets that hang in the air a few moments, then uncrosses her left leg, and instead crosses right over left. "Are you concerned about the survival of humankind at all?"

"Yes, of course. And I do everything I can to help mankind survive. I gladly give blood every two years, and I'm not opposed to organ donation. I just want it to be a choice, not mandatory." The last sentence comes out whiny and pleading, like a crazy person pleading for the sane to believe her. That's what I feel like, here. Like a crazy person. Part of me wonders if I am crazy. If Dr. Grant has somehow warped me like a strange Svengali.

But, in my heart, I know I am not under any spell. I am doing what is right, even if the world thinks I'm crazy. My mother's lack of choice literally cost her her life. Susan almost paid with her life. I have no intention of being like them, even if FoSS thinks I'm crazy or, worse, evil. I wish I'd made it to Peoria. In Peoria, what I'm saying would play as well as the best ever Vaudeville show.

"May I ask you another question?" the lady doctor coos with false sincerity.

As she's been asking already without permission, her requesting it now seems odd. Perhaps it is some psychological move to make me feel I'm in control again. Or perhaps she's just weird. Her reasons don't matter, I suppose. "Go ahead," I say evenly.

"What if you were the only match for this man? What if no one else were able to give him a kidney?"

"If no one else could give him a kidney?" I repeat, turning the idea over in my mind, trying to grasp such a foreign concept. There is always someone else, always another match. Not as good as the first, but good enough. Good enough to save a life.

The phrase "Life First" dances in my head. The words are connected with every memory, every synapse, like an intricate web. I've heard the phrase so often, lived it, breathed it. Yet, when she asks the question like that, the familiar mantra seems meaningless. What would happen if there were no one else? The answer pops into my mind clear as day, and I blurt it out before I can stop myself. "Then he would die."

"If it were your choice, you would choose for him to die?"

I shake my head. "If it were my choice, I would choose for me to live without injury to my body. Whether he lives or dies only relates to him. My choice is about me."

"Even though it kills him."

"His failing kidneys are killing him, not me."

She narrows her eyes and gives me a death-ray stare. If looks could kill, I'd be dead, and Lady Klein would get to see what this room looks like from the other side.

Finally, the man, Dr. Slate, stands. The lady startles, as if she's forgotten he's there, then stands also. He smiles at me and says, very friendly, as if we've just been discussing what to have for dinner, or an upcoming outing, "Thank you for talking with us, Kelsey."

And with that, he turns off the recorder and hands it and the tripod to Dr. Klein. Then he picks up both chairs, turns and exits. Dr. Klein follows close behind.

Alone again, my insides feel like they've been flooded with ice as the realization of what I've done hits me. I've blown it. Shit. They are going to deem me a sociopath, take my kidney, and then scavenge every useful organ I have left.

16. JOKE'S ON YOU

A half hour later, Dr. Slate returns. This time, he is alone. He brings in a chair, sets it on the floor not far from where I am perched on my rubber block, then sits.

"How are you, Kelsey?"

This has to be a trick question. How is one supposed to be after having her head shaved; being stripped, prodded and given useless medical tests; spending a sleepless night; and being asked a bunch of questions by a doctor who clearly hates her? "As well as can be expected," I murmur.

"I want to ask you a couple more questions, if you don't mind."

I have no idea why he is here or where this is going, but I look him in the eye and nod.

He leans forward, gives a sheepish half smile, looking almost bashful. It's as if he is trying to endear himself to me. "I know this is an awkward place to be brought to, and everything seems very harsh, especially us doctors. And sometimes it's hard to feel like you can open up."

He pauses, looks at me as if awaiting a response. I nod, then he continues. "You can trust us, here, Kelsey," he says earnestly enough that I want to believe him. It is not true, I know. I can't trust him. This is certain, based on our last interaction. I trusted them with the truth; that was a mistake. Now, he wants me to believe I can open up. I nod, a sign to show I accept his lie. He smiles, showing pearly white teeth this time.

"When we asked you before about your reasons for not wanting to follow through with the donation, did you leave anything out?"

Now, that is an odd question. Not at all what I expected. I think for a moment. Nothing springs to mind. My reasons are clear. "No," I say, shaking my head.

He nods, sits up straighter, bites his lower lip, thinking some apparently deep, silent thought for several moments. Finally, he leans forward again, looks me in the eye, lowers his voice slightly. "I know your father is a state senator running for governor, and you may not want to embarrass him. If that's the case, don't worry about his career or any impact what you've done will have on that. What you say will stay between us. Just tell me if you have another reason."

This is, by far, the oddest conversation I'd ever had (and that's saying something, given the weirdos I've met at my father's campaign stops). I have no idea what this doctor is talking about. He thinks I have another reason, something unsaid. Something I think would embarrass my father. My mind draws a blank. Nothing. It is awful that when you need your brain to work most, to think of logical answers, nothing happens. Is he giving me a second chance? A second bite at the apple to improve my situation. If so, I have no idea what to say. I need more help. I study his face looking for clues. Green eyes, auburn hair, strong jaw bone, angular face. Nothing to give me a clue. I look up at the ceiling, then back at him, down to the floor, racking my brain, begging it to give me the right answer. But nothing is forthcoming. Finally, I simply shake my head. No hidden agenda. Besides, what could be worse for my father's career than his daughter fleeing? I basically gave the middle finger salute to the state he is seeking to govern. I can think of nothing worse than that.

The doctor gives me a resigned look and adjusts himself in his chair. We stare at each other, playing a verbal game of Chicken, each waiting for the other to say more.

I break first — cluck, cluck. Any other time, I could sit here and stare him into oblivion, but not now. I have a question. It's clear I totally blew my previous interview. And while I sorta like the ignorance-is-bliss mode, I know it will be better to have an answer so I can prepare myself mentally. I clear my throat so I am sure I have his attention. "When are they going to do the transplant?"

"They're not," he says, matter-of-factly.

Now, I am utterly confused. If I'd gotten a better reception from the doctor and his colleague earlier, I might think I'd succeeded in swaying them. But, it is clear telling the truth has not helped my cause. While they've been gone, I've been bracing myself for the moment they would tell me I am a pariah and they are going sedate me, and take my kidney, even though I've said no. "I don't understand," I say, pleading with my eyes for explanation.

"You're not eligible," he says with such perfect clarity that I can't even pretend I've misheard and ask him to repeat himself.

"Why not? I thought I was the perfect match."

He watches me closely now, evaluating me. Astonishment settles on his face. "You don't have any clue, do you?"

I shake my head.

He laughs. "Well, there's certainly irony in that. Isn't there, Kelsey?"

I don't like his laugh. It is harsh and cold and means something is very wrong. "Irony in what?"

"If you'd come in to do the procedure, they would have turned you away."

Is this some sick joke? Is this was why inmates try suicide, because of crazy taunting doctors like this one? "I — I — I don't understand."

He takes a deep breath, leans forward and begins speaking in a patient, even tone. "When you came in, we did a health evaluation, a urine sample."

I nod.

"This morning, we did a blood test and the ultrasound. You remember?"

Is he kidding? Of course I remember. "Yes, you did an ultrasound and blood tests to look at my kidneys, to make sure they were still in good condition."

He shakes his head. "No, that's not why. I mean, we can use the ultrasound to look for that. But that's not why you got one. You got the tests because of your urine sample. After we found the markers in your blood, we were pretty confident we had the right diagnosis, but it was the ultrasound that confirmed it. The blood tests had given us the right prognosis. It had not been a decoy."

I feel alarm. They found something wrong with me during the blood test. Something so wrong I am no longer suitable for the transplant. "What did you find in my blood?"

"Human chorionic gonadotropin, also known as HCG."

It sounds familiar, but I can't quite figure out why. "What is that?"

"A hormone."

A hormone. We all have hormones. How could a hormone make me ineligible? Is it a sign of cancer, a brain defect, or maybe even a kidney defect? Talk about irony. I feel like all the air has been sucked from my lungs. My voice comes out raspy and frightened, when I finally pluck up the courage to speak. "This HCG — it's bad?"

"Nope," he says, standing up, then grabbing his chair. "It's good. A woman only produces it in these quantities when she's pregnant. Ultrasound confirmed it wasn't a hoax. Wasn't something you'd injected yourself with to keep us from doing the transplant. There's a little guy or gal attached to the wall of your uterus. You're about four weeks along."

And with that, he walks out the door. It closes with a bang, followed by the click of the electronic lock.

I am dumbstruck. Pregnant. I hadn't considered, hadn't even thought of it as a possibility. Luke and I are always careful. But, obviously, nothing short of abstinence is 100 percent foolproof. I don't know what went wrong, but I feel overwhelmingly glad for whatever folly it is. Luke is going to be a daddy, and I am going to be a mommy. A smile spreads across my face as the thought sinks in.

I don't notice the electronic click that signals the door being unlocked. But, it must've sounded, for I look up to see the door open again and my father enter. I am shocked. He is the last person I expected to see at this moment, and a complete mood shifter. My surprise and happiness over the baby are immediately tempered as I see the results of my betrayal up close. My father has several new gray hairs. And he doesn't smile at me, not the genuine one or the public one.

I feel the guilt pile on like bricks as he walks towards me. I have hurt him immeasurably. And despite how sorry I feel, seeing him makes me realize I have done this to him. I have cracked the implacable man who has been there for me whenever I needed him. I walk over and hug him. "I'm so sorry, Daddy."

His arms stiffly embrace me for a moment, then he pulls away. He turns and won't look at me. It's all I can do to keep myself from crying. He's cutting me off and I deserve it. After Mom died, it was just me and him. We were all the family we had left, and we were always supposed to be honest with each other. Always supposed to be there for each other. I broke my end of the bargain when I sneaked away in the middle of the night.

I thought my note could explain it, that he might understand when he read it. That what was happening right now would never happen. But, clearly, I was wrong. His eyes were ice when he walked in, and he won't look at me now. It is apparent that my actions mean more than my explanations. I close my eyes, trying to keep the tears at bay. I tell myself that he came. That means something. He came.

"I'm glad you came," I say, hoping he will tell me I am misreading him, that he does not feel as wounded as he looks.

He nods curtly, stares at my head. The lack of hair must be jarring. I rub my hand over my head. "It's going to be all the rage in the salons, soon. I'm at the forefront of the trend."

He smiles at that, a genuine smile. "Well, at the very least, this hasn't affected your sense of humor," he says.

I roll my eyes. "I wouldn't say that, but you can't give up everything just 'cause you're locked away for refusing to give up a kidney you weren't actually going to have to give up anyway."

He is stiff and uncomfortable. "So, you didn't know about the baby?"

I shake my head. "Looks like you'll be a grandpa."

"Looks like," he says, offering a public smile.

I want to say something, to say I am sorry again, but that seems utterly inadequate. I've ruined everything for him, both his career and personal life. No one will vote for a candidate whose daughter dodged her responsibility. And I've created a rift between us that has never been there before. That rift feels as wide as the Grand Canyon as we stand in the tiny white rubber room.

"Did you get my note?"

He looks at me for a moment without speaking, then says stiltedly, "I did, but the chip was corrupt."

No! He has to hear Mom's message. I feel what little color I have drain from my face. That is the most important part, the thing he needs to see most. How could it be corrupt? I checked it myself earlier that day. Mom's video was on there.

Seeing my dismay, he edges closer and puts a hand on my shoulder. "The note was enough, Kelsey. I didn't need the chip."

I study his face, wanting to believe him, but his eyes seem so distant, so foreign to me, that I know he is wrong. He needs to really see it to understand. I take a deep breath, then sit down on my block. I close my eyes.

My father takes the two steps over to me and kneels. "Kelsey, don't upset yourself, not in your condition."

"I'm fine, Daddy," I say, hoping saying it will make it true. "It's just I wanted you to understand, understand that I'd never intentionally hurt you, that what I did, I did for me, and I really am sorry that you were hurt by my actions."

He proffers a genuine smile. "I understand, Kelsey, really." He hugs me, and pats my back the way he did when I was little and had fallen and scraped a knee. The familiarity of it is very comforting. Then he lets go and gives me a piercing look that reminds me that I have let him down. I am a failure as a child. I wonder if I'll be a failure as a mother, too. Then, a thought occurs to me. Luke.

"He doesn't know, Daddy," I sputter. "He doesn't know I'm pregnant. You have to tell him."

My father looks confused. I changed subjects without telling him. I pause, preparing to explain, but at that moment, my father seems to get it. "The baby's father?" he asks.

"Yes, you have to tell..."

"John," he says, cutting me off. I stop cold. John? John works in Dad's office, and I went on one date with him. It wasn't even a real date. He just accompanied me because Dad hadn't wanted me to bring Luke. My father is now giving me a significant look, one that says to go along with him.

"Yes, John," I say, as it dawns on me my father is right. Bringing Luke's name into this, bringing him into the fold, into the authorities' purview is idiotic. He's saved me. Even though I've so wronged him, he's saved me, and I am grateful.

My father breathes out a sigh. His face is ashen. Something is wrong. I still can't figure out what. One moment he's loving, fatherly, saving me and Luke from my idiotic big mouth, and the next he's cold and aloof and distant. I'm trying to read his face, but this isn't like anything I've seen on the campaign trail. It's a bit like when Mom died; a persevere, despite all odds, stoicism. I bite my lip.

"Honey," he says, looking down at the floor, not at me. "The things you said have not helped your case. They'd like to transfer you to the long-term unit."

My lips part and my eyes widen with incredulity. He can't be serious. I'm pregnant. My hand instinctively touches my belly. They can't move a pregnant woman to the long-term unit. Those places are only for people who society has written off. I haven't even had a hearing. They can't transfer me unless someone has made a decision. Someone other than a prissy psychiatrist. Another look at my father's face reveals I've been mistaken. His demeanor hasn't been anger or disappointment or resentment or some other awful thing my guilt has led me to imagine. His demeanor has been dread. Dread at telling me I am being railroaded.

"What about my hearing?" I manage to ask.

He doesn't answer immediately. More dread seeps into his bluish-gray eyes. "Dr. Slate would like to convene a hearing in two days. Then, he'd like to take the baby and have you transferred."

That doesn't make any sense. I don't understand. "Take the baby?"

Dad joins me on my rubber block. He takes my hands in his, meets my eyes, and speaks firmly, clearly. "You're familiar with the Grant Research Lab on campus, headed by Dr. Stephen Grant?"

My entire body tenses in shock. I pull my hands free of his, stand, and back away as the horror of what he is saying sinks in. "No," I shout.

He stands, too, reaching his hand out to me. "I understand how this would be upsetting, Kelsey," he says, calmly.

"NO!" I scream, shaking my head, wrapping both hands around my abdomen. "No, no, no, no, no, no, no."

He tries to get closer to me, but I back away to the corner. I sit on the floor, pull my knees to my chest, tuck my head, use my hands to cover my ears and just kept saying, "No." This can't be happening. This is the worst of all possibilities.

17. DR. GRANT'S LAB

Three Years Ago

After meeting Dr. Grant in his hotel room, I hadn't wanted to see him again.

He'd shattered everything I'd known and believed about my mother's death, about the inherent purity of Life First. I'd watched my mother again and again, in her last moments of life, urging me never to put another's life before my own. Urging me always to choose my life first. It was so odd to hear. The idea that society was wrong, that protecting life as a whole, as a general concept, wasn't so important. That even though something didn't theoretically cost much, the reality could be quite different, and if it was more than you were willing to give, you shouldn't give it. It was the antithesis of Life First.

Before I saw her recording, I'd felt confident in Life First. After, I had doubts. At what cost did life come first? It wasn't as simple as statistics. It was something the government didn't have a right to decide.

A month after he'd given me the recording, Dr. Grant called. He wanted to show me his lab. My mother had inspired it, he'd raved. It would honor her memory for me to see it, he'd insisted. I'd begged off, not wanting more upheaval in my life. I couldn't deal with having more of my most basic truths shattered like porcelain.

Another month passed, and he called again. It was after I'd seen him with Luke. My curiosity about the work and about Luke took over. I wanted to know: what had my mother inspired? And what did this handsome assistant actually assist him with.

So, I agreed to meet him.

"I'm so glad you came," Dr. Grant told me when I arrived in the large warehouse-like building with gray cement floors. The main room was separated in two. The first space, closest to the entry, was a work area. There were desks, computers, and tables holding data logs. The other half of the room was clearly where the real work was being done.

There were several areas separated by large cloth partitions, the kind you saw in old movies featuring makeshift hospitals. The partitions were black, and the experiments were hidden behind them.

Dr. Grant walked me toward a table and said, "This whole lab is all because of your mother. What happened to her shouldn't have. She should have had an option. Something other than them both dying, or just the baby dying," he said.

He was about to speak again, when the door to the room opened. Luke walked in, striding toward us with a sense of urgency. "Dr. Grant," he said. "I'm sorry to interrupt. There's a problem with Mrs. Mitchell. She's holding on your private line."

The two exchanged a glance full of some hidden meaning. Then Dr. Grant turned to me, smiled apologetically. "I'll be back in one minute. Luke, why don't you show Ms. Reed around?"

Dr. Grant took a few quick strides and was out the door. I turned to Luke, who flashed me his best grin, full of dimples and that mischievous twinkle in his eye.

"So we meet again, Ms. Reed," he said.

"Yes, we do," I replied, trying to keep cool, even though the way he stared at me with those dazzling blue eyes was heating me to thermonuclear levels on the inside.

"I think this may be a sign."

I grinned and raised an eyebrow, hoping to look coy. "A sign? Of what?"

He flashed a crooked smile that made me wonder if his lips were as soft and kissable as they looked. "That you and I are meant to have dinner together."

I liked that he cut to the chase, but I wasn't quite ready to say yes. "Aren't you supposed to be showing me around?"

"Of course," he said, holding out his arm to me, like an old-fashioned gentleman. "That doesn't mean I can't ask you out, too."

I smiled. "Why don't you tell me what you do for Dr. Grant?"

"I assist him," he said, purposefully vague, but never losing eye contact.

I tried to be equally bold, holding his gaze. "With what?"

"Whatever he needs," Luke said cheerfully.

Even more vague. It was irritating, yet alluring at the same time. "Are you a doctor?"

"Nope." He shook his head

"A med student?"

Another head shake, chased by a sly grin. "Nope."

"Researcher?"

He laughed this time. "Nope."

"Are you going to tell me what it is you do for him?"

"Maybe at dinner," he said, this time winking.

I couldn't suppress my smile. He knew he had me. I could tell by the look in his eye. He knew I would go to dinner with him. Instead of confirming it, I said, "You're persistent."

"Of course," he replied, cocking his head slightly. "I'm supposed to be showing you around. What is it that you'd like to see?"

He wasn't going to tell me what he did, and now he'd changed the subject. Figured I'd go with it. What did I want to see? "No idea," I told him. "I don't even know what Dr. Grant is researching."

He stopped cold, regarded me, genuinely surprised. "You don't know?"

I shook my head.

Skeptically, he asked, "Truly?"

I nodded.

He shrugged, finally accepting my ignorance. "You know Dr. Grant is an obstetrician?" he asked, looking a little uncertain that I knew anything about the doctor.

"Yes."

Appearing relieved, Luke continued, "Well, he specializes in high-risk patients. One of his early patients died of pre-eclampsia, a fairly rare disease. But the only cure is to deliver the baby. No one knows exactly why, but the symptoms subside fairly quickly once the pregnancy ends."

He started walking us toward the screened area. "Well, right now, it's tough to make the correct call and get permission from the medical board to deliver a baby that can't survive if the mother's vital signs look pretty good. Unfortunately, things can go downhill quickly and without warning. So, Dr. Grant has been looking to develop an artificial womb. One you can remove the fetus to, so it can survive, but that will allow the baby to be delivered."

An artificial womb would have saved my mother. They would have easily taken the baby if they'd known it would survive. No weighing whose life was more at detriment. I felt both a sense of regret that no one had accomplished such a feat in time to save my mother, yet a new sense of hope that others might not lose their mothers the way I'd lost mine. "Has he had any success?" I asked, hopeful they were on the brink of perfecting it.

Luke sighed. "Not quite," he said, as we approached the other area of the lab, where several cloth partitioned cubicles were. Luke pulled back the curtain of one, and I saw what looked like a glass barrel containing clear liquid with a translucent sac at its center. Inside the sac was the outline of a baby. It was upside down and had clearly developed arms, legs, hands, feet and a head. But, something about the baby didn't quite look right.

"What is it?" I asked, marveling at the wonder inside the cylinder hooked to so many tubes.

"It's a womb, supported artificially," Luke said. "Dr. Grant can remove the entire uterus and keep the baby alive, at least in some primates. This is a chimpanzee."

An ape. That's why it didn't look right. The head was not the right proportion for a human baby. The body and extremities, though the right general shape, were too long.

"He uses chimps because of their similarities to people," Luke continued. "It's not exact. We're not allowed to do human trials here. The ones on the apes have shown good progress. If the placenta's fairly developed, he can remove the womb, and the baby can grow outside a mother. But, he hasn't figured out how to support the fetus without the uterus."

I looked at the tiny sac, completely awestruck. There was a baby in there, living without the aid of a mother's body. "You can save the baby, but you have to take the uterus?"

He sighed. "Yes. It will be better than death for both, but it means a woman can't bear any more children. It's a heavy price to pay."

I nodded. A heavy price indeed.

18. GOOD NEWS

Present

At some point, my father gives up on getting through to me. Maybe it is 10 minutes or two hours; I'm not sure. All I know is, after a while, he simply leaves me here careening from his news.

When he finally returns, I am still rooted to the floor, my arms hugging my knees. It feels comfortable this way. The floor isn't as soft as the block that is supposed to be my bed, but feeling comfortable is the last thing I need.

My father kneels in front of me, looks me over. I hear another set of footsteps behind him, but don't bother to look. Probably the doctor. Probably going to tell me about the procedure Dr. Grant will do. How the doctor will plunge a scalpel in my abdomen and rip my baby from my carcass, still wrapped safely in my womb. Only my womb will be gone forever, and I'll never have another baby.

I shudder at the thought, and my father tenses. I don't even care anymore. I close my eyes and tuck my head, still wondering how I didn't realize this before. How I didn't realize it would come to this. I mean, all long-term holding facility inmates are sterilized. No passing on corrupt genes. The last thing a society that has already been decimated by disease needs is a bunch of sociopaths and murderers corrupting the gene pool. FoSS wants good people. Being sentenced to a holding facility means your genes are bad and will produce bad people.

"Kelsey," my father whispers.

I lift my head enough to see his face. He is right in front of me, staring at me, eyes filled with fear and anxiety. An avalanche of guilt smacks into me. My father looks like his whole world is dependent on whether I'm OK. I hate that. He should leave me here to get what I deserve. But he isn't. For that, I owe him more than I'm giving. I need to say something, so I bury my despair for this moment. "Yes, Daddy," I whisper.

He's been holding his breath awaiting my response. He exhales in relief. "Are you alright?"

And then my selflessness is gone. I cannot be brave for him. I shake my head. "Daddy, you can't let them do this to me," I splutter, the panic palpable. "They can't take my womb!"

He's nodding his head before I've even finished the sentence. "OK, sweetie, OK," he says in a lullaby-gentle voice. "I need you to calm down."

I still, returning to my senses slightly, surprised by his response. It is not quite right, and I don't know why. I scrutinize his face: solemn, eyebrows squished together, lips pressed firmly together, and eyes of steel. Strength. He is trying to convey that I must be strong. Yet, he is the strong one. I'm just the daughter.

I even my breathing and try to take on a calm tone. "Daddy, you have to help me."

"I will," he says with conviction. That is no lie. He is going to help, but still there is something he is not saying. "First, I want you to get up and come sit on your bed, dear."

He is calmer than me, much calmer. I am not sure why he wants me to move or if it is useful, so I stay put for a minute. Then, I reason that he is strong, and if I am to be strong, I should do as he asks. I stand and follow him to the rubber block. We both sit, me closest to the doorway but with my back to it, where our watcher lurks. My father sits next to me, facing me. His eyes dart over to the doorway, then back to me. "I'm going to try to help you, Kelsey. Clearly this has been an ordeal for you," he says patting my shoulder. "First thing you need to know: your hearing is the day after tomorrow. In preparation for that, I'm going to hire psychiatrists to come in and evaluate you, to see if there is something the people here missed."

I nod. My defense. I need a good defense, and the psychiatrists could help with that. Good move, Daddy.

I am glad my father is thinking for me, that he hasn't given up on me, written me off. The best thing for him politically is to cut me off, but he doesn't seem to care. He seems intent on helping me through this. He cannot comprehend how glad that makes me, especially since I feel so desperate at this moment.

"Second thing," he says, taking a deep breath. "I don't think you're doing well in here. I know the procedures are such to prevent anyone from hurting themselves, but you seem overly despondent to me."

I want to protest, to say something in my defense, but the truth is, I feel overly despondent in here. But, I will not hurt myself nor even try, not when I am carrying Luke's and my baby. I touch my belly. "Daddy, I would —" I start to say, but he shushes me.

"I'm sure you'll make every effort to be OK, but I've asked and received permission to have a guard stationed inside the room here with you. If you're ever feeling overly despondent, just ask him, and he'll call a doctor to see you."

Now this is crazy. I am in a facility that has doctors readily available. Why the middle man? Why not just call for a doctor? Why station some guard in my room? Someone inside my room for heaven sakes — watching me all the time! I am about to protest, when he says, "Mr. Geary, would you come over here, please?"

My heart skips a beat. Did he just say what I thought? I am afraid to turn my head and look, afraid the hope building inside me is going to dissipate, afraid that I misheard my father. Afraid that I have somehow misconstrued what is happening.

"He comes highly recommended," my father adds. "His father worked here for 30 years."

Two black shoes are now standing beside us. I stare at them for a moment, then follow the blue pants line upward, past the belt, past the starched shirt and black tie knotted at the neck, to the face, the dimples, those blue eyes and those brown locks peeping out from under his cap.

"Just let me know if you need a doctor, Ms. Reed," Luke says, giving me a wink and a crooked grin, then walks back to the door.

With willpower I didn't know I had, I manage to suppress the smile trying to claw it's way onto my face. In fact, I want to jump for joy. But, I know that will put the kibosh on this guard ruse. I don't know how my father and Luke pulled it off, but they did. I lean in and hug my father. "Thank you," I whisper in his ear.

"Anything for my Kelsey-pie," he whispers back.

My father stands, gives Luke a curt nod, then exits the room. Luke closes the door behind him, and stands just inside the doorway. I rise, prepared to walk over and greet him properly.

"Sit down," he barks sternly. Though affronted by his tone, I follow his command. He watches me, but does not move. I don't understand why he is doing this. I want both to scold him and wrap myself in his arms at the same time.

He speaks softly, less sternly now. "There are cameras in the room." He inclines his head slightly upward to the corner. "The sound is usually muted, unless they want to hear a specific room. We can talk, but you have to lie down. Turn your face to the wall. Maybe cover your face with your arm, like you want to block out the light so you can sleep. If the monitor guard sees your mouth moving, he's going to want to turn up the sound, hear what you're saying."

Of course. Luke is only protecting me from cameras. I do as Luke says, adding a touch of my own, giving a big yawn first with both arms outstretched. Then I open my mouth and pat it a couple times with my hand. I lie down, facing the wall, and form my arms into a sort-of pillow, tucking my face in.

"So," I say. "Can't he see your lips moving and realize you're talking?"

Luke chuckles. "Nope. I'm standing just out of camera view. That's why I haven't come into the room. He can see my feet in the frame, maybe a bit of my lower body, but my head is hidden."

Clever. "How did you guys pull this off?"

"Your father is surprisingly effective when he wants something done. I think he called upon everyone who's ever owed him a favor, and promised out a 100 more."

That sounds like my father — a wizard at political deal making. "So, do you think he'll be able to get me outta here?"

Luke doesn't speak for a moment. I am not sure if he is thinking, if perhaps someone is coming into the room, or if the answer is no and he doesn't want to tell me.

"I hope he can," Luke finally responds. "It's just an uphill battle. Your father thought things were going our way when they got the pregnancy test results. He wanted to see you before the interview, so he could give you a heads up to say you left because you were pregnant, but he couldn't get in."

I roll over to see Luke so I can respond. He gives me the stink eye, so I roll back the other way. This weird, don't-look-at-me communication is frustrating. I want to see his expression, see what I am missing. Head resting on my arms, mouth facing the wall, I ask, "Why couldn't he get in? He got you in. He's got plenty of clout. What happened?"

"The big guy, Dr. Slate," Luke says. "He's Michael Nimmick's brother-in-law." Crap! That explains a lot. Michael Nimmick is the current governor, and not too happy my father is trying, fairly successfully until now, to unseat him. Nimmick would like nothing more than to see me locked away as a menace to society. No wonder Slate is rushing things.

I start to tilt my head toward the door, toward Luke, but think better of it. "Well, how did he get you in here?"

"Political savvy. The tide is definitely turning against your father over this, and Slate was afraid that if you somehow managed to hurt yourself in here, the tide would swing the other way. That your dad would spin it as people letting his pregnant daughter get hurt, and he'd appear more sympathetic. So, right now, Slate's willing to give in on a guard, but he definitely wants you convicted and sent long-term."

I breathe out, praying some of the tension and stress I'm feeling will sail right out of me with that breath. No such luck, though. This is horrible news.

"Kelsey," Luke says. "We should probably cut the chatter for a bit. I want to get settled in, give the appearance of doing a good job. I'll be here overnight. We can talk more at lights out, OK?"

This is disappointing. Luke is here, just a few feet away, and we can't speak or touch or even look at each other. "Just one thing before we go silent?"

"Sure," he says, tension in his voice.

"Are you happy — about the baby?"

"Immensely." I don't even need to see him. I can hear the thrill in his voice.

19. YES

Like the previous night, the lights go out at 10 p.m. Instead of feeling fear and anxiety, I feel pure bliss. Luke is here with me, and we can now talk freely.

I sit up on my block. "Luke?"

"Yeah, I'm here."

"Come here," I say, reaching my hands out, grasping at the air around me in hopes that he'll walk right into my eager arms.

"OK, but it's dark. I can't turn on my light, or they'll see in the security room."

I hear his shoes clacking on the rubber floor, then I feel a hand on the shoulder of my outstretched arm. A joyful tremor passes through me at the familiar touch. It's been fewer than two days, yet it seems like a lifetime. I reach my own hand up and take his in mine. His is strong, sturdy — and hairy on top. It's also cool to the touch, probably because the room's a little chilly. "I'm so glad you're here," I breathe out.

"Me too," he responds, giving my hand a squeeze.

I scoot over on the block, making room for him. "Sit with me."

His fingers go rigid within mine. "I shouldn't," he says. "The guard in the security room can turn on the lights. Thanks to my Dad, I've taken care of the sound, pretty much. A closet near the monitoring room holds the circuitry that links the audio from each cell into the central hub. I manually pulled the circuits for this cell. If he hits the button, he won't be able to hear us. He won't leave his post to check it out without announcing it over the radio. So we'll know if he leaves to check the sound closet.

"But, he will be able to see us, Kelse. My father thought killing the

92

light switch would be too suspect. Guards rarely want to listen, but they do like to watch. So, I probably shouldn't have even come this close. It's just, sometimes you thwart my better judgment."

I squeeze his hand tighter, not ready to let go. It feels warmer now, after just a few seconds of me holding it. Luke slides his hand out of my grip, and I can hear him step away. Then, a slight swishing followed by a thud. He has gone further away, but not back to the doorway.

"Where are you?"

"On the floor, next to your bed. Lie down, with your head nearest the door. You'll be closer to me that way."

I do as he says, making sure I don't fall, as the bed block is fairly narrow, only wider than a person by a few inches on each side.

"So, how are you feeling?"

"Truthfully?" I ask, but don't wait for a response. "A little nauseated."

"Already?"

"Apparently so." I chuckle. "I've been feeling this way the past week, but I thought it was stress related. Now, I'm thinking not."

He drums his fingers on the rubber, but as it is pitch black. I can't tell if it is the floor or the wall, or the base of my block he's chosen to tap on. "You've felt this way for a week and didn't say anything to me?"

"It wasn't anything that bad. It wasn't worth worrying you with."

He exhales a long breath that sounds like a swoosh. I wish I could see his face. That way I would have a sense of what his long breath and silence mean. I wonder if he is brooding over me not mentioning the nausea. I wish I could light a candle, or there were a sliver of moonlight or hallway light able to peek through, so I could have even a silhouette to see.

I could wait for Luke to say something more, but I've waited so long to talk to him, I want to hear him speak. About something. Something good. Happily, I ask. "So, who told you? About the baby, I mean."

"Your dad."

I can't imagine that going well. "Was he mad about it?"

"About me knocking up his daughter?" he chuckles. "If he was, he didn't show it. In fact, he seemed pretty happy about it."

"I am too," I say a little too loudly. I am giddy and it shows, even in the darkness. "I can't believe it. I was so surprised when the doctor told me. I can't even imagine the shock you felt. I bet you about passed out."

I wait for his chuckle, his, "me too," his confirmation that he was as surprised by the news as I was. Instead, all I hear is his steady breathing. In and out, in and out. But no words. Slowly, the obvious sinks in: he had more of an inkling than I did that I could be pregnant.

He speaks softly: "Remember the night after I proposed, the night we made up?"

It would be hard to forget that night. After I put off his marriage proposal, he left, fairly upset with me. He went silent: no calls, no texts, no nothing, and I began to think I'd made a huge mistake. But, he came over the next night, and we talked. He seemed at peace with waiting until things were settled. And then he made love to me, the kind of lovemaking that seems to last an eternity and leaves you breathless for more, but too tired to continue. I smile at the memory and start to nod in response to Luke's question, then I realize he won't see me. "I remember," I say.

He breathes in again, deeper this time. "Well, when I was taking the condom off, it was broken. I wasn't sure if I did it taking it off, or if it happened earlier. You were already stressed out about being marked, so I didn't say anything."

My breath catches in my throat, and my body tightens with shock. He's known it was possible. He's known it and decided not to share it with me because he thought it would stress me out. "Why," I ask, cocking my head to try to see him better in this awful darkness, though it is futile. I shake my head. "Why did you think I would be more stressed?"

"Kelsey, after you wouldn't agree to marry me, I wasn't sure what to think. I thought for sure you were going to say 'Of course I'll marry you,' and I was wrong. Devastatingly wrong. If you'd asked me before I proposed how you would have felt about being pregnant, I would have said you'd be surprised, and ultimately happy. After I proposed, I realized I didn't understand you as well as I thought. I just didn't know what you'd think. So, I didn't say anything. I convinced myself I didn't need to say anything. I mean, even if the condom had broken early-on, it wasn't likely you were pregnant. Even if you were, I figured you'd find out in Peoria, and then you could make whatever decision you wanted about it. The laws would let you do whatever you wanted to there."

I can't help but gasp. He thinks I'd get rid of our baby. A wave of nausea hits me. I turn back to the wall, finally glad for the darkness. I can't face this Luke who thinks for a moment that I would do that.

Not saying yes was a mistake, such a huge mistake. I let him down on that one question and after that he doubted everything else about me. To doubt that I would want our child. I feel so awful, I start to cry — low, soft sobs, hoping he won't notice. In the absence of seeing, there is nothing to do in this room but listen to the noises.

"Kelsey, are you crying?"

I can't respond. I don't want him to feel bad that I am crying, but answering in the negative isn't an option either because I am, in fact, crying and can't stop. A moment or two goes by and then I hear the shuffling of fabric and gentle thud of his shoes. Luke is standing over me, as I lie curled up on my cold, sterile block. "Scoot over," he says.

Through sobs, I manage, "What if they turn on the lights?"

He sighs. "Then, they'll think I'm molesting an inmate. It's not the first time it's happened." It takes a minute, but I gain some composure — or at least shirk off the blubbering mess I've become — and do what I'm told: sit up and scoot over. Luke sits and wraps an arm around me.

"I wouldn't have done anything in Peoria that I wouldn't have done here," I say softly, though with conviction. I'm still fighting off the urge to cry, so I'm not sure how it sounds to Luke. I wipe my wet face with my hands, and try to see his face as I talk to him, but it's still too dark.

Luke leans in and kisses my eyelid. I'm not sure if that is the spot he intended or if his aim is affected by the darkness. "I know you wouldn't have, Kelsey. At least, I know now. But I was unsure then. And not because I thought you didn't ever want a baby. But, we were using condoms for a reason. Neither of us wanted a baby going in that night, and if you felt that way still, I didn't want to stand in your way. Plus, I've seen enough of Dr. Grant's patients to know that pregnancy is nothing to sneeze at. It can put you at tremendous risk. If you weren't ready for that, I wanted to give you the space to make that decision."

"Luke, I didn't need space. I wouldn't have —" I start, but he cuts me off.

"Shh. Kelsey, I realize that now," he says. He pats my shoulder. "I also realize that pregnancy is not necessarily easy. I've seen the complications Dr. Grant's patients have. Some are very dangerous. I considered that maybe being pregnant, after what happened to your mother, after seeing her in her last moments like you did, that maybe it made you wary of pregnancy."

Luke always thinks of everything, considers every perspective. Perhaps, I should be more ambivalent at the prospect of pregnancy after what happened to my mother. But I'm not. The prospect of me, Luke and baby makes me happier than I've ever been. Yet he understands that it might not make me happy, and he's able to accept that, too.

Then it hits me, like being doused with cold water. "The baby, is that why you wanted to wait to come to Peoria?"

He swallows, and the arm he wrapped around me feels a little heavier now. He waits a few seconds before speaking. When he finally does, his voice isn't the strong, sure Luke I've always known. It is an emotion-filled whisper. "Kelsey, I could understand — in my head, at least — I could understand the reasons you wouldn't want to be pregnant. And I couldn't begrudge you any of them or any choice you made about your body. But while my head could get it, my heart never really could, you know. I decided I would let you go down there without knowing, and I would come two months later. You know, if I showed up, and you weren't pregnant, I could tell myself you never were. If you were, then I'd know that you were genuinely happy with the choice. What I couldn't take was going down there with you and having you tell me a week later that you didn't want to have our baby, that you were going to end the pregnancy. It was your choice, but I wasn't prepared to face it: you not wanting to be pregnant. So I wanted the two months."

He pauses, takes a breath, then starts again. "That night when I got down on my knee and proposed, I would have bet my life that you were going to smile that beautiful smile of yours, wrap your arms around me and say 'yes.' I was wrong about that. You didn't tell me 'yes.' You gave me an answer I didn't expect at all. And that's fine. I could take being wrong about the proposal. I couldn't deal with being wrong about how you'd feel about a baby. So, I gave myself the two months."

I pull him tighter. "I'm sorry, Luke," I say. "I'm so sorry I put you through that." I'd been such a fool. I wish I hadn't been. I shouldn't have cared what his reasons were for asking me to marry him. Shouldn't have worried about whether he would change his mind later. Luke is always there when I need him, and he'll make a wonderful husband. He isn't going to change his mind. He isn't going to regret his decision. Neither am I. And I should have realized that when he asked me that night. But, it isn't too late.

"Yes," I say.

He caresses my arm lightly. "Yes, what?"

"Yes is my answer to the question you asked me that night. I should have said it then." He leans in and kisses me, his lips finding mine perfectly. "I'm sorry I made you wait."

"No, it was my fault. I should have known the perfect time to ask you would be in complete darkness in a holding facility while you awaited your hearing. Things are clearly much more settled now."

We laugh, and sit there holding each other. After a few minutes, Luke says we really shouldn't live dangerously and he returns to his spot on the floor.

Almost as soon as he does, the lights flick on. A beep emanates from Luke's belt. I don't look up to see exactly what he does, because I don't want to draw attention to myself, but he must pick up his guard's radio.

"Geary," he responds in a militaristic voice he's never used with me.

"Thomas here," crackles the voice over the radio. "You OK in there?"

"Yeah, just moved to the floor to keep a closer eye on her."

"Need the light on all night?"

Luke laughs. "So the senator could claim we're torturing his kid? No thanks."

The lights disappear. Just like that, blackness is back.

"'K," says the radio man. "I'll check in later."

I wait a few minutes, then say. "Close one."

"Yeah, get some sleep, Kelsey."

I close my eyes, intent on obeying my fiancé's request.

20. JAVELINA BOY

I am groggy when Luke wakes me. It is still dark. Barely able to open my eyes, I feel his hand on my shoulder.

"Lights come on in about 10 minutes," he whispers, his breath warming my face. "I have to leave at 8 am, because guards can only work twelve-hour shifts. I just wanted to tell you good-bye. I won't be able to later."

My mind manages to click on, to claw it's way from the fog of sleep. "You're leaving?"

"Yes, but don't worry," he whispers, then pecks me lightly on the cheek. "I'll be back tonight."

"Alright," I whisper, but it's not alright. I don't want him to go.

"I just want to let you know the day guard may not be so nice. Some of the guys who do this are assholes, OK? No matter what he says, don't get upset. It would just give Slate more ammunition, alright?"

"OK," I say, not wanting to think a minute more about Luke leaving. "I'll be fine." I reach out and touch his shoulder reassuringly.

"Alright," he says, his voice more cheerful than earlier. "Go back to sleep, if you can. You need your rest."

I close my eyes, and, amazingly, fall right back to sleep. I am tired. When I awake, Luke is gone, as promised. The guard who has replaced him whilst I snored is short and rotund, with a face resembling a pig. Even though overtly high-fat, unhealthy foods are banned in FoSS, some people still overeat and don't exercise enough. This guard is one of them.

His complexion is ruddy and pink, and his bulbous nose has wide nostrils. He has little black eyes with wild, bushy eyebrows sprouting above them. When he sees that I am awake, he does not smile, wave hello, or even nod. None of the things I have been so used to in polite society. Instead, he looks me over from head to toe with complete disdain. He stands in the same spot as Luke, and I fear he chose that spot for the same reason — it is hidden from the camera. The man's jowls quiver slightly, and I think for a second he is about to spit on me, but he merely purses his lips slightly and stretches his neck, as if stiff. Then he returns to watching me with his cold, wicked eyes.

I look up at the clock. It is 8:50, and I wonder how I could have slept for 50 minutes with a man filled with such contempt standing so nearby. It radiates from him like heat — only it's cold, chilling me to the bone. I stare at the ceiling, trying to ignore him, trying to forget he is there. I imagine how Luke would look changing a diaper. I mean, he is the baby of the family. Would he have any clue? Gosh, what am I talking about. I am the only child of my family. I'd have as little clue as he. We'd be ignorant together, fumbling around trying to figure it out. But, we'd laugh and enjoy it because we'd be in it together.

I do not realize I have begun to smile, as my thoughts instinctively filter down to my face muscles. "Imagining how you'll kill your baby, are you?" the guard says coldly. "Or is it someone else you're imagining killing? Is that why you're so happy."

I turn to look at him, wishing he would move out of Luke's spot, tarnishing the one bright spot I have in this place. I remember Luke's words: Don't get upset. I say nothing, just put back to him, so I now face the wall.

"You want to kill people?" he asks, his voice thick with venom. "Not just the people you deprive of life by running off, but others too?"

I wish I could run over there and slap him across his face. I know it is violent and wrong, but I wish it right now. However, I do nothing. I say nothing. I lie still.

"I've been a guard for 25 years. I've seen people like you before. Pretending you're exercising some choice, some wonderful thing you deserve. But, all you are doing is being selfish. You're a selfish whore is what you are."

He chuckles. Must be his idea of a fabulous joke, calling someone a selfish whore. "I hear you're knocked up and not married. A real piece of work you are, Ms. Reed. Not fit to be the state's first daughter. Do you even know who the father is? Probably some piece-o-shit, no good pro-choicer, too."

Luke told me not to get upset. I have failed. I am upset. However, I will not fail the spirit of the advice. I will not do something to make myself look any worse than I already do. I close my eyes and begin to hum, trying to tune him out. He speaks louder. "You know, my great-grandmother was the only survivor in her family. Twelve years old and the only person of the 100 close and extended relatives she knew to live through the pandemic. Entire family was wiped out. She thought life was worth saving. She made a video for her children to watch. Made them promise to show it to their children, and them to show it to theirs and so forth. She thought it was important that our family never forgot how precious life is. The world almost comes to a standstill. But, people keep surviving, we keep moving on. We keep struggling and living and striving to do right, to keep society alive. Finally, we get a world where people do everything to make sure each other can stay alive, and sick bastards like you come along to ruin it. Sickos like you come along and try to drag us down, drag us back to the brink of extinction.

"It's people like you that make this world a bad place. But, the joke's on you, missy. You're gonna help society, yet. They're gonna make sure you help out the neediest of society and then they're gonna take your carcass and burn it. It'll burn just like your soul is gonna burn in Hell."

I stop humming, for the tune I was thinking of left my head. I am silent now. Fortunately, so is he. Pig Face turns his eyes back to the door, and away from me. I hope he is finished for today.

I will not say another word, or utter another sound while he is here, I decide. I will lie here and wait for Luke to come back, or my father or his psychiatrist.

I want to cry, but I will not, as this will give Pig Face satisfaction. As I lie here, trying to appear unaffected, I realize just how wrong I had been. Luke told me holding facilities were bad. I had thought it was all his colored view of things. I was wrong. I am wrong. It is not the nothingness, the white walls, the rubber floors, the bland, nutritious food that make this place such a nightmare. It is the staff. I had assumed them all moral and kind, like Luke's father. But that assumption was wrong. They are not like that. I wonder if most are like this man.

I pray they are not, but suspect I am wrong. I close my eyes and hope the day will pass quickly.

* * *

When the psychiatrists come, they kick Pig Face out. My father hired these doctors, and they are thorough, which leads me to believe they are good. They ask me a slew of questions. Not just about my reasons for not wanting to do the transplant, but about my child-hood, my mother's death, Susan, even my pregnancy — though I have known about it for less than a day now, so there isn't much on that front. We spend much of the day talking. There is a break, dur-ing which Pig Face brings me lunch. I don't eat it. I'm afraid he poi-soned it. Or just spit in it. I know I need to eat for the baby, but I am scared to eat what he's brought. He who wants me to burn in Hell.

By the time my father comes at the end of the day, I am tired, famished and wish to talk to him privately. But he is not alone. Uncle Albert is with him. Technically, Albert Harrell is not my uncle. He is my godfather and a judge in the local circuit court.

Uncle Albert takes a disapproving look at me, then brushes his hand over his own hair. "When you get out," he says, "You should switch to a new stylist."

I laugh, my fatigue overshadowed by delight at his presence, and give him a hug. Uncle Albert is a roly-poly man with a gruff face, but the sweetest disposition you'll ever find. He is on the shorter side for a man, the same height as me, but he has never seemed bothered by it. Uncle Albert always exudes self-confidence.

"It's nice of you to come," I say as we pull free of the embrace.

He scowls, waves his hand as if shoeing away my concern. "This isn't nice, sweetie. It's work."

I give him a puzzled glance, then look toward my father.

"He's your attorney," Dad says.

"Aren't you a judge?" I ask, confused.

"All judges are lawyers," he says flatly, with a trace of his native Mississippi twang. "I retained my bar license, and I can practice in Maryland. Just because it's highly unusual doesn't mean it can't be done, my dear."

I look at Daddy and wonder if this is a good idea. I love Uncle Albert, and I've been told he was a pretty good criminal defense attorney in his day. But he's been a judge for more than 20 years now, and hasn't tried a case in as much time. I retreat to my bed block, then look back at them both. It's best not to pull any punches with Albert.

"It's been a long time since you've tried a case," I say, looking him in the eye.

He holds my gaze. "Your father surely didn't raise a fool," he laughs. "It's wise to raise this point. I can assure you, I'm still quite qualified to try your case, dear. I wouldn't have agreed to your father's request ... Hell, he wouldn't have asked me, if I weren't able."

I nod. He's right on both accounts. Well, perhaps I should ask the better question. "Are you sure you want to do this?" Part of me wants to look away, afraid of his answer. "I'm sort of a political albatross. I've probably killed my father's shot at being governor."

He laughs. "Dear, if you think I care what strangers think, then I've done a piss-poor job of being a godfather."

I shake my head. "No, I know you don't care," I say. "That doesn't mean you shouldn't care what they think, sometimes."

"Well, I care what you think." Uncle Albert's gaze says the rest of the world be damned. He turns to my father. "What about you, Lewis? Do you care what strangers think?"

"Nope," my father says firmly. "I care about getting Kelsey home safe."

"Thank you," I say, looking first at Albert and then my dad. If someone were to say I could only have three people on my side, I have the good fortune of having the best three people in the entire world: Luke, my father and Albert.

I pull my legs up onto my bed block, criss-cross applesauce, and Uncle Albert steps out and asks Pig Face to bring in chairs for him and daddy. As Pig Face returns to his post outside, they pull their chairs close to my bed block, and take a seat. Albert says my father may stay, only because he is an attorney, too, and my statements to him are privileged as well. Albert begins by reviewing the information he has so far.

My statements are bad, he declares. And if they were to come before his court, he'd toss me in a holding facility and throw away the key. Not a good start. But, there are two good points, Albert asserts. First, I am pregnant.

"This is good because you technically weren't eligible for the transplant," Albert says, giving my father a significant look.

"Why does that matter?" I ask.

"The statute specifically makes it a crime for an eligible donor to flee a marking," he says in a rather subdued tone for such good news.

"Why don't you sound as happy as you should," I ask, as his face looks like he's eaten a rotten lemon.

"Because this goes to interpreting the law," my father interjects. "And judges at this level don't like to do that."

"I don't understand," I say. "This sounds like it should be good news. I wasn't eligible, right?"

"Under the exact wording of the statute, yes," my father says. "But people have tended to look at this as meaning eligible at the time you were marked. At the time you were marked, you were eligible. But, technically, the way the statute is written, it refers to eligibility at the time of the surgery. At that time, you weren't eligible."

"Kelsey," Albert says severely, "this is our most promising legal avenue, but don't get your hopes up."

I wonder if I look like I've been chewing the same rotten lemon as Albert at this point. "But, it sounds like I should be set free."

My father sighs, leans in. "You should, according to the statute. But, like I said, lower court judges don't like to set new precedents. They don't like to interpret the law. They want appeals courts to do that. So, I'm not sure we'll get a decision in our favor. Granted, there aren't a lot of people fleeing donations, but given the recent upswing in this choice movement, I don't think a lower-court judge is going to rock the boat. "

"Plus," Albert adds. "There's public opinion. Even if a judge doesn't mind setting new precedent, I don't think he will do it in such a public case. There are several reasons for this. One, judges are elected, and if it's an unpopular decision, the judge won't be re-elected. Second, the judge has to work with these prosecutors day in and day out. We judges don't like to talk about it, like to pretend it's not true, but these prosecutors are our colleagues, and sometimes it's easier to punt on an issue than make a colleague look like a fool for bringing a case he legally shouldn't. This is our best legal argument, Kelsey, but it may not work. If I were the judge in your case, I'd let you go."

I smile at that. "Why don't you just stay on as a judge and hear my case?"

He gives me a hard look. "That would be wrong, Kelsey," he says, drawing out the word wrong for emphasis. "Even if I didn't recuse myself on my own, I'm sure the prosecution would demand it."

I shake my head in exasperation. "My best hope is not an option."

Albert nods. "Let's move on, Kelsey. I'll write the motion, and then it's out of our hands. What we can control is the defense at your hearing."

I nod. "What are our options?"

"Susan," Uncle Albert says succinctly.

"You can't do that to her," I protest, slapping my hand down on my thigh for emphasis. "She's already been through too much."

"And so have you," Albert retorts. "Plus, what happened to her was wrong. If the panel could hear that, see what you'd been exposed to, they would understand why you went crazy."

I raise an eyebrow. "Crazy?"

"Pregnancy psychosis," my father says.

I look from him to Albert and back to my father again. I feel my face screw up in confusion as I ask, "Pregnancy what?!"

"Psychosis," Albert says. "It's a rare pregnancy disorder that typically emerges in the third trimester and involves psychosis related to harming the baby. But the psychiatrist suspects you may have an extreme form of it. This psychosis, coupled with your knowledge of Susan's situation, caused you to flee."

I let it sink in a minute. My stomach churns lightly. I look down at my feet and ask the question I am not sure I want an answer to. "You think I'm psychotic?"

"Of course not," my father says, leaving his chair, taking a step toward me. "It's just a defense, sweetheart. Saying what you feel, taking a stand isn't going to help at this point. What you need is a defense to get you out of here, and pregnancy psychosis may be all there is."

I raise my eyes to meet his. My father is squatting so we are at eye level. His expression has a genuine quality about it that I can't quite describe but know when I see it. I feel relief now that others don't think I'm bonkers. My father joins me on my block, sitting next to me, and wrapping his arm around my shoulder, offering a gentle squeeze of reassurance.

I look at Albert. "So, do you think a panel will believe I have this pregnancy psychosis?"

"It's a long shot, dear," he says, his Southern twang thickening, "but it's all we got, so we're gonna aim, and hope we hit the bulls-eye."

With that, Uncle Albert and Daddy begin saying their good-byes. I give Albert a hug, then ask my father to stay a moment longer, as Uncle Albert calls for the guard to release him. I wish I had such an easy way out.

After Uncle Albert has trundled through the door, I take a step closer to my father and whisper. "Dad, is there any way to get another day-shift guard?"

He furrows his brow. "What's wrong?"

I am not sure how far to go with this. In the end, I can ignore the fiend, but I don't want him in the room with me anymore. It is hard enough being in here without someone telling you what a sick bastard you are. "It's not a big deal," I say, trying to sound casual. "But the guy today just said some unkind things to me, and if it's not too hard, if you haven't exhausted all your favors, maybe just a new guy, or maybe see if you can get him to stand outside during the day."

As the words tumble from my mouth, I realize how ridiculously whiny this is sounding. I am in a holding facility, not a spa. I feel like a spoiled child seeking just one more thing from my indulgent father, and it smarts to think it. "Just forget about it, Daddy. I'll be fine. It's not a big deal."

I hug him, and then go back to my block. I sit, and he stares at me. My stomach growls, then my father looks over at the tray of food on the floor in the corner. "Why didn't you eat, honey?"

I wish he hadn't asked. Now he will think I've gone crazy. I momentarily debate not answering, then finally spill. "It was just... I just thought ... the guard, he seemed kind of nasty..." I fidget with my hands and cast my eyes down, as I struggle with how to explain my concerns. "I thought maybe he'd tainted my food."

I glance up at my father. He's got that I'm-dealing-with-a-crazy-person look on his face. "I'm just stressed in here," I tell him, hoping he'll stop giving me that fake smile he uses with ranters on the campaign trail. I could deal with just about any political face but that one. "I'll be fine. Forget I asked about the change, OK?"

I wait a moment, then look up to see he has his worried face on. And now I wonder if maybe I liked the I'm-dealing-with-a-crazy-person face better.

"I'll get you some food, Kelsey. I'll bring it myself, OK," he says, reassuringly. "And I'll see what I can do about that other matter, too."

Even though what I asked for is more than I deserve, I feel complete euphoria that he said he'd try. "Thank you, Daddy."

21. PERSPECTIVE

It is night, and Luke has replaced Pig Face, to my immense pleasure. Other than him giving me a significant look upon his arrival, he does not speak to me. The lights cut off, and to my surprise, he walks over immediately, beckons me to scoot over and slides in next to me on my bed block.

Sitting beside me, he wraps an arm around me. I lay my head on his shoulder and wonder why he has chosen to show such little restraint. "Aren't we living a little dangerously?"

"Charlie's monitoring the security room, tonight," Luke says, planting a kiss on my neck. "Word has it, he never turns on the lights. He apparently likes to watch porn on a little portable image player."

I pull away slightly, raise an eyebrow, then remember he can't see me. Trying not to sound too naive, I ask, "How does he get porn? Isn't that illegal?"

Luke laughs — a, "you're joking, right?" laugh. One that shakes us both, as he's still got his arm wrapped around me loosely. "Holding Facilities are different, Kelse. Let's just say, he gets it." He places his hand on my knee and gracefully begins sliding his fingers up my thigh. "And besides, that wasn't the point. The point is I feel confident you and I are due some privacy."

His hand stops on my buttock, and he pulls me up onto his lap, and plants a kiss on me. His lips are soft and his mouth is warm, with his tongue passionately probes mine. It is hot and entrancing, and then I remember where we are, and pull my face from his. "Luke, what if Charlie gets bored and turns on the light."

"Then he'll probably assume I'm having sex with you and watch a little," he says as he kisses my neck.

I whack him on the shoulder. "Be serious."

"I am serious," he says, sighing. "Why do you think I got your father to get me in here, Kelsey? It's not safe in here."

"And nobody cares if the guards break the rules?"

His body bobs rhythmically and I can tell he is shaking his head, though I can't see it. "Nobody cares, and half the prisoners are so insane they don't know what's being done to them."

I shudder.

He gently strokes my neck. "I'll be here with you every night," he says. "I promise."

I scoot off his lap. Not as a result of his reassurance that he'll be with me, but for the general realization that I have gotten myself into a real jam. While Luke always expressed disdain for holding facilities, I never quite understood why. I always thought it was more of an inherited distaste. His father hated holding facilities, so Luke, by virtue of growing up in that household, soaked up the hate and took it on as his own.

I always assumed that because most people saw nothing wrong with holding facilities, those people were right. I had never heard complaints about the facilities or their treatment of inmates. So, I assumed society was right and Luke was just biased. But, being an inmate now, and hearing Luke talk, it is finally settling in just how desperate my situation is. I'd initially thought that a short-term wing would be different from the long-term ward, yet that is proving to be untrue. This place is awful, and no one cares but the people trapped inside.

I feel Luke's hand groping along in the dark as he pats his way down my arm and eventually finds my hand and takes it in his. "What's wrong, Kelsey?"

I am not sure how to put it, but I try anyway. "I just wonder why nobody cares that holding facilities are so bad, why nobody talks about it."

He squeezes my hand. "I think nobody cares because it would force them to look at the hypocrisy of the situation. This isn't Life First, Kelsey. At least for the people in here. Their lives are meaningless to the outside world. So no one talks about it. They just pretend it doesn't exist. Not to mention, the population in here isn't that vocal. Their family shuns them, writes them off as menaces to society. They've got no one."

I nod. "I don't know how your father could stand working here for 30 days, let alone 30 years."

Luke breathes out, and leans back against the wall. I feel his body shift next to mine, and decide to lean back, too. "He compromised, Kelsey," Luke says flatly. "He wasn't proud of it, and I always thought he was wrong to do it. But, he had a family to support, to care for, to be there for. I mean, no one ever starves in FoSS. We'd have gotten government assistance if my father hadn't been able to work. But, he didn't want that, didn't want the intrusion. Once you ask for help, the government comes in and starts telling you how to raise the children, and what values to instill and all those things. With my mother's condition ...."

I imagine he has closed his eyes and is trying to steel himself to move past these words, though he has never really been able to move past what happened. I reach out and stroke his arm gently, wondering if he is grimacing, or just sad, lamenting that he never knew the woman his mother had been when she married his father. Only the mentally ill woman she had become before she drowned in a neighborhood pool.

He rubs his thumb gently along the top of my hand, then continues. "With my mother's condition, and especially after she died, my dad wanted to keep the government out of our lives. I resented him then for keeping her condition a secret, for pretending she'd drowned by accident, for leaving Emmie with so much responsibility. I realize now he was doing the best he could. I thought it was weak back then, that he failed to take charge of the situation. But he hadn't. He took charge the only way he could. He made sure we were safe, then came here every day and did his job and came home every night and had nightmares. I got used to the screams from his bedroom, waking from some dream about this god-awful place. Even so, he came back everyday so he could afford to take care of us. For that, he's a good man."

I have met Luke's father only once, but he seemed meek. He is tall, like Luke, and handsome and fit. But, there is a certain something about him that makes him seem overly gentle, overly docile. I wonder if my impression of Luke's father has been clouded by what Luke told me about him. The two don't get along. Luke always thought his father hadn't been strong enough.

"You respect your father more now that you're here, now that you've actually seen his working environment first-hand?'

"No, working here hasn't affected me that way" Luke says quickly, surprising me. "I respected him more after I found out you'd been marked. I realized that sometimes compromise isn't as bad as I thought it was. That I'd rather compromise and have you, than risk it all, and not have you. Realized that maybe we were more important to him than I'd ever thought. Realized his sacrifices were from love, not cowardice. I guess maybe I should have always known that. But, I was too bitter."

I scoot closer and lay my head on his shoulder.

"I love you," I say.

"I love you, too." He clasps my hand and squeezes tight.

"You must," I chuckle. "Otherwise, I think you'd be anyplace but here."

"Yeah, it's about as bad as my father described. I thought he'd told me some of the stuff just to scare me, but it was all true."

"I didn't realize he talked about it with you." I always had the impression that Luke knew it was bad from his father's demeanor and offhand comments. Something about the way he spoke makes it seem like they talked at length.

"When I was younger, he didn't tell me about it. When I started working for Dr. Grant, he decided I should know details. Wanted me to know what I was getting into, what would happen to me if they found out what we were doing on our trips to Peoria."

"And it didn't scare you, the idea of being put in here?"

He pauses, and when he resumes his voice takes on a steely tone. "Of course it scared me, Kelse. But, I thought I'd be stronger than him, and do what was right, instead of what was easy. Turns out, he wasn't doing what was easy. He was doing something hard, something that was right. I was taking the easy way out. I was breaking the law on some principle that may have helped some women I barely knew. But, the biggest sacrifices we make should be for those we love. That's what my dad did."

I lean in and wrap my arm around him. "Thank you for doing this for me, Luke. I don't know that I could survive in here without you at night."

He squeezes me closer to him. "I couldn't survive out there, wondering what was going on in here at night."

He holds me for a few moments more, then strokes my peach-fuzz head. "It's late. You should get some rest."

I close my eyes and try to clear my head. Then a thought pops in. "Luke, I have a question."

"Go ahead," he says, still stroking my head.

"Were you mad that I left you at the gas station?"

"Hmmmm," he says, stopping the gentle stroking and resting his hand on my shoulder. "Where'd that come from?"

"I have a lot of time to think in here," I say, gently guiding his hand back to my head. "I was wondering about it this afternoon."

"I see," he says, then is silent for a moment. "I wasn't angry. I hadn't expected it, but I figured you thought you'd be caught."

"The man in the store recognized me, I was sure," I tell him. "I just wanted to put some distance between us, so you wouldn't end up in a holding facility, too. When I asked you to buy the antacid, I was so afraid you were going to realize I was faking."

He starts laughing. Big belly-shaking guffaws. Not a fitting reaction. "What is so funny?"

"I've felt very guilty these past few days, and apparently for nothing," he says through pauses in his laughter. "I thought it was my fault you'd been spotted. I thought someone outside recognized you while I was inside the store."

"Oh no," I say, raising a hand to my mouth in embarrassment. "I'm so sorry."

"No, no reason to be sorry. I shouldn't have spent so long reading the medicine labels. The antacid said you're supposed to consult a physician before taking if you're pregnant. I was looking for something with a safe label, and debating if I should just say they didn't have any. Debating whether I'd made a mistake by not telling you about the condom breaking. Then I started worrying you'd eat the wrong thing in Peoria. I realized I'd been in there too long. When I went out and you were gone, I figured someone had spotted you."

The idea of Luke poring over labels is sweet. It makes me smile, but also, it makes me sad, too. "Hey," I say in a serious tone. Luke stiffens a little, as if bracing for the new direction the conversation is going to take. "This made me laugh, in retrospect, but there's an underlying problem in this story. We weren't honest with each other. I should have been more honest about my reservations to your proposal, and you should have told me when you realized the condom broke."

He sighs and starts to say something, but I cut him off. "It's water under the bridge, Luke. I just don't want more water and more bridges. Let's just both promise to be completely honest, even if we're concerned about the other person's reaction."

Luke kisses my forehead. "I promise," he says.

"Me too."

He holds me in his arms for a while, then kisses my head and tells me. "You really do need to get some sleep."

"Alright," I say and close my eyes.

22. PREPARATION

The psychiatrists my father hired return and question me again. I tell them everything again, same as before. I asked Uncle Albert if there was any way to put a better spin on things, but he insisted I say everything the same. "Changing your story midstream makes it look like we're trying to gaslight the doctors. Exactly the same," he said. So, I tell them everything the same, remembering that this all goes to pregnancy psychosis. "One of the hallmarks of the condition is the person believes they're being perfectly rational," Albert said.

It seems like we've been over the same ground a dozen times when the doctors finally pack their things and leave. Uncle Albert returns. The day guard, a different one from Pig Face, carries in Albert's chair, then leaves. I am not sure if the new guard is my father's doing, or if it was Pig Face's turn to move on. Either way, Pig Face has not been back since I mentioned it to my father. The day guard also has been standing outside, hopefully my father's doing, too. Even if he was stationed inside, he would've left, as attorneys and clients are due privacy.

Albert sits in his chair and leans forward, a severe look on his face. "I have news," he says, clasping his hands together in his lap as he pauses to see my reaction. I remain expressionless and nod. "First, like I thought, the judge denied my motion to dismiss because you weren't technically eligible to donate when you fled."

I nod, and try to look steely, strong, even though I am not. It is deflating to hear him say the words, despite knowing this was the likely outcome.

Uncle Albert, his two hands held together by interlaced fingers, begins to tap the lonely thumbs against each other and continues. "Now it's all about the hearing. You and I have some decisions to make."

I shift my position on my bed block, as it suddenly feels horribly uncomfortable. I brace for what will probably be more bad news. "Like what?"

"Well, as you know, they scheduled your hearing for tomorrow. They didn't do it just because you're guaranteed a speedy trial, but because they hoped we'd balk and ask for more time to prepare. That way they could drag this out, get some more bad press for your father and get more prepared."

He looks like he's awaiting my response. I am not sure what to say, so I nod my head for him to continue. "While some attorneys would seek the continuance, I'm inclined to go tomorrow."

I lean back slightly, and reach up to tug at my hair, which is no longer there. Even though it has been three days since I've become bald, and I don't have the weight of the hair or the feel of it brushing against my face and neck, I sometimes forget it isn't there. "Why do you want to go?"

"Because, the prosecution only gets better with preparation. If there is a crime that involves lots of witnesses to interview and evidence to collect, you can't go. You just have to suck it up and postpone or you'd be doing your client a disservice. However, in a case like this, where the facts aren't going to change much, where you're not going to learn anything earth-shattering or new, it's best to just go ahead. You get a less prepared prosecution."

"Aren't you less prepared, too?" I ask.

"Yeah," he shrugs. "But, I know enough to know where I can poke holes in his case and where I can't. The burden of proof falls on him, not me."

Albert sits up straight, adds, "Plus, we're at the beginning of a jury cycle. This jury has only been empanelled a week, so they've probably only heard a couple of cases. Towards the end of any jury's six-week term, they're tired of it, and tend to be more willing to convict."

I sigh and drum my fingers on my block. I am not sure if I am on board with going quickly, however, the consequences of a wrong choice are dire. "If juries convict more often in the later weeks, why don't they shorten the session?" I ask.

Albert hunches his shoulders, and blows out a long breath. "It's been suggested by some people that we should. It just hasn't happened. The six-week system was fine when FoSS began and there were so few people left. Empanelling a jury for each specific trial, like they did in the United States, required too many people coming in for vetting, and wasn't stable enough. The six weeks system worked fine, then. But, now, it's like getting professional jurors after that amount of time. There's also a high bias toward conviction anyway."

A high conviction bias. Wonderful. "And you think going tomorrow will reduce the chance of that?"

"Yes," he says emphatically. "We'll catch the prosecution off-guard. I'm sure he's expecting us to seek a continuance, for at least two weeks. But, that will put us later into this jury's term. If we're gonna have the same set of facts in two weeks, I'd rather go now than then."

I nod, then manage a smile. "Let's do it, then."

"One down, one to go," he says. "The other question is whether you testify."

I freeze, bite my lip, as I digest his incongruous suggestion. "Shouldn't I?"

"No, you still have the Fifth Right. You don't have to testify for or against yourself during a trial."

I remember one of my professors declaring the Fifth Right one of the more important carryovers left from the old U.S. system of justice. Yet, I've always thought it a weird one to carry over. It seems imprudent not to testify on your own behalf. I try to read Albert's expression. It is neither sad nor happy. Looking into his face gives me no clue what to do. My gut says I should testify, but the fact that he would even suggest I not, leaves me second guessing. "Shouldn't I testify? I mean, how else will they know what I was thinking?"

He crosses his arms, leans back and ponders. A slight frown forms as he looks at me. "Kelsey, I'm not sure we want people to know what you were thinking."

Ouch, that hurt. Clearly my expression said as much, for he gives me an apologetic look. "I don't want to hurt your feelings, but I do need to be honest and give you a realistic, legal perspective on this. Hearing your thoughts in your own words might turn the jury off. I think it would be better just to let the psychiatrists speak. To let others speak, and for the jury to assume you're too mentally incompetent to speak at the hearing."

Albert takes a deep breath, then speaks again, softer now. "Plus, I can't allow you to lie on the stand. Not knowingly, at least."

I am both stunned and offended. "I wouldn't lie," I protest.

He shakes his head, and gives another apologetic look, leaning forward in his chair. "I misspoke. I don't think you would lie. It's just that there is an issue that the prosecution is going to want to address, and your father has indicated you would like to keep the information to yourself."

"What?"

He points to my belly. "The father."

Well, yes. That's a problem.

"If I put you up there, the prosecutor is gonna ask. And as an attorney and a judge, for that matter, I'm an officer of the court. I can't knowingly let you lie up there. Now, I don't know for sure who the father is. I have an idea, from what Lewis has said to me over the past few months. But, I can't be sure, so I couldn't definitively say you lied about it, and wouldn't accuse you of it. But I have to warn you, whomever you name, the prosecution is going to go talk to and make sure you're not lying. And if you take the Fifth when they ask, I think it would make you look conniving and duplicitous. And a person who is conniving and duplicitous is able to fake mental illness. Juries don't like defendants who are only willing to tell part of the story."

Well that makes sense. "But, do they like defendants who don't talk at all?"

With an understanding glance, he says: "No, they don't like that either. However, this may be a case of bad versus worse, rather than good versus better. And, I think I can hint at you being not stable enough to testify. But, I can't hint too much or even come right out and say that, or else they'll delay the trial because you're not stable enough to testify."

I guess this is what the inside of a rock and hard place feels like. I lean back against the wall and pull my legs up so knees are under my chin. "I'm sorry," I say to him. "I'm sorry I talked to them, that I said things that have made it so I can't even testify. I was tired and unsure. It was stupid to think I should just say what was on my mind."

Uncle Albert reaches out and pats my shoulder. "Kelsey, trust me, lots of people talk. They say much worse. People in custody say all sorts of things they later regret. I've seen plenty of cases like that.

Right now, you have to let it go. What's done is done. We have to deal with the statements we have and move on. We can't change the past, so let's not worry about it. All we can control is what we do next."

Gee. He knows just what to say, and he's right. We've got to deal with what we've got. No regrets. "Let's go with your gut, Uncle Albert," I say. "I won't testify."

"Okay, well that takes care of the major hurdles," he says. "I'm going to let you eat lunch, while I look over the psychiatric reports. I'll be back in an hour, okay?"

I nod my understanding. He stands, leaving behind the chair, and walks to the locked door. He knocks, and a moment later it opens. The guard lets him out and removes the chair. I am alone, yet again.

* * *

When Uncle Albert returns, I have finished up my lunch: a turkey sandwich, flanked by baby carrots, grapes, and a cup of spinach soup. A prenatal supplement came alongside it. Without Pig Face, meals are turning out fairly well at the holding facility.

"How was lunch?" Albert asks.

"The best part of my day," I respond truthfully. Perhaps it is the pregnancy hunger, but I've never had such a satisfying meal. I could almost forget why they want me so well-fed and healthy in the first place. Almost. "So, what now?"

"The psychiatrist's report is about what I expected. She's good and was able to do me a favor by seeing you. She's testified in cases in my court, so she'll do fine on the stand," Albert says, leaning against the wall. "I want to talk to you about potential witnesses that could help our case, in terms of your character."

I study his frank expression, in an attempt to avoid thinking about where he is headed with this. "My character?"

"Yes, our goal will be to show that this is out of character. That this is strictly the pregnancy psychosis talking here. So, I'd like a character witness. Do you think there's anyone willing to do that for you?"

Well, hmm. That is a good question. No one, and I mean no one, wants to be linked to a criminal. Once you are on the inside, or let's face it, once you've been accused, it is as if you have the plague. No one will vouch for me, willingly at least. Well, almost no one.

"Susan," I say.

He shakes his head. "Susan's agreed to testify about her own marking. And while she'll say good things about you, she'll come off too biased. I was hoping for someone less attached — someone you haven't been best friends with for the past decade."

I search my brain thinking of anyone who might still be willing to say something nice about me at this point in my life. Someone who isn't afraid of getting tainted with the stench of my crime, and worrying about their own reputation. I have friends, but they're not good friends, friends whom I could call anytime, anywhere. I suppose, having found one in Susan, I never searched out another, and now the only people I could even consider are no more than robust acquaintances.

There is no one. I feel like a fool for being unable to come up with a name for Albert. He is doing all the heavy lifting with preparation and strategy. All I am asked to do is come up with a name. "Maybe Mary Grimm," I say, though I doubt she'll agree to it. "She teaches the kindergarten class across the hall from mine. We've gotten to know each other pretty well this year. She might do it."

Uncle Albert reaches into his satchel propped open on the floor, pulls a notepad from it and jots down the name. Then he comes over to his chair and sits.

"I just want to go over a few things with you about court, the proceedings, make sure you understand everything."

Well, it is nice he wants to explain, but I already understand. The justice system in FoSS is simple and swift. It carries over some of the tenets of the former U.S. system, but streamlines them a lot. This modification was done because crime was almost nonexistent at FoSS's formation. Crime rates have risen, but I don't believe there's been much change in the court system.

The most basic right is to a fair and speedy trial. One can go with a jury or simply a judge. Once convicted, you get two appeals. Those appeals must be completed within six months, and then the sentence is carried out.

That simple. But, I don't want Albert to leave, so instead of suggesting I know enough, I decide to keep him as long as I can. Only white rubber walls await me once he leaves. "What should I know?"

"Well, let's start with the charges, Kelsey," he says. "The punishment for not showing up for a surgery after you've been marked is pretty clear. A trial isn't even needed. You simply get a hearing before a judge to ascertain whether you were in fact marked, and in fact didn't show up for your surgery. Once those things are shown, you're sent in for surgery."

I give a stiff nod.

"After the surgery, you're typically evaluated to determine if you're sociopathic or simply having mild psychiatric trouble. The evaluators recommend charges for your hearing. If you're having mild psychiatric trouble, they suggest a six-month stint in a short-term facility with an extra blood donation and counseling. If you're sociopathic, they ask you be remanded to a long-term facility and used for life-saving procedures for others."

I lower my eyes. That is not the possibility I want. Albert has paused, seeing I have stopped looking at him. I lift my eyes to see him again, so he continues.

"Because of your pregnancy, they can't do the transplant. So, now they've moved to the next step. The prosecution is asserting you're a sociopath, Kelsey, and they want you sterilized and sent away."

I know this. It doesn't sound any better coming from Albert's mouth.

"This is a fairly rare predicament, to be honest with you. Very few people flee after being marked, and even fewer are deemed sociopaths. That label is usually saved for murderers and child molesters."

This bothers me. "Why? Why are they pushing so hard on me?"

"To set an example," he says. "Your father was two weeks away from being governor before this story broke. He was going to be the highest official in this state, if the polls were accurate. They can't let that go."

I suppose he is right. But, it doesn't feel fair that I am being punished because of who my father is. "So what do you think my chances are?"

He waves me off. "It's not good to try to calculate the odds in this situation, Kelsey," he says. Though, this is practically a blasphemous thought; in FoSS, statistics are everywhere. Albert seems to realize where my thoughts are headed, and speaks again. "There are too many variables. You've taken enough statistical analysis classes to know that too many variables produce unreliable answers. All we can do right now is put our best foot forward and look at the things we have on our side."

Ha! Things on our side. "And what would those be?"

"One, you're a mother, or going to be. And this society, above all, loves its mothers, its givers of life. And two, you've got a disease. One that will go away as soon as you give birth. Maybe the jury will just decide to let you go."

"You think?"

He shakes his head. "Not really. But, it's your only shot."

23. GETTING READY

It is the morning of the hearing, and I am filled with anxiety. It is not allayed by the news Uncle Albert brings.

I've lost my job. Kindergarten teachers — well, teachers in general — are expected to exhibit high moral turpitude. While I knew I'd be fired, it is not the best way to start the day. Albert does not tell me this to be cruel, but as part of letting me know that Mary Grimm will not help. She is afraid she will lose her job if she testifies. I do not believe it is an unreasonable fear. It's not just the holding facility that gets you depressed. It's the public shunning, as well.

"Is there anyone else we can use," he asks me.

At this point, I mention the only other people I think might be grateful enough to me to risk the negative fallout: Anakin and Patsy Spencer.

"I saved their son's life," I tell Albert, and his eyes widen with a why-didn't-you-tell-me-sooner look. I sigh, as I'm about to get to why. "Ethan was in Mary's class last year, and we were on a field trip at Montgomery Gardens when he was stung by a bee. He'd never been stung before, so no one knew he was allergic, but he began swelling immediately. It was quite obvious he wouldn't last long. His face was puffing up, his fingers bloating, and he was gasping for air like a fish out of water. He needed an epinephrine pen."

Albert listens intently, clearly waiting for the "but" that makes this story no good. I look at him briefly, then find my hands. "We were at least a couple hundred yards from the building. I wasn't sure how long it would take me to get there. Even if I sprinted, they might not have one available. So, I looked around and saw that Julie Merman, a girl in my class, had her pocket pouch around her waist. She's allergic to practically everything and keeps two emergency epinephrine pens in the pouch. I took one of hers and used it on Ethan."

I look up. Uncle Albert grimaces. "It saved Ethan's life, the doctors said. The reaction was so severe, he would have suffocated. The Spencers were really grateful. Especially the father. He works for a hospital and seemed to understand I'd been instrumental in saving his son's life."

Uncle Albert is quiet for a moment. Finally, he says, "I'll consider asking, but I'm not sure."

I understand his hesitation. "Yeah, the Mermans weren't happy."

"You endangered their child when you took her epinephrine."

Yes, I'd been told this: by the principal, by the Mermans and by an administrator from the central office. "I guess one could argue that, but she kept two in the bag. Really, what were the odds she'd need two pens before we could get her a replacement?"

He gave me a hard stare. "You already had one bee sting, so clearly bees were around and she might need it."

"Fine," I said. "It's not the best example of my good character. But, it's all I got. Without the Spencers, I don't have anyone else."

He nods, and tells me the other unfortunate news of the day. The prosecution has hired Dr. Grant to testify against me.

"He can't," I protest.

"He can and he will," Albert shoots back.

He lets the shock settle in, then launches into an explanation of why this is fine. "First, we don't think they've made the connection between Dr. Grant and Luke. We don't want the doctor to try to get out of testifying and have authorities research more about Dr. Grant and find his former assistant was Luke. Your father had Dr. Grant wipe out any records that Luke worked for him, so he could get him the job here at the holding facility. But, it would only take someone asking around to connect Luke to Dr. Grant. And if they make that connection, they'll eventually find the connection between you and Luke."

While I can't argue with the logic, I still don't like it. I scowl, as he opens his mouth to continue.

"Second, Dr. Grant is also associated with your mother. It is in a negative way, so that is on our side. However, I don't want authorities to go delving deeply into that connection either, and trying to get him to back out of it would probably not be successful and raise more scrutiny."

I'm still not quite on board.

Uncle Albert speaks again. "Third, he's not an expert in pregnancy psychosis," he says, flashing me a wicked grin, "so I can tear him apart on the stand."

Part of me likes that, yet part of me doesn't want to see Dr. Grant on the stand, let alone torn apart by Albert.

"If he's not an expert," I ask, "why'd they pick him?"

"Because he's a Nimmick ally," Albert states flatly. I give a resigned look. I knew my father hated Dr. Grant. So, I hadn't been surprised that Dr. Grant had allied himself with Nimmick. Dr. Grant and I never discussed this. Governor Nimmick cut the ribbon for the opening of Dr. Grant's lab on campus. Nimmick doesn't have the personal animosity toward Dr. Grant my father feels, and he doesn't mind that Dr. Grant's reputation lurks between pregnancy miracle worker and obstetrics charlatan. Grant's work with the "pagan" Peorians and some of his writings, which hint at "pro-choice" leanings, don't sit well with some in society. But, Nimmick never seemed to mind. Now I suppose he wants Dr. Grant to repay the support by burying me.

I want to ask Uncle Albert more about Dr. Grant testifying, want more time to let the news sink in, but he looks at his watch and declares we must leave for the hearing, or we'll be late. He hands me the clothes he's brought and tells me he'll step out so I can change. Since the clothes are covered by a garment bag, I assumed he'd come with a standard suit. When I open it, I find a black skirt suit with pink silk shirt. Upon closer examination, I realize the top flares out at the waist and is designed for a pregnant woman. A woman more pregnant than me. The skirt has an elastic-band waist also meant to stretch for a pregnant belly.

I catch Uncle Albert's eye as he is heading out the door, and give him a "Really?" look.

Unfazed, he says, "You're a mother. Don't forget that."

* * *

To be truthful, I've never been in a courtroom before. My father abandoned law and moved onto politics by the time I was three. I've never been arrested before or even fought a traffic citation, so I've never had occasion to be in one. Entering one for my own hearing today is a little jarring. On some level it is what I expected, similar to what I've seen in movies, but on a smaller scale. The room is tiny and divided into sections by small, but noticeable barriers. There is an area in the rear, for spectators. There are none in the room yet. I'm sure people are interested in my hearing, but the courtroom will not open for the public until right before the proceedings begin. Media will mainly attend.

In front of the spectator area is a waist-high wooden wall. Just beyond the wall are two tables. One on the right, one on the left. There are two chairs at each table. I can only presume one table is for Albert and me and the other for the prosecutor. In front of that, behind a wide-berthed wooden podium, a tall winged-back chair is positioned behind it where I presume the judge sits. Adjoining it is a boxed-in area that contains a chair for witnesses. It is a chair I will never sit in, I realize, given the decision I've made. I turn my head to the right. Perpendicular to the judge and witness area is a set of chairs for the jury. Ten seats for the ten people who will decide my fate.

Albert, standing beside me, places a hand on the center of my back and gently urges me forward. We move deeper into the courtroom, and take our spots. Albert repeats all the things he told me earlier. Look maternal; don't let anything said phase me; and remain calm, no matter what happens. Soon, the prosecutor enters, then the jury and finally the judge. My father shuffles in and grabs a seat behind us in the audience area, as do several onlookers who I assume are with the media. A few minutes later, the judge calls the courtroom to order.

24. TRY ME

The prosecutor wants me dead. He'd like to see my carcass sliced open and emptied of all the useful parts — given to some kind soul who wouldn't dare flee. This is clear from the moment Evan Bickers opens his mouth.

He plays a single line from my recorded interview with Dr. Klein — the one where I'd answered what would happen if no one else could give the Virginia man a kidney. "Then he would die," my video self says more firmly than I remember. But, the video doesn't lie.

With that, Bickers proclaims I am a sociopathic murderer who must be convicted.

It is a rough start. I feel like we have lost, but I try to look neutral, yet maternal. I place my hand on my belly, settling it on top of the loose fabric which might make it seem as if I am sporting a tiny baby bump. Uncle Albert stands, walks over to the jury and begins speaking in earnest, his drawl and friendly smile making him seem more neighborly than lawyerly.

"This is Kelsey Reed," he says, pointing at me with outstretched arm. "She's pregnant. Going to be a mother. A giver of life, something that should be revered. Yet, for her, this pregnancy has brought something more than just a wonderful new life."

Albert pauses, frowns: "It's brought a disease. An almost unheard of disease."

Albert looks back toward me sympathetically, then to the jury. "Our psychiatrist will show that Kelsey suffers from pregnancy psychosis, a rare disorder where the mother-to-be acts irrationally, though she feels perfectly sane. Ms. Reed believed she should not give her kidney, that it would end her life, and she fled. This was not the anti-Life First sentiment of a rabble-rouser," Albert continues, shaking his head in the negative.

"With the right treatment, Ms. Reed can be helped. It would be wrong to keep her in a holding facility, take her baby and sterilize her, when she suffers from a disease, a very curable disease. Ladies and gentlemen of the jury, I'm going to ask you to listen to the evidence carefully, weigh it in your hearts, in your minds and with the law. And then, I'm going to ask you to find Kelsey Reed not a sociopath."

* * *

The next hours bring Bickers showing the most damaging sections of my video interview with Drs. Klein and Slate, along with Dr. Klein's testimony that I am a sociopath, and not suffering from psychosis. Dr. Slate does not testify, as Albert would pick at his obvious bias. Clearly, he avoided questioning me, letting a junior doctor take the lead, so he would not taint the case. Uncle Albert has almost no questions for Klein, except a couple that expose she's only been practicing a year, enough to hint she isn't qualified to render an opinion on my mental condition.

When she exits the courtroom, Bickers stands and announces, "I'm calling Dr. Stephen Grant to testify."

My stomach clenches as he says the words, and, despite what Albert has said to me, an anxiety-borne grimace emerges. A moment later, a guard opens the door to the courtroom, and Dr. Grant walks in. He marches up the center aisle, through an opening in the barrier, and right up to the witness chair, where he swears to tell the truth, the whole truth and nothing but. The idea that he is testifying for the prosecution still rubs me the wrong way. Dr. Grant has been my friend, and seeing him up there to say bad things about me feels like a betrayal.

Despite what Albert said about tearing him apart on the stand, I still have a bad feeling in my gut. And it isn't the nausea of pregnancy, either.

Bickers goes through a series of basic qualification questions with Dr. Grant: his education, where he's practiced, his experience with high-risk pregnancies. It is dull, but necessary if Bickers is going to use Dr. Grant's words to lock me up, take away my baby and throw away the key.

"So, Dr. Grant," Bickers says cordially, "You've been in obstetrics for nearly 15 years, and you've seen a half dozen cases of pregnancy psychosis?"

"Yes," Dr. Grant says dispassionately.

"And did you review the interview recording between Dr. Klein and Ms. Reed?"

"I did."

"And in your medical opinion, is Ms. Reed suffering from pregnancy psychosis?"

The moment of truth. Dr. Grant pauses, sensing the tension in the room, as we await his answer. "No," he says, definitively, looking directly at me.

Damn! He could have at least hedged.

Bickers smiles ever so slightly, then asks. "Have you ever seen a woman suffering from pregnancy psychosis exhibit any symptoms similar to Ms. Reed's?"

Another definitive, "No" from Dr. Grant. And it goes on like this, with Bickers asking Dr. Grant in every imaginable way if it is possible that I am suffering from pregnancy psychosis. Finally, Uncle Albert objects. "Your honor, this question seems to have been answered already," he says, almost apologetically. "If we could move on."

While Albert told me earlier that the hearing room is about showing respect for the judge while being thorough for your client, I'd like to see a little more fight from him.

The judge tells Bickers to move on. Instead, Bickers sits, indicating he is finished with the witness.

Uncle Albert strides over to Dr. Grant, flashes a humble smile. "I won't take up too much more of your time here, Dr. Grant. I just have a couple of questions for you."

Dr. Grant acknowledges this with a curt nod.

Albert walks toward the room's side wall, and leans on it, forcing everyone in the room, Bickers, the judge, the jurors, myself, my father and Dr. Grant, to turn and watch only him.

"Did you ever treat Maya Reed?"

Dr. Grant looks hesitant for a moment, and then says, "Yes."

"And she was Kelsey Reed's mother?"

"Yes," he says, more quickly this time.

"Maya Reed died under your care?"

There is a dramatic intake of breath from the jury. Bickers stands and objects, saying it is irrelevant. We all turn to look at him.

Uncle Albert does not. He looks at the judge. "Your honor, this goes to the defendant's medical history. If I could get a couple more questions, the relevance will become apparent."

"Go ahead, Albert," the judge says, revealing a familiarity that I didn't realize they had. Though, it makes sense that Albert would know plenty of other judges.

Albert acknowledges the judge's remark, but remains coolly leaning on his wall. "So, Dr. Grant, did Maya Reed die under your care?"

The doctor shifts in his seat slightly, and taps his fingers on his thigh. "Technically, she was under Dr. Johan Rice's care, as he signed the death certificate, but I was the primary caregiver during much of her last day."

"I see," Albert says, somehow shoving condemnation in those two words. "And the death certificate said she died of heart failure due to a previously undiagnosed heart condition. Did you agree with Dr. Rice's finding?"

"No," he answers quickly.

"What was your conclusion?"

"I believe she had an extremely rare medical condition called preeclampsia, which led to a seizure, then heart failure."

"And as a physician whose life's work is to study pregnancy and maladies that impact it, who researches all over the world, even getting special dispensation to travel to the heathen country of Peoria, would you say that rare pregnancy-related conditions tend to be hereditary?"

He pauses a moment to think. "Yes."

"So, if you correctly assessed Maya Reed's condition before she died, isn't it possible that her daughter could have inherited a gene disposing her to rare pregnancy-related problems?"

Dr. Grant shifts again in his seat, seeming to wonder what he should answer. "It's possible," he admits hesitantly.

"Also," Albert says casually. "Are you an expert on pregnancy psychosis?"

"No," he says, quickly adding, "However, I have seen it firsthand in patients."

Albert leaves his perch on the wall and moves steadily closer to Dr. Grant in his chair. "When do you typically start looking for pregnancy psychosis in your patients?"

He takes a moment to consider the question. "I wouldn't say I specifically go looking for it, but around the eighth month, if the patient exhibits symptoms, I might start to suspect psychosis."

"Have you ever attempted to diagnose it in a woman with Kelsey's gestational state, less than two months into the pregnancy?"

"No."

"And in the patients who you eventually diagnosed as suffering from pregnancy psychosis, did they appear any different to you at this point in their child's gestation, than Ms. Reed appeared in the recording?"

"I can't say they did."

"So, a woman could have been suffering from pregnancy psychosis the entire pregnancy, and you wouldn't have noticed or looked for symptoms until the eighth month?"

"I would like to think I would have noticed..."

Albert cuts him off, smiling the entire time. "Doctor, I'd like a yes or no answer, please. Would you have looked for symptoms of pregnancy psychosis in a woman who was fewer than six weeks pregnant?"

"No."

"Do you know what those symptoms would look like at this gestational age?"

"No."

"So, are you really qualified to say Ms. Reed is not suffering from pregnancy psychosis since you've never looked for it in patients at this stage of pregnancy?"

Bickers objects.

"Never mind, your honor," Albert says, looking up at the judge. "I'll strike the last question."

Albert then turns back to the doctor, with an apologetic expression. "Just one more thing, Dr. Grant. Did your lab receive a special $8 million allocation in a funding bill that passed the state legislature last night, and was signed by the governor this morning?"

"Yes." Dr. Grant says, as Bickers objects, saying it is irrelevant.

"Goes to bias, your honor," Albert says.

The judge tells him to proceed, which Albert does happily. "Did the governor promise you this funding if you would testify against his political rival's daughter today."

"NO!" Dr. Grant says with enough indignation to make it look like he has clearly been part of a payoff.

"I'm done, your honor," Albert says, then returns to my side.

And for the first time, I realize just how glad I am Albert is sitting next to me, and not across the aisle.

* * *

The prosecution spends the rest of the day adding to its case. They call witnesses who explain that my LMS data was changed and suggest I some how hacked in and did it myself. Though, even those witnesses admitted it would take someone of extreme knowhow — knowhow I likely did not have — to accomplish such a feat. I am glad the people we paid off have not been caught. That the prosecution thinks I am a hacking whiz.

The prosecutor also mentions there were several pro-choice rallies on the campus while I attended. Albert points out there are no photos of me at rallies or any pro-choice literature found among my belongings.

Then the prosecution rests. Just like that. Albert was right, I realize. The short prep time had hurt them more than it had hurt us. With very little time, there was very little information they could offer the jury. The psychiatric testimony was strong, but everything else was weak. Giving them short prep time meant they didn't have a massive case to put on. They had what they had. No time to get more. Going now, at least, keeps us even.

Our turn is next. The first witness Uncle Albert plans to call is Susan. Albert thinks Susan will be pivotal to the jury understanding how my pregnancy psychosis developed.

25. SUSAN'S STORY

This is the testimony I have most dreaded. It seems unfair to make Susan tell her story to these people; it is none of their business. Testifying means she must relive the mistakes the system made. I suppose she lives it every day, so perhaps my concern for her is unwarranted. Still, I feel guilty that my hearing will dredge up the senseless mistakes yet again. That it will remind her it all could have been prevented; remind her that at one point in time she was just like the rest of us: vibrant, walking, running, kicking, swimming, moving her legs. Instead, she will be tormented with this again today, reliving it one time more than necessary. Sometimes in life it's easier to just move on with the results we have, not to keep going over what led us there.

Steeling myself for Susan's appearance, I tune out what's going on. Albert says something, then I notice all eyes have converged on the door that leads into the courtroom. I turn to watch, too. The guard is holding the door open as Susan wheels herself in, past the rows of spectators, past my father, past the table where I sit with Albert and the one opposite mine where Bickers sits. She continues toward the chair where the other witnesses sat, where she can be seen by the jury and the opposing side. Once she turns her chair in the proper direction, she smiles at me. Instinctively, I smile back.

The deputy walks over to swear Susan in, presuming she will remain in her wheelchair, hovering in front of the elevated seat where everyone else had testified. But, he doesn't know Susan. "A little help," she says to him, as she begins hoisting herself out of her wheelchair and into the testimony seat. The deputy seems astonished for just a moment, then grabs hold of her arm and helps heft her into the elevated witness chair. Susan catches her breath; the maneuver, even with the help of the deputy, has left her winded.

We all watch, mesmerized by Susan's determination to do things the same as everyone else. Mesmerized by her calm, by her projection that this is the norm, when it is not. The deputy watches beyond when Susan catches her breath and seems ready to be sworn in. The judge clears his throat, jolting the deputy back from his trance-like observance, and he swears Susan in.

When the deputy returns to his post, Uncle Albert approaches Susan and gives a respectful nod. "Ms. Harper, how long have you known Kelsey Reed?"

"Since we were five. So 18 years," she says in a firm voice that carries across the room clearly. She wants the jury to hear her answers, to make no mistake about what she is saying. Susan obviously has none of the ambivalence about her testifying that I do.

"And how would you describe your relationship?"

"We're best friends."

Uncle Albert nods, then his expression turns serious, almost grim. "Ms. Harper, I'm going to cut to the chase here, and I know this may be difficult for you, but I'm going to ask a few frank questions about your medical condition. Is that alright?"

She nods. "Yes. Of course."

"Have you always been in a wheelchair?"

Emotionless, she says, "No."

"How did you come to be in a wheelchair?"

Susan takes a fortifying breath before answering. "It is the result of a bone marrow transplant operation, after I was marked." Some members of the jury raise an eyebrow, but no one gasps. I keep watch on Susan's face, which seems dispassionate, unemotional. I wonder if she's practiced to keep herself from becoming emotional, or if she has gotten there on her own, after being wheelchair-bound for a year now.

"Please explain, Ms. Harper," Uncle Albert says, leaving things open-ended.

"About a year ago, I received notice that I had been marked. I was the best match for a man in need of bone marrow, so I was scheduled for surgery. I had the procedure two weeks later. Everything went normally. I seemed to be recovering fine, and was released."

"You were fine, when you left the hospital?" Albert prods.

Susan swallows, and answers, this time showing the first tremor in her voice. "I seemed fine," she corrects. "Sometimes, there are complications from the surgery. The one doctors particularly worry about is infection. At the first sign of infection, you should see a doctor because the procedure is done so close to the spinal cord, the cord can become infected. I was out of the hospital for more than a week, when I started running a fever. I went in immediately. My regular doctor was away due to a family emergency. The doctor on call was new. He didn't take the necessary blood tests. Instead, he imaged the site of the surgery and concluded all was well. The new doctor thought I'd picked up a viral infection from my cousin's six-year-old daughter, who I'd visited and now had the flu. I was given some antiviral medication and sent home.

"After following the doctor's instructions, and taking my medication meticulously, I still felt like crap. Finally, Kelsey called an ambulance and had me taken in. By then, I could barely move. The infection was bacterial, not viral. It was from the surgery, which was fairly near the spinal column. The way the infection spread caused permanent damage. I don't remember much of it. The infection was so severe they had to induce a coma during my treatment. When I woke up, I couldn't feel my legs."

The jury is watching closely. I can see sympathy in the eyes of every person on that panel. What happened to Susan was so wrong. The room is deathly silent as Uncle Albert gives Susan a sympathetic look, but says nothing, letting the weight of her words really sink in with all those hearing it for the first time.

"And was Ms. Reed a good friend to you during this time?" Albert finally asks in the firm, yet friendly, tone needed for this situation.

"Of course," Susan scoffs, as if suggesting otherwise is blasphemy. "Kelsey and I were roommates at the time, and she was wonderful. She stuck with me through one of the toughest times in my life. Going from able-bodied to being in a wheelchair and having health problems resulting from the infection was difficult. A lot of people feel guilty about still being able-bodied, or feel awkward about being around you when you're so different from how you had been. And not that Kelsey didn't have some initial pangs of that. But, she got over it, quickly. And she's remained my friend. My best friend."

Uncle Albert gives a reverent nod, then presses on. "And did you ever tell Ms. Reed that you blamed the transplant for your problems?"

"Yes, I did. I told her I wished I'd not been marked, and that if I had it to do over, I'd refuse," she says bitterly. I try to keep my face neutral, try to hide my surprise at her blatant lie. Susan never said anything like that to me. She never told me she felt bitter. She'd always tried to move forward, deal with the hand she'd been dealt. I always thought she felt at least some bitterness beneath the bravado, but she never expressed it. I think saying it aloud to me would have crushed her spirit. Yet, now she wants to help me by saying she filled me with bitterness toward the prospect of donation. She didn't need to fill me with bitterness. I gleaned that on my own.

I look down for a moment, trying to make sure my face is composed, then back up at Susan, as she continues to lie.

"You can call it a fluke, with statistical odds so entirely fantastical that you'd be more likely to be struck by an asteroid, but the truth is that infection was a complication from surgery. The misdiagnosis of my fever, of my type of infection was, well, just a poor job by the doctor. But, I shouldn't have been in the position to be misdiagnosed like that. I was only compromised because I had been marked. My health was perfect before then. I had a full evaluation before surgery. There was nothing wrong with me. Nothing. The only reason I'm in a wheelchair is because of the surgery."

Albert's face oozes empathy as he nods affirmation to Susan. "So, when Ms. Reed told you she had been marked, how was she?"

"Scared. Scared that something crazy and statistically unlikely could happen to her, too. And I don't blame her. I don't think she should have to jeopardize her health, if she doesn't want to."

Uncle Albert doesn't nod in agreement this time. In fact, he doesn't move. He asks simply. "What did you suggest Ms. Reed do?"

Susan swallows, looks briefly at the jury, then casts down her gaze. "I lied to her. I told her I thought she'd be fine and that she should go through with it, that I was an aberration, and she shouldn't use me to evaluate her situation."

"And what did Ms. Reed do with your advice?"

Bickers objects, claiming hearsay.

"Your honor," says Albert. "I am not asking Ms. Harper what Ms. Reed said. I am asking about Ms. Reed's actions. Those are witnessed, and go to my client's state of mind."

The judge allows Susan to answer.

"Kelsey ate very little, slept very little and ignored what I said. She was incredibly agitated about the upcoming surgery. And when I finally confronted her about it, she moved out of our apartment."

"She packed all her things and left?" Albert asks, as if this were the craziest thing a person could do. Perhaps if I'd done that, it would be an indication of crazy. But, I hadn't left like that. I'd packed a few clothes and went home to my father's. It was part of my escape plan. I told my father I felt more comfortable staying with him. That I thought it was bothering Susan for me to be there in anticipation of the surgery. That I was bringing back awful memories for her, and that it would be best to spend the last week at his house. For his part, my father was quite happy to have me return home. As it was campaign season, he didn't cancel any of his scheduled meetings to spend time with me. I was home alone with Haleema. And she was rarely there, for she often attended my father's campaign functions. It was a perfect place for Luke and me to get things ready.

Susan gives a sigh of weariness and shakes her head lamentably. "I wanted her to be with me, where I could keep an eye on her. She said she wanted to be with her father, at home. But, I think she just wanted to be away from people, away from people who would know something was wrong. Her father is a wonderful man, but he's been so busy campaigning, there's no way he could have noticed that Kelsey wasn't alright. She packed up and left on one-day's notice and went to be in a house where no one else would be around. Where no one would see that she had become unhinged."

"Objection," Bickers shouts, standing. "Ms. Harper is not a psychiatrist and has no way to know why Ms. Reed chose to live with her father in the days before her surgery."

The objection is sustained, and part of Susan's statement stricken from the record. But, the jury has already heard it. There will be no way to strike it from their memories.

Uncle Albert asks a couple more questions of Susan, but nothing of note. When Bickers stands up, his face seems sympathetic, and he approaches Susan gingerly. "Is it possible that you misinterpreted Ms. Reed's odd behavior and desire to return home as someone who was worried? Isn't it possible it was the behavior of someone cold and callous who wanted to be alone to plot her escape?"

To which Albert objects, even as Susan protests that she had not misread me.

26. PREGNANCY PSYCHOSIS

Susan's testimony leaves the jury shaken. Some are shocked by her appearance, others by what she said. On her way out of the room, she stops her wheelchair in front of me, then grabs my hand. I flash her my widest grin, then hug her. Testifying must have been hard for her, and I am grateful for her support.

Uncle Albert wastes no time after Susan. The psychiatrist testifies immediately.

Dr. Melinda Winters's first task in the chair is to explain pregnancy psychosis, which she does succinctly: "When a pregnant woman enters into an alternate world that she believes is real. It is characterized by strange and delusional thinking, often entailing thoughts of harming her baby."

Uncle Albert asks questions emphasizing that the delusions don't have to deal with the baby, and that there is no way to know when pregnancy psychosis sets in. He also ties in Susan, asking if my knowledge of her problems could embed itself into my psychosis.

"Yes," Dr. Winters says. "The psychosis is often based in some nugget of reality. It is very likely that Ms. Reed's psychosis was rooted in her friend's ordeal. That she somehow internalized this struggle as her own."

Albert nods his head, then shoots a sympathetic look my way, as if staring at an indigent child. He returns his gaze to Dr. Winters. "While pregnancy psychosis usually emerges later, isn't there typically some inciting incident that triggers symptoms?"

Dr. Winters crosses her legs, then looks at the jury studiously. "Yes, of course. In many cases, the trigger is the impending birth. Sometimes it's a bout with premature labor."

"Could a trigger be learning you'd been marked?"

"Certainly. In most pregnant women, they would know that they were pregnant and could not participate. But, Ms. Reed is so early on, that she would not have known that and been very stressed by the marking. That, I'm certain, was the inciting incident for Ms. Reed."

Uncle Albert tells the judge he is finished and resumes his seat next to me. It sure does sound convincing. At least for this brief period before Bickers stands to dismantle Dr. Winters' testimony.

Dr. Winters cannot cite a single case of pregnancy psychosis in any woman at this stage of pregnancy. This is expected, though, I think. But, it is only the beginning of Bickers' cross.

"Have you ever seen a case of pregnancy psychosis like this before?"

Dr. Winters answers, "No."

"When diagnosing pregnancy psychosis, is there a checklist of symptoms you go through to make the diagnosis?"

"Yes," the doctor replies.

"And how did Ms. Reed do on the checklist?"

"She had many of the symptoms, enough to justify the diagnosis," the doctor says, slightly defensive.

"Isn't it true she had fewer than half the symptoms on the checklist?" Bickers asks.

"Yes," the doctor says, quickly adding. "But she had the most significant symptoms."

Bickers glares at her a moment, then asks: "If so few of Ms. Reed's symptoms actually meld with the standard pregnancy psychosis definition, isn't it possible she doesn't have pregnancy psychosis?"

"Yes."

On that damning note, Bickers returns to his seat.

27. NIGHT AT LAST

I am glad when the shift-change rolls around. Luke takes his place in the doorway and smiles at me. That simple act sends my heart soaring after the day I've had. Luke says, "Hello," and I respond in kind. The exchange is only two words, but it is enough. Enough to make the whole rest of the day, the hearing, melt away. I am certain I will be fine until lights out, when Luke will next speak to me.

When the lights go out, Luke walks over to my block and asks me to scoot over. I do. He puts his arms around me, and squeezes gently. "How are you feeling?"

I smile, though he can't see it in this dark abyss. "Good. Me and the little guy are feeling much less nauseated today."

Luke kisses the peach fuzz on my head. "Your dad said it was rough going but he thought overall, Judge Harrell did a good job."

"Yeah, he did," I say, wearily. "But, I don't want to talk about the hearing, if it's OK."

He seems a little surprised, his body stiffening ever so slightly, but then he relaxes again. "That's cool. What do you want to chat about tonight?"

"How about being Mrs. Lucas Jeremiah Geary?" I snuggle into him.

"See, this is the reaction, I was hoping for the first time I asked."

"Well, I may be a little slow, but I'll make up for lost time," I say, turning to kiss him on his chin. "Do you know, are the marriage laws very different in Peoria?"

He takes a moment of thought before answering. "I think they're about the same. So long as we're not brother and sister. And preferably not first cousins, though I think first cousins can get a waiver depending on genetic testing."

"Well, we're not first cousins, so it doesn't matter." I grope in the dark to find his hand. There it is. I scoop it in mine, and hold it. "As long as we get married and get to spend our lives together."

"Yeah," he says, wistful.

Marriage to Luke would be great, even in Peoria. I know I can't stay in FoSS even if Uncle Albert gets me cleared, which I am not sure he can do. I won't stay in this country and wait to be marked again, or wait for Luke to be marked. We have to leave. I try not to think about what will happen if Uncle Albert can't win the case. About being stuck here forever.

So my thoughts are only about leaving here, going to Peoria, and getting married. The only downside is that my father won't be there. This past year, it seemed all his friends' daughters were getting married. He'd come back from the ceremonies with some pronouncement about how my wedding would be different or similar. "You know, Kelsey," he'd say, "when you get married, we'll have a much classier shebang than that." After one of his friends arrived by horse drawn carriage to walk his daughter down the aisle, my father decided that was what he'd like to do when I got married. I feel bad that he'll miss this day he's so been looking forward to.

"You think my father will be able to come see us in Peoria?"

"Where'd that come from?" Luke asks, giving me another gentle squeeze.

"I just thought maybe he could come for the wedding. I'd hate for him to miss it."

"Maybe," he says, rubbing my arm lightly. "Dr. Grant is able to make the trips. But, first things first. We gotta get you outta here. Either Judge Harrell will do it the legal way, or we'll fall back on the contingency plan."

My heart skips a beat, and I bolt upright, breaking free from the arm Luke had wrapped around me, though still clinging tight to the hand I am holding. "What contingency plan?"

He chuckles. "Breaking you out."

"You said nobody's ever broken out of a holding facility before."

"No one ever has," he agrees. "But no one's ever loved anyone as much as I love you."

The bravado is sweet, but it is also insane. "Are you suffering from pregnancy psychosis?"

He laughs. "Of course not. But, your father and I have been doing a little strategizing." That startles me. Luke and my father getting along, even strategizing together — that is something new, and, for lack of a better word, weird. "We have one advantage this time that we didn't have before. No LMS broadcasting your location. They're not going to replace it until after Dr. Grant has done his procedure."

I involuntarily shudder when he says it. Luke feels it and pauses.

"I'm sorry, Kelsey, I shouldn't have said it that way. Dr. Grant is not going to operate on you. It's not gonna happen. I won't let it happen, and he won't either. OK? I just meant, that for now, Dr. Grant has convinced them it would be more effective to wait until he does his procedure to replace the LMS."

I take a deep breath. "But he won't do it?" I ask this more to convince myself than anything else.

"No, Kelsey he won't. Trust me."

"I do," I say. "With my life." He gives me a reassuring squeeze, and I nestle back into his arms. "So, you were saying you had a plan to break me outta here?"

"Yeah, sort of. We looked into getting you out of here, and there are a few security holes we can exploit with success, but I think the logistics of it might be too difficult to pull off. So, your father and I were thinking we could take you from Dr. Grant's lab, instead. We could send you over the night before the scheduled procedure, then get you out. The security is very lax at that place, and without the LMS, there'd be no indication you were gone."

I take a moment to take it in. That plan seems OK, but there is one problem. "Won't we have the same problem as before. Of getting to the border before they initiate a search."

"Nope," Luke says, confidently. "We're gonna fly."

"Nighttime flight is prohibited," I say, instinctively.

"For passenger planes. We'll be on a medical supply plane. They're allowed to do overnight runs, so as not to congest the air during the day."

Part of me doesn't want to hear anymore, doesn't want to get my hopes up that I can get out of this place, get to Peoria, and keep my kidney. Even if it does mean flying, which I hate. I can withstand a little takeoff anxiety if it means I can have everything I want, plus a baby too. I don't want to hope that the seemingly impossible might come true. But, the other part of me wants to hope, wants to believe in Luke's plan with all my heart. "When do you think you would get me out?"

"If they find you guilty, and the judge orders the procedure, we'd probably wait two weeks. "

The idea of being free of this place makes me smile, makes my heart do somersaults. But I wonder if Luke is being overly optimistic about this. "Do you really think it will work?"

He doesn't answer right away, taking a long inhale before he speaks. "I think it will, Kelsey." He kisses my forehead. "The key this time is going to be that we won't have to try to deal with the security here. Only at the lab. And with Dr. Grant on our side, it'll be perfectly possible."

Perfectly possible. I hope so. I hope Dr. Grant will be a better savior for me than he was for my mother.

28. EMMIE

In the morning, before lights come on, Luke wakes me. I am groggy and still feel like a lead weight, unable to lift myself off my bed block. Luke waits for me to get my bearings and appear lucid.

"I'm sorry to wake you, Kelse," he whispers.

I smile, though he can't see me in this darkness. He is kneeling in front of my block, and I can feel his warm breath on my face. It is nice having him so near. Slowly I sit up, and stretch. Sensing my movement, he finds his way next to me and embraces me.

"Did you sleep well?"

"I always sleep well when you're with me," I say. It is true. I am so glad he is here with me at night. I don't think he can ever understand just how grateful I am. It is a bit of sanity in an otherwise insane place.

"I'm glad," he says, pausing. "I'm sorry I woke you. I just wanted to tell you something. I meant to mention it last night, but the time just didn't seem right."

I tense. The time didn't seem right? It has to be something bad. He rubs my right arm and speaks softly. "Relax," he says, clearly feeling my tension. "It's not bad." He pauses. "Not too bad, at least."

"What?" I says.

"Emmie wants to see you."

I wait for more. How could that be bad? I still wait. There is nothing more. "Well, of course," I say. "I'd love to see her."

Luke is shaking his head. I can feel the rhythm of it as he holds me, and I imagine what he might actually look like, the way his hair would bobble ever so slightly as he swung his head sided to side.

143

Stern no, or lighthearted expression, I wonder. "She can't come," he says, sounding regretful. "It was hard enough for your dad to get me in here without arousing suspicion. Having my sister show up to see you would be living a little too dangerously, don't you think?"

I nod. And of course he can't see me, but I'm sure he feels the movement. "Yeah, too dangerous." I wish it weren't. I like Emmie. Not just because she is Luke's favorite family member, but because she is a nice lady. She has a good heart, is honest and fun. In some ways, she is a female version of Luke.

"So," Luke says, breaking my train of thought. "Emmie understands why she can't come, but she still wanted to — er — communicate with you."

"Communicate how?"

"She wrote you a letter."

I pull away from him, startled by the news. I want to see his expression, but of course, I can't. "Where is it?" I ask impatiently. "Give it to me."

"I don't have it," he says, grabbing hold of my hand. "I'd have a hard time explaining why I was passing you that note. Albert's bringing it today. It will be part of some documents he wants you to review before your hearing."

I lean back into him. Albert will bring it. Everyone is now doing wrong on my behalf. I feel more guilt. I wish it didn't have to be this way. I wish everyone didn't have to try so hard to help me because I decided to flee. If I'd gone in for the transplant like I was asked, I wouldn't even be in this position. They would have said I didn't need to do it. But, instead, I'd left, tried a grand escape, and now Albert is being complicit in giving me contraband papers. I sigh.

"What's wrong, Kelsey?"

I think about saying "nothing." I would have before we made our pact. But, I promised to be honest with Luke. "I just wish I hadn't been so principled. Wish I'd gone in for my transplant. Then Emmie wouldn't be passing me notes surreptitiously through my attorney, and heck, I wouldn't even need an attorney, and you wouldn't be sitting in here in the dark where I can't see you. Instead, we'd be planning our wedding and thinking about baby names."

He leans in and kisses my neck. His hair tickles my face, then he pats his hand along my body until he finds my hand. He wraps his fingers around mine. "I meant what I said, Kelsey," he says. "I should never have asked you to go in and have the surgery. I love you for who you are, and you did the right thing."

"It doesn't feel like the right thing," I say.

He gives a humph. "I suppose it doesn't," he says. "But, it's not because it wasn't the right thing. It's because it didn't get the result you wanted. You wanted to be in Peoria and not face the prospect of giving up your kidney. Just because this isn't that result doesn't mean you made the wrong choice. And, it may still work out. That's why I'm here, and Albert is here, and I think, what Emmie wanted to remind you."

He kisses the back of my head. It tickles a little. I've never felt his lips on that part of my skull before. Not with so little hair, at least. This hair prickling kiss sends a warm trill all the way to my toes. Despite the pleasantness of this new sensation, I will definitely not keep this hairdo if I get outta this place.

We sit a few minutes more, then Luke kisses my peach-fuzz head again. "It's almost time, sweetie. I have to get up." I scoot away from Luke. He stands and heads back to his station. I lay my head back down. About five minutes later, the lights spark to life. We are prisoner and guard again, and it feels rather lonely. I hope Luke is right. I hope I have done the right thing, even though everything feels wrong.

* * *

When Luke leaves, I feel again like a normal inmate: scared. Scared that I will be here forever. Scared that I will soon wake up and find out it is my last day on earth — that they are going to send me to an eternal sleep so that someone else might live. Scared that I will never see Luke again, and our baby will be taken from me.

I try to put the fear out of my mind. It is easy to do at night, with Luke by my side. But, during the day, when I am here alone, when Albert isn't prepping me, when I don't have something tangible and distracting to think about, I feel the fear, and know I won't last long if I am sentenced here permanently. I don't think my sanity will remain intact for more than a day.

I look up at the clock, trying to distract myself from these thoughts. It is 8:11, and Albert isn't due until 9. We will have all morning to prepare, and the hearing will resume following lunch. It seems like an odd schedule, but it is designed to give the jury the occasional half-day of rest. It is good for us, as it allows more prep time.

While waiting for Albert, I try to focus on something other than this place, something tangible. I think about Emmie. She is tall and trim, with jet-black hair. Her eyes are the same intense blue as Luke's. And they both have a thin layer of brown freckles on their noses and cheeks. In many ways, she resembles him. Not just in the overt ways that a person who happens to see a picture of them together might notice. But, in the small ways that families often resemble each other. In the way I probably resemble my father. It isn't so much about looking physically alike, as it is the whole package. They have a similar gait, loose and free-flowing, as if they don't have a care in the world. They bite their lips the same way when they are tense. And when they have a joke to tell, some secret funny thing, they both get a crooked half-smile that makes you want to know exactly what is on their minds.

I've only met Emmie a few times. But our first meeting was momentous — at least for me. I was more nervous about meeting her than anyone else in Luke's life. She is ten years older than Luke, and more like a mother to him than a sister. With their own mother descended into madness and a father always working — at a place he hated, no less — Emmie was the family caregiver. She took care of herself, of Luke, and of his older brother Chase. Luke thinks the world of her. She is the reason Luke began working for Dr. Grant. And when we met, she was the person whose opinion he valued most. So, I was nervous beyond belief.

Yet, I shouldn't have been. Emmie loves Luke with all her heart, and she would have loved anyone Luke introduced to her. To be honest, he'd said as much, but of course I worried I would be the one person Emmie wouldn't like. That I'd make such a bad impression, she'd break her longstanding tradition of accepting Luke's friends and say I wasn't worthy. I suppose everyone has such fears when meeting their significant other's family.

But Emmie put me at ease. She and her husband, Greg, were both funny and kind. After dinner, I offered to help in the kitchen, but Luke and Greg suggested Emmie and I relax a bit while they did the dishes. The two of us decided this was a splendid idea and adjourned to the living room. Emmie and Greg had a small Cape Cod style house in Takoma Park, MD. It was sparsely decorated but still felt homey.

We were about to sit, when Emmie stopped suddenly and motioned upstairs. "Come with me. I want to show you something."

I followed her out of the living room, up a staircase and onto an upper floor landing. The ceiling was low there, and we had to crouch a little to keep from banging our heads. Three doors flanked the tiny landing. The open one directly in front of us was a bathroom, and the two on each side were bedrooms. Emmie turned to the right and entered a small room with a sloped ceiling. It, too, was sparsely furnished: a rocking chair, a dresser, and a chest clustered near the window. Emmie sat on top of the chest and motioned for me to sit across from her in the rocking chair.

I wasn't sure why she'd asked me here, so I sat silently and waited for her to start. Finally, she did, looking at me with an intensity that had the power to suck you in or force you to turn away. I was sucked in.

"I'm so glad we've finally met, Kelsey. You've made my brother so happy, and for that, I'm really grateful."

I blushed at the unexpected compliment. "You have a wonderful brother, and he makes me very happy. I feel lucky he's in my life."

She nodded. "Well, you two are clearly a good fit. Luke has always had a side to him that wasn't...." She trailed off searching for the right word, finally coming up with, "settled. I always worried he would never be settled. It was tough on him growing up with a mother who wasn't well. The rest of us were older and understood more, but for him, it was hard, and I don't think he ever felt a natural sense of peace. The sense of what normal could be that Chase and I had. But, since he's met you, he's gotten that."

Her confiding this in me could have felt awkward, yet it didn't. It felt special that she could tell me this. The content of her statement was odd in that it was surprising to me in many ways, yet not at all. In the time that we were dating, Luke always seemed confident and strong and at peace. Like an anchor. Yet, I knew the Luke I'd met the year before was different. I hadn't known what had changed. I'd always thought it was whatever happened to Emmie that led Luke to work for Dr. Grant. But, Luke had never told me what that was. He just said that Dr. Grant had helped Emmie, and it wasn't really his place to tell me what had happened to her.

It didn't bother me that he didn't tell me. I admired that he kept his sister's confidence. And I understood, too, that many of the things Dr. Grant did were illegal, and telling me would expose that. Not that I didn't know some of the things, but perhaps what he had done for Emmie was something I wouldn't want to know.

Emmy's stare was burrowing into me as I pondered what she said. "I appreciate that you think so much of my influence. But I think Dr. Grant, and you and me and his life this past couple of years have ultimately helped Luke gain that peace."

She nodded. "You're right. I was probably the first piece. What happened with me, that led me to Dr. Grant. Did Luke ever tell you what happened?"

I shook my head, no. Anything more would have felt like I was asking her to tell me. While I wanted to know, it wasn't my place to ask. It was clearly something personal that she would tell when she was ready — or perhaps never. So, I looked out the window of the small room.

Emmie spoke in a low voice, and I turned back to her. She looked resolute, yet a bit frail. "I didn't think he had," she said. "That's why I brought you here. I thought you should know."

I gave her a look I hoped was reassuring, that let her know she could confide in me. "A couple of years ago, Greg wanted a baby. I did, too, on some level. But, I was ambivalent. I'd helped raise Chase and Luke and knew children required a lot of effort. Part of me was ready. Part of me wasn't. But, since Greg wanted it so much, I went into it with the attitude that we'd try. No huge plan of what to do. My friend Jenny had even suggested taking prenatal vitamins while trying would give the best results. But, I just wanted to see what would happen. Not do any artificial encouragement. After two months of seeing what happened, we realized I was pregnant, and I was extremely happy. I went to the doctor, got a prenatal supplement, started preparing myself mentally."

She had a certain sadness in her eyes when she spoke, and I knew it had not ended well as Luke was not an uncle. She looked around the room, staring momentarily at a shelf with nothing on it, perhaps remembering something that had been there and was now gone. Or remembering what she had planned to put there. After a moment, she took a deep breath and returned her focus to me. "We were going to put the baby in here. It was pretty early on when Greg bought that rocking chair. He thought I could sit in it while the baby was still in the womb, and the baby would be used to the familiar swaying by the time he or she came out.

"When I was 16 weeks, I went in for an ultrasound. We thought maybe we could see the gender of the baby. We expected the ultrasound tech to tell us all about the baby: fingers, toes, nose, everything we were seeing on the screen. Instead, our technician was completely silent during the procedure. He seemed not to share in our marvel at the baby. When the doctor came in, he told us the baby appeared to have a neural tube defect."

I took a small breath in, tried not to gasp. Luke had told me of one of Dr. Grant's patients with a neural tube defect. It was a horrible complication of pregnancy that could produce a baby with no brain, or such a severely damaged one he would be in a persistent vegetative state for most of his life, and likely die by the age of 10.

"The baby had only a portion of his brain and my doctor thought it unlikely to survive beyond a month or two. The time he would be alive would be hooked to monitors and in incubators and untouchable. He wouldn't know what was going on. He'd be just there, a body, a life form, but without soul, without life.

"It was then that I had a mini meltdown — right there in the doctor's office. I began screaming, throwing things, and hyperventilating. Finally, I passed out. They took me in for an evaluation. I spent three nights in a psychiatric ward," she said looking directly at me, and I could see the fear, the loneliness, the terror that experience had caused her. "I was afraid I would become like my mother. She was always different, but what pushed her over the edge was the stillborn. When Luke was one, they had a girl named Sophia. But she was dead when she was born. And after that, my mother went downhill.

"So, I was afraid it would happen to me, but I couldn't tell anyone. Not the doctors at the psych ward or they'd keep me there, keep me locked away. Greg knew. I couldn't talk about it with him, though. Speaking it made me worry he'd take me back to the institution. So, we didn't speak about it. I worried and Greg worried without talking. Luke was beside himself, worrying that I would become like Mom. It was a bad time for him, but strangely it was Luke who rescued me."

She smiled and I leaned in slightly, curious what Luke did. "He was drowning his sorrows with liquor, when he met you at a bar. He told me he'd been 100 percent obnoxious to a complete angel, though he didn't remember exactly what he said. He thought maybe you were a regular, and went back the next night, hoping he could apologize. He didn't see you. But, on the TV screen behind the bar, there was an interview on, an interview with an obstetrician who specialized in tough cases — Dr. Stephen Grant."

My mouth opened in shock, but it quickly closed. I hadn't known Luke had found Dr. Grant for his sister, or that he'd found him when looking for me. It was odd to hear, yet right in a sense. It seemed to me that Luke and Dr. Grant and I were all connected in some unseen way, some way I couldn't quite put my finger on, and this just confirmed that. Emmie looked briefly at me, then continued her story.

"He told me about him, told me that maybe my doctor was wrong and I should see this guy." She paused a moment, then let out a cynical laugh. "Luke was right. My doctor was wrong. Dr. Grant said it was much worse than my doctor had described. My baby would probably die in utero, around eight months, and that I'd probably have to birth the corpse. While they could remove the baby through surgery, birthing the corpse is the preferred method because it carries lower risk for the mother.

"Of course, that was not what Greg or I wanted to hear. Greg was beside himself. He looked at Dr. Grant and said that was crazy, that I couldn't take that. Wasn't there any other way? That's when Dr. Grant confided there might be another way, one that wasn't quite legal, but that we could pursue if we were interested. Before I even had a chance to process it all, I said, 'yes.' I knew in my heart that was right for me, for this baby who couldn't survive.

"Greg and I went home and talked about it. We both agreed we wanted to just end the pregnancy if that were possible. I've known Greg my entire life, you know. He lived three houses down. He knew my mother went insane after the stillborn. He saw firsthand how hard it was on me. And he knew I couldn't live through birthing a corpse.

"It was such a strange situation to be in. Knowing the life you helped create wouldn't really get a chance at life. No matter what you did. I just wanted it to be over, to be over and done with, so I could move on. We had another appointment with Dr. Grant, and he gave me pills. They weren't anything harmful to me, but they would decrease oxygen supply to the baby, and then he'd be gone. Once that happened, since I was fewer than 20 weeks, Dr. Grant could remove him surgically. They call it a D&C. And so, that's what I did. I took the pills. I went to Dr. Grant a week later, he did a sonogram and determined the baby had died. As such, he did the D&C, and sent me home. And I was sad, but grateful. Grateful that it was over, and Greg and I could move on. Grateful that Dr. Grant gave me a choice to give me some peace, and the baby some peace."

She paused, her hands in her laps, quiet, contemplative. "We named him Philip," she said. "You have to name them, even if they don't survive, you know. I hadn't ever really realized that, until it happened. That you had to name the baby, if it's beyond 14 weeks, no matter what the cause of expiration, even a late spontaneous abortion, they require a name and a death certificate. Even though the baby never lived to take breath outside the womb, it's considered alive, and its passing is considered a death."

Her eyes were moist, and there was a torrent of emotions sitting just beneath the surface of her voice, but she had spoken her entire story steadily and clearly, and seemed to be holding together for the moment. I felt honored that she had confided in me. Telling that to the wrong person would land all of them in a holding facility: Emmie, Greg, Dr. Grant.

I left my rocking chair and crossed over to Emmie, keeping my head low to avoid banging it on the ceiling. I knelt in front of her. "I'm so sorry about what happened, Emmie," I told her, as I patted her knee. "I'm glad you confided in me."

She smiled as a single tear ran down her cheek. She used a hand to wipe it, then took both her hands to grab one of mine. "Of course I can confide in you. You're the reason Dr. Grant does this. The reason he helps women like me."

I joined her on the chest, and shook my head. "He does it for my mother, not me."

She shook her head in protest. "Yes, your mother started it. She was the spark. But, it's you he does it for. He told me that once."

I stiffened at her words, cocking my head slightly towards her, to make sure I'd heard her correctly. Why would he be doing it for me? We'd never even met until the year before, and at that point, he'd been doing this already. I bit my lip, and crinkled my brow as I tried to figure out why she'd think that. Clearly realizing she'd brought about this state, Emmie spoke.

"He went to your mother's funeral," she said. I stared, wide-eyed. I hadn't realized. Those days were a blur in my mind, all running together, the sadness, the emptiness. Only random, disconnected moments remained clear — my father standing over her casket, the way her hair had turned a slightly darker shade of auburn after she died, so it didn't look right as it brushed against the favorite red dress she'd been buried in, the apple crisps Haleema would cook each night and let me eat for breakfast every day for the week following the funeral, how I didn't go to school at all during that time, but Susan would come over and we'd do the homework assignments together, Susan leading me through the stuff I didn't understand.

After the montage of my past finished playing in my head, I noticed Emmie was staring, waiting. I nodded for her to go on. "He'd never told me your name or your mother's name, but said he started doing this after a patient died because she wasn't given a choice about how to handle her life. He said he went to the funeral and he saw this woman's daughter, and she was so sad. She looked as if her life had been ripped apart. She looked like she was burying her own soul when they lowered the casket. The little girl seemed hollow. And that, he said, is when he vowed he would never let any of his patients die because they didn't have a choice. He would do everything in his power to make sure they were given choices, even if it didn't take into account everyone's life at stake. To him, he would put one life first: that of his patient. No one else."

* * *

When Albert arrives, he tells me there are papers for me to review, and notes that page five is worth studying. Then, he leaves to get some coffee. "I think better with a little caffeine in me," he says on his way out. I open the folder he's left and turn to page five.

There it sits, Emmie's letter. I shake my head and chuckle. I had expected more because Luke said it was a letter. But, what I have is so Emmie. It is four lines in neat script, signed at the bottom with an elegant E.

> *The doctor was wrong. That little girl didn't bury her soul that day. She still has it, and she's using it to fight for what she believes in. Keep fighting, Kelsey. You're doing the right thing.*

— *E*

I smile. She knows just what to say. I hope she is right.

29. A FOOL FOR A CLIENT

Uncle Albert and I agree I should not testify. Putting me on the stand is too risky. First, I might come off unsympathetic. But more importantly, I can't risk questions about my baby's father.

However, in the absence of my own testimony, we need someone to fill in the blanks: a character witness. Susan did a great job in both testifying about me and her own condition. But, Albert also wants someone to testify about me as a person. Someone who knows me well and will come off in a good light. He's rejected the Spencers, as they were hesitant when he talked to them, and the fact that my saving their son had possibly endangered the life of someone else.

In these last few minutes before we go into court, before my father arrives, Albert gives me one last reminder about today's testimony.

"I know we talked about this earlier. I just want to say again, it was a tough choice between your father and Haleema," he says, trying to reassure me. "Haleema would be a better witness, in terms of drawing sympathy for you on the jury. She's great. She comes across matronly and loving and could accurately describe your warmth, your personality, acts of kindness and generosity."

He trails off a second, and brings on the buts. "But, I don't have time to prepare her. I just worry that if she says something wrong, something I don't anticipate, it could really hurt us."

He looks as if he thinks I'll argue it, but I say nothing. "So, your father, I think is the best we can do. Men generally don't play as well with juries, but I've seen your dad's internal polls. He has a really high likeability quotient among men and women. You can't underplay that. I think it will make up for anything we might have lost with Haleema. It will also give us your father's skill, both as a politician and a legal mind. He'll have a better instinct of what to say and what not to say, and where the pitfalls are."

I nod. This sounds the same as before. The fact that Albert feels the need to discuss it again worries me. "I'm sure my father will do fine," I say, trying to sound reassuring — for both my own and Albert's sake.

Uncle Albert points at my belly. He never says Luke's name. "They won't expect your father to have an answer to that question. He can say as much." At this point, Albert pauses. "Just one more time, I want you to think on this, because this is important, for both in the courtroom and in here," he says significantly, looking around at the four white walls. "There is no indication of any relationships out in the general sphere that Bickers would have heard of."

I shake my head no. I've been over it in my mind dozens of times. Luke and I flew under the radar. Because of the nature of the work they did, both Luke and Dr. Grant were low profile together. Also, with my father's political issues, I kept my private life as private as possible. We had not meant to have a secret courtship, but looking back on it, we had, and it is working to our advantage now. A quick survey from the prosecutor of those who knew me would not turn up my relationship with Luke.

There may be evidence that I have been to Dr. Grant's lab on a few occasions, but given his testimony against me, that would hardly seem a problem. However, it is important no one make the connection between Luke and me. It would be nightmarish if Luke got tossed as my guard, especially now that I know what guards do to inmates at night.

Uncle Albert gives me a final onceover, looks at his watch and says, "Alright, let's head over."

* * *

My father's direct testimony goes well. He manages to paint a nice picture of me as the all-American girl who was a good student, a good teacher, had friends, and dated occasionally. More importantly, he says I am a good daughter, and that we have a close relationship, especially since I am motherless. He plays up the devastating effect my mother's death had on me, and how I overcame that to try to lead a normal life. He says after I was marked, I seemed to be in a haze similar to the one I fell into after Mom died. He tells the jury he assumed it would pass after the transplant, then he puts on his public look of regret for not having seen the depth of my anguish.

I must admit, my father is good at this. When Albert finishes, Bickers begins his cross.

"Senator Reed," Bickers begins, respectfully. "I have just a couple of questions for you."

My father motions him to continue.

Bickers moves closer, smiles, pauses. "You mentioned that your daughter dated occasionally?"

"Yes," my father says.

"Was she in a serious relationship?"

"Not that I know of." The lie comes out smoothly, effectively; it seems fairly honest. I wonder briefly if Uncle Albert feels compelled, as an officer of the court, to report my father's perjury. Though, it occurs to me at this very moment, Albert told me that to put me at ease. He was never worried about his duty as an officer of the court to report perjury. He was worried that I would not be able to lie effectively. It is why he chose my father to testify. Haleema is better at being honest, forthright and sincere. That would come through to a jury. But, when she tried to force a lie, if she were even willing to do that on my behalf, it would come through to the jury, too. My father, on the other hand, is better at lying, while appearing honest, forthright and sincere.

Bickers freezes and stares at my father a moment. "You did just tell us that you and your daughter were close. Would it be possible for her to have a steady boyfriend and you not know of it?"

My father raises his hand to his chin, as if to ponder the question. This is a great stalling tactic he uses often during the campaign. He smiles, then almost chuckles. "We're close," he says to Bickers. "But, I have to admit, like a lot of fathers who want to protect their daughters from unsavory characters, I have not been the most inviting to men who try to woo her. Therefore, she tends not to bring them around unless they're ready for a little serious scrutiny."

It's a good answer. Close, but not so close my daughter brings me every dreg she dates.

"So," Bickers says in a voice that is a little too condescending, even in just that one word. "You and your daughter are not close, when it comes to her love life?"

My father smiles, and tries not to appear defensive. "Well, I'm not sure how much other daughters tell their fathers about their love life. But, I don't think Kelsey was any more reticent than other women her age. It's not really the subject she wanted to discuss with me, unless necessary."

Bickers nods. "Do you know who the father of your grandchild is?"

My father pauses. "No, I don't."

"Really?" Bickers demands.

My father's face flushes slightly, clearly irritated. "Sir, I do not know."

Bickers smiles briefly. He walks to his table, takes a paper from his briefcase, walks back to my father, and hands him the sheet. "Please read the top line, Senator Reed, then read the highlighted section."

My father pulls a pair of reading glasses from his suit-jacket pocket and puts them on. Whatever he is on the paper has turned him incredulous. He looks to Uncle Albert, then the judge. "Your honor," my father says to the judge, "this is a transcript of a privileged conversation I had with my daughter. This is not admissible."

Uncle Albert stands, then approaches the bench. The judge bangs his gavel, and calls a short recess to discuss this matter. My father sits in the witness chair, while Uncle Albert, Bickers and the judge leave the room. The men are gone five minutes. When they return, Albert is wearing his game face, but his eyes seem dejected. He sits next to me and writes a note: "Your father's first conversation with you was not privileged. Will explain later. May mean trouble. No matter what happens, don't show any emotion. Game face, Kelsey."

I want to scream. Game face! How am I supposed to keep on my game face when things are clearly falling apart.

"Senator Reed, please read the transcript," Bickers says crisply. "This is not privileged."

Uncle Albert stands, opens his mouth to speak. The judge waves him down. "Harrell," the judge says. "Your objection in my chambers is duly noted for the appeals process. However, I do rule this to be admissible." Albert sits.

My father begins reading. "Transcript of conversation, Thursday, May 14, for inmate Kelsey A. Reed."

"And the highlighted section," Bickers prods.

My father reads the brief snippet of our conversation that first time he saw me, the conversation where he and I discussed notifying the father of the baby, and I admitted it was the boy I'd introduced him to, John.

"So, Senator Reed," Bickers says, smugly, triumphantly. "When I asked you if you knew who the father was, why did you lie?"

My father has been caught in the lie. There is no denying it now. "I didn't lie," my father responds.

There is a moment of stunned silence among the courtroom, as everyone appears riveted by my father's words. Then Bickers narrows his eyes, sharpens his voice so it comes out almost shrill, and definitely accusatory. "You're saying this transcript is inaccurate?"

My father looks him in the eye. "No, it's accurate."

Annoyed now, Bickers asks. "Then you know the father is this John fellow."

"No," my father says firmly, in a tone hinting Mr. Bickers is an idiot for not understanding. "I spoke with John. He said he and Kelsey dated briefly, but had not been intimate. Given John's state of mental clarity and Kelsey's state of psychosis, I took him at his word, and feel confident he is not the baby's father. As I stated before, I do not know who the baby's father is."

If my father's answer has flustered Bickers, he doesn't show it. He simply takes the transcript from my father and returns it to the table. Then, he walks back to where my father sits. "Do you think your daughter knows who the father of her baby is?"

"Somewhere in her mind, yes. I think she does. I think the psychosis has hidden it, though."

Bickers laughs. "Pregnancy psychosis does not create memory loss, Senator Reed. Is it possible your daughter hasn't told you who the father is because she sleeps around and doesn't know?"

"My daughter is not promiscuous," my father shouts. Bickers has clearly roiled him with the last statement. It is rare for my father, public man that he is, to appear so angry in front of the voting public.

"How would you know? Didn't you say your daughter didn't discuss all of her paramours with you?"

"I did say that," my father says, managing to have calmed himself that quickly.

"Then, isn't it possible, she was having sex with many different men and you wouldn't know."

"It's possible she was secretly discovering a cure for cancer too, but I think it's highly improbable."

Bickers sighs with impatience. "This a yes or no question, Senator Reed. Is it possible your daughter was having sex with several men, and does not know who the father of this baby is?"

My father responds quietly. "Yes."

Bickers smiles ever so slightly, then returns serious. "Isn't it true that you thought your daughter's promiscuity that resulted in pregnancy is what caused her to flee her marking?"

"No," my father declares.

Bickers gives him a disapproving look. "Did you tell the psychiatrists who initially interviewed your daughter in the holding facility that you thought she ran because she feared her situation would be a detriment to your campaign?"

My father does not answer immediately. He is trying to figure out how to spin this, but he knows he doesn't have a lot of time. Hopefully, no one but me, who has seen so many of his expressions, sees the moment of uncertainty cross his face before he answers. "Yes, I did, but the situation I was referring to was her pregnancy."

Bickers nods curtly. "I see," he says, then turns toward his table, walks to it, and sits down on the edge of it, facing my father. Bickers raises a hand to his chin, as if he were the model in that famous Rodin sculpture, the Thinker. "Hmm. Wouldn't fleeing a marking be more of an embarrassment to your campaign than an unplanned pregnancy?"

"Yes, but I knew Kelsey wasn't thinking clearly. I believe I stated that earlier."

Bickers stands, then walks back toward my father. "Would a pregnancy where your daughter didn't know who the father was be more detrimental to your campaign than one where she was happily in a relationship and on the path to marriage?"

Albert objects. "Your honor, my client is not a psychic or an expert in public perception."

The judge tells Mr. Bickers he can't ask the question, and strikes it from the record. But, it is clear the jury is looking at me in a different light now. It is as if a wave of disgust is now emanating from the jury box. It is a noticeable and rapid change from how things were just moments ago. I am now a whore. That is about as antithetical to Life

First as you can get. Most sexually transmitted diseases have been eradicated, but being a society borne from the survivors of pandemics, we are well aware that diseases don't stay dormant forever. Monogamy and marriage are high values because of this. Deadly STDs are a concern, and anyone who values life would not be promiscuous and risk spreading disease. It's just the way things are. And now, I've been painted with this label. This is awful. I try to keep my game face on as I watch Bickers return to his seat, then say pleasantly to the judge. "I'm done, your honor."

Uncle Albert stands and attempts damage control. "Do you think your daughter knows who the father of her baby is?"

"Yes," my father says, quickly.

"Have you ever seen any indication your daughter is promiscuous?"

"No," he says emphatically. "She values herself and others. She would not be promiscuous."

"When you told doctors you thought she fled due to the pregnancy, it was simply because you thought she was concerned the unwed pregnancy would negatively impact your campaign?"

"Yes, absolutely," my father answers quickly. "Even when she was young, I told her that how she behaved could and would affect my campaign. I thought maybe she took it too much to heart, that she thought being pregnant and not married would hurt me and she tried to flee. I have never been concerned about promiscuity."

Uncle Albert nods, then sits. This is the best he can do, I guess.

The judge orders a recess. When the jury is gone, my father joins us at the table. "I'm sorry, Kelsey," he says.

I shake my head. "Nothing to be sorry about, Dad," I say. "You did the best you could in a bad situation."

Albert sighs, nods as if in agreement. But, it is clear by his posture and the barren look in his eyes that he thinks this is bad. If Albert gave me confidence earlier, he is giving me the exact opposite now: fear. I have to shake it off. "Why?" I ask. "Why were they able to use the transcript."

"It wasn't privileged," Albert says, clearly distracted by thoughts of what happened.

"The judge said that," I remind him, though more frustration seeps out than I want. I try to temper my next statement. "Why wasn't it?"

"There are two types of bar licenses: active, for people who are practicing attorneys, and inactive, for people who have practiced, but are not practicing now and want to be able to practice law again, at some point in the future. Keeping an inactive license means you pay a fee, and don't have to take the bar again when you decide to return to practicing. Being active means you do stuff like pro bono work, etc."

He is rambling. My father's testimony was worse than I thought if it has sent Uncle Albert into fits of rambling. "I get it, but what does this have to do with anything?"

"Up until last week, your father was inactive, which meant he couldn't practice law. That's one reason he couldn't get in to see you. He tried as your attorney, and they said his bar was inactive. He went through the hoops to reactivate it, and then they let him in to see you. But, they let him in initially as your father, because his reactivation didn't occur until the following day. Therefore, the conversation wasn't privileged."

"I'm sorry, Kelsey," my father says, meaning it completely.

I shake my head. "It's not your fault. It's mine. I wanted you to tell him about the baby, and I didn't realize it would be a problem. You saved me. It's not your fault."

My father closes his eyes and hangs his head. Finally, he looks up at me. "Still, I feel like I should have done something differently. I didn't want anything from that day to come back to hurt you."

I lean forward and hug my father. "It's OK, Daddy, really." I say, trying to sound soothing. I turn back to Uncle Albert, and the weight of my lie sets in. It isn't OK. Really, it isn't. But contributing to my father's guilt is even more not OK. So, I take the lesser of the two evils and try to make him feel better. But, I fear my father's testimony is going to lead any waffling juror to the conclusion that Kelsey is a bad person and needs to be convicted.

30. CLOSING ARGUMENTS

Bickers stands, his pinched face drawn into a vengeful scowl. "Kelsey Reed has refused to do her duty. She refused this duty because she is a sociopath who wants to hurt society. The law is clear on what must happen. She comes in here, hoping to feed on your sympathies and talking out of both sides of her mouth."

He walks in front of the jury box, looking at each juror as if trying to connect. "Her attorney and psychiatrist tell you she is suffering from an obscure condition known as pregnancy psychosis. That she is deluding herself. Yet, you saw her on the video, you heard her. She isn't suffering from any psychosis. She just doesn't want to do her duty. Doesn't care if Mr. Lyons lives or dies. Not her problem," he says, throwing a contemptuous look my way.

"This is a free society, one people choose to live in, to be a part of. If Ms. Reed didn't believe in Life First, she was welcome to leave. Welcome to go off to Peoria or Nuriland, or some other place where civilization is on the decline and every man or woman is for himself. She had every opportunity to say good-bye. But, she didn't do that."

Bickers shakes his head in disgust. "Instead, she stayed here, took advantage of our society, of our excellent health care, of our food and policies dedicated to preserving life. She didn't run off to join those Peorians. She stayed here and reaped the benefits of our society.

"That is, until she was called upon to perform her civic duty, to help her society survive and thrive, as it has done for the last century. Then, she decided our rules were bad and she didn't want to follow them. She tried to flee, and didn't give a damn that Mr. Lyons might die because of it.

"Now, her attorney will tell you that her fleeing didn't matter in the end, that it was alright because Mr. Lyons required a new donor anyway. Ms. Reed, due to her pregnancy, was unable to give a kidney.

"He parades her out here, tells you she's pregnant, reminds you that she will be a mother, one of our most revered roles in society: giver of life. He plays on your sympathy for mothers, plays on your regard for their safety and well-being. But, Kelsey Reed is not the normal mother of FoSS. She is not married or in a loving relationship that can nurture and raise a child. She is unmarried, and likely someone who is reckless with her body."

Bickers pauses, then looks back at me, letting the jury savor his words a moment before continuing. "Her father testified. He told us she was a wonderful girl. Yet, he knew few of her suitors. And could not identify the father of her baby. The man she told him was the father was not. Does she sleep around? Whore herself? Disrespect her body? Potentially spread disease?"

Two people on the jury gasp. I hold my face as steady as I can, though I feel the anger rising in me. The idea that I am a whore who doesn't know the father of my child is incensing. Especially when I know he is the sweetest, most caring person I've ever had the good fortune to meet.

"Her father admits it's possible she is promiscuous. Though, he can never really know. And while her attorney claims this pregnancy psychosis disorder, Ms. Reed does not appear the least bit mentally distressed. Not as she sits here in this courtroom. And not in the recording where she was interviewed by Dr. Klein. Do you remember what she said when Dr. Klein asked her what would happen if they could not find another kidney for Mr. Lyons? Kelsey Reed looked at that doctor and said, 'Then he would die.' She was cold and callous and didn't care. That was not pregnancy psychosis. That was a killer. A person who does not put Life First."

Bickers waits the appropriate amount of time for his words to sink in, for their weight to resonate with the jury, then continues. "Please, look at the facts here. Doctors Klein and Grant have called it right. Ms. Reed is not suffering from psychosis. She is a sociopath. Cold and hard at heart. A moocher from society. Please find her guilty, so she can pay her due. Save Ms. Reed's child from her. Find her guilty and allow the court to have the baby removed. Then, Ms. Reed can dutifully pay the society she loved so much until recently, what she owes it."

And with that, he returns to his chair.

I want to convict me. This is hopeless. I turn to Uncle Albert. He stands slowly, deliberately and walks toward the jury. His countenance is sober, yet he manages to not be grim or foreboding.

He takes in a deep breath, turns slightly, angling himself so the jury can see both me and him, and then he motions to me. "Mr. Bickers is trying to paint a picture of Kelsey Reed that just isn't true," he says with conviction.

"He wants you to think she's a sociopath. That's a lie. Ms. Reed is the backbone of our society. She is a giver of life. Right now in her womb, a life waits to be nurtured and loved. Unfortunately for Ms. Reed, with that new life has also come a sickness. A disease that has caused Ms. Reed not to be herself."

He looks my way again, lamentful, then continues. "You've heard testimony from the psychiatrists, from Susan Harper, from Senator Reed. This is not the Kelsey Reed they know. This woman who fled is the result of psychosis. Think back to Ms. Harper's testimony. You remember?" he asks, making eye contact with several members of the jury. "Ms. Harper pulled herself into that witness chair and told us how being marked caused her paralysis. Ms. Reed saw the result of that paralysis every day. Ms. Reed heard her friend lament going in for her procedure every day for almost a year. Then, Ms. Reed learned she would have to do the same thing.

"And due to her psychosis, she snapped. She internalized Ms. Harper's plight as her own. She feared it and she fled. It was a mistake, a mistake caused by disease. This disease destroyed her reason. Don't let it destroy her life, too."

He turns and points to me. I try my best to look sympathetic. "Please do the right thing. Find Ms. Reed guilty but treatable so that she can get well and help bring another life into FoSS."

With that, Albert returns to his seat. It was short, simple and to the point. It was eloquent, too. But it doesn't seem like enough. The rest of the hearing is a blur to me. The judge issues some instructions, the jury leaves, and I am taken back to my cell.

31. DON'T WORRY? HA!

Uncle Albert tells me not to worry, that there is nothing I can do at this point. Once things are in the hands of the jury, all I can do is wait. So, I try that. I sit in my cell and try not to worry. I rub my belly and talk to the baby, who I've dubbed Peanut. I'm not sure if it's a boy or a girl, obviously, but Peanut seems like it could go either way.

The hearing ended at 4 p.m., so I eat, talk to Peanut a bit, and pretty much wait for Luke. When he arrives at 8, he doesn't speak to me, not even, "Hi," which is weird. Then, at 9:40, he turns on his guard's walkie-talkie and asks permission to go on a 10-minute break. Once permission is granted, he leaves and doesn't come back until 2 minutes 'til lights out.

I lie on my bed block, anxiously awaiting the darkness, so I can break our silence. Once the lights fade, I sit up and speak. "What's going on?"

He shushes me.

I sit there and wait for what feels like an eternity, but in reality may be just 5 minutes, before Luke finally comes over. I slide over to make room for him on the block.

"What happened?"

I hear him swoosh in a breath, then he adopts a cheerful tone. "Kelsey, you worry too much," he says. "Nothing happened. I just needed to check my messages."

I worry too much! He has to be kidding. "Since when do you need to check your messages after you've arrived?"

He answers too quickly, as if he had it already prepared. "I was waiting on a call, and it hadn't come. That's it. I just wanted to check for it."

What could be that important? "A call from whom?"

"Dr. Grant."

"Oh," I manage. Well, I suppose that makes sense. I'd wondered from the moment I'd seen him with the good doctor, what exactly Luke did for him. Our first encounter in the lab made his job seem mysterious and secret. On our first date, he'd told me he really just did filing, talked to patients who were concerned, and escorted patients to Dr. Grant's lab in Peoria. I asked him why he'd made it sound so mysterious earlier, and admitted it was just so I'd go out with him. I sorta bought that explanation. But, then on our fourth date, I got a glimpse of what Luke really did for Dr. Grant. It was what he said, but in a more intimate way than I had expected. He had two mobile phones: one for personal calls, and one for calls related to Dr. Grant. And that phone, he was often replacing. He'd say he needed a new number, or new information associated with it. It didn't matter, though, he said, because only Dr. Grant's answering service had the number.

On that fourth date, he received a call from the answering service, and even though we were hot and heavy in a make out session, he took the call. He up and left me. Went to the other room to call a patient back and then spent 45 minutes talking with her on the phone. I was more than a little miffed when he returned. He apologized profusely and said his job involved talking to the patients when they were having a hard time with something. And this patient was.

He gave me that apologetic face, the one with the sad eyes, those beyond-appealing dimples, the face that makes him look like he ought to be forgiven anything. So, I forgave him. It wasn't until I realized he and Dr. Grant helped women who needed treatment that would likely end their pregnancies that I became aware of just how important Luke's job was. These women were alone in a society that told them what they were doing was the ultimate wrong. They had no one to turn to, except Dr. Grant and Luke. Often not their husbands or family members. So, Luke would often take their calls, chat with them, help them. And on occasion, he would ferry medications to them — things they couldn't go to a pharmacy to get, things Dr. Grant had put together himself in his lab. On rare occasions, Luke would accompany a woman who wanted to defect to Peoria. Any FoSS citizen can renounce his or her citizenship and move to Peoria, with two exceptions: a person who has been marked but not yet donated and a person who is pregnant. In both cases, you had to wait to leave FoSS. The marked person had to make their donation first. And the pregnant woman had to give birth to the child first. FoSS found it acceptable to allow a mother to leave with her new child, but not until it was safely outside the womb and protected from Peoria's "pagan laws."

Once in Peoria, a woman is welcome to stay at the Grant House before moving on. He's only done it twice, but it is enough that Luke knows the ropes and wasn't afraid to accompany me there when I decided to flee.

Dr. Grant and Luke always worked so well together. It is odd he wouldn't call Luke back. "Is it very important, the reason you need to talk to Dr. Grant?"

There is a second of hesitation, then, "Not really." Luke shifts a bit in his seat, jostling me. "I've just gotten used to him returning my calls. With him and me keeping our distance so the connection isn't made to you, it's probably for the best, him not calling me." He is using his reassuring voice, yet his comments don't reassure me.

Luke wraps his arms around me, gives me a gentle squeeze, then kisses my ear. "So, how are you? I heard they closed on your case today, and the jury will start deliberating tomorrow. Does Albert have any inkling which way they might go?"

I shake my head, and because I am nestled in Luke's arm, end up rubbing against his chest. "No," I whisper. "He said it's out of our hands now. I think he did a pretty good job with what he had. The question really is whether they want to give me another shot, me and Peanut."

"Peanut?"

A little giggle slips out. I guess it is a silly name. "Yeah, I've started calling the baby Peanut."

A moment of silence, then he lets go of me and backs away slightly. "Wait," he says, perturbed. "You named the baby without me?"

"No," I counter quickly. I hadn't expected that reaction. I try to recover, grabbing hold of one of the hands he'd moved away. "No, of course not. This is just the in-utero name. We'll pick an outside world name together, once we know if it's a boy or a girl. I just think Peanut goes either way and is nice. But, if you don't like Peanut, we can pick something else for in-utero."

More silence from him, then finally a chuckle, as he resumes his earlier position, wrapping his arms back around me. "Peanut's nice," he says. "For in-utero, at least." He hesitates. "Unless you like Ingo?"

I scrunch up my face, glad the darkness hides my expression. Ingo! Is that a boy's or a girl's name? Either way, it is sooooo not right for Peanut. Hopefully he's joking. "Umm, I think I like Peanut," is all I say. Ingo? Seriously? He has to be joking.

He rubs my tummy, and I am so glad Luke is here with me. The closeness we are sharing now suddenly gives way to the terror that it will be gone tomorrow if the jury deems me a sociopath. "Luke, what do the people on the outside say about me, about the trial?"

With a shove-it-under-the-rug tone, he says, "I don't know, Kelsey. It doesn't matter. Don't worry about what other people think."

I take his hand off my belly and tuck it into my own. "You do know what they're saying, Luke! You go out there every day. You have to hear something about it. We promised no more secrets. Tell me," I say. Softly, I add, "Please."

He sighs, then speaks in a voice so low I can barely hear him. "I don't want to say, Kelsey, because what they think about you is my fault."

I am taken aback. I don't understand. "What are they thinking? And how can it be your fault?"

He continues in the whisper. "Your father didn't talk about me, and you didn't testify because you couldn't talk about me, and now they think you're promiscuous and probably faking the illness."

The fact that people think I am a whore is not great by any means, but I find it more disturbing that Luke is blaming himself for it. "It's not your fault, Luke," I tell him. "I'd gladly let everyone think I'd single-handedly brought back HIV if it meant you could stay in here with me at night. I couldn't be in here without you, so I don't care what they think."

He gives me a soft kiss on the top of my head. I squeeze his hand. "It's alright, Luke. We knew it would be an uphill battle," I say. "Besides, we've got your backup plan, right? Even if they convict, we've got an alternative."

"Yeah," he says with an utter lack of enthusiasm.

"Don't get down, Luke. I know it's tough to keep your spirits up when something doesn't go our way, but we have to. And I know your plan will work. We just have to get to Dr. Grant's lab, and then you can break me out. The sentence won't matter?"

I smile and rub my thumb in gentle circular motions on his hand, hoping to restore his confidence. I don't want him to feel so down. I want him to have a positive outlook. It is the only thing that is keeping me sane in here, knowing that Luke and my father have a backup plan. That even in the face of the worst, it will be OK.

"Kelsey," he says softly. "You should probably get some sleep — you and Peanut."

He starts to gently ease himself away, yet it feels abrupt and ominous. It worries me. "Are you getting up because you want me to get some sleep or because you're worried about the backup plan and you don't want to tell me?"

Luke stops moving, and for a few seconds, we are both completely still as the question hangs in the air. Finally, he says, "I'm not really worried, but, understandably, I have anxiety as things get closer, Kelsey. It's not for you to worry about, OK?"

"'K," I manage to say, though it isn't. I am the one who will be spending time in a long-term facility if things go wrong. But, they do have a plan, I tell myself. Luke, my Dad, and Dr. Grant: they have a plan.

Then a horrible thought occurs, and I pull away from Luke. "You don't think Dr. Grant is backing out on us, do you? You don't think that's why he won't return your call?"

More silence, as if all life has been sucked out of this tiny cell. As if it is truly a vacuum, not just pitch black due to the absence of light, but pitch black due to the absence of everything. "Kelsey," he says after too much time has passed. "You worry too much. Dr. Grant does what he does because of your mother. He would never let you down."

The words come out forcefully, yet something in his tone makes me doubt them. And why is he so desperate to talk to Dr. Grant if he isn't worried? "He took that money, that grant money from the governor."

"Of course he did. That made it look like he was cooperating with authorities," Luke retorts. "His testimony was fine in the end, wasn't it?"

Luke's words make sense, but something about them, about the way he says them, rings hollow, as if he doesn't really believe it, but hopes I will. Seeking to cut to the heart of the matter, I ask plainly: "Are you sure we can trust Dr. Grant?"

He finds my hand again rubs it lightly. "It doesn't matter if I'm sure or not, or if Dr. Grant is on your side or isn't. What I am sure of is that you won't go into a long-term facility, and they won't take Peanut from us," he says. "I promise."

He isn't sure of Dr. Grant, but he is promising the impossible: that I will somehow escape, no matter what. "You can't promise that, Luke," I say weakly.

"Yes I can. I've never broken a promise to you, and I promise you I will get you outta here."

Those words have Luke's confidence, but for the first time, I am not sure I believe him.

* * *

Luke can tell I am unnerved by the Dr. Grant situation, even though he insists I shouldn't be. He decides to live dangerously for much of the night, holding me as I drift in and out of sleep and promising me that I won't die in a holding facility, stripped of my child and then my organs. By the time morning comes, I am hoping he is right, hoping I am not foolish to believe.

Right before he leaves, he whispers to me: "I'll be back tonight. Promise. And no matter what else happens, I'm going to get you and Peanut outta here."

32. WAITING

After Luke leaves, there is nothing to do but wait. There are no meetings with Albert or my father. There is nothing to discuss until the jury comes back.

So, I am alone, and it feels like a slow form of torture. Luke was right. The short-term unit of the holding facility can drive you as mad as the long-term. The white walls, the lack of any movable objects, not even a piece of paper, is driving me mad. I want to pick something up, to hold something, yet there is nothing. Not a pencil, or a blanket, a piece of paper, a magazine, a yoyo. Nothing.

I would play with my hair, but, of course they have taken that, too. My God, this place is awful. Staring at four white walls is insanity. I wish I'd received television or reading privileges. That would at least help pass the time. Instead, I sit alone with my thoughts. And my thoughts are all about my fate. Will I be sentenced here permanently? Will my womb be ripped from my abdomen? Will I be gutted of all usable organs?

Being alone with my thoughts is so not working. I need to figure out how to center myself, to think of better things. Finally, I decide to think of Luke. To imagine what life will be like if I get out of here. Luke and I in Peoria. Happy, together, with four kidneys between us. Six kidneys, once peanut is born.

There is a knock at the door. I look up. Saying "come in" would be the appropriate thing to do in modern society. The polite thing to do. But this place is far from modern society, or anything polite. The person — whoever it is — will enter whether I consent or not.

I sit silently on my block, staring at the door, waiting for my father or Albert to enter. The door opens a moment later.

I grin as wide as the moon. "Susan," I say, leaping from my bed block and barreling toward her, as she rolls herself into the room. I kneel in front of her wheelchair, lean in and hug her. She kisses my cheek, then rakes her hand across my fuzzy head.

"Nice look," she says.

"Yeah, I did it just so I could say 'I'm peachy' when people ask how I'm doing."

She laughs, then coughs, then laughs again. "That was a really bad joke."

"I know. Only my best friend would laugh at such an awful joke." I beam at her, elated she has come to see me. I take a step back get a good look at her.

She seems weaker than I remember. Her red hair is darker, more the color of dried leaves than a flaming inferno. There are circles under her eyes, and her complexion is pale and wan. I wish she were her old self, that this hadn't happened to her. Everyone else's life was put before Susan's. Now she is like this, a shadow of her former self. The government that commanded she put life first said hers didn't matter. It only cared if she were going to die, not if her quality of life were poor.

I feel the anger rising in me, still, after more than a year, and determine I must let it pass. Susan doesn't want me angry. She's moved on.

"So," I say conversationally, "What brings you here, today?"

She raises an eyebrow and gives me a cat-ate-the-canary grin. "Didn't you know? Holding Facilities are like the new malls. Everyone just pops right in to visit an inmate, see what organs are available, pick one up."

I chuckle. "Now, who's making bad jokes?"

She gives her trademark tooth-filled smile. I respond in kind.

Part of me doesn't even care why she is here. I have missed this, this thing we have, this easygoing wonderful place we go to when we're together. I am glad to have it back, even in here. Yet, the other part of me wishes she had not come. This is no place for her.

The room is quiet, neither of us quite knowing what to say to each other in a place like this, a place where neither of us belongs, a place neither of us wants to be. Finally, Susan clears her throat, and our eyes meet.

"I have a question," she says. "And I want you to be honest with me."

What an odd request. I am always honest with Susan. No, not about how I feel about what had happened to her. That is not something I can really be honest with her about, and not make her feel bad. I think she knows I put on a front for her. If you put her life on the line and asked, "how does Kelsey feel?" she could tell you my true sentiments. This is one subject we negotiated a comfortable lie on. But, in other things, in the important things, I am always honest with Susan. I agree to be truthful, not sure what she could possibly want to ask me about.

"What were the chances of your survival when you jumped in the lake to save me?"

I am stark still, frozen momentarily by the question. I hadn't expected it, but I know where she is headed. I used to wonder if she'd realized what I'd done that day. In the end, I assumed she hadn't, that my story had fooled her just like it had my father, the camp director, and everyone else.

"The chances for an average swimmer to survive were 87 percent. Well within the acceptable range."

She sighs, then says, "I asked you to be honest with me."

So, she is looking for the answer I don't want to give. I promised honesty, so I have to 'fess up. "I was a below average swimmer, and based on the results of the swimming test I'd taken two days earlier, my chances were 56 percent."

"Did you know that at the time?"

I shrug, look down at the endless white I'm standing upon. "I don't know. Maybe the thought ran through my head, but I knew I could hit the average swimmer's speed. So, I went with that."

Her face remains expressionless. I still have no inkling why she brought this up today, of all days. "Why do you ask, Susan? After all these years, it doesn't matter. What matters is that you're alive and I'm alive. The odds on that day aren't important."

A single tear begins rolling down her cheek. If I had a tissue or a handkerchief — but I don't in this stupid goddamn room — I would give it to her. Instead, she reaches a hand up and wipes the tear away. "I just always wanted to know if you made a mistake when you jumped in, or if you made a choice."

A mistake or a choice. I made a choice. Saving someone's life should always be a choice. And I would always choose to save Susan.

"I made a choice. The right one, Susan," I tell her. Exasperated with why this should matter, I ask, "How long have you wondered this?"

"Since my leg cramped and I couldn't swim anymore"

Shock runs through me as I realize she'd known even that day. "While you were in the water?" I ask, still a little stunned.

She nods. "I thought my drowning was a foregone conclusions. I was sure you wouldn't come in, that you knew your survival likelihood was only 56 percent. That you would hit the alarm, and I would drown as you watched and waited for help that would arrive too late."

She looks up and smiles at me. "I've never been so happy as when I saw you jump into that water. I thought there was a possibility that I might survive. That's why I kept trying to stay afloat. Before then, I was debating just letting it happen, just sinking. I didn't think I had that much more to give. I'd been at my limit when the cramp hit. It was supposed to be my final lap, and then I was going to collapse on the pier with you."

I take Susan's hand. It is warm. "I'm glad you kept your head above water," I say, meeting her familiar green eyes.

"Me too."

I am glad Susan has come, but wish she hadn't brought up Camp Picklewick. It is a reminder that even then, even as a child, I had shirked my duties to the Life First mantra. Even then, I hadn't done what society deemed right. "You're alive and I'm alive, so, let's not think about it anymore, Susan. It's in the past."

She shakes her head. "Why did you do it?"

Now I am confused. The answer to that is quite obvious. "Because you were going to die if I didn't"

"But, you could have died, too," she retorts. "Your chances of surviving the kidney transplant were better than your odds of surviving when you saved me. Why did you do it, despite the odds?"

"Because you were going to die," I repeat. "Because you were my best friend, and I didn't want to lose you. The odds were good enough. Maybe not for the survival statistics teacher, or for that poor old balding camp director or my dad, but they were good enough for me. And it worked out. So, we don't worry about it."

Susan composes herself, wiping away another tear. "Well, I just wanted to say thank you. I always thought you knew the odds, that you'd risked it all, even though you shouldn't have." She pauses, sincerity brimming in her countenance, says, "I never really thanked you for going above and beyond."

I feel awkward getting Susan's thanks for something that happened a decade ago. Something she already thanked me for. "You're welcome. I'd do it again, and I think you'd do the same for me."

She nods, and we sit there staring at each other for a moment. Then, she looks at the door. "Listen, I should go," she says, wheeling her chair backwards, then angling it to turn around.

"You just got here," I protest.

"I know, but I have a few other things to do. I'm going to come back, OK?"

"OK," I say. She wheels herself to the door and knocks. A guard appears and then she is gone.

33. BETRAYED

I am once again alone with my thoughts, which constantly veer toward what will happen if I am stuck here. If Luke can't break me out. With great effort, I push those thoughts out of my mind, and decide to focus on something else: my father.

And I see a silver lining. My conviction might actually help my father. Not emotionally, but politically. Perhaps he will get a boost in the polls if he denounces me for the traitor I am and tells the world I am getting what I deserve.

My attempted escape has caused so much trouble for him politically, maybe a conviction will assist him in getting some of his career back. It had been such an uphill battle for him to get where he was before I messed everything up. My father had so many strikes against him, yet he'd overcome them all. No one seems to care that he is a widower who hasn't remarried, that he only deigned to bear one child for society, not three to five, as is common. It all seemed to fit him, that it was OK for him to be different. But, in a good way. Since my attempted escape, everyone is re-examining everything about him, and his poll numbers are plummeting.

My father would never tell me such things, but when I asked Albert, he told me. I have always appreciated Uncle Albert's candor, and never more than in here.

I stand and stretch. I want to clear my mind, so I pace the cell, back and forth. I make 243 trips across the room and back again. Focusing on other things, the simple task of counting my trips, allows me to stop thinking of the things that worry me.

I am six steps into trip 244 when the door to my cell glides open. Uncle Albert enters. He is pale and looks as if he needs a few good nights of sleep.

"Jury's back," he says deliberately. He holds my gaze only for a second. In that time, I read his despair.

This is not good. I debate asking, and finally decide I must. I need to steel myself for the verdict. "You think it's bad?"

He doesn't say anything, or move at all. He stands there, some internal debate filling his head. Finally, he looks me in the eye and admits, "Quick verdict is usually bad."

I am standing near Albert at the door, but the sudden weightiness of the situation forces me to stagger backwards and find my seat on the block. I knew this was likely, but had hoped, really hoped, for the best.

I take a few deep breaths, and try to center myself. Being a wreck when they deliver the verdict will serve no purpose.

The guard stationed at the door clears his throat to urge us on. Albert stretches out his hand to me, though he is still a few feet away. "We have to go, Kelsey."

I take a deep breath, stand and reach for his hand. I feel better when my hand is in his, like he can somehow shield me, protect me. But, I know that isn't true. The only people who have the ability to protect me are in the courtroom waiting for me to return. And I have the distinct impression they are going to throw me to the wolves.

The walk to the hearing room is fairly quick. A few corridors, outside on a walkway, another building, then we are there. Uncle Albert is still holding my hand, and it is wet with sweat now. I let go, more so he won't feel uncomfortable than for any desire I have to be free of his reassuring touch. I'm sure I am pale as a sheet. My stomach feels hollow as we enter the room. It is as if I already know that I am walking toward the gallows. I wonder if this is how all long-term inmates feel? Is it like this for them every day? The knowing what will happen, but wondering if this will be the day? No, for them, it has to be worse. Right now, I just suspect. I don't really know anything. I have a bad feeling, a feeling that probably isn't wrong. But, there is still hope, still a chance. Once you've been sentenced to vital organ donation, there is no reprieve.

I sit, and Uncle Albert whispers something in my ear. I am not sure exactly what. The gravity of the situation, combined with my own internal panic, have left me unable to think clearly or comprehend what he is saying. I think he is asking me to remain calm, no matter what. He said that on the walk over. Several times in fact. I wonder if I don't look calm. I wonder if I look as panic-stricken as I feel.

My father comes in and sits in the chair behind me. His hand touches my shoulder and I can tell that he's standing and leaning in towards me. In my ear, he whispers, "No matter what, I love you, and I will get you out of the holding facility."

I smile. He sounds like Luke. How odd is that? How can that be? I pegged them as very different because they didn't get along. But, now as they surround me in my hour of need, I realize they are alike in the ways that count. They both stand by you. They are both loyal. And they both love me immeasurably.

My father's hand slides from my shoulder, and I can only assume he's returned to his seat. The jury members enter the room and take their places. Many don't look at me. The ones who do have contempt in their eyes. This is bad. I look down at the table. I can't face them. The judge enters the room, and Albert whispers, "Stand up, Kelsey." I do. Looking up at the judge clad in a black robe and somber expression makes it all sink in again. I close my eyes. The judge bangs his gavel and we all sit again.

"Do you have a verdict?" the judge asks.

The jury foreman stands. "Yes, your honor."

Judge Dahlberg nods in return, then says, "Please read the verdict."

"We, the jury, find Ms. Kelsey Anne Reed guilty of willfully violating the law of mandatory donation. We find that she was not insane under the law at the time of the violation, and is in fact a sociopath. We recommend the punishment of death through organ donation."

My father is silent, as is Uncle Albert. I, on the other hand, begin sobbing incoherently. The tears stream down my face, hot and salty. I try to stop, to be calm, like Uncle Albert said. But, it isn't happening. I'm going to die, and I don't want to. And no one can protect me from that. My body trembles as the tears continue to flow, and strange, guttural wails emerge from somewhere deep within. I feel someone, perhaps Uncle Albert, put an arm around me and pull me close. It is Albert; he is patting my shoulder and saying things in my ear. Things I can't make out because he is speaking softly and my sobbing is too loud. The judge bangs his gavel, thanks the jury and orders a short recess so I can compose myself.

* * *

Uncle Albert, my father and I adjourn to a private room near the hearing room. Once inside, I calm down after a few minutes, so Albert can explain what will happen next. While I was neither emotionally nor mentally prepared for the verdict, Uncle Albert and my father are legally prepared.

They'd expected a guilty verdict and plan to appeal. The process will take no more than four weeks, and if I am granted a new trial, it will have to occur at the end of an empanelled jury's time, Albert says. They feel it is fairest to squeeze in appeal trials at the end of a session.

Albert isn't sure that a new trial, if we luck out and get one, will be that successful. But, he does think the appeal has a better chance in the higher court. If nothing else, the appeal will buy us more time. "Time for your friend to solidify his plan." Albert says of Luke. Nothing explicit. Vague and simple, but enough to pull me from my stupor.

I feel more alert now. I tune in, perking up to hear better. "The good news is Dr. Grant's new assistant signed off on a treatment procedure for you," Albert tells me.

"And this is good news, how?" I ask. I feel like going glassy-eyed again. A plan to have my uterus removed is not a good thing.

Albert pulls out a document and hands it to me. I look at the words on the paper, but don't read them. "It explains that due to your genetic predisposition to a high-risk pregnancy, the safest course of action for the baby is to move you to Dr. Grant's facility to perform the procedure. As you know, his facility is not secure, so a guard would be sent with you. It also recommends moving you in the next few days so he can monitor the pregnancy, but waiting until you're 16 weeks to do the procedure. The 16-week mark is healthiest for the baby."

I say nothing. It is with mixed emotions that I let this information settle on my brain. Moving to Dr. Grant's facility takes me away from the holding facility. But it also means I will be closer to a misunderstanding, confusion or some situation in which Dr. Grant will actually perform the procedure on me. A situation in which my womb will be forcibly removed. Albert calls Dr. Grant's recommendation "a saving grace," as such reports often greatly influence the judge, and can't really be objected to by the other side.

I feel helpless as I sit here caught between emotions: despair that I have been sentenced to die to insane hope that Luke or Uncle Albert or my father or an appeals court can save me. I am about to put my head down and cry again, when I notice my father staring guiltily at me, and realize I can't do that.

Instead, I try to look optimistic for his sake. I feel increasingly worse for him, as he is standing by me, when so many others abandon their accused family member. Most run for the hills, and hope they will not be tarnished by the stink of the traitor. Yet, here is my father, sitting in this room with me, his career falling apart because of what I did and not holding it all against me. Not a single drop of ill will.

My father has lost my mother already, and now he is going to lose me, too.

* * *

We are adjourned for an hour. We can delay sentencing until tomorrow, but Albert wants to move forward with it, since we have Dr. Grant's treatment plan on our side. With any luck, I can be transferred to his facility in the morning.

Things start off fine. Bickers goes through his litany of reasons why I am a menace to society and should go long-term immediately with the baby taken. Uncle Albert just listens. When it is his turn, he has two things to discuss with the judge: my appeal and Dr. Grant's report.

When Albert asks to submit the report to the court, Bickers stands and objects. All eyes turn to him. Albert is about to speak when the judge clears his throat and turns to the prosecutor.

"This isn't really something you can object to, Mr. Bickers," the judge says, scowling.

Bickers bobs his head in agreement; still, he opens his mouth to speak, with that "but" expression on his face. "Under normal circumstances, that's correct, your Honor. However, I have learned that this report was falsified."

More silence. Not that there was a lot of talk before, but there was shifting in seats and rustling of clothing. Now, there are no sounds. It is as if everyone has stopped, collectively holding their breaths, waiting for more.

Finally, the judge says venomously, "Are you suggesting Albert Harrell falsified this report?"

Bickers eyes widen as he realizes his mistake. He takes a step back, as if wanting to both literally and figuratively backtrack. "Your Honor, forgive me," he says, sounding like the weasel he is. "Falsified is the wrong word. The report is no longer accurate. Dr. Grant has changed his mind."

"What?" I hadn't meant for the word to leave my mouth.

Albert puts his hand on my shoulder, a subtle reminder for me to remain quiet. Bickers draws up the corners of his mouth into a dastardly smile, flashes it at me briefly, then turns back to the judge with a more deferential, though no less triumphant, expression. "Dr. Grant called me an hour ago saying new research indicated his recommendations are no longer accurate."

Albert gently squeezes my shoulder in a move to calm me. In the corner of my eye, I see my father stand and walk toward the exit. He will find out what is going on.

"Your Honor," Albert says respectfully, but with conviction. "This is the first I've heard of this." He turns to Bickers. "If Dr. Grant made this call to you, did he also send you an affidavit?"

Bickers shakes his head. "I'm afraid there wasn't time," Bickers is saying, when a commotion outside the room causes him to stop abruptly.

From the hallway, I hear my father's voice shout: "You sick, charlatan bastard. How could you? How could you kill her mother and now doom her to this?"

All eyes turn to the courtroom doors. A moment later, those doors swing open, and in walks Dr. Grant, looking grim. He looks directly at Bickers and the judge, but avoids eye contact with Albert or me.

My stomach wobbles and lurches. I think I might vomit.

"Dr. Grant came to testify, rather than providing an affidavit," Bickers says as Dr. Grant stands alone in the now-open hearing room doorway. I watch in silence as Dr. Grant takes the stand and swears again to tell the truth and nothing but.

Bickers doesn't bother reminding the judge who Dr. Grant is or of his qualifications. He simply launches into questions.

"Dr. Grant, do you recognize this report?" he asks, holding out a few sheets of stapled paper.

Dr. Grant looks at it, then assents. "Yes. It's the treatment recommendation my assistant sent to you and Judge Harrell."

"What does it say?"

"It's based on my previous research and recommends we wait until week 16 of Ms. Reed's pregnancy to remove her baby."

Bickers gives a quizzical look. "But you say this is now incorrect?"

Dr. Grant nods, looking briefly at Bickers, then his hands, but never gazing in my direction.

"Could you speak your answer for the court record," Bickers asks.

"Yes, it's now incorrect." Dr. Grant says loudly.

"How?"

"Well, we've been running human trials in Peoria for the last year," the doctor says, looking to the judge, and for the first time smiling. "We've had success removing a baby as young as six weeks. The woman learned she had pancreatic cancer that needed to be treated aggressively and quickly, to give her any chance of long-term survival. So, we removed the baby. This was eight months ago. The woman died four months ago, but the baby survived. We delivered him two weeks ago without incident. It was our first human success taking a baby so early. We also have had good success with the four babies we removed following week 16."

"This procedure would be safe for Ms. Reed and her baby?"

Dr. Grant doesn't hesitate. "I believe it would be safe. And more importantly, FoSS believes it would be safe. As you know, I have not been licensed to do this procedure in FoSS, except provisionally on inmates like Ms. Reed. However, I received approval this morning from the Medical Board to use the procedure in high-risk FoSS citizens at least 16 weeks along, as well as approval to teach the procedure to other obstetricians and certify them to perform it. Also, I was given provisional approval to use the procedure on non-FoSS citizens and FoSS holding facility inmates with fetuses as young as six weeks gestational age."

I let out a small gasp, and he looks at me for just a moment, probably less than a tenth of a second. But in that time, when our eyes lock, I see a familiar look. It was there the day he told me the details of my mother's death: guilt.

Then, as if it hadn't happened, Dr. Grant focuses on Bickers again.

Bickers, oblivious to our exchange, goes on with his questioning.

"So this new approval invalidates your previous report?"

"Yes. We could take the infant as early as tomorrow under the provisional approval I've been granted."

Tomorrow. That is insane. He can't take my baby tomorrow. I am not far enough along. I grab the sleeve of Albert's suit jacket and tug. He has to do something. He has to stop this.

Albert doesn't say anything, but he does find my hand and squeeze it gently. Bickers is still up there with Dr. Grant, asking him questions about the procedure, and where it will be done.

Finally, Bickers ends with a request for the judge. "Your Honor, I request that the court order the procedure performed on Ms. Reed tomorrow."

"I object," Albert finally says. If he hadn't, I would have leapt from my seat and done it.

The judge looks at Albert, motioning him to continue. Albert clears his throat. "Judge Dahlberg, first of all, Ms. Reed is not far enough along for this procedure. At present, she's only four weeks. So, tomorrow is too soon. It's not within the confines of Dr. Grant's provisional approval, even."

Dr. Grant looks at Albert, and while I sit next to Albert, he manages to not look at me. He seems to be avoiding any connection to me. I am so disgusted and angry, I can't think straight.

The judge looks at Bickers, then Dr. Grant.

"Well, your Honor," Dr. Grant says. "The baby's actual age is probably 4 weeks. We however, base the procedure on gestational age, which is calculated based on the date of the last menstrual cycle. That typically adds two weeks. And if I've checked the records correctly, Ms. Reed's last menstrual cycle was six weeks ago, making the baby's gestational age six weeks."

I close my eyes. This isn't happening, I tell myself. Bad dream. This has to be a bad, bad dream. I open my eyes. Everything is as it was when I closed them. This is not a bad dream. It is not something I will awaken from scared, but glad it was just a dream.

"Your Honor," Albert says gently. "Even if Dr. Grant is correct, my client is still due an appeal, so mounting a procedure for tomorrow would violate her appeal rights. If the verdict were overturned, the court would have wrongly ordered this procedure. The court can't undo the removal of her uterus."

The judge looks to be weighing this in his mind. I hope he will put off the procedure. Put it off long enough for Luke to think of a new plan, some way to escape without the aid of Dr. Grant, who has clearly betrayed me. Then Bickers, in his snake-oil salesman voice, chimes in again.

"Your Honor, I'm not sure the appeal matters for the purposes of this procedure. If Ms. Reed is found to be suffering from pregnancy psychosis, sterilization is still recommended. It's a psychiatric disorder that threatens the life of another that could be transmitted to the offspring. And if she is found, as this panel found her, to be a depraved sociopath, sterilization would be mandated."

Albert glares at Bickers, then turns to the judge, looking humble. "Your Honor, Mr. Bickers is generalizing. While he's correct that sterilization is often recommended for psychiatric disorders that threaten others and can be passed on genetically, it is not a requirement. There are exceptions made. Therefore, nothing should happen until the appeal is finished. At most that would take two months, and in that time, the baby would grow more and be stronger and healthier for the procedure. I don't believe there is any harm in that."

Bickers appears prepared for this. He doesn't miss a beat when he turns to the judge and responds. "Except, your honor, that Ms. Reed is possibly suffering from pregnancy psychosis. If that is in fact the case, then she might try to hurt the baby during the delay."

"That's inane," interrupts Albert. "You just convinced a jury she doesn't have pregnancy psychosis. You can't argue she does now in your attempt to carve her up."

Bickers narrows his pointy eyes and retorts. "Your Honor, the only issue up for appeal would be whether Ms. Reed has pregnancy psychosis. Presuming the appeal finds she does, then she would be at risk of harming her baby. While the holding facility is a generally safe place, we can't stop Ms. Reed from failing to eat or finding some other way to harm her baby. And since her LMS is gone and cannot be safely replaced at this time, I think it would be in the baby's best interest to be removed."

The judge looks at Bickers, then Albert, weighing what they've said.

"Your Honor," Albert says, giving one last attempt. He sounds humble, pleading. "It is well within your power to sentence Ms. Reed to this procedure. I just ask that you let the natural appeals process work out and not rush it. This procedure isn't even approved for

FoSS citizens! Please consider that in your decision."

The judge orders a 15-minute recess. During the break, Dr. Grant leaves the room, and my father returns and sits at the table with Albert and me. "What happened out there?" I whisper. He looks at me, then around the hearing room, with Bickers staring at us from his table. My father looks for a moment like he will answer, but then waves me off. "We can't talk here."

Albert chimes in that it is just as well, as there is nothing we can do right now but wait for the judge. I've always thought the FoSS system of swift justice was great. That is, until sitting here facing it. This is too swift. I knew this could be coming, but there was always that hope of escape. To use the worst possibility — Dr. Grant's lab — as our platform to escape. But, with Dr. Grant betraying us, his lab is looking like the worst place for me to go.

I'm sorry, Peanut, I think, touching my belly.

The remainder of the break is spent in the courtroom. Albert offers to get the guard to take me to the public restroom, so I can walk around a bit. While the idea of walking around is slightly appealing, I am not in the mood for media. I want to keep a low profile, for the sake of my father. Reporters roam the hallways, and I have been fortunate to use the restrooms for inmates in a nonpublic side corridor, so as to avoid them.

"Kelsey," my dad whispers in my ear. I notice now that the judge is returning to his seat on the elevated podium. "No matter what happens, remember I love you and we'll figure something out."

I nod, though I don't look at my father. I can't quite muster up enough strength to put on a brave face and pretend his words were helpful.

The judge bangs his gavel, then turns his attention to me. "Kelsey Anne Reed, please stand."

34. SENTENCE

Judge Dahlberg fixes his eyes on me and I know he is going to let them do it. There is nothing but contempt in his eyes. "Ms. Reed, before I announce my decision, do you have anything to say?"

Albert looks at me with a reminder warning. A reminder that I am only to say that I love my baby. And that is it. It will remind the judge I am a mother and will not address the issue of whether or not I was in my right mind when I tried to flee.

I rub my hands along my skirt. I hope it looks like I am smoothing it, but it is really a gesture borne of anxiety. "Your Honor," I say, trying to speak loud enough that he will hear me across the room, but without the shakiness I feel inside bleeding into my voice when I speak. "I want you to know that I love my baby, and want him or her to have a good life. I would ask that you don't risk him or her by sentencing me to this procedure prematurely."

The judge motions that he's heard me. "Ms. Reed, your actions have shown an utter lack of consideration for your fellow man. The panel has found you guilty of violating your duty to donate because you are a sociopath. As such, I am sentencing you to a life sentence in the long-term holding facility and sterilization. This sterilization may be carried out as early as tomorrow at 2 p.m."

He turns, almost apologetically, to Albert. "You may seek an emergency appeal of this decision, if you would like. I'm sure the appeals court would hear you before 2 p.m."

He is about to bang his gavel, when I yell, "Wait!"

He looks at me disapprovingly. "Your time for speaking is over, Ms. Reed."

He bangs the gavel, yet I continue. "When my baby is born," I say. The judge stops banging and stares at me, shocked by my defiance. Or perhaps he is shocked that I have my child's welfare on my mind. Either way, curiosity overrules his better judgment and he motions for me to continue.

"When my baby is born," I repeat. "I want him or her to be loved and cared for in a safe, happy environment. Somewhere away from here, away from a place where they force you to donate organs and murder you if you don't. Somewhere where doctors don't steal children from their mothers' wombs. Someplace where life involves choice, not mandates. Send him or her somewhere where his or her life will be put first."

I'm not sure if I would have said more or not, but the judge begins banging his gavel again, then Alfred grips my arm tightly, and mutters, "Kelsey, stop now."

The judge orders me returned to my cell. Albert reluctantly interrupts, asking that we be allowed a minute in an adjoining attorney room to discuss my emergency appeal. The judge grants the request, clearly out of courtesy to Albert. If it had been my request, I'm not sure I would have gotten beyond, "Your Honor."

We enter the private room for attorneys and their clients. It is a small room with a gray square table in the center, and three chairs tucked underneath it. In the far corner is a lone chair, and I decide to go there and sit. Albert sets his briefcase on the table. He seems to briefly consider pulling out the chair tucked underneath and sitting. Instead, Albert grips the back of the seat tightly, his knuckles going white, then lets loose on me. "What were you thinking?" he yells. I am stunned. Albert never yells.

I don't know what I'd been thinking. Part of me snapped. "That it doesn't matter," I say, trying not to feel consumed with anger. "Those people are going to send me up the river no matter what. So, it doesn't matter what I say. And if it doesn't matter, I might as well say what I'm thinking."

Albert sighs, lifts his hand to his forehead wearily, and rubs for a moment. Putting his hand down, he inhales, exhales slowly, then speaks. "Kelsey, you're right that those people are going to do whatever they want to do, but you're wrong about what you say not mattering. It matters in our appeal, and it matters to your father."

As if on cue, the door opens, my father scuttles in, and shuts it behind him. "I'm sorry. I just needed a minute to make a call," he says, striding toward me. When he gets to the seat against the wall I am perched in, he reaches for my hand. "Sweetheart, you shouldn't have said that."

He looks like my saying it has somehow wounded him. I turn to Albert. "Could we get a minute alone?"

Albert doesn't seem to mind my abruptness. Without a word, and looking relieved, he exits the room.

My father stares a moment at the closed door, then at me, worry lines crowding his eyes. "What is the matter, Kelsey?"

I shake my head. "Nothing's wrong," I start, then stop myself as I realize how foolish that actually sounds given the circumstances. "Nothing beyond what's going on today, I mean."

A sigh escapes his lips, then he puts on his "keep your chin up" face. I've seen that one on the campaign trail. It is quite convincing, usually. "We've got the emergency appeal. Just keep that in mind."

I don't give a damn about the emergency appeal. It isn't going to work. Nothing will work. He has to stop helping me and help himself, now. "Tomorrow, I want you to publicly denounce me."

He stops breathing. His face is still, and he seems frozen in time. "What?" he breathes out.

"Denounce me. With that little speech today, I've made myself the perfect villain. Distance yourself from me and see if you can salvage something of your career."

He doesn't speak. It is an odd way to see my father; he always seems so utterly composed, as if nothing fazes him. Yet, now, he appears truly frazzled. I'm sure his advisers suggested cutting me loose immediately. Only Dad was clearly too stubborn to do so. Well, now I've given him ample reason. The silliness of the pregnancy psychosis can be done away with. I am a bad person for sure, or at least I will be when they report about me on the news. So, he can do what so many others whose family members end up in holding facilities do: say good bye and shun me.

He sits on the edge of the table, then put his head in his hands. "I'm so sorry, Kelsey," he says, his voice breaking.

"Sorry?" He isn't the one in a holding facility because he refused to give up his kidney. He hasn't ruined his loved one's career. "Dad, you have nothing to be sorry for."

He shakes his head in refute. "I do, Kelsey." He sighs. "I saw the video on the chip. I saw what she said to you. I saw the condition she was in."

I gasp. "You said it was corrupt."

"I just said that because I wasn't ready to talk about it. I didn't want to acknowledge the role I'd played in it." He shakes his head in anguish. "Your mother shouldn't have died. I should have demanded they do something. Not just wait and see. I didn't stand by her against a system that didn't have her best interest at heart. I didn't listen to her, really listen, when she called and asked for my help. And she died because of it. I didn't listen to you either. I could tell you didn't want to do this. Instead of listening, I ignored all the signs and just kept trying to reassure you it would be alright. That was the wrong choice to make. When you ran, when you were caught, I vowed that I would stand by you, and support you in the way I had failed to do for her."

"Oh, Daddy," I breathe out, as I go to him and pat him gently on the back. He lifts his head from his hands and looks at me. "Daddy, you have been here for me. More here for me than anyone could ever have expected. I've never felt alone. I will be eternally grateful for you hiring that guard."

He takes my hands in his. "You're a brave girl, Kelsey. Don't despair in here. Albert and I won't give up. I'm going to do better for you than I did for your mother."

With that, he stands, briefly hugs me, and walks toward the door. As he grabs the door handle, he turns back. "I'll come by first thing in the morning."

35. MURPHY'S LAW

Having been returned to my cell, I am now crawling the walls. All I can do is walk back and forth across the room and think about why things have gone to hell: Dr. Stephen Grant.

He isn't on my side anymore. For some reason, he has forsaken me. Part of me wonders if he's ever really been on my side. How could someone who had really been on my side take my baby and my womb?

I stop pacing for a moment and take a deep breath. Clean, cool air in; bad, negative thoughts out, I tell myself. Negative thinking never helps. It is just hard not to have these thoughts, after today's hearing.

I want Luke to come. I need him to come. He can help me get rid of some of my anxiety, maybe. He can help calm me. Or, if not, at least help me understand what is going on. Help me understand why Dr. Grant betrayed me.

I glance up at the clock and realize the day guard's shift is almost over. I am so glad my father was able to get rid of the pig-faced guard who'd so enjoyed taunting me. Today's day guard stood outside, and said to knock if I need him. What I need is for him to go, to get outta here when his shift is over, so I can talk to Luke.

I need to find out if Luke has another plan. Something that could be executed before I am transferred to Dr. Grant's lab. Maybe he even knows more about the appeal. Maybe it is a sure thing. Bribery and political corruption are generally considered a thing of the past, but if Michael Nimmick can make such efforts to destroy me, perhaps my father has a few tricks up his sleeve to get the appeals board to delay things.

In the courtroom, I felt bravado, a nothing-to-lose haze, but as I stand here in my cell, it is very clear how much there is to lose. I don't want Peanut taken away from me. And if he or she is taken away, I need to know that Luke will find a way to claim him or her.

I look at the clock on the wall again. Two minutes until 8 o'clock. Luke will be here in just two minutes, maybe he is even telling the other guy to take a hike right now.

I decide to lie down facing the wall, my head tucked down so the guard in the monitor room won't see me speak to Luke when he comes in.

Closing my eyes, I try to think good thoughts, happy thoughts, insane thoughts about the appeal working out, and Luke figuring out a way to get us safely to Peoria. Finally, I hear the door open, the dull thud of the shoes on the rubber, then the door shut. I start to turn and tell Luke how glad I am he is back, how I've been impatient waiting for 8 o'clock to roll around.

But the chuckle stops me. It is more of a cackle, really, the kind you associate with black-and-white movies where dastardly villains twirl their moustaches in advance of evil deeds. I've heard that laugh before and hope my memory of when is deceiving me. Then he speaks. "Guess who's back, darlin'?"

I finish turning and see Pig Face standing in the spot where Luke is supposed to be. My face must be ghostly pale, because his smile grows wider as my panic sets in. He likes the look in my eyes. I can tell my fear is giving him pleasure, but I can't shake the fear, nor can I hide it. Where is Luke? He is the reason I haven't lost my mind in this god-awful place. I need him, not this monster.

"Wondering where the usual guy is?" he asks me.

I don't want to give him the satisfaction of answering, of knowing that he has read the look on my face completely, but I also want the answer. I nod.

"Called in sick. So, it's just you and me tonight. And when lights go out, I got a little something special planned," he says, a glint in his eye. Then he lets out another wicked cackle.

I am too stunned to move. Lights go out in two hours. Where is Luke? What happened? Is this Dr. Grant's fault, too? He betrayed me in court, but has he also told authorities about my connection to Luke? Is that why Luke isn't here?

I close my eyes. I want to know what's going on, but I can't focus on that. The more urgent question is: what does Pig Face have planned for me?

This is like Murphy's Law on steroids. What I need is a dose of Luke's Law. Though, that is not going to be forthcoming. So, I will have to come up with Kelsey's Law.

I turn to face the wall. I will go into a full-blown panic if I look at Pig Face. Dr. Grant, who has decided his pledge to help me is inconvenient to his own career, has sent things spiraling down. Neither Luke nor my father, who've been my lifelines during this ordeal, are around to help. I need to figure out some way to cope on my own. And apparently, I only have two hours to do it. Two hours till lights out, and I get to see what Pig Face's idea of "special" is.

* * *

The wall clock says 9:59. I have less than a minute before the room goes dark. My plotting for the last two hours has made me realize one thing: my father wasted his money on that handful of karate lessons I took when I was 11. I can't recall a single useful thing the teacher said about technique or skill. My mind is drawing a blank. Yet, I need to figure out some way to defend myself.

The eyes are a good target; so are the ears and neck. I remember that from a self-defense course I took in college. Crime is rare in the post-pandemic world, but it still happens. Susan, of course, signed us both up for the class. At the time I doubted I'd ever get the chance to use what they taught us.

I still might not. This is a totally different situation from being attacked in an alley. This man is supposed to be here. Thanks to Luke's microphone antics, no one will hear me scream and come to my rescue. And even when I fight back, Pig Face's training should have taught him the best way to subdue me.

Everything we learned about defense said get away and save yourself. The instructors said not to worry about a minor injury, so long as you survive. But, I can't do that. Peanut is in there counting on me to protect him or her. I have to worry about any injury the baby might sustain.

I wonder if Pig Face will care about hurting the baby. He said he's about Life First. But, he doesn't seem to think my life falls under that banner. I wonder if I can appeal to his reason. Just as I finish that thought, the lights go out.

In less than a second, he is right here with me. He must've started toward me before the lights went out, because he has climbed on top of me, like he was standing here, waiting.

He crouches over me, pinning me to the rubber block, and puts his face so close to mine I am assaulted by his warm onion-scented breath. "Aren't you glad I'm back?" he asks.

I am not sure if his question is rhetorical or if there is something I can say to avert whatever plans he has for me tonight.

"You know," he says. "You tried to fuck the system. Well now, sweetie, you're gonna see how it feels when the system fucks you."

I struggle beneath him, but I am pinned. I feel him grab at my pants waist. "Please don't do this," I beg. "You believe in Life First, right?"

"Don't talk," he says. "I don't like it when the girls talk."

Figures. I push on him hard, and he moves slightly. He laughs. "I like it when you're feisty like this."

"Stop it!" I plead, giving another apparently useless shove. "I'm pregnant, for God's sake. This could hurt the baby. Please, don't do this."

He scoffs. "I heard about what happened in court. You don't even know who this baby's father is. You're a dirty whore. But, I won't hold that against you tonight."

I struggle futilely for a moment, then decide to stop, to let him think I am cooperating. It works. He's gotten my pants down to my knees and is pulling his own down, when I ball my free hand into a fist, and lunge my arm, as best I can, from the hip, straight into where I believe his groin is. I make contact with something soft and fleshy, and hear an awful wail as he collapses on top of me.

Not the best plan, though I am glad something from those karate lessons has finally come back to me. I push, and he topples onto the floor. I get up, pull up my pants and head to where I think the door is.

"Fuckin' bitch," I hear him spit from the floor. I am not sure what to do. I am still locked in the cell with him.

"Help," I call out, banging on the cell door. "Can someone help me, please?"

This is stupid. No one is going to hear me. No one is going to help.

I hear rustling from the middle of the room. A zipper zipping up.

Then a beep. The crackle of a guard's radio.

"Monitor room, this is Mr. Lawrence in holding room 211. Please turn on the light."

Suddenly the room is illuminated. I close my eyes reflexively at the sudden brightness. After a moment, I open them and he smiles at me, a truly evil smile. Pig Face — or, perhaps I should call him Mr. Lawrence now that I know his name — is standing in the middle of the room, his belt undone, staring at me lustfully.

He lifts the radio to his mouth again, pressing the button, and a beep emerges. "Please make a note that the inmate became violent at," he pauses, looks at the clock, "10:03. She had to be subdued." He winks at me, then speaks into the radio again. "Now, please turn off the lights for the rest of the night. I'd like a little privacy here."

After a moment of silence, there is a gruff "OK" from the speaker.

He looks right at me, taking in my position, then there is blackness again. As disorienting as this lights-on-lights-off sensory experience is, I have to ignore it. Blinking to adjust my eyes, I run away from where I was just standing, hoping to give myself more time. I know the inevitable is coming. The room is too small for him not to catch me. I've spent enough nights in here with Luke to know that eventually your brain adjusts. Sound becomes as useful as sight in figuring out where someone is.

Even if I am as quiet as I can be, he'll still hear my breathing or the soft thuds of my feet hitting the floor as I walk. It is just a matter of time.

"I usually like to get my workout during," Pig Face says. "But I'm willing to get a little exercise before."

I don't speak, trying to disguise my location for as long as I can, taking shallow breaths I hope he cannot hear.

"You asked me if I believe in Life First," he says, getting closer to me. I can tell from the sound of his voice. I take two soft steps away and bump into the bed block. Using all my self-control, I avoid the instinctual yelp that would normally accompany my stubbed toe.

"I do," he continues. "I just believe in Life First for those who also believe in it. Those who don't believe it. ... Well, they get what they deserve." He is getting closer. "We started out on the wrong foot here tonight, Kelsey. I understand that you're pregnant, and apparently that baby in there means something to you, I think. The way you mentioned it earlier, it makes me think maybe even a monster like you has a soft spot in your wicked soul for that baby."

He is getting closer, so I climb onto the bed and slowly crawl across it, stopping at the opposite end. "I think maybe you and I should make a deal," he says, his voice sounding friendlier, but still deliberate. "You be nice and cooperative here, and I won't accidentally whack you in the abdomen with my club while subduing your violent outburst."

The idea that he would intentionally hurt Peanut stops me in my tracks. I am not sure what to do. I don't know if he is telling the truth about not hurting me if I cooperate, but I believe wholeheartedly that he will hurt my baby if I don't.

I am still in a moment of indecision, when I feel thick, flabby hands grab my waist. "Gotcha," he shouts, triumph in his tone. "And you're right where you need to be. Lie down."

In the absence of a real plan to escape, I do as I am told.

"That's more like it," he says. "Pull your pants down and your underpants, too. All the way to the ankle, but don't take them off. I like it better that way."

Again, I comply. This won't be so bad, I try to convince myself. Not so bad, not so bad, not so bad, I repeat silently in my head. It is better than the alternative, better than him hurting the baby. I can do this. If I just think about something else, it will be OK. I can do this, I tell myself again. Just lie still and let him do it. Luke will understand. And it will be OK in the end. It is just sex. I've had sex before. It won't be so bad. I can do this, I repeat in my head.

He says, "Turn over."

I don't move. I am not sure I can do that.

"Turn over," he says again, impatiently. I hear the swift motion as something heavy slice through the air, then a hard cracking sound. "That's the billy club on the rubber. Imagine what it sounds like crossing the flesh of your abdomen. You know a six-week-old baby is only the size of a lima bean. Just barely tucked into the uterus. Feels any blow its mother does."

I turn over. He orders me onto my knees. The sound of the Billy club echoes in my mind, and I reluctantly move to my knees.

"You like to say FU to the system, don't you, Kelsey? Want to fuck them up the rear, don't you?"

I can't speak. I can't believe this is happening. Part of me wants to bolt, but I can't stop thinking of the reverberation of the billy club against the rubber. I imagine Peanut feeling that. I am frozen with fear and disgust.

He puts his hand on my bare bottom, and rubs. "Nice," he says. "Now, I must warn you, this is gonna hurt. A lot."

No, I can't do this! I feel him edge closer, and I scurry forward, crawling to the edge of my block, then leaping down to the floor and scuttling to the corner. I pull up my pants, put my back to the wall, pull my knees close to my chest and tuck my head, hoping this position will most protect the baby from any blows. Ideally, I would protect my head more, but any position with my head out of harms way seems like it would just expose the baby to injury.

I hear him coming toward me, full of glee. "Doing this the hard way can be fun, too," he sniggers. "At least for me."

That's when the door opens. We both look up, as light from the hallway pours into the room. Pig Face is standing inches from me, red-faced with sweat beading on his forehead. He is as surprised as I am to see Luke, in his guard's uniform, sprinting toward us. In a moment, Luke reaches us and pulls Pig Face away from me and toward the center of the room. Then, Luke raises a fist and before I can even gasp, he's slammed Pig Face so hard with his fist, the guard crumples to the floor. Luke kneels down and begins pounding Pig Face with both hands clenched tightly. I find myself mesmerized by the sight. Normally, I'd look away. Normally I'd tell Luke to stop, but I don't have it in me. Luke raises his fists again and again, meeting flesh or bone. I hear a crack, a gurgling, a squeal of pain.

Finally someone says what should have been said long ago.

"Stop," Susan calls as she wheels her way into the room.

Luke hits Pig Face once more, then stops. I am beyond confused. Luke spits on Pig Face then walks over to me. Kneeling down right in front of me, he wraps his arms around me. "Kelsey, are you alright?"

"Yeah," I say, starting to feel the relief spread through my body. "He hadn't started yet."

Luke breathes out, relieved. "OK," he says, his whole body shaking. "OK."

Susan closes the door. It is dark again. We sit there in the silence for too long. Susan speaks. "Luke," she says. "There's limited time. We have to go with the plan, or else it's not going to work."

Though I feel safe wrapped in Luke's arms, I am also not sure what is going on. Luke slowly pulls his arm free from me, turns on a flashlight he'd brought, and sets it on the floor with its beam pointed straight up to the ceiling. I can see his face better now. He looks concerned, but determined. "Kelsey, can you change clothes."

I nod. He goes over to Susan, who has some type of bag in her lap. Luke takes it from her, and pulls some clothes out for me. I pull off my shirt and put on the new one. I reach toward my pants, but find I can't make my hands move to pull them off. It is too much a reminder of what just happened.

Luke comes closer to me, "Kelsey," he says. "I can help if you need it."

"No!" I say, a little startled by my own vigor. Luke moves away. I manage to get my old pants off and slide on the new ones. Luke is waiting with a pair of shoes in his hands when I finish. I slip those on too.

He hands me a red wig. I put it on, still just going through the motions. I am probably in shock. It isn't until I look over at Susan in her wheelchair that I realize I need to come out of this haze.

"Why is your head shaved?" I ask her, as it dawns upon me the red wig I am wearing is the exact same color of Susan's normal hair. In fact, if I had to bet money, I'd say she'd actually been wearing this wig a minute ago.

"I liked you better quiet," she says, proffering a weak smile.

I look to Luke, then back at Susan, who starts to explain. "Luke needed a quick plan, and this one fits the bill," she says to me. Then to Luke, "Come on, help me out of this chair."

Luke goes over, lifts her up, and carries her over to the block. Once he's set her down, she pulls off her red shirt to reveal the white holding facility garb — just like mine. "Help me with this, Luke," she says, pointing to her pants.

I turn to Luke, completely alarmed now. "You can't mean to leave her here?"

Susan answers. "Yes, you two are going to go, Kelsey. I'll be fine."

I ignore her and stay focused on Luke, who is gently removing her brown baggy pants to reveal the HLFM clothes inmates wear. "Luke, you can't do this. You can't leave her here!"

Luke briefly meets my desperate pleading eyes, then looks at Susan. "If you've changed your mind, I understand. We'll figure something else out. Just tell me if you've changed your mind," he tells her firmly.

She shakes her head. "I'll be fine — as long as you take him with you," she says pointing to Pig Face, who is curled in an unconscious lump on the floor. "And lock the door."

"The other guards have keys," I say to Luke, my voice high and panicked. "What if there's someone else like him?"

Luke looks from me to Susan. "Let me think a minute."

He walks back and forth in the tiny room, then says. "I can jam the lock. It will lock Susan in, and no one will be able to get in or out. My dad mentioned it's happened a couple of times, mainly through inmate machinations. They're scheduled for a heart transplant and don't want to go. They have to open the door from the outside by removing the hinges." He looks at Susan. "You okay with being stuck?"

"I was OK with being stuck before, and I'm OK with it now," she says, plainly. "Luke, the two of you need to hurry."

He nods. "First I have to take care of him."

We all look down to the floor, where Mr. Lawrence — no, Pig Face suits him better — lies. I wonder if he is dead, but don't verbalize it. Susan, apparently thinking the same thing, asks. "He's still alive," Luke says, checking Pig Face's pulse, then hoisting the man into Susan's wheelchair.

"Where are you taking him?" Susan asks.

"There's an empty cell down the hall. I'm going to lock him in. When they find you, they'll go looking for him."

Susan nods. Luke wheels the man out. I stand there, not sure what to do.

"Kelse," Susan says, "come here."

I take the two steps closer, then sit on the block next to her.

"You OK?" she asks.

"Yeah," I whisper. I'm not sure why. No one would hear, but her.

She pats my shoulder. "We came in time?" she asks. "Luke's not here. Tell me the truth."

"Yeah," I say, then I start crying uncontrollably. They'd come just in time. A moment later and I am not sure I could have dealt with it. She hugs me and strokes my back, and says it will be alright. And I feel like sitting here forever, like not getting up. But, that is wrong. I have to pull myself together and convince Susan this is insanity.

"You can't stay here," I say through tears.

"Yes, I can," she says. "I'll be fine."

"No, you can't," I say. "They'll make you stay, for helping a fugitive escape."

She laughs. Laughs at my words. I pull away from her, look at her in the low light. "Why are you laughing? This is not funny!"

"I think you're being overly dramatic," she says. "Plus, I'm going to take a sleeping pill in a minute. I'm going to tell them I have no idea what I'm still doing here. That a friend arranged for me to come see you, and that I woke up in here, and have no recollection of what happened. I'll be fine. You'll be fine. And we'll be even."

I want to throttle her. "Is this about the lake? We don't need to be even. And this is so much riskier than me jumping in the water?"

"Seriously, Kelse, how did you not flunk survival statistics? This is so much less risky than the worst swimmer in the class jumping into a barely warm lake to rescue someone from drowning."

I shake my head. I can't believe this. This is ridiculous. She has to come with us. I stand and move closer to the door. Luke will be back in a minute. He will help me convince her.

"Kelsey, this is the last time we're probably going to see each other. Luke is taking you to Peoria tonight. Please don't end it on a sour note. I didn't tell you stay ashore, don't jump in. I didn't fight you in the water. I let you rescue me. Let me rescue you."

I don't like the idea of tit for tat or her staying here, or anything like that. Yet, she seems so determined, so stalwart, so wanting to do this, that the idea of not letting her do it makes me feel cruel. I walk back over and hug her. "Only if you really think you're safe, Susan. If you don't think it's safe in here, you can't stay. We'll figure out a way for all of us to go."

Susan hugs me again. "It's safe. Luke will jam the door."

"I love you, Susan."

"I love you, too, Kelsey."

The door opens, letting in more light. It is Luke, bringing the wheelchair back. He reaches in his pocket, pulls out a zip top bag squished full of something. He pulls open the bag and dumps the contents on the floor near the door.

"What's that?" I ask, though I think I know.

"My hair," Susan responds. "He thought it would be best if it looked like you shaved my head here, after you drugged me."

I sigh. They have thought of everything. This feels wrong, yet inevitable. "Susan, you don't have to do this," I plead.

"I know," she says. "I'm making a choice."

I hate when she uses my own words against me. Luke clears his throat, and when I turn to him, he points to Susan's wheelchair. "Kelsey, please get in."

I hesitate a moment, then hug Susan. I stand and walk over to the wheelchair. She lies down. "You sure you'll be okay?" I ask, one last time.

"Positive," she says reassuringly.

"Blame me, please. Remember this was against your will. We forced you to stay, drugged you, cut your hair. I don't want them to put you in here for helping. I don't want you to spend one extra moment in here, Susan."

"All the blame goes to you, Kelsey, and your awful accomplice."

I wave good-bye.

"Good luck in Peoria ," she says as Luke opens the door and wheels me out. I look back, and she smiles at me. Then, he closes the door, and begins doing something with the key-lock system. I can only assume he is jamming it. He backs the wheelchair up, then angles it until I am pointing in the right direction. And we are off.

36. ESCAPE AGAIN

Getting out of the holding facility is easier than I'd ever have imagined. I keep my wig on and my head tucked down. A blanket over my legs. No one asks anything. Luke signs us out, wheels me to the parking lot, then hoists me into Susan's van.

And that is it. We are out. After putting the wheelchair in the back, Luke comes to the driver's seat, starts the van and begins to drive.

It seems too simple. A perfectly executed plan. One person in and one person out. Unfortunately, Susan is still in there. I feel guilty about leaving her, even though she wanted to do it. "You locked the guard in the other cell?" I ask for the fourth time as I crane my neck to look out the rear window toward the holding facility, though it is long past us.

"Yes, Kelsey," he responds reassuringly. "He won't hurt Susan."

We are silent for a minute, and then the panic hits after a thought occurs. "Luke, they're going to find him and then Susan. It's not going to work. His LMS, Luke? His LMS is going to bring someone calling." As the words leave my mouth, I realize his LMS should have already brought someone calling. Pig Face's vital signs from being pummeled should have sent authorities to assist him.

"That's kind of what took so long, Kelsey. His LMS is off. It is almost impossible to do, but I got the tech to turn it off."

"They can do that?"

He nods, keeping his eyes on the road. "They're only supposed to do it when a person is dead. So, we changed his status, and my guy could get in such trouble if someone figures out it was him, but we

200

think we've covered our tracks enough. I actually was supposed to knock him out using chloroform, but I knew that would mess with his vitals enough to call for help, so we turned it off."

So, no one would come to help Pig Face with his injuries. He'd rot in his cell until someone found him. No help for him tonight. I know it is wrong to enjoy his misery, but I am glad no one will help him.

Luke is driving down a main thoroughfare. We've gone at least three or four miles since leaving the holding facility. He pulls the van into a convenience store lot, and parks.

"Why are we stopping?" I ask. But, he doesn't answer me. Doesn't look at me. He just takes a few deep breaths, as if preparing himself for something awful.

Finally, he looks at me, a piercing, desperate stare that frightens me a little. "We got there in time?" he whispers, never taking his eyes off my face.

I nod. "Yeah."

"You're not just saying that to me?" he asks, his eyes softening slightly. His voice breaks just a little, but he is trying to look and sound reassuring. "If I didn't get there in time, you can tell me."

I shake my head. "I'm not just saying that Luke," I tell him, still a little shaky at the memory. "I don't think I could have held it together this long if you hadn't gotten there in time."

He nods, then lets out a long breath. "I'm sorry I left you in there with him tonight."

I reach out and touch his hand. It is trembling. "It's not your fault I was in there with him, Luke."

He shakes his head no, but doesn't say anything more. Then, he puts the van in gear and we leave the parking lot. We are driving again. In silence. I consider asking where we are going, but realize, ultimately, I don't care. I know Luke won't take me anyplace bad. That he will do everything in his power to keep me safe. I trust him with my life. Already tonight, he's beaten a man senseless in his quest to protect me, and broken me out of a holding facility. Whatever else he has in store has to be alright.

We've been driving for about 20 minutes by the time I recognize where we are headed: Susan's and my apartment. We live downtown on the first floor of a high-rise building. The place is wheelchair accessible on all floors via an elevator, but Susan preferred not to be dependent on the rumblings of a machine to get her to and from her abode, so we live on the first floor.

"Why are we going to the apartment?" I ask.

"Well, that's part of the plan, for one," he says. "Though, that's just part of it. I'd like Dr. Grant to check you out."

"Dr. Grant!" I spit. "He betrayed me."

Luke shakes his head, eyes me briefly, then watches the road. "No, we just wanted it to appear that way. We wanted it to look like he really had an axe to grind with you, that he wanted to bury you. He didn't betray you, Kelsey."

"I don't understand," I say, totally confused. "He moved up the date. He changed the recommendation for the procedure."

Luke nods, but keeps his eyes on the road as he speaks. "He found out Nimmick wanted to do the procedure at the holding facility hospital, not his lab, if we waited until you were 16 weeks."

I let that sink in a minute. The holding facility is not what we wanted. Seeing that I'd processed this, Luke continues. "Dr. Grant was already on track for conditional approval to do the procedure in FoSS. He asked Nimmick if he could speed up that approval, and explained that if he could get the conditional approval to perform 6-week procedures in the lab, they could get you done in the next week — right before the election. Nimmick went for it. We thought we could break you out of the lab, but then, I realized if we let Nimmick think he'd won, his guard would be down and it would be possible to get you out tonight. I'd always thought we could get you out if there was someone to switch places with you. I just never wanted to ask that of anyone. But, when I was bouncing escape ideas off Susan, she said she wanted to do it. I called Dr. Grant and he agreed to suggest fast-tracking you. He thought that it would throw off any future suspicion he was on our side."

"Yeah," I say. Dr. Grant had certainly done that well. It had been a believable act. I am glad, perhaps even ecstatic, that Dr. Grant has not betrayed me. A promise from him is a promise. He promised to help me and he has.

I put my hand on my belly and let it sit there for a moment. Things are going to be OK. "I don't think the guard hurt the baby," I tell Luke.

Luke doesn't respond immediately, then says. "It's better to be sure, especially before we get on a plane."

"A plane?"

"Yeah, we're flying out tonight."

"Supply plane?"

"Nope, medical emergency for Susan Harper," he says, eyes on the road. "We'd better go ahead and get there."

37. HOME

We pull into the lot of the apartment building and park. Luke makes no move to get out. He glances my way, then back at the steering wheel. He seems to want to say something to me. I wonder if he still thinks I have not been honest with him about what happened in the cell.

I would have told him if more had happened. At least I think I would have. Right now, I am trying to put those memories behind me. I might break down in Peoria and spend the next three weeks weeping, but tonight I need to keep moving, keep going, escape. And that means not looking back. Not at Susan, stuck in that damned cell, and not at what might have been if Luke had arrived even 30 seconds later.

"So, Dr. Grant is here?" I ask, breaking the silence.

He chews his lip a moment, then says. "And so is your father and Judge Harrell." He pauses to see my reaction. "They wanted to say good-bye."

I am caught between stunned and overjoyed. I want to say good-bye to my father, but I thought I wouldn't get the chance. The quick verdict and ruling by the judge followed by the thrown-together breakout plan that involved Susan staying in a holding facility overnight left me thinking I'd be doing nothing but escaping.

"You've thought of everything," I tell him, grinning from ear-to-ear. "Thank you."

He should be happier at my reaction, but he isn't. Maybe I am reading too much into it, but he seems to still be holding back.

"There's one other thing, Kelsey," he says, alternating glances between me and his hands tightly gripped on the wheel. "It seemed like a good idea this afternoon.... But now, after tonight, it's probably not a good time for it."

"What?"

"Well, I kind of asked Judge Harrell to marry us," he says without looking up. I blink in surprise. Wow! "But, we don't have to," he adds when he sees my face. "I just suggested it because, the other night, it seemed like it would mean a lot to you to have your father at our wedding. And since we're flying, time didn't seem like it would be that much of an issue. But, you know, given what happened with Lawrence, if you don't feel up to it, I understand."

Even now, he thinks about my needs first. It is why I love him so. And he's right, too. There's a part of me that doesn't feel up to it. A part of me that feels like curling into a ball and climbing under the covers. But, that part of me can't win out. Not tonight. Not when I only have an hour or two more with the people I love before leaving them behind forever.

"You know what," I say. "I once told this guy that it wasn't the right time to do something. And he told me I was full of shit. That there was never a perfect time for anything." I grin. "I think he was right, and I couldn't think of anything that would make me happier than to marry you tonight."

He looks up, a huge, deep-dimpled smile on his face. He takes my hand. "Then, let's do it."

* * *

When we get to the apartment, my father is waiting. I am so excited, I hop from Susan's wheelchair, bound forward and hug him. He feels so warm and so soft, just like he did when I was a child and would fling myself into his arms for a hug. "Daddy," I say. "I'm so glad you're here."

"Where else would I be?"

Nowhere else, I suppose. I let go of him, and smile as I look him over. His suit is baggy on the sides, and it's clear he's lost too much weight recently. His face is more wrinkled. My failed flee attempt and trial have taken their toll on him. I thought he'd looked bad after my mother died, but that seems like a day at an amusement park compared to how he looks now.

He takes my hand, and leads me across the room, past the sofa along the wall, and to the opposite corner, away from Luke and the others who had assembled there: Dr. Grant, Emmie, Haleema and Uncle Albert.

"How are you?" he asks quietly.

It is a good question. I want to say fine, but the truth is I am shell-shocked. The holding facility was a horrible ordeal, but I can't let that color my view right now. My father wants to know how I am for his own peace of mind, so I tell him the truth, at least the part of the truth that is crucial for him. "I'm happy, Daddy," I say. "Very happy to be out of there, and looking forward to being with Luke."

"You love him?"

A grin breaks out on my face and I blush. "Yes, very much."

He hugs me again. "And you want to go to Peoria with him?"

I don't look up at him yet, just delighting in the feeling of the hug. I don't want to speak the answer. Yes, I want to go to Peoria with Luke, but that also means leaving my father, and I don't want to say yes to leaving him, not just yet. I'd finally come to terms with leaving my father behind before my failed escape attempt. Now that it looks like my escape is going to succeed, all the emotions I'd struggled with earlier have come back. And before this all happened, my father was fine. He looked good and healthy, and had Haleema there to help him and a fairly vigorous career. Now he looks weak and tired. His name is tarnished. He's risked it all to save me, and I am going to leave him with nothing: not his daughter, not his grandchild, not his reputation.

"I don't want to abandon you, Daddy," I say softly, still clinging to him like a child.

He pulls away from me, a genuine smile appears on his lips. "Honey, don't worry about me. I'll be fine. I just want to know you're doing what you want here, what's going to make you happiest. Does Luke make you happy?"

That is an easy one. "Happier than I've ever been."

"Good," he says, winking at me. "He asked me to do him a favor."

"Luke did?" I say, surprised. Clearly, they've gotten closer while plotting to free me.

"Yes, he did. But, I told him that it was really up to you. So, if you say, yes, I'll do him the favor."

I crinkle my brow. "What does he want you to do?"

"He'd like me to walk you down the aisle. That is if you're OK with marrying him tonight. Albert will do the ceremony, if that's what you want, Kelsey."

I look over at Luke, who is standing near the door chatting with Emmie, Haleema, Dr. Grant and Uncle Albert. He catches my eye and grins, flashing those gorgeous dimples. Then I look at my father, whose smile threatens to spread beyond ear to ear.

"I would love it if you would walk me down the aisle, Daddy."

He squeezes my hand gently, then adds softly, "I'm not sure how legal it will be," he says. "You can sign the marriage certificate as if the two of you did a solo ceremony. It's still legal to conduct your own ceremony, and send the certificate to the court, but I think it reminds people too much of how bad things were after the pandemics so it's not very common."

I hadn't really thought about the legality of the ceremony until he mentioned it. But now that he has, I'm glad there is a prospect of legality. "So, if we signed a form, and sent it in, it could be legal?"

He shrugs. "Potentially," he says. "But, technically this option is only open to citizens in good standing. Given that you're a fugitive, they may not accept it. Either way, I think doing this tonight is a good omen."

"I think you're right," I tell him. "Legal or not, I'm glad to have everyone here for us."

He smiles, turns to Luke and offers a thumbs up. Luke bolts across the room to join us. Once at my side, Luke pulls me close to him, then looks earnestly at my father. "Thank you, Mr. Reed."

"I'm always happy to do anything for my little girl," my father says, then he reaches out, shakes Luke's hand and meets his eyes. "I know I'm leaving her in good hands."

I watch my father, wondering if he is sad to let me go, to leave me with Luke. Yet, there is no trace of sadness on his face, only happiness, happiness that Luke and I are so happy. I turn to Luke. "You ready to get hitched?" I ask.

He scowls. "No way."

Huh? Now I am baffled. "What are you talking about? I thought you just said…"

He cuts me off, with a finger to my lips. "Shh," he says, then kisses my cheek. "Two things, very quick."

I nod, wait for him to continue.

"First, Albert wants to know if you want the standard ceremony, or if you want to say something first."

I am a little taken aback. Things are moving so fast, I wasn't quite expecting that.

"You don't have to say anything," he says, gently squeezing me closer. "I think he just asks all couples that."

Despite my initial anxiety, I tell Luke, "I'd like to say something." Ever since I'd accepted Luke's proposal, my mind has wandered to what our wedding day would be like. And I always envisioned saying at least a few heartfelt words to Luke.

He kisses my forehead. "OK, one down."

"What's the other thing?"

"You and I have to get dressed," Luke says.

I look down at the red shirt and brown baggy pants I am wearing. Not perfect wedding attire, but it seems fine. "What's wrong with this?"

"For a wedding?" He shakes his head. "Susan left you some stuff in your bedroom. Go on."

I can't help grinning. "A dress?" I ask, inching away from him. He nods. I start off toward my bedroom. "I'll be out in a minute," I say. "Don't go anywhere." That request sounds ridiculous the minute it leaves my mouth. Why would he leave? Why, after all he's been through to be with me, would he go? I'm not sure why I even said it.

But, his answer reminds me why I love him. He simply smiles and says, "Never. Wouldn't go anywhere without you."

* * *

The bedroom is as I remembered it: wood floors, a blue spread on a full-size bed, a dresser and a few photos.

On top of the bed tonight, though, is a flat, black garment bag, zipped up, with a hangar protruding from the top. On top of the bag is an envelope. I move closer to it, and can see Kelsey spelled clearly in Susan's handwriting.

My hands are shaking a little. I pick it up and hold it tight in my hands, as a wave of guilt washes over me for leaving Susan in that nightmare of a place. For letting Susan sacrifice herself for me. Part of me wants to lie on that bed and have a good cry. But, Susan wouldn't want that. She wouldn't want me second-guessing her decisions, treating her like a child, like an invalid. She is strong and brave and makes her own choices.

I sit on the bed. The mattress is firm, like Susan. I take a deep breath, open the envelope, and pull out a single sheet of white paper filled with loopy cursive:

Kelsey,

I'm so happy for you and Luke. I'm just sorry I can't be there to see it myself, though Haleema promised me a play-by-play.

I hope you like the dress (and the shoes! — I know how much you love shoes!). Luke asked me to pick something you'd like, but there wasn't a whole lot of time. I lucked out and found this. It practically screamed from the rack, "Kelsey would look great in me!" At the very least, I know the size is right. Thankfully, you're not so pregnant that it won't fit! I know you'll make a great mother.

Know that I love you. You have always been my best friend, and especially, this last year, you have been my lifeline, giving me hope in my darkest moments. You deserve all the happiness in the world and I know you and Luke will find it in Peoria.

You will forever be my friend, and I wish you nothing but joy on your journey and in your new life. I will miss you terribly, but know you will always be in my heart, and I am happy that you are getting your happily ever after. Don't be sad I'm not there. Enjoy your day today and your new life.

Love,
Susan

Warm tears run down my cheeks. I love Susan, she loves me, and I won't see her anymore. I feel as if there is a hole in me because of it. I lift my hands, wipe away the tears and take a deep breath. As guilty and sad as I feel about Susan's absence and my impending departure, there is nothing I can do about it. All the choices I have made mean that I can't stay here in FoSS anymore. I have to put on my big girl britches and deal with the consequences.

I set the letter on the bed, then unzip the black bag. Inside is a full-length, long-sleeved, white silk dress. The fabric is soft and thin, shimmering slightly when touched, and hanging just perfectly. It is elegant and simple, and just what I'd have picked myself. Susan knows me too well. On the floor next to the bed is a shoebox. I pick it up and look inside. White heels with an open toe, and a bit of something sparkly embedded in them. They glimmer in the light. Perfect.

There is no veil, which is good. I have never been partial to them before, and now the idea of one is particularly unpleasant, as it screams: "bride is bald." Though, I suppose that will be pretty noticeable anyway.

I look to the dresser, where a bouquet of white lilies sit. There are a couple dozen buds in bloom tied together with a white ribbon. It goes exquisitely with the dress. I am about to change when there is a knock at the door. I move quickly, opening the door just a crack.

"May I come in?" Dr. Grant asks.

I open the door wider, and he slips in carrying his medical bag. I close the door quietly behind him. "Luke said you might have been injured and he wanted me to check on you and the baby," he says quietly, adding, "without alarming your father."

"Yes." Luke is right. I don't want my father to worry. Dr. Grant does a quick check of my vital stats, asks me a few questions, listens to my heartbeat as well as Peanut's, then pronounces us A-OK.

"Thank you," I say, giving him a hug.

"I should go," he says, pulling away and heading toward the door. "You need to get dressed."

Once he is gone, I follow his advice, quickly slipping into the dress, and grabbing my bouquet. I look in the mirror. Bald, but still bride-like. It will do. And, the truth is, I don't actually care that I look like a Q-tip in a wedding gown. I care that Luke and I are getting married, and my father will be there. Though, Susan's absence is like a missing puzzle piece in what would otherwise be a perfect picture. But nothing in life is ever perfect.

There is another knock on the door. My father speaks. "May I come in?"

"Yes," I call out.

He enters, then beams a genuine smile. "You look beautiful."

"For a bald woman, you mean," I tease.

"No, for any woman," he retorts. "Besides, Luke's not marrying you for your hair. He likes you with or without it."

"Yeah, I think he does," I say. "So, do you like Luke more now that you've gotten to know him better?"

"I've always liked Luke, Kelsey." And while the statement is a complete contradiction of what I've believed up until now, I don't think it is untrue. My father's tone is frank. "I wasn't effusive about Luke because I wasn't quite ready to let you go, earlier. I wasn't sure if he would take good care of you. But, I think he's shown he's more than capable of taking care of my baby girl."

Luke is very capable. My father reaches out his hand to me. "You ready?" he asks.

"Definitely," I say, slipping my hand into his.

38. I DO

After the pandemics, as part of society's rebuilding process, some traditions were abandoned; others became more deeply entrenched. Weddings fall into the latter category. They symbolize the uniting of families, the building of more families — everything a rebuilding society wants and needs to encourage. Society will always survive if our families are strong and plentiful.

So, the idea of a wedding in such a short time in such a small space with so few people feels out of place. Yet, at the same time, I am ecstatic. Especially when I think about the lengths to which Luke has gone to make it happen.

It is time. My father sticks his head out the door, issuing some signal and then, seconds later, I hear Mendelssohn's Wedding March begin. My father gives a simple smile, holds out his arm to me. I take it, looping my arm through his, and we walk out the bedroom door, to the center of the living room, where my husband-to-be stands waiting in a handsome black tuxedo, cummerbund and all.

Uncle Albert welcomes everyone. "Thank you for coming today to witness the joining in matrimony of Kelsey Anne Reed and Lucas Jeremiah Geary," he begins. "You all know that it has been a long and difficult journey for them to arrive at this point." He stares solemnly at us. "And they still have more difficulty ahead. But, they will not face these difficult times alone. They will have each other. Tonight, we are here to unite them. They will solidify their bond so that they may spend the rest of their lives together."

Albert smiles, then says, "Luke and Kelsey would like to say a few words."

Luke and I smile in unison, then Luke takes my hands. His ocean blue eyes find mine and everything else fades away: tonight's horrors, the past two weeks, Susan's absence, my father's presence, all the other people in the room. It feels like just Luke and me, together, forever, as I know it should be.

"The first time I saw you, I knew you were special," he says, his lips curling up into that sweet smile, as dimples emerge from their hiding place. "I knew you were someone I'd never forget. What I didn't know was that you would change my life."

His hands squeeze mine tighter, and he looks down briefly, but then finds my waiting smile again. "When I was younger, my home life was difficult because my mother was ill and eventually she died. And we coped and moved on with life. I certainly wasn't unhappy my entire childhood, but I still knew there was something missing, something I didn't have. But, when I met you, I felt it. I discovered what I knew all along was missing. I felt peace. I felt complete, like a hole in me had been plugged, a hole I hadn't even known was there.

"And even though I knew this peace was new and wonderful and everything I wanted, I didn't realize it could be taken away," he pauses, shakes his head lamentably. "Not until last month. Not until you'd been marked, and I realized that everything we had could go away. Poof. Just like that. And worse, I knew that I could not live my entire life without you. Kelsey, I couldn't imagine not seeing your smile, not hearing your laugh, not watching you light up when you get excited about some new project.

"I'm so very happy you've agreed to be my wife. I promise to be there for you every day for the rest of our lives."

Luke keeps my left hand in his, but releases his right hand to reach for the ring my father is holding. Once he's taken hold of it, he slips the little gold band on my finger.

The ring is warm. Not the cold you expect metal to be. I am a little surprised, yet it seems fitting. After the month we've had, a little warmth is nice.

I am so happy to be here with Luke. His words are so poignant, so touching, I am not sure I'll remember what I want to say. When I envisioned saying a few words, I thought it would be short and simple. What we lacked in elegance would be made up for in sentiment. Yet, Luke has not lacked eloquence. I hope what I have to say won't pale in comparison. But, even if it does, I know Luke won't care, so long as I say one thing. So, I figure I'll lead with it.

"Luke," I start; it sounds more like a long breath than a name. "I love you. From the moment I met you, I felt a connection. And ever since then, it's grown. You are sweet, strong and loving. You have been my knight in shining armor, my friend and my confidante. I often wonder how I got so lucky to have you in my life; and then I realize it's best not to question your good fortune; just to go with it. So, that's what I am going to do. For now and for every day for the rest of my life: go forward with you. I promise to love you always and to always try to make you as happy as you have made me."

I reach out my hand toward Emmie, who obliges me with the simple gold band, and slide it onto Luke's finger.

We both turn to look at a joyous Uncle Albert, who says, "Luke, do you take Kelsey to be your lawfully wedded wife, for as long as you both shall live?"

"Yes," Luke says.

"Kelsey," Albert says, turning to me. "Do you take Luke to be your lawfully wedded husband, for as long as you both shall live?

"Yes," I say.

"By the power vested in me, I now pronounce you husband and wife."

With those words behind us, Luke leans in, wraps his arms around me and presses his warm lips to mine, in a kiss that makes me tingle all the way down to my toes. We could stay like this forever, locked in each other's embrace. It is the applause, the gentle clapping of the small assembled crew that gets us to break free. I smile and turn to see almost everyone who matters. I feel a pang of sadness as I think about Susan.

My father comes over first, shake Luke's hand. "Congratulations," he says. "Take care of her." Luke nods. Then, Daddy hugs me. Albert, Dr. Grant, Haleema, Emmie all offer their well wishes.

Then, my father looks at his watch. "Dr. Grant, go ahead and make the call," he says. He turns to us, next. "You should say your good-byes."

Dr. Grant departs for a moment, mobile phone to his ear. Luke and I together say good-bye to Haleema, Emmie and Albert. Then there are two left, my father and Dr. Grant. I don't want to tell my father good-bye, so I postpone it a moment more by walking straight toward Dr. Grant, Luke following a step behind.

I hug him. "Thank you," I say. "You have put a lot at risk for us. I want you to know I appreciate it so much. Your help is the reason we're able to get out of here tonight."

He gives me a gentle pat on the shoulder. "After your mother died, I promised myself I would help you in any way I could. I'm glad I've been able to keep that promise."

I feel like I should say more, but Dr. Grant ends the conversation. "Good luck, Kelsey, Luke," he says, then shakes both our hands. He turns and walks toward the others milling about on the other side of the room. Sad to see all those I'm leaving, I look in the other direction, only to see my father standing near the door waiting. I sigh.

There is no avoiding it. I have to tell my father good-bye for good; tell him good-bye and know I am not going to see him again.

We walk over and meet my father at the door. Luke speaks first, thanking my father for all his help getting him into the holding facility as a guard, and promising him he will take very good care of me in Peoria. "I've been there on many occasions, with Dr. Grant. It's very safe and I will make sure your daughter and grandchild are happy."

My father claps him on the back like an old friend. "I know you'll take good care of them, Luke. You've already done a fine job. I'm glad Kelsey will be with you."

Luke offers us a moment alone, then walks over to his sister. I wonder momentarily what private good-bye he will say to Emmie. Then I turn back to my father, who looks expectant.

"It's OK," he says, flashing a genuine smile.

"What's OK?"

"That you're leaving and not coming back."

But it isn't OK. I am leaving him alone. He'll really be alone now. I look down, find a circle to stare at in the grain of the wood floor, not quite wanting to face him. "It's not OK, Daddy. I know it's necessary at this point. But, I want you to know how sorry I am that I have to leave you." I finally lift my head to see him. There is understanding in his face.

"Kelsey, you feel guilty because you feel like you're leaving me alone," he says. "I don't want you to feel bad. Of course, I'll miss you, but what I want most, what I've always wanted most, is for you to be safe, healthy and happy. If you stay here, there is no happiness, health or safety in your future. Going to Peoria means you'll have all three, and that's what I want."

I nod in agreement. Still, it is hard. "I love you."

"I love you, too, Kelsey."

We hug, and then, somehow Luke is beside us. He clears his throat. When I turn, his expression is apologetic. "We've got just eight minutes to get to the roof."

Wow, that's not a lot of time. Luke and I head to my bedroom, and change quickly. Me out of the simple silk dress and back into Susan's clothes and wig. Luke dons black slacks, a plaid shirt, white doctor's overcoat, and a plastic ID tag around his neck identifying him as Dr. Stephen Grant. We sign the solo marriage form and seal it in an envelope my father will drop in the mail. Luke shows me a small black waist pouch filled with Peoria currency. I wonder when he had the time to get it, but he"s found the time to do everything else.

Luke signals that he is ready, so we leave the room, wave a final good-bye to everyone, and walk out the door.

Standing in the hallway, the weight of the situation hits me, making me feel as if I am being pressed down by a thousand pounds of sand. I stop, even as Luke tugs gently on my hand, guiding me to the elevator.

I drag behind Luke. Finally, he nudges me. "Kelsey, we'll get way behind, maybe arouse suspicion, if you don't move." He gives another tug on my hand, leading me to Susan's wheelchair stationed by the elevator. Motioning for me to get in, he says, "Come on, we need to get to the roof."

39. ROOFTOP ESCAPE

The helicopter lands on the roof, and Luke pushes me toward it. As Luke wheels me closer to the helicopter, the wig feels ridiculously wiggy. I worry that it will blow off due to the massive gale created by the helicopter's rotors. Or, at the very least, the pilot will immediately spot it is fake hair and send me right back to the holding facility.

My eyes are closed, as I pretend to be asleep, trying to look unmemorable. Luke introduces himself as Dr. Grant and says he will be flying to the airport with me, where we'll pick up a medical plane to Georgia. I open my eyes in time to see the paramedic nod, then start toward me. Seconds later, I am hoisted out of Susan's wheelchair, carried onboard the copter and placed flat on a gurney. I open my eyes again, and watch the paramedic strap me down, as Luke climbs aboard. I close my eyes again and lie still.

The entire flight to the airport, I keep my eyes closed, listening to the sound of the rotors as they whirl above and praying my wig won't dislodge. On occasion, Luke — or at least I think it is Luke — grabs my wrist, as if checking my pulse.

The flight to the airport is shorter than I expect. When we arrive, the paramedic and Luke heft me, still strapped to the gurney, off the helicopter and onto the ground. Then the gurney is moving, being wheeled someplace new.

Keeping my eyes closed and head tucked down for fear that someone will realize I am not Susan is irrational. No one here knows Susan. But it seems best to come into eye contact with as few people as possible. To go unnoticed, blend into the scenery.

The pilot greets Luke. "I'm Dr. Grant," Luke lies. "Thanks so much for coming out. Ms. Harper really needs to get to Georgia tonight."

"I'll get you there," says a gruff-sounding man, though I can barely make out the voice over the noise of the aircraft nearby. "Due to regulations," the gruff sounding man is saying. "She'll need to be properly in a seat."

"Will do," Luke says. "Ms. Harper is able to sit up."

The gurney is wheeled a few feet, then stops. "Susan," Luke says. I open my eyes. "I'm going to help you onto the plane." I glance around, but do not see the pilot. He must have climbed onto the plane already.

Luke looks confident, reassuring, as he lifts me off the gurney and carries me onto the plane. Even though the pilot isn't near, I shut my eyes and tuck my head into Luke's shoulder, keeping only my red wig visible. Once ensconced in my seat, I look around to see a small plane with seats that back along the plane's hull.

It is sparse, yet comfortable. There are four seats bolted to the fuselage on my side of the plane and four pull-down seats on the opposite side. The seat portion is tucked into the fuselage at the moment, in case one wants to put medical equipment there. There are hooks on the floor, that I assume let you bolt the equipment down.

A small opening with a curtain separates the cabin from the cockpit. It is more comfortable than I thought a medical plane used to transport patients would be. But, what do I know? I've never needed medical transport before.

In a short time, Susan's wheelchair is stored on-board and we are ready to go. The take off is fine and we glide through the air without an ounce of turbulence on our way to flying altitude. Luke and I sit with one seat in between us, so we will appear like doctor and patient. Luke leans over once and checks my pulse to look doctorly. But he also puts his face close to my ear and whispers, "I love you, Mrs. Geary." I can't help grinning from ear-to-ear.

As we cruise through the air, I can see the end of the road. We just have to get to Georgia, and drive across the border. Luke looks at his watch. "It's only an 80 minute flight, and we've been flying for an hour."

I grin and take his hand. Just 20 minutes and we land. Twenty minutes and the hardest part will be over. I squeeze his hand and give him an excited look, then release him. I'm sure the pilot's too busy flying to come out and look at us, but you can never be too careful.

Just now, the plane intercom crackles to life. It is the captain. And when I hear the voice, hear it without the background noise of the airport, hear it without trying to bury my head and hide my face, hear it while alert, I know we are sunk. I know it is over.

"This is Capt. Anakin Spencer," his voice says smoothly, almost as if he is talking to us, his passengers. But it is clear he isn't. "I have reviewed the files you sent, and they confirm my initial suspicions: fugitive Kelsey Reed is impersonating a Susan Harper, and an unknown man is impersonating Dr. Stephen Grant. I will land the plane at the Hartsfield Regional Airport, where authorities will meet us."

A different static-filled voice now rumbles through the loudspeaker. "Thank you, Captain Spencer. If you hadn't recognized Ms. Reed, we would never have known she escaped."

"You're welcome, sir," Spencer responds, pride in his voice. "I want all fugitives brought to justice. Over and out."

Luke doesn't speak, but the look on his face is dejected and confused. I shake my head in horror and can feel warm tears forming at the corners of my eyes. Luke takes my hand, says, "Kelsey, we'll figure something out." But he doesn't mean it.

We are going down, and it is all my fault. I am about to put my head in my hands and weep outright, when a gloved hand peels back the flap of fabric separating the cockpit from the passenger area. Captain Spencer emerges. He looks pretty much like the last time I'd seen him: tall, with dark eyes, short black hair, and a rim of stubble on his jaw. The main difference is now he is dressed in a pilot's uniform. And he isn't full of gratitude toward me. He looks serious and unhappy.

Luke appears to be considering throttling him. Sure, that would make landing tougher, but landing and facing the police is going to be pretty hard anyway. I grab Luke's arm, and give it a gentle squeeze. I hope he knows it means it is time to give up. I have to face the music.

Captain Spencer looks at me. "I'm glad you're alright, Ms. Reed," he says, offering a stiff smile.

I nod, not sure what to say. "I'd be better if you hadn't turned us in. But, I guess I should have expected you would."

Luke looks confused. "You know him?"

I am about to explain, when Captain Spencer responds. "Yes, she saved my son's life. And now I'm going to return the favor."

40. A FAVOR REPAID

"What?" I blurt out.

Luke appears as confounded as me but doesn't say anything.

"Kelsey, you rescued my son that day at school. We met several times. I wrote you a profound thank you letter," Captain Spencer says giving me an apologetic look. "I couldn't pretend I didn't recognize you. So, I had to call in that you were on the plane."

"I'm not seeing how this is returning the favor," Luke says incredulously.

The captain gives Luke a cold look, then offers me a warmer countenance. "I couldn't pretend I didn't see you. I couldn't pretend I didn't recognize you," he repeats, more forcefully this time. "I had a decision to make. I thought about pretending to be sick, calling in backup, but then there was a chance that person would recognize you and turn you in."

"So you decided to turn her in?" Luke says, still full of venom.

"No," he shoots back. "I decided I'd fly you to Peoria. That's gotta be where you're going, stopping in Georgia, then to Peoria. But, if you stop in Georgia, you'll never make it to Peoria. Kelsey's face is everywhere. She has to go straight into Peoria."

Luke gives him another hostile look, and in a sardonic tone, asks, "If you want to fly us to Peoria, why would you turn us in?"

Captain Spencer takes a step closer to Luke, glares slightly. I don't know him well, but Captain Spencer is clearly not someone who is going to be pushed around. "First, it shows that I'm a cooperating citizen. Second, it buys you more time. Third, it makes my story believable when I fly you right into Peoria."

"What story?" I ask.

"In a few minutes, I'm going to radio in that you were listening to the conversation where I turned you in. I'll say the Dr. Grant impersonator — who I'll estimate is 5'7" with blond hair, and a wiry frame — held me at gunpoint, demanding I fly the plane to Peoria."

Luke, who is 6 feet, broad and strong, with not a speck of blond, smiles, then scoots closer to me. "I told you, we'd figure something out."

Luke's enthusiasm for the situation is too quick. It isn't thought out. I look from Luke to Captain Spencer. "What happens when we get to Peoria? Won't they arrest us and send us back to FoSS? Not to mention, won't they realize Luke didn't have a gun?"

"I'll say I threw it out the window," Luke says.

"From 30,000 feet, you opened a window?" I ask, expressing the insanity of that statement with tone alone. But, just in case he doesn't get it. "Luke, that's the most ridiculous thing I've ever heard."

Captain Spencer sighs, interrupting us. "Actually, that's the part I need to tell you about."

Something about his tone leaves me uneasy. Both Luke and I look at him warily. "What do you need to tell us?" Luke asks, his face tight with dread.

The pilot looks past us, eyeing two compartments in the back. "I actually can't land the plane with you two on it. Ms. Reed is right. Under the FoSS/Peoria Fugitive treaty, you two would have to go back because you would be holding me hostage while transporting me to Peoria."

"So how are we supposed to get to Peoria if you don't land the plane?" I ask through clenched teeth.

"There are parachutes," he says, nonchalantly.

"No," I blurt out. This is insane beyond belief. This man is crazy. Certifiable. No way in Hell I am jumping out of a plane.

"Are they medical chutes, the ones that deploy automatically?" Luke asks as if this is the most normal thing in the world.

I can't believe it. He can't be seriously considering this. I grab his arm and pull him close to me, so we are eye to eye. "Luke, we can't jump out of a plane." Why is the person who supposedly has pregnancy psychosis the sanest person on the plane?

He nods, puts his hand on top of mine, patting it gently. "Yeah, we can. These chutes for emergency medical aircraft allow you to get a lot of patients out. Rather than landing, you can parachute them to their destination below, right?" He looks to the captain for confirmation.

"That's right," Spencer says, in a silken, calm voice. "They're designed to work with a gurney or chair. You simply strap the patient in, then program in the airplane height, and drop the person. The chute deploys automatically."

I keep shaking my head. "I cannot jump out of an airplane," I screech. "Peanut cannot jump out of a plane, either."

Luke tries to pull me into an embrace; I resist, though I still clench his arm tightly. "Kelsey, you can do it," he says. "Peanut can do it." Then he pauses, as if rethinking it. Addressing Captain Spencer, he says, "Why wouldn't they send us back if we parachuted? Don't we still have the same problem?"

Well, no, we don't. I know the answer but, before I can speak, Captain Spencer fills in Luke. "No, Peoria has no extradition for people who flee a medical procedure. The issue with me landing the plane is I am your hostage and have been taken to Peoria 'against my will'." He uses air quotes for that last part. "The treaty says you can't forcibly bring someone to Peoria soil. If you do, you and that person have to be returned to FoSS. Once you're off the plane, and presuming I don't land — I'm sure I've got enough fuel to get back to Georgia — you've not forcibly brought me on their soil. They have no reason to deport you from Peoria. I think you'll have to file a request for asylum, but they shouldn't turn you over to FoSS."

Luke throws a friendly nod in the direction of the captain. "Thanks for your help," he says. "Could we have just a minute to discuss it?"

The captain returns the nod. "Sure, but, in 5 minutes, we'll be approaching the area where I need to start our descent for Hartsfield. I'll need you to have a decision at that point."

Spencer returns to the cockpit. As soon as the little curtain closes, I give Luke my most desperate look. "He can't be serious, Luke? There has to be some other way."

Luke shakes his head. "His plan is pretty good for something on the fly, Kelse," he says, pausing, looking aside for a moment, as if he'll find inspiration in the fuselage. He pries my fingers from his arm, then takes both my hands in his, looks into my eyes, his blue pupils glinting with hope. "I think it might actually work, Kelsey."

I shake my head. Jumping out of a plane! Ummmmm, no! I don't particularly like flying as is. I put that aside for the purposes of this escape. But, now he wants me to jump out of a moving airplane. "We'll die — you, me and Peanut," I say, ripping my hands from his and putting them over my belly.

He takes a deep breath, and I can tell right now he thinks I am having a meltdown. He is bracing himself to calm me. But, this is no pregnancy tantrum. This is me being the only person to exert reason in a room — no, an airplane — full of lunatics.

He reaches out for my hand. I reluctantly give it to him. With sincerity, he says, "You know I would never, ever suggest you do anything that would hurt you or Ingo."

I have to laugh when he says Ingo. "Really? You really like Ingo?" I ask, purposely sidetracking.

"Yeah. And it's a real name — one for people — which is more than can I say for Peanut."

I frown. He looks serious again.

"Kelsey, we don't have much time to figure this out," he says, bringing us back to the topic at hand. "I know planes scare you. And I know the idea of jumping out of one has to be even scarier. But, think of the alternative."

Splatting to my death after dropping from a plane or back to a holding cell, having Peanut Ingo forcefully removed, and then me being killed? What wonderful choices to have. I sit there for a bit trying to come up with reasons jumping is bad, but the cons of jumping are nothing compared to what will happen if we don't jump.

"I know what you're saying," I finally whisper to him. "And you're right. Jumping is the best option. But, I don't think I can do it."

That sounds insane, even as I say it, but it is true. I am afraid I'll freeze, that I won't be able to jump when he says to.

Luke leans in closer, then wraps his arms around me. "Kelsey," he whispers just loud enough for me to hear over the plane's engines. "I'll be with you the whole time, and there's nothing to do. These chutes are made for injured passengers. The chute will deploy on its own. You will land safely."

I so want to believe him. With everything in me, I want to believe him. Still, my heart is pounding in my chest like it is on fire, and I keep envisioning me dropping through the air, accelerating toward the ground but no chute deploying. Just me and Peanut going crash, bam, splat. Closing my eyes, I take a few deep breaths.

"Kelsey, you can do this," Luke says.

I can't do this.

But it doesn't appear there are other options. "OK," I say. "Tell him we'll do it."

Luke marches over to the cockpit, sticks his head behind the curtain, and confirms that we're in. I don't hear the exact words he is saying, as the engines are roaring so loudly. I stand and walk over to the two of them, wobbling a bit as the plane shudders across the sky. It is easy to remember why I hate flying: so high up in the air, balanced precariously by thrust, lift and drag — as we were taught in school. Miscalculate any of those factors, or enter another variable like wind shear, and you drop of out of the sky, plummeting to your death.

Statistically, I know flight is very safe. It's been at least five years since a passenger plane has crashed. But I never feel safe when I am up in the air. I take a deep breath as I near the cockpit.

Luke is standing in the tiny doorway. He stops speaking. Initially, I think it's because of my approach, but then I realize it's because Captain Spencer is speaking. The radio handset is to his mouth, and he is speaking in a voice that breaks with fear.

"He has a gun," Captain Spencer says. "I'm pretty sure he's going to use it. He wants me to land in Peoria."

There are a few moments of silence on the other end. Then the radio gives a static burp and a voice emerges. "Do as he says," man on the other end cautions. "Land in Peoria." Then the voice dashes off some coordinates, presumably for a Peoria airport where authorities will be waiting.

So it is set. He'll fly in and we'll jump somewhere before the Peoria airport. Luke turns to me. I must look as queasy as I feel, for my husband's eyes brim with sympathy, as if I am a lost child. In an instant, the look dissipates, and he puts on a solemn expression, one that exudes everything is serious, but fine. "You heard?" he asks.

"Yeah."

Captain Spencer sees me next to Luke, smiles, then presses a few levers on the control panel. "It's on autopilot," he says, standing up. I glance at the controls uncomfortably. I prefer a real pilot. Luke steps aside and I follow suit, heading back into the main cabin, as well. Luke and I are wedged against the fuselage wall as Captain Spencer enters the cabin. He points to the wall at the right rear of the plane. "We better take a look at your chutes."

Luke and I follow as Spencer trudges to the area he just pointed toward. Mounted on the interior fuselage are two rows of seven squares that look like backpacks with electronic keypads and small screens. Captain Spencer pulls one from the wall, and shows it to us.

On the backside is a metal ring with brackets coming out from it. "It locks into place with a chair or gurney from the plane if necessary," Captain Spencer explains, pointing to the brackets. Then he lifts straps dangling from it. "You can use these straps to harness around the patient, if necessary. But you're both able-bodied, so you won't need them." He detaches the straps, which were held in place by a sturdy-looking metal clip.

"I will program in the drop height here, and the computer will determine when to deploy the chute." As he speaks, so calm, so deliberately, I wonder if he normally watches the chutes while speaking; or if he does it this way tonight to avoid staring at the dread and fear clearly emanating from me. "These are emergency devices and therefore intended to be used in emergencies. Drop heights can be pretty low. But, because of the topography of the area we'll be flying into, I'll be dropping you a little higher – from 12,000 feet. This means your free fall time will be longer."

"How long?" I ask, but it comes out more like a demand.

He takes his eyes off the chute, looks briefly at me. "Two minutes."

Two minutes of plummeting through the air to my potential death. "Isn't that kind of long?"

He seems torn between ignoring me and answering. After a moment, he says with forced calm, "A little. But, you'll be fine. It's not too high. Your chute should deploy around 2,700 feet. If it doesn't, there's a backup…"

Cutting him off, I squawk, "What do you mean, if it doesn't? I thought these were perfect."

He looks to Luke, perhaps for some clue as to how to respond, but then looks at me. "Ms. Reed, your chute will deploy. I'm just telling you what we tell everyone. Just precautionary. If your main chute doesn't open, the backup will open at 1,000 feet. If that doesn't open for some reason…."

I am about to interrupt him yet again, but he cuts me off with a stern look. "If that doesn't open," he continues, "pull this yellow lever with all your might and it will manually deploy the backup chute. This is a fast-launch chute which will keep you from dying if deployed as little as 200 feet above the ground. You won't die, but you'll have a hard landing."

A hard landing. He grimaces when he says it. If he grimaces, a hard landing has to be bad.

"But that's a worst case scenario," Luke chime in, patting my back gently. "These things deploy properly like 98 percent of the time, right?"

"Of course," Captain Spencer agrees, looking at me with rehearsed confidence. "I just needed to let you know the possible pitfalls. You won't need this yellow lever."

I nod, hoping they are right.

Captain Spencer offers some more advice on what to do, but I can't help tuning him out. And it isn't 'cause I don't want to know. I am just trying to perpetuate my denial a little longer. If I just don't listen, maybe it won't really happen in a few minutes. Or maybe I can just put off dealing with it until I have to, until I have to get out of a moving airplane.

"You alright, Kelsey?" Luke asks.

I must look terrified, but I offer a weak smile, and say, "Mmmhmm." I'm sure Luke knows I don't mean it, but he's kind enough to pretend I'm going to be OK and not ask me again.

"In five minutes, we'll be in Peoria airspace," Captain Spencer says. "I'm going to show you a map." He heads back toward the cockpit, and Luke and I tag along behind him. As we get to our original seats, I sit, realizing not standing in the wobbly plane will make me feel better. Luke sits next to me, and takes hold of my hand.

Captain Spencer reaches into a wall compartment near the entrance to the cockpit and pulls out a computer map tablet. He turns it on and a color-coded map of the area appears. It shows lots of brownish blue area. I don't remember everything we learned about these types of maps, but I have a feeling what I am looking at isn't good.

Luke scowls. "That's swamp," he says, leerily.

"I know," Captain Spencer says. "Peoria is swampy. Why do you think FoSS gave it up?"

"Is it safe to parachute into a swamp," I ask. "What if our chute starts to sink or something and pulls us under?"

Captain Spencer shakes his head impatiently. "I'm not dropping you in the swamp," he says curtly. "That's what we're flying over now, but I want you to know you're going to be adjacent to swamp, so there's still a chance you might see a gator or two."

A GATOR OR TWO?! I take in Captain Spencer's facial features carefully to see if this is a joke. Set jaw, open, honest eyes, firm stance. Is Captain Spencer great at deadpan? He doesn't seem the joking type, I decide. "You want us to jump into an area full of alligators?"

He shakes his head. "Near a place inhabited by gators. And you probably won't even see one. This drop spot is on the flight path to the airport, but not so close they'd actually push for me to land in Peoria."

Luke looks a little skeptical himself, but chimes in. "I'm sure they'd be sleeping, Kelsey. No doubt, even if we saw an alligator, it would be asleep and we'd just mosey on by."

MOSEY ON BY! I am not sure what to even say to that. Does Luke really believe that? That we can just mosey on by a bunch of hungry alligators? Given my current luck, alligators are probably nocturnal feeders. We are probably being dropped right in the middle of suppertime. I can't speak. There are no words to express my feelings at this very moment.

Captain Spencer leans toward me more. "It's not to worry you, Ms. Reed. It's just so you know. I'm sure you're worried, but given what you've done, you'll have a better life dropping into Peoria, than if I have to land you guys there or back in FoSS."

He is right. Gators are nothing compared to the doctors and politicians who want me to pay. Though, I wonder if I am being fair to Peanut? Surely it is better for him or her to be alive and well and raised by someone else than to be gator chum.

As if he can read my mind, Luke looks at me, then my belly. "Honey, this will be fine. You, me and the baby will be fine. We will not be eaten by gators."

Captain Spencer clears his throat, getting our attention. "Listen, we've detoured here, with this discussion of alligators. You're not likely to see any. And if you do, I can give you two emergency, single-use defibrillators. You can use them like weapons. The gator won't like the charge. They're meant for emergency, so they've got one charge. Just pull the red lever, wait ten seconds, then, it will emit an electrical shock when you press the button. That would daze any animal and send it scurrying."

A weapon. For some reason that makes me feel better. In FoSS, deadly weapons are generally only for military use. The idea of having one here and now, of being able to defend myself, is very comforting. Like a security blanket for the big bad swamp.

Both men seem to notice my anxiety level has fallen, so Captain Spencer continues, pointing to the map. With his pointer finger, he touches the screen, sliding the image over. Now it is fresh green, no marshy mess. He pans further over, revealing a solid expanse. "This is farmland. There are some houses around, but they're pretty spread out. You should be OK in this area to make a clean drop. And it looks like there's a hospital and some other businesses within a mile of the drop zone. The airport is about 80 miles from here, which is where they're expecting us to arrive. Simply drop here, and walk to the hospital."

Captain Spencer hands the map tablet to Luke. "You can use this once you're on the ground," he says looking him directly in the eye. Then, catching my eye, he adds, "It'll be about 10 more minutes until we're at the drop zone."

He shakes my hand, then Luke's. Finally, he turns around and disappears behind the fabric concealing the cockpit.

41. THIS IS OUR STOP

Luke spends the final 10 minutes of our flight getting me ready. He straps the parachute around me, checking things are properly tightened and buckled. He puts on my helmet, straps it snugly, which is easy to do because I am bald, and checks the strap. Then he checks me again. When he finishes, he equips himself with a chute and helmet, then comes back to me. He begins pulling on straps and levers on my chute to make sure it is properly fitted.

When he pulls on a strap around my waist for a fourth time, I swat his hand lightly. "I don't want it to deploy in here," I say. So, he nods, and we both sit on the seats that line the plane's fuselage. Side by side, but not speaking. I suppose we each need a moment to mentally prepare ourselves.

When I do look over at him, he is leaning forward, his hands clasped together with his forehead resting on them. I think for a moment he is simply in thought, but I can see his lips moving ever so slightly, and it dawns on me that he is praying. It is a fitting idea, and I know instantly it is one I should imitate.

I bow my head, close my eyes and take a cleansing breath. *Dear Lord, first let me say, I appreciate all the wonderful things you've given me in this life. I've had a wonderful father, great friends like Susan, found Luke, got Peanut now. So, thank you for all that. And you've done plenty for me, that's for sure. But, now, if I could just ask for a safe landing with these parachutes, that would be the icing on the cake. If not, that's fine, too. But, I'd appreciate a safe landing. Thank you for listening. Amen.*

I open my eyes and lift my head. Luke is staring at me.

"Praying?"

"Yeah, I stole your idea." I smile and reach for his hand. "I feel better. It was a good thing to do."

He smiles. Then, we hold hands and listen to the steady drone of the plane's engines. The warmth of Luke's hand, the slow realization that this is it: sink or swim — we'll either be safe or dead by morning — brings me strange comfort. The unknown is always difficult, so knowing there'll be an answer to whether this will work out or not in less than an hour makes it easier to deal with. Sometimes choice is refreshing — the idea that you can pick and choose your own destiny. But, sometimes a lack of choice is refreshing, too. There aren't too many options. My choice is to jump off this plane or go back to FoSS. That isn't much of a choice. I am going to jump off this plane. And I am starting to see myself do it. Close my eyes, take the leap into the night, land right next to an alligator, and make my way to freedom, moseying on by, just like Luke said.

I take a couple of empty swallows to avoid my eardrums exploding — a clear indication the cabin pressure is changing as the plane descends. I wonder if this is as difficult for Captain Spencer as it is for us. No, he doesn't have to jump, but he does have to sell a lie. He has to tell authorities something that isn't true, and be completely convincing. Most accomplices are not prosecuted, but I worry what will happen because this has been such a public case. It can't be easy for him to take such a risk, yet he is.

I open my eyes in time to see Captain Spencer emerge from the cockpit. "We're at 12,000 feet," he says. "This is your stop."

My legs feel like wet spaghetti noodles. Yet, I pull myself into a standing position, imagining myself going through the reverse of the cooking process — from soft and flexible to rigid and sturdy. Luke stands, too, though I doubt he feels, even for a moment, the wet noodle mindset I am experiencing.

"Thank you for your help, Captain Spencer," I say, taking a step closer, then hugging him. "You're saving my life, Luke's life and this baby's life. I'll be eternally grateful."

He gives me a gentle squeeze in response, then lets go. "You saved my son, and I'm glad I can help you now."

Luke leans in, shakes Spencer's hand, and offers his own thanks. Then, Captain Spencer motions to the door opposite us. It has a white metal lever that runs flush against it, with a red arrow indicating you turn the lever clockwise to open the door.

"It's on autopilot, but I don't want to leave it like this too long with the changing cabin pressure when I open the door. You should each grab hold of a bar there, as it's going to get windy in here," he says, indicating a metal rail alongside the door. Luke and I each grab onto it, then the pilot continues. "I'll want you two to jump quickly, then I'll shut her up."

We both nod. There isn't much to say to that. At least not for me. Everything that happens now is simply something that has to happen. It is the next logical step. And when you're out of other choices, it's easy to follow the next logical step.

Luke looks to see if I am ready. I am not, of course. But it doesn't matter. I take a deep breath then give him a "go" look. Spencer opens the plane door, and the wind is immediate. There's a tugging like an ocean current and I feel like I might be sucked right off the plane. And perhaps I would have been had Capt. Spencer not told me to hold on. I am standing there feeling the pull of the wind — no the pull of gravity, the pull that will suck me down to earth. The pull that will crash me onto a piece of hard, flat earth, where I will go splat unless this chute works.

I let go of the bar, take two steps forward, and my third sends me off the side of the plane. I'm not sure what I expected to feel when I left the solidity of the plane. But, what I do feel isn't it. I feel — for lack of a better word — freedom.

There are a million sensations I could describe, and they would all be accurate. But none would convey the feeling, the true sense that I feel, better than freedom. There's wind sweeping across my head, running through my fingers and billowing around me. I feel it all at the same time like I have everything in my control and nothing. The air is gentle and pleasant. The air is cool as my body slices through it.

I close my eyes and feel the wind whip around me, imagine what it would be like to kick my shoes off and have this wind slide through my toes and across my feet. While I feared it, I shouldn't have. The sensation is exhilarating in every way possible. And Peanut! I wonder what Peanut thinks of this. "Your first roller coaster ride will pale in comparison to this," I tell our baby as I fall through the sky. "I wonder what your father thinks of this?"

I tilt my head back, looking straight up to see if I can find Luke. I expect him to be descending slightly above me somewhere. He was to jump a few seconds after me, and we will land within feet of each other, or that is the plan. The sky is black, but the moon is out, and there is enough light to see a silhouette of him, up there. Just then, though, just as I think I've spotted the outline of his form, there is a sudden jerk, a stilted hip-hop as my parachute deploys. Now, above me is a large green billowing mass. It reminds me of a quilt. A beautiful safety blanket that will glide me to my new life.

I am no longer speeding downward in a surprisingly pleasant free fall. I am now floating downward, softly, gently, the parachute rippling in the night wind.

I laugh. I can't help it. I've been worrying, panicking that I couldn't do this. That I couldn't jump out of a plane, deploy a parachute and land safely. Yet, it is all going so well, so easily, so effortlessly. It is as if the heavens have finally smiled upon me. As if things are finally going to be all right.

That's when I hear it: a whoosh. It has come from nearby. I have been so focused on my own green chute as the air pushes it into a perfect curve above me, I haven't been looking around. But the noise forces me to refocus. I look in the direction the sound came from in time to see a red helmet just like the one I am wearing sliding farther and farther beneath me. It is Luke, and he must have passed me very quickly.

Why? Why is he going so fast? It doesn't make any sense. His chute should have deployed. Shit.

Shit! He is going to crash. His chute isn't deploying. I watch the dot that is him accelerate faster and faster toward the ground, waiting for the chute to open. A backup, something, anything. I hold my breath waiting for a puff of colored fabric to shoot above him and slow his descent.

My God! He is going to die! Nothing is happening. We will have done all this, suffered all this, come so far, given up everything, in hopes of living a life together, only to have him die now. No. No, no, no no. "Luke," I call out frantic.

It doesn't help, it doesn't stop his descent. It seems only to speed it up, to make things a blur, harder to see. It is so dark already. And the further away from me he gets, the harder he is to see.

Part of my brain says I should close my eyes now. That I don't want to see Luke die. That I don't want to see his body explode when it hits the ground below. Force is mass times acceleration. His speed is only getting faster. There will be a sound, a horrible, crashing sound when his body hits. I wonder if he will speak, too, or if his jaw will shatter or his lungs pulverize before he can produce sound.

I should close my eyes, but part of me is still hoping for a miracle. That damned emergency chute will open, and he will be saved. I watch, my heart screaming for a miracle my brain says won't come.

Then, it does. A pink cloud mushrooms above him. It slows his descent, not as slow as mine, but some, and then, a few seconds later, bang, he stops. He must have crashed. But, was the slowing enough? Or is Luke dead? How fast was he going when he crashed?

I won't know until I land.

42. THE GROUND

The ground is harder than I expected. It isn't a terribly harsh landing, I don't think. More like the landing you'd get if you jumped off a low retaining wall. Still, it is harsher than I thought it would be, as I'd been floating so gently down to the ground.

I immediately begin detangling myself from the chute's harness, and head toward Luke. He's drifted about 15 yards away, or perhaps I've drifted away from him in my fall. I am not sure. I just know he isn't close to me. I can't tell how badly he is hurt. I can see his chute on the ground, and he is in a heap next to it.

The harnesses are harder to unlatch and remove in my hurry to get to Luke. While I could try to get to him without getting loose from the chute, I worry if I don't free myself, a strong gust of wind will pull it — and me — further away.

Once unstrapped, I sprint toward Luke with a singular focus. The ground is soft and marshy, much softer than it felt when I landed. Almost as if I could sink right in. So, I make an effort to lift my knees, practically to my chest, as I run, so I won't get bogged down or stumble.

When I reach Luke, he is on the ground, with the pink chute tethered to him and blowing around at his side. Panting from my sprint over, I stop in front of Luke, then manage to hold my breath, silencing my body for just a few seconds, long enough to look and listen. To see that his chest is moving up and down, and hear the slight whoosh he makes as he inhales and exhales.

Luke is alive. With great relief, I open my mouth and breathe again, gulping in mouthfuls of air, as I drop to my knees on the ground next to him. "Luke," I say gently, then reach for his hand, pulling it into my own. "Luke," I say, louder and less gently. "Luke, can you hear me?"

No response. He doesn't seem to hear me. He isn't stirring at all. I pat his hand and call his name again.

Nothing.

He is half on his side, as if he had been trying to turn when he landed. I gently roll him onto his back and lean in over his face. I can feel the warmth of his breath. He is breathing. He is alive. This is good. What's bad is that he isn't speaking. "Luke," I say again, this time trying to sound gentle, enticing, inviting enough for him to answer me.

But nothing.

"Luke," I say, trying to mask the panic erupting inside me. Other than being unconscious, he appears fine. No cuts and scrapes or bruises. None that I can see, at least. There are no tears in his clothes or open wounds. Nothing that indicates there is a serious problem.

I let go of his hand, unstrap his helmet, gently remove it, and set his head in the grass. I turn the helmet in my hands, examining it. My hands freeze when I see it. A thin line jutting across the back. A cracked helmet is bad. My entire body quivers with fear, and I feel like all the air has been sucked out of me. I take a couple of gulps of air, then try to force the panic from my brain. Even though a cracked helmet is an indication of tremendous force on the helmet, it also means the head has not suffered the full force of the blow. So maybe Luke is alright. I just need to remain calm.

My trembling hands toss the helmet aside, then I steady myself enough to run my fingers through his hair, feeling out injuries. His hair is a little damp — perhaps sweat, perhaps from the dewiness of the grass. But, there are no obvious lumps or cracks that I can feel along his skull. That is good. Though, one can get a concussion without damaging the skull to the point that it is manually felt, or seen with the eyes. The Life Saving 202 instructor drilled that into our heads. I need to get Luke checked out at a hospital. Unconsciousness is bad. I take a deep breath and tell myself again, "don't panic." I look at and feel both his ears, searching for signs that any fluid might be seeping from them. Clear liquid is very bad. It is a sign that the fluid around the brain is leaking. I can't see or feel any fluid. Another good sign.

I gently touch his face, running my fingers along his forehead, then cheeks, and finally chin. Nothing feels out of place. This has to be good. I slide my fingers under his head, so I'm cradling his skull.

Luke's head turns ever so slightly, moving so it lies uncomfortably on my middle and index fingers. That slight bit of discomfort brings me more joy than I've ever known.

"Luke," I say, leaving my hands in his hair, gently supporting his head.

His eyes open and he smiles at me. Dimples, a glint in the eye, and pure love radiating from his face. Then he does a slight double take, and appears confused.

I put my face closer to his. "Are you okay?"

He doesn't answer immediately. He just looks strangely at me and then at the surroundings. The blackness, the tall grass. It must seem odd; he is disoriented.

"Did you hit your head?"

At this, he sits up, with a bit of effort, and a gentle push from me.

"Hey," Luke says, offering up his smile again, but not answering my question. "I'm fine. I just got confused for a minute."

I nod, try to look reassuring, though I am worried. Luke being unconscious was bad. "We should get you to a doctor," I tell him. "Do you think you can walk?"

With a look that suggests this is the silliest question in the world, he replies, "Yeah, I can walk."

I nod again, but don't move from my spot on the ground next to him. He doesn't look ready to walk. He looks hurt. "Do you remember what happened?"

Luke lifts his hand, rubbing his forehead. I wonder if I missed that spot when evaluating his head. Is there a lump there? It doesn't look like it. Luke tilts his head back and stares straight up at the sky, then at me. "We jumped," he says, blowing out a long breath. Then he shakes his head. "And my chute didn't open. I had to pull the emergency one."

"I saw," I say, trying to shake the horror I'd felt as I watched him slam into the ground. Even from above, it had been frightening. "Did you hit your head? You were unconscious."

Still rubbing his forehead and now the front top of his head, he looks at me and hesitates. It's as if he is deciding whether or not to be honest with me. Deciding whether to hold back or lay it all out. "I think I did hit it." He looks to the helmet lying a few feet away. "But I was wearing that," he says, pointing to the helmet. "I'll be fine."

Maybe, I think, examining him for myself. Then, he leans toward me and kisses me. His lips feel soft, supple, and happy, even, if lips can feel that way. Then he pulls back, and grins.

"We did it," he yells. "We made it."

His smile, his enthusiasm are infectious. I can't help but mirror his look of goofy, unadulterated happiness. "We did it. You, me and Ingo."

He laughs. "Name's grown on you, eh?"

I shake my head. "Not really, but given that you almost died when your chute didn't open, I thought I'd throw you a bone."

He squints in mock disapproval. "I won't comment on whether or not I almost died, but I will say, someone who almost died should get the chance to pick the baby name in its entirety."

I scoff at that. "Nice try, buddy, but no." I stare at him, taking him in, in all his good form. He doesn't appear badly injured. Maybe he isn't. Maybe he is going to be alright. I smile. "Whenever you're ready," I say, "we can walk to the hospital."

I think he'll take awhile, work up the strength, test his steadiness. Instead, he springs up, as if nothing had happened. Standing steadily, assuredly, he holds out his hand to me. "Come on," he says. "You ready to start our new life together, Mrs. Geary?"

I stand, my heart finally beating at a normal pace this evening, and take his hand. "Yes," I say. "Yes, I am."

THE END

Second Life
(Preview)

Please enjoy a sneak peek at the first three chapters of the next book in the Life First series.

1

KELSEY

I wake up with a gasp, my breathing heavy. I sit up in bed, pulling the blanket with me. Luke turns beside me, disturbed by my sudden wakening and the lack of covers. "Are you alright, Kelsey?" He slurs his words, half asleep.

"I'm fine," I lie. "Just had some gas that woke me. I'm going to the bathroom."

Luke pulls the blanket back over him as I slide out of bed, tiptoe to the bathroom and shut the door. I pee; this is something I have to do all the time now. I wipe, but don't flush. Instead I stand, lower the seat cover and sit back down. I need a minute to recover from the dream.

This same vision has invaded my sleep every night for the past few weeks. It's like watching a movie of the life I could have had. Luke and I in a grand wedding at my family home; my father and I arriving by horse-drawn carriage; Dad proudly walking me down the aisle; Luke and I moving into our first home; decorating as we prepare for a baby; my best friend Susan and I laughing like giddy children together; and Susan helping me pick baby clothes out. Then the dream descends into a nightmare. Susan is yanked away by some unknown force. One moment she's showing me an infant onesie. The next she is gone — evaporated into thin air. There is nothing but red, bright, dazzling red like her hair. The red darkens, thickens and congeals until I realize it is blood. A pool of blood and Susan is at the center.

During the day, I can force these images from my mind, but at night nothing drives them away. They keep coming back, stronger and more vivid than before. I have put on a brave face for Luke and tried to have a good attitude. Tried to convince myself that all is well, that this is the life I wanted, that this is the life that is best. That everyone is alright. After I fall asleep, though, my thoughts and fears run free in my mind. They seed my dreams, transforming both my wishes and regrets into living, breathing visions.

I always wake up second guessing myself. I escaped the Federation of Surviving States (FoSS) nearly two months ago. I was scheduled for a mandatory kidney transplant; the government would take one of my healthy kidneys and give it to an ailing stranger. FoSS is what remains of most of the former United States, following a pandemic 100 years ago that wiped out 80 percent of the population. The survivors live under the policy of Life First. Each person is expected to help his fellow man survive, even if it means donating his own body parts. After I was determined to be the best match for a sick man, I was officially "marked" for donation. Once marked, your only choice is donation or death. Most people choose donation. I risked death, and fled instead.

I barely escaped to Peoria, a bordering country located mostly in the former state of Florida. The country also includes some coastal areas that used to be part of Alabama and Mississippi. Peoria did not want the Life First policies of mandatory donation and seceded from FOSS many years ago.

While I call Peoria my home now, it didn't have to be that way. There were other choices, ones I'm regretting not making. Luke asked me to go through with the donation, instead of trying to flee. If I'd just said yes to him, if I'd just gone in for the surgery, I would have learned I was pregnant, and they would've cancelled the donation. Instead, I followed the pipe dream of a flawless escape.

I glance at the little clock on the wall. It's 2 a.m., and instead of sleeping, I'm holed up in my bathroom regretting my decisions.

I touch my belly, hoping it will give me some comfort. Even though I know I'm not far enough along to feel movement, part of me hopes I will. Hopes I will feel some semblance of joy that tiny flutter of life within is supposed to bring. But it's too soon. I sigh as nothing happens. Most first-time mothers don't feel movement until the fifth month. I'm only three months along. I blow out a breath, lean forward, rest my elbows on my thighs and place my head in my hands. My pregnancy has been healthy and uneventful so far; that is the one bright spot in this whole mess. I must find joy in that, if nothing else in my new, uncertain life.

I lift my head and look at the closed door. If my husband was more than half awakened by my departure, he will now start to wonder why I haven't come back to bed. If he was just barely awake, as I suspect, he has fallen fast asleep and I can have a moment more to myself.

I sigh. Whether Luke is awake or not, I should go back out. I need to sleep for the baby. I stand up and peer into the mirror above the sink. I look awful. Leaning forward, I scrutinize my reflection: there are dark circles under my eyes and thin red lines mar the whites. My haggard appearance isn't helped by my hair, which is a little more than an inch long. My head was shaved three months ago when my attempt to escape landed me in a FoSS holding facility. Sort of like prisons, holding facilities are places for lawbreakers, only you wait there to die. Inmates are used for life-ending organ donation. The government takes everything: heart, lungs, pancreas, corneas and whatever other usable parts unhealthy law-abiding FoSS citizens need. Inmates are prone to suicide, so they're allowed nothing that can help them achieve that end — including hair, which early inmates used to weave into nooses. The spiky brown tufts of hair that have grown back since my imprisonment sit atop my head like a poorly shorn lawn. It is a dreadful, unpleasant look. Part of me prefers the peach fuzz I had when I escaped the facility to what has sprouted since.

I turn on the sink's hot water, grab a wash cloth and hold it under the tap until the entire cloth is warm and wet. I wring it out, feeling the water trickle through my fingers. Raising the cloth to my brow, I wipe my face. It is soothing to do this. In fact, I must do this if I am to have any chance of getting back to sleep. I can relax now, I tell myself. I will go out, have a good night's sleep and wake up at peace in the morning. I repeat the process, trying to force the nightmare down the drain with the water, letting the heat from the cloth warm my face, and hopefully my soul.

Deep breath. I'm going to be fine. This new life is going to be fine. I hang the wash cloth on a rack opposite the toilet, then lean over to flush, telling myself again that I will have a good night's sleep.

As I straighten up, a sharp, searing pain shoots through my abdomen. God, what was that? Another pain, fast and angry, follows the first. I grab my belly as I double over. My gut tightens in agony. Peanut! Not my little baby. I kneel on the floor, and the sharp pain diverges into hostile throbbing. I can't move.

"Luke!" I scream, then lie down on the cold tile floor. "Luke."

2

KELSEY

The ride to the hospital is a blur in my memory. Coping with the pain took the bulk of my concentration. The acute anguish subsided shortly after I arrived, but the doctors don't have a lot of answers. The physician on-call examined and admitted me, saying I was a bit dehydrated. Now, I get to experience a standard hospital room, an intravenous fluid drip and machines that go beep in the night.

If I were solely at the mercy of the doctors here, I don't think I would be as calm as I am. Luckily, I am not at their mercy. Dr. Grant happens to be in Peoria, and I am glad for it. Dr. Grant aided my escape from FoSS and has been a good friend to me, despite my fugitive status. While the Peorians say their doctors are excellent, I still have a FoSS mentality. One that says the people here do not have the same advances in medical technology. I feel better that Dr. Grant has come to check on me.

"The doctors who examined you earlier are right, Kelsey," he says, looking up from the electronic tablet he's reading my medical chart on. "The baby's vital signs look good. The baby also looked good on the ultrasound. There's no bleeding. Normal heart rate. I agree with them: you should stay here today for observation, and if everything remains normal, head back to the compound."

I cringe when he says "compound." I hate that place. It's supposed to be for my own safety, but it feels like a prison. I push thoughts of the compound from my mind. I have more important things to think about. I touch my belly.

"Peanut will be alright, then?" I say.

Dr. Grant smiles at my nickname for the baby, then says reassuringly, "Peanut is fine."

I let out a whoosh of air and adjust myself slightly in the hospital bed. Dr. Stephen Grant is a world-class obstetrician from FoSS. He also has a clinic here in Peoria, where he is free to do more medical procedures than FoSS allows. While FoSS generally has better medicine, its Life First policies that try to preserve human life at the utmost mean slow approval processes for new procedures. Dr. Grant perfected a procedure to remove a uterus containing a fetus and support the unit until the fetus reaches full term. He had to test it here in Peoria, because FoSS felt it too risky for its citizens, even though the procedure can be used to save the life of both a mother and baby if treatments to one would harm the other. One of his first Peoria successes was a woman with pancreatic cancer whose two-month-old fetus was able to continue to grow with artificial support while the woman received treatment. Those cancer-killing drugs would have killed the baby had he still been inside her body. So, Dr. Grant truly is a miracle worker.

I return my hand to my belly and decide to pick Dr. Grant's brain about what went wrong. "I'm glad everything is well, but what do you think caused it?"

Dr. Grant shakes his head, sympathetically. "It could've been anything, Kelsey." He glances back at my medical file. He looks intense as he scrolls through the pages of what the doctors here have recorded. After a few moments, he tosses his head in bewilderment. "Pregnancy is wonderful, but sometimes strange things happen that are perfectly ordinary. It could be a pulled muscle, overstretched ligaments, or just stress that caused this pain."

Stress. I try to look normal, as if that don't feel like I've just been slapped across the face. The idea that my regrets, my unhappiness here are causing stress that could hurt my baby cuts me to the core. "Stress?" I ask tentatively.

"Yes, stress is never good for you, Kelsey," he says, pausing, paying careful attention to me. "When you're pregnant, it's not good for your baby."

I nod.

"Is there something worrying you, Kelsey?"

I bite my lower lip, knowing I need to be honest about why I am stressed. Pushing my hesitancy aside, I speak words I have been unwilling to say to Luke. "I haven't been sleeping well. I can't stop thinking about Susan."

Luke walks in at that moment. He has brought me a can of sardines. It's one of those weird pregnancy cravings; I totally love sardines, and my husband was willing to venture from a hospital after being up with me all night just because I craved them. "What about Susan?" Luke asks, his brow furrowed.

Dr. Grant looks from me to Luke and folds his arms. "I was just telling Kelsey that stress can bring on incidents like last night. When I asked if anything was stressing her, she said Susan."

Luke's face falls. I'm not sure if it is learning that stress may have caused this or that Susan's disappearance continues to weigh so heavily on my mind. Luke starts toward me. Dr. Grant, who was at the foot of my bed, backs up to give him a wide berth. Luke sits next to me in the chair he vacated forty-five minutes ago. A cloth grocery bag dangles from his arm, and I am sure the sardines are in it.

He sets the bag in my lap, leans in and takes my hand. "Sweetheart, I know you feel guilty about Susan, but there is no way we could've known

—"

I cut him off. "Known that they would take her somewhere that no one would be able to find her? Not her uncle and aunt, not my father. Known that she was held captive at one point, and right now she might be dead or worse because she tried to help me?" I hurl the words at him. "No, I couldn't have known, but that doesn't make it any less my fault, Luke."

What I have done to Susan is what haunts me most, what makes me unable to sleep, unable to do anything but dream constantly of what would have happened if I had simply made a different choice. I close my eyes and bring my hands to my face, as tears seep out. My decisions have hurt everyone who has tried to help me, Susan most of all.

"Kelsey," Luke says softly, rubbing his hand along my arm. "I asked Susan to do this. It's my fault, OK? Please don't do this."

I wipe the tears from my eyes and open them in time to see Dr. Grant slipping out of the room. He's probably running for the hills, not wanting any part of this domestic drama. I look at Luke. "It doesn't matter that you brought her there," I tell him. "She came because of me. She stayed and let me escape. We left her in a prison, Luke!"

"Holding facilities aren't prisons," he says weakly.

"Semantics, Luke. We left her there. And now she's … she's… God only knows where she is."

Luke looks down, pauses. "Kelsey, I didn't realize Susan's disappearance was stressing you out so much," he mumbles.

Didn't realize. How could he not realize? Oh, I suppose because I've been trying to put on a good show. Trying to act normal, hoping I might feel normal. I sigh. "I guess I broke our rule," I say. He looks at me, half smiles, probably remembering when we promised to always be honest with each other, even if it wasn't something the other person wanted to hear. "I don't think I've been honest with myself, on some level. I've wanted things to work, and I've tried to put the bad things out of my mind and focus on Peanut. But, it's not working."

"I know, Kelsey," he says, commiserating with me. "I've been trying, too. And it's not working as well as I want, either."

I close my eyes again. I wish I could tell Susan I'm sorry for all of this. That I could make it up to her. "I just wish I knew she was alright or what they'd done to her."

"Well, about that, Kelsey," Luke says, stumbling over the words slightly. "Your father, he, um, didn't want to get your hopes up falsely. But —"

"But what?" I demand.

"He thinks he knows what happened to Susan."

3

SUSAN

~ FIVE DAYS EARLIER~

I learned a little more than a year ago that regrets aren't worth having. It was obvious after a surgical error left me paralyzed from the waist down that regrets don't change anything. So I've stopped indulging in them.

Therefore, it would be wrong to say I regret helping Kelsey.

However, I did miscalculate. I thought switching places with her so she could escape the holding facility would lack consequences of significance. I thought claiming I'd been drugged and taken against my will would get me deemed an "innocent bystander," and I'd be sent home.

I wasn't. Two months later, as Kelsey enjoys freedom in a new country, I am trapped in a government facility with no clue why I was brought here or when I will be released.

My captors say they believe I wasn't involved in the escape. They tell me I was used by Kelsey and will not be punished. But they don't let me leave. Instead, I have been subjected to therapy where I have to talk about my life with a psychiatrist. I've also had a couple of medical exams and been told it's important for me to stay healthy.

I am given three meals a day plus a snack, and allowed to go into the courtyard to get fresh air. I can watch certain recorded programming, but nothing live. I was given an electronic reader and a tablet to keep a journal in. I believe the journal is monitored, so I write nothing meaningful in it: what I do each day, how I yearn to be home. I do not write my true feelings. I do not write about Kelsey or Luke.

It is frustrating and lonely here. I want to see someone: my uncle, my cousins, hell, even my aunt. Yet, I've had no visitors. I received a note from Sen. Lewis Reed, Kelsey's father. It had almost a dozen words: "Trying to get you out. Stay strong. You are not forgotten."

That was it. Enough to inspire both hope and despair. Sen. Reed has lost the bulk of his clout since Kelsey fled after being marked. Being the father of someone so entirely antithetical to the Life First doctrine tarnished his name so much that I'm not sure he has any political favors left to call in. As "not forgotten" as I am, I fear he can't help me.

That means I'm stuck here, even though I don't know why. If they said they didn't believe me, that they were prosecuting me for helping Kelsey escape, I would at least know what to do. Know I was entitled to a hearing, an attorney. Something. Now, I know nothing, except that I am not free to leave.

I am less bothered by being here than I am by not knowing when they intend to release me. If I knew there was an end in sight, I could simply bide my time and wait it out. The surroundings are more than comfortable. I'm in a suite. Furnished like a fancy hotel, it includes a living area, kitchenette and bedroom. It's inside a villa-style building: a completely enclosed rectangle with an inner courtyard. While the architecture style is Romanesque, I'm pretty confident it's a government building, as evidenced by the men in FoSS military uniforms who stand sentry at the exits.

The villa is surrounded by an eight-foot high stone wall. Out front, there is a driveway with a wrought-iron gate in the center. I suspect the property is secluded on several acres.

When I first arrived, I was allowed out front. One day, I screamed as loud as I could. The guards looked put-out, at most. They didn't rush me back inside, and there was no evidence that anyone on the other side of the wall heard me. Not even a less-than-neighborly, "Shut up; you're making a racket." Since then, I have not been brought to the front of the villa again. Based on the fact that no one can hear me scream — or that no one cares when they do hear — my prospects of outside help seem dim.

The only place I have been allowed to roam freely is my suite, which is on the first floor. I've been taken to exam rooms on the first floor, as well. While I have passed a staircase that leads to a second floor, the upstairs is a mystery to me because no one has taken me there. I'd try to check it out myself, but I'm sure my captors would notice if I attempted to heave myself up the stairs, my paralyzed legs flailing behind me.

As I was brought here while unconscious — transferred from the holding facility while still drugged — I'm still not certain where I am exactly. The people who work here are taciturn, but when they do utter a few syllables, they are laced with Southern accents. It is also warmer here than when I left Maryland, so I suspect I'm somewhere further south of the Mason-Dixon Line, perhaps South Carolina.

While their accents suggest I'm due a certain amount of down-home hospitality, the people I've encountered have provided almost no information. The guards say nothing. I asked the man who took me to the medical exam room, "Why am I here?"

He flashed an apologetic smile and said, "I really don't know, Ma'am. I'm just the advance technician." An advance technician? That's the most meaningless term I've ever heard.

In my time here, I've only seen one other person who didn't look like a worker: a woman being wheeled on a gurney. It was about a week after I arrived, and the woman had olive skin, a trim physique and long black hair that mainly lay pressed beneath her. A handful of glossy black strands rested on her arm, stopping just beneath her elbow. She wore a hospital gown and was covered from the waist down with a blanket. She turned toward me, deep brown eyes watching me curiously, probably the same way I was looking at her. When the man pushing her gurney caught us staring, he told her to close her eyes, and quickly rolled her down the corridor.

When I play the memory in my head, it seems like the exchange — our eyes locking as we examined each other — was lengthy. In reality, it was probably no more than a few seconds. Had I not been so surprised to see her, had I been thinking clearly, I would have called out to her, shouted something to see what response she gave.

Instead, as I saw her gurney turn the corner out of view, I asked the technician with me who she was and why she was here. "I can't say, Ma'am," he sputtered.

Useless. No one here is willing to explain anything. It is frustrating beyond belief. Barbara, the woman who cleans my room and brings me food, is willing to talk a little. She always smiles and asks, "What are you reading?" Probably because whenever she comes, I pick up my reader and act like I'm completely enthralled. I do read. There's not a whole lot else to do. The reader came loaded with thousands of books, and it bothers me that there are so many. How long do they intend to keep me? The thought of being here long enough to celebrate my 25th birthday next February makes me cringe. It's been two months; how much longer?

The reader is in my lap now, as I sit in my wheelchair looking out a window facing the courtyard. In the center of the courtyard is a large magnolia tree with hefty white flowers blooming. The surrounding lawn is so well-manicured, I am certain that even if there were another side to see, the grass wouldn't be any greener over there.

I hear an electronic click, a sign that someone is about to come in. The suite door is always locked, so I cannot leave unless someone lets me out with an electronic keycard. I have considered trying to steal a card, but the keycard reader is conveniently about six feet off the ground, next to the door. I cannot reach it from my wheelchair. Barbara assures me that if the fire alarm is pulled, all doors in the building will unlock, and I'll be able to wheel myself to safety. I'm not entirely sure I trust that. I'm sure Barbara believes it, but anyone inclined to hold me against my will is probably inclined to let me perish in a fire so I don't talk about it.

The door opens just a crack, and in slides a man I've never seen before.

He is tall with dirty blond hair, and wears blue jeans and a long-sleeved white shirt that hugs his muscular torso. He gives a backward glance at the door as if afraid he's being followed, then scans the room until he sees me.

His eyes widen slightly once they settle on me, like he's shocked to find me here. Though I can't imagine what he thought he'd discover here, if not me.

"Who are you?" I ask.

His warm hazel eyes fix on me, and he parts his lips slightly, as if he intends to reply. Instead, he closes his mouth and takes long, purposeful steps toward me. Some part of my brain is telling me I should be alarmed. I mean, a strong, furtive stranger just snuck into my room and is coming straight at me. But, another part of my brain — the part that's winning — says to stay put, this will be worth my while. My heart quickens in anticipation until he stops right in front of me. "Rob," he says, tipping his head respectfully. His voice is strong, self-assured and kind. "My name is Rob."

He doesn't reach for me, make any sudden movements or do anything that makes me think I should be afraid. I offer a nod in return, but not my name. I am intrigued by Rob, whose eyes seem to have flecks of green in them, and whose hair is sun-streaked in places. His skin is smooth, he has a strong jaw and his expression and demeanor say, "Trust me." Only I know I can't trust anyone here, because no one is telling me anything. However, he is the only person here I've even been tempted to trust.

"You're Susan," he says, half question, half statement.

"Yes," I respond, not sure if I've given into this urge to trust him, or if I'm simply unable to break the habits of polite society.

He kneels so he is on eye level with me, and while the movement has brought him closer to me, I don't feel a desire to move away. Rob's face is a mix of curiosity and distress. "Do you want to be here?"

It is the first time anyone has asked me this, and though I know I don't want to be held captive in this place, I feel an intense need to clarify his question. "Do I want to be here with you right now? Or do you mean in general, in this place?"

He raises an eyebrow, and one corner of his mouth ticks upward into a half smile, but it melts away momentarily. "Here in this facility. Did you come here of your own free will, or are you kept here against your will?"

"Against my will," I say fervently. He nods, rises, then heads back to the door as quickly as he came. He lifts his arm, waves his key card at the reader to the left of the door, waits for the click, and opens the door slightly. He peeks into the hallway, then turns back to me.

"I will help you get out of here. I will come back for you. I promise." With that, he slips out and gently pulls the door shut. I am alone and dumbstruck. I feel certain of one thing, though. He spoke the truth: he will come back for me.

~ End Preview. If you'd like more, you can purchase it at Amazon, http://amzn.to/18lzWS1, or Barnes & Noble, http://bit.ly/18hrk1I. ~

Book Club Questions

Enjoyed the book? Suggest it for your book club. And you don't even have to come up with questions. Here are 9 great questions for you to use.

1. The book's title is *Life First*, the mantra of this futuristic society. Having completed the book, what meaning do you take from the title?

2. In the book, there is much discussion about body rights, and whether a person should have their healthy body operated on for the sole purpose of saving the life of someone else. What is your opinion on body rights? Would you donate an organ to a friend, a family member or a stranger?

3. In the book, lingo used in the current abortion debate (such as pro-choice) is used by this anti-mandatory donation faction. Do you find there are comparisons between this debate and FoSS's organ donation policy?

4. Kelsey is reluctant to give up her kidney, and in the beginning of the book we aren't exactly sure why. What was your opinion of Kelsey in the first few chapters of the book? What was your opinion after you learned more about her personal history?

5. Given what you know about the society where Kelsey lives, would you choose to live in FoSS or would you defect to Peoria?

6. Dr. Grant's character straddles the line between a good guy and a nefarious guy. When all is said and done, where would you put Dr. Grant: ultimately good or ultimately nefarious?

7. Lewis Reed sacrifices his career to assist his daughter. One of the reasons he gives for this is his guilt over his handling of Kelsey's mother, Maya. What role do you think he played in what happened to Maya? Is it something he should feel guilty over?

8. Luke is a stand-up guy. Afraid the two weren't on the same page after Kelsey said no to his marriage proposal, he withheld important information from her, information that could have drastically changed her predicament had she known about it. Do you think Luke made the right decision, given what he knew? If you had been in Luke's situation, what would you have done?

9. Susan was a true friend, making a huge sacrifice to help Kelsey escape. What do you think of her agreeing to participate in Luke's plan? Do you have any friends you'd make such a sacrifice for?

NOTE TO READER

Thank you so much for purchasing this book. If you enjoyed it, please tell a friend about it and leave a review on Goodreads, Amazon or Barnes & Noble.

If you liked the book enough that you still want more, check out my website, http://rjcrayton.com and click on the Extras tab. I've included two scenes that I wrote for the story but are not in the book: *After No* and *Rocky Road at Midnight*.

If you still want more, be sure to sign up for my newsletter, and I'll email you when I post a special preview of the second book in the *Life First* series.

-RJ Crayton

ABOUT THE AUTHOR

RJ Crayton grew up in Illinois and now lives in a Maryland suburb of Washington, DC. She is a fiction writer by day and a ninja mom by night (What is a ninja mom, you ask? No idea, but it really sounds like a much more awesome job than regular mom, so she's going with that). Before having children, Crayton was a journalist, so all the stuff she wrote had to be true (sniff, sniff). She's worked at big publications like the *Wichita Eagle* and the *Kansas City Star*, and little publications, like *Solid Waste Report* and *Education Technology News*. *Life First* is her first published novel. The sequel to this book will be out soon, so she hopes you enjoyed it enough to want more.

RJ Crayton loves connecting with readers. If you talk to her, she'll talk back, so please check out her:

Website
http://rjcrayton.com

Facebook
www.facebook.com/rjcraytonauthor

Twitter
https://twitter.com/RJCrayton

Goodreads
www.goodreads.com/author/show/7111348.R_J_Crayton

Pinterest
http://www.pinterest.com/rjcrayton/